SENTINELS OF SOLITUDE

SENTINELS OF SOLITUDE

A SUSPENSE THRILLER OF LOVE, LAND, AND LEGACY

RAE RICHEN

Sentinels of Solitude

Published in the United States of America by

Back Beat Publications
an imprint of Lloyd Court Press
3034 N.E. 32nd Avenue
Portland, Oregon, 97212
www.lloydcourtpress.org

Cover design by Diana Kolsky
Book Design by Amit Dey

ISBN: 978-1-943640-23-2 (Paperback)
ISBN: 978-1-943640-24-9 (E-book)

Publisher's Cataloging-In-Publication Data
(Prepared by The Donohue Group, Inc.)
Names: Richen, Rae, author.
Title: Sentinels of Solitude: [A Novel of Suspense and Love] /
                    Rae Richen.
Description: Portland, Oregon: Back Beat Publications, an imprint of Lloyd
                    Court Press, Second Edition 2024 | Subtitle from cover and
                    copyright page.
Identifiers: ISBN 978-1-943640-23-2 (paperback)
                    ISBN 978-1-943640-24-9 (ebook)
Subjects: LCSH: Women landscape architects--Fiction. |
                    Sheep ranches--Oregon--Willamette River Valley--Fiction. |
                    Boundary disputes--Fiction. | Murder--Investigation--
                    Oregon--Willamette River Valley--Fiction. |
                    Crimes of passion--Oregon--Willamette River Valley--Fiction. |
                    LCGFT: Romance fiction, American. | Thrillers (Fiction)
Classification: LCC PS3618.I34 S46 2024 (print)
                    LCC PS3618.I34 (ebook)
                    DDC 813/.6--dc23

FOR THE STUDENTS

of the Willamette Valley Schools who taught me about your lives and your hopes. Thank you for your patience with those who don't farm, raise sheep, hunt food, and who otherwise need your help to understand life as you live it. Now that you are grown, I can tell this story about where city and farm life meet.

PROLOGUE

SPRING, SAWTOOTH MOUNTAIN, IN THE CASCADE RANGE

Bronwen Llewellyn recognized the dark red shape in the snow one hundred yards above her. Red meant Ben's backpack. That meant Ben lay somewhere nearby.

She pushed forward, clicked open her radio phone, and forced herself into solve-it mode when her heart pounded, and her head knew.

"Backpack at four thousand feet," she said to the team. "I'm headed there now."

Ben, please hang on. Please.

The voice of Frank Bauman came over the airwaves. "Bronwen, wait for the rest of us. I see it, too."

She answered. "I can't let him be alone any longer." She hoped silence meant Frank understood.

Ben, loving, impetuous, laughing Ben had been missing for two days.

The cold in Bronwen had crept over her as soon as they found the body of his friend, Larry, deep in a dry gulch. She had looked up at the striations on volcanic rock at the summit and had seen the place Larry must have slipped, the long fall that would have yanked out their safety pitons and ropes. And his fall had started an avalanche, not huge, but big enough.

She had known then that the weight of snow, and the swiftness of Larry's fall would have brought Ben down as well.

But she had hope. Ben was strong, resourceful. He had equipment. As she had continued the search, part of the rescue crew stayed at the crevasse to lift Larry from that rock-ragged depth, tied to a litter, a rescue sked.

Bronwen whispered, "Ben, Ben, be alive. Ben, I'm coming."

Maybe he's built an ice cave, she prayed as she approached the red pack in the snow. His sleeping bag is goose down. He'll be cold, but all right. He'll be …

Each step raised the smell of ancient rock and annual layers of glacier. Each step sped her closer to the backpack and the possibilities she feared. One of Ben's backpack straps lay far out from the pack, disengaged from its mooring grommets.

And the large flap still covered the main pack compartment. Ben had not used the things inside the pack – the matches, the phone, the flares. Still tied to the upper frame, the sleeping bag.

Deep fear gripped her, sped her steps even more. She crunched over white snow corn that concealed loose rock. She topped the rise and approached the backpack but looked beyond it. Another small dark shape lay three hundred feet further on.

Ben, inert, partially covered with snow from the avalanche, his back to her, his ice axe on the snow near him, his legs at improbable angles.

She ran across the ice to him. "I'm coming. Please don't …" When she fell in the freezing cold next to him, she knew.

His gray skin color told her the truth, but still, she took his beloved face in her hands, felt for his neck pulse. She yanked off her pack and pulled out the sleeping bag to warm him.

Ben, part of her since they were children, her playmate, then her challenger, and finally her lover and husband – Ben.

However, she tried to deny fact, she saw that his normally bright and laughing brown eyes stared at her, not moving, not clear, but glossed over with icy film.

She stopped working to warm him, chanting a low, "No. No. No."

A moment later, Frank knelt on the other side of Ben's body. His whispered "Oh" poured out the grief for both of them.

Bronwen knew.

I should have been here. Not at work.

But she stuffed that thought down into her boots and did the next thing that had to be done. She wrapped her husband's body in the sleeping bag for the trip down the mountain.

And then she shoved the ski patrol leader away and grabbed the rope to guide the back end of the rescue litter – the sked. Ben was not going to suffer any more because she would make this last trip down safe for him.

Bronwen knew she acted crazy. She saw Frank touch the arm of the ski patrolman and whisper to him. The man didn't try to retake the rope.

She hoped Frank had told him she knew what she did. She and Ben had served on the ski patrol every winter during architecture school.

After the grueling climb down, guiding the litter, she paced inside the ski patrol offices near Timberline Lodge awaiting the ambulance that would take Ben's and Larry's bodies back to Portland.

Frank Bauman, senior partner in their architecture firm and their mentor, sat on a wooden bench, his head in his hands. Frank, like a father to both of them, needed to cry.

That meant she had to be in control.

She held a grip on herself as they followed the ambulance to the morgue. She held herself in a tighter grip as the medical examiner determined that Larry died of the fall, but Ben died of exposure, too broken inside and out to get to his pack, dig a cave or do any of the things that might have saved him – things she could have done if she'd been there with them.

"Bronwen," Frank said, "You cannot blame yourself."

"But if I had been there, Ben would have chosen a safer route, not that rotten rock they were climbing."

Frank closed his eyes and rocked himself. "No." he said. "If you'd been there, I'd have lost both of you."

Afterward, she called Ben's parents in Beaver Creek, Oregon, and told them what had happened. Their disbelief became horror. Ben was the strong one.

After struggling to stay calm as she visited Ben's mother and father, and after planning for and pushing herself through his memorial, so that she could take care of his mother and father in their deep loss, Bronwen found herself walking all the time.

Two weeks went by. She never talked about any of it to anybody, even Frank – especially not poor, lost Frank. Instead, she just walked around west Portland near her apartment and the offices of Bauman, Grant and Llewellyn where she worked.

She figured she must be trying to rid herself of the image of Ben's broken legs and his internal injuries.

At noon, on a Tuesday, she strode from the architectural offices where she and Ben had worked with Frank. She walked straight across west Portland. She walked up onto the Morrison Bridge. She thought she must be planning to walk across the Willamette River and into east Portland. Walk on, and walk on, until she could think and remember no more.

At the apex of the bridge, she looked down. The grid of the bridge roadway allowed a narrow view of the river far below. And there, she stopped.

Down. Down. The water flowing as an avalanche flows, but faster and faster, and she couldn't move.

Minutes passed. She remembered gripping the rail, trying to look anywhere but down, maybe out at the office buildings on the west side, maybe across the river to the science museum, maybe up at the bridge towers, but she couldn't move her attention from the flowing river.

When the ambulance came, she finally knew that people had been speaking to her, that someone had taken her backpack purse and called the emergency number in her wallet, that Frank Bauman had come, and that she needed help.

CHAPTER ONE

TWO YEARS LATER, IN PORTLAND, OREGON

In the Bauman, Grant and Llewellyn Architectural Offices on the fourth floor of the Dekum Building in Portland, Oregon, the ring of Frank Bauman's office phone didn't interrupt Bronwen Llewellyn's work.

Frank knew that, because he glanced beyond his office door to watch her as he answered.

He also knew almost nothing could break Bronwen's focus when she reached this point in a landscape design.

As he listened to this client's requests, Frank closed his eyes and ran his free hand over his face. The lilting Scots voice at the other end of the telephone line brought up old warmth and old regrets.

"Yes, Margaret, I think you're on the right track with that idea," he said.

"I don't want to discommode your staff," Margaret MacGregor said. "But I hope to create this change during the spring, before Janet and her family come to visit."

Relief flooded through Frank when he realized his client's request could be handled by Bronwen rather than by himself.

And then he smiled to himself when he realized he had not heard the word 'discommode' in forty years. How like Margaret Campbell MacGregor still to be using that word.

"No discommoding," he laughed. "We'll send the best. Bronwen Llewellyn."

When he mentioned Bronwen's name to Margaret, Frank watched. Bronwen didn't even glance up.

"Yes, Margaret," Frank Bauman said. "Bráhn-oo-wen. Welsh name. Best there is. A superb landscape designer."

As he talked to Margaret about the project, and then about the ranch and her family, Frank saw that Bronwen bent ever closer over her slanted desk. Her gold-brown hair, always braided, had been stuffed into the back of her shirt collar to keep it out of the way. Whenever she rolled up her blouse sleeves and hooked her left foot into the rung of her desk stool, Frank knew she created something worth waiting for.

As their conversation moved to family matters, Frank whispered, "I think both of our families have been hurt. Mauled, more like."

He thought, but didn't say, the girl hasn't driven or walked across a bridge in almost two years.

But emotionally mauled or confined by unreasoning fear, Bronwen Llewellyn still was a top designer.

She shunned the confining computer program that most designers used. She loved the motion of drawing, the smell of pencil lead and shaved wood. And after the first penciled layout of dimensions, Bronwen poised over the T-square, and worked from top to bottom in pen and ink. Erasure? Unnecessary. She always seemed to have her landscape complete in her mind.

Her hand-drawn designs became framed works of art on the walls of her clients' homes.

She was the best, but, as with himself, the death of Ben had changed her. She didn't just stuff her hair into the back of her shirt. She also stuffed her grief and her loneliness. If anyone on earth could assuage grief and dispel loneliness, Frank knew it would be Margaret MacGregor.

So, Frank told Margaret, "I'll talk to Bronwen about your project. We'll see what works in her schedule. How about if I have her call you in the morning?"

And after he hung up the phone, he sat very still, holding in his own sadness. He worried about sending Bronwen one hundred miles down the highway, but he knew Margaret could be just what Bronwen needed, a gentle lady with steel-strong loyalty, and a way of opening others with her listening and her observant hearing of the unsaid.

Well, he hoped Bronwen would accept the challenge of this job.

Getting to the ranch would be her first obstacle.

*   *

Bronwen glanced over her design, studying the park in southeast Portland, Oregon, its sunken garden, the playground for small children, basketball courts and the community house with its swimming pool; the beautiful light-filled building was the creation of her senior partner, Frank Bauman.

This project proved easy to reach by taking the light rail over the low Tillicum Bridge. No need to walk across a bridge or drive.

Frank Bauman and her late husband, Benjamin Llewellyn, were among the few Northwest architects who had used a landscape architect right from the beginning of a design. And despite her hang-up with bridges, Frank kept her on.

Bronwen smiled, remembering earlier times.

Ben, beloved Ben, used to watch her as she worked. When she created a drawing of elevation changes, he had joked about her "nice contours".

Warm memories came to her often now. Two years after his death, she recalled the finer times more clearly.

"Grief casts a shadow over your mind," Frank had told her after Ben's death. "It keeps you from too much awareness. As grief withdraws, you'll remember even what his jackets smelled like and how he always put his booted feet on the coffee table."

Frank had been right, of course. Lately, when her thoughts moved to Ben, they were like this, humorous and loving.

He'd died when they were both twenty-six. She'd felt cheated and guilty – guilty because she hadn't been with him in his last hours of agony, cheated because she had so much love to give and no one to give it to.

At twenty-eight, she still had the love, but somehow in the two years since, she hadn't wanted to offer it to any who'd grown interested in her.

She hadn't offered it to the charming, but insistent, Leonard Parr, Vice-President of Parr Development. For some, his attractiveness appeared magnetic, and he used it adeptly, but Bronwen's shields had been up and her distrust of him apparent from day one of their business acquaintance.

Leonard had been oblivious to all the negative signals. She'd never forget the night she'd come home to find him asleep on her sofa.

"Money buys entree to everything," He'd smiled, dangling the landlord's master key.

Money had bought her a new set of door locks to which her landlord did not have duplicates.

*   *

At last, Frank's soft voice intruded into Bronwen's consciousness, but she hadn't heard what he'd been telling the client on the phone.

She turned her attention back to her park, but a moment later, Frank stood next to her.

"Time to clear the desktop for the day, Bron."

She glanced up and saw the shine of pride in his eyes as he looked at her park. Even when she'd been a summer apprentice, he'd made it clear he appreciated her work. As she watched, his look of pride turned into a small furrow of concern.

"What is it, Frank?"

"Bron, I had a call from a very good friend this afternoon. She has a beautiful old house on a large sheep ranch down the Willamette Valley near Eugene. You'll enjoy Margaret MacGregor very much and she could use your deft hand. Could you call her tomorrow?"

Bronwen glanced with worry at her park design. The crowded days on her docket loomed in front of her.

"When would I fit in another landscape? We'll have all those design approval meetings for this park next week. We've got to get the machines moving in that TECH park for Parr Development near Portland. And Standard Investments is taking bids for its Multnomah properties. It's spring, Frank and things will be hopping around here."

His gently lined face took on an earnest determination. "And there'll be frisking of lambs at her place. If she's willing to landscape during lambing time, we ought to be able to help."

Frank turned his face away from her as he finished. "Bron, please talk to the lady. We'll work something out."

His avoidance of eye contact telegraphed a message to her. He didn't want to admit the importance of this request.

"Of course, I'll take care of her," she said. Frank, the senior partner, rarely asked favors of his team. "Leave me her phone number," she said. "I'll call her tomorrow morning."

Frank's shoulders relaxed as he turned back to her. The creases in his forehead softened, as if at some lovely memory – a Frank she almost never saw.

"We'll make time in your schedule," he said. "You haven't taken a day off from work in more than a year. Being with Margaret will be like a vacation for you. You'll enjoy the ranch and the lady."

Bronwen thought, for a moment about the best way to arrive in Eugene. One hundred miles to the south. She hadn't driven a car over a bridge for two years.

But Frank seemed to have forgotten that fact in his anxiety to have this Margaret taken care of. Bronwen wondered why that was.

Frank continued trying to convince her. "Besides, I'm sure you aren't anxious to attend those meetings with Leonard Parr about his Eugene development, so I'll handle him."

Bronwen laughed and mimicked a coquette, complete with fan and batting eyelashes. "What? Miss Poor, Dear Leonard?"

Frank grinned, "Tsk, tsk, young lady. He's a quarter of our income for this year."

Bronwen's imaginary fan snapped shut. "I'd rather be working with Standard Investments. At least Standard knows how to plan a real community with parks, pedestrian access and other amenities unheard of by Leonard Parr."

"I'm with you there, but Bauman, Grant, Llewellyn, et cetera, have thirty-four families to feed and we need major projects like Parr's to keep everyone working steadily."

Suddenly, Bronwen remembered the best part of her schedule. "Our little park! Ground-breaking will be . . ."

"That ground-breaking can still be overseen by the old man, you know."

Bronwen relented, laughing with affection. "I don't see any old men around," she said. "How about if you see to it, Frank?"

Frank chuckled, "Thanks for taking care of Margaret MacGregor, Bronwen." He turned out her office light. "Now, leave that desk as is," he said.

Frank walked Bronwen to the elevators, discussing other things. But she felt his gratitude underneath the careless guise. She figured she'd look up the bus schedules to Eugene this evening and call Margaret MacGregor early tomorrow.

CHAPTER TWO

IN THE HILLS NORTH OF EUGENE OREGON

Douglas MacGregor scanned the ridge of black firs across the ravine. He saw no hint of his stolen sheep. The foothills of the Oregon Cascades seemed as placid as the spring sky above them.

Seventy-eight-year-old George Conall lowered his amber bottle and wiped his sleeve across his mouth. "Spot anything?" he asked.

"Nothing. No Blackwatch, and no sign of the thieves." Douglas hoisted his rifle, frustrated. "Let's head on into the ranch."

With a stubby forefinger and thumb, George replaced the Glenlivet Whiskey in the side pocket of his backpack, and grandly waved his tall companion ahead of him down the trail.

"Let's get on wi' it, then," George urged, bowing.

Raising one dark eyebrow, Douglas grinned. He accepted his sheepherder's parody of deference, adjusted his Kelty backpack, hoisted his hunting rifle into the crook of his arm, and moved down the trail. Their companionship was quiet and easy, as it had been since their first hike together when Douglas had been five years old and

George, forty- eight. Thirty years later, Douglas still recalled that first hike with love.

During this recent hike, Douglas had become aware of George's hesitant step and labored breathing, so he slowed his long legs to accommodate his aging mentor. In spite of worry over his stolen, experimental flock, he settled into the relaxed pace and let himself enjoy the quiet of the Cascades foothills.

A crack of gunshot echoed across the ravine. Pivoting toward his companion, Douglas saw the glazed look in George's eyes and knew he'd been hit.

With a grunt, George fell into him and they both went down over the steep pitch toward the stream. The rifle ripped from Douglas's hands as the two men tore through the branches of a pine, smacking into each other with all the weight of their gear. Part of Douglas's conscious mind watched his rifle spin away like a child's whirligig.

He yanked his arms from his backpack, aware that its frame posed a danger to both of them. It bounced into a rock, and cartwheeled out of sight. As the steep earth rose to hit Douglas, he instinctively tucked, landing and rolling across the rocky ground. He couldn't see George, and became too disoriented to do anything more than brace himself for each bone jarring contact with dirt and rock, until the whip of vine maple across his face and the smack of George's boot on his back announced their arrival at the bottom.

Silent seconds passed as Douglas regained his breath. He scrambled up to find George. The old man lay nearby in the thicket of vine maple, blood streaming down his chest.

Praying and cursing, Douglas unsheathed his Buck hunting knife and pushed away the thick woven straps of the old man's pack. He cut into George's bloody shirt and found the source, high in the muscle across the top of the shoulder – the clavicle had been smashed.

Close, he thought, too damn close to the artery! He glanced at his friend's weathered face and felt its lax creases, then pulled off his bandana to apply pressure on the wound. Stop bleeding! Come on, come on!

One dark eye opened. "Pillow?" George asked.

Douglas's laugh felt tight. "For your feet or your head?" He knew George would face down the devil with a jest rather than acknowledge fear.

"Both, now you mention it." Humor trailed off, but the other eye opened.

Keeping pressure on the bandana, Douglas searched George's pack for enough clothes to pillow his head. When the bleeding subsided, Douglas felt the man's body and legs for other breaks and found none.

"You're a homely nurse, MacGregor." George's impassive black eyes hid in folds of weathered skin as thick as the Scots brogue which still colored his speech.

Relieved, Douglas continued applying pressure and cursed George for getting in the way of the bullet. By the time he'd stopped the bleeding, he'd gotten enough response to know the man wasn't in shock – yet. But given George's years, who knew how long he could hold up. It grew cool in the early spring shade, too cool for a man in pain and losing blood, and their sleep mats lay strewn under the pine they'd first hit, thirty-five feet above them.

Douglas saw that his own pack and rifle were within ten feet of each other, a few yards up the scree. Without giving George a chance to protest, he darted uphill. Dust greeted him, and then the whine of bullets bouncing off the granite. He scrambled from rock to rock, grabbing up his rifle on the run.

Followed by the angry buzz of death, he snagged his pack, and zig-zagged back to the maple brush, circling it to enter where the maple hid him from above.

"Don't do that, boy." George's voice weakened. "What would your mother say to me?"

Douglas snorted. "Frightening, having to answer to Margaret MacGregor, isn't it?"

"An ogre, she is."

Something warm ran down Douglas's arm. Perplexed, he watched a trail of blood drip from his hand. A near thing and he hadn't even felt it happen. Before George could notice, he rolled down his flannel sleeve and reached into his pack for a tee-shirt to wrap the flesh wound.

Bantering as if the burning pain were not growing on him, he said, "If you'd learn to dodge lead, George, I might get both of us home in one piece."

"One piece? Ha! The Glenlivet's broke already."

"I know. You smell worse than usual."

"A waste . . . a sad waste."

"Did it cut you?"

"To the quick." One eye winked.

Douglas smiled with relief. The old man exhibited his usual flinty self. At least George's wound had stopped bleeding.

Their situation had little to recommend it, Douglas noted as he glanced around. They'd rolled to the bottom of a ravine, next to a small stream. Their attacker shot from a grove near the top of the opposite slope. The sniper's back faced the lowering sun, which put Douglas at a disadvantage.

"But, 'tis a boon we're in the shadow of the ridge," George whispered.

Douglas had grown used to having his thoughts read by George. "Some boon!" Douglas said. "But we'll turn this small thicket to our advantage yet."

At that moment, two more shots rang out across the ravine. Douglas flattened himself over his friend.

Beneath him, the old man grunted. "I'd say we've finally flushed him, Lad."

"Aye. You could put it that way." Douglas pushed himself off of George.

Douglas hauled out his cell phone, and as expected, had no connection to the outside world or possible help. Nevertheless, he dialed anyone who might hear. Six numbers later, he gave up and faced their isolation.

"At least we know for sure it's not been a four-legged animal takin' those poor ewes," George whispered.

"We knew that anyway," Douglas said. "Only a greedy human would have taken 'em, never a cougar."

"Cougar?" George laughed. "No self-respecting cougar'd be run to ground in this valley – liable to get flattened by a Parr-dozer or a concrete mixer. I spotted Parr Land Development trucks going in and out of Mary's Peak . . ."

"Yeah, I saw 'em, too." The mere thought of Leonard Parr made Douglas angry.

He shifted his weight to fuss over the man, pulling George's jacket around his shoulders. "Enough talk George. Get some rest."

He didn't like the cool, wet feel of George's skin. With George showing signs of shock, they couldn't afford to be trapped long. There had to be a way to sneak up on the grove where their assailant holed up. Stretching his six-foot frame next to George, he scanned the cliffs opposite him.

Douglas's attention caught the stillness of a single figure – an eagle, high on the cliff, the alert silence of her a warning.

Beside him, George stirred in discomfort. Pointing out the bird, Douglas whispered, "She's got her eye on lunch."

George squinted into the distance. "Aye, Lad. I'd nae be her prey." He shaded his old eyes with a gnarled hand as he watched. Both men, immobile as the bird, listened to the last scuttling rodent make a frantic dash. Tiny scratching feet echoed in the forest's dread silence.

Without warning, the eagle plummeted from sight. Moments later, she whirled aloft, her wings beating a rhythmic Te Deum. A small rabbit hung limp in her talons as she returned, triumphant, to her eyrie.

Douglas' low voice held awe, "And like a thunderbolt she falls." George glanced at his companion, "Always got the poetry in yer head, nae?"

Douglas nodded, "Even Tennyson had some good ideas. I'm goin' up there."

"Now, Lad . . ."

"She showed me the way, flying into that draw to the north. We couldn't see her until she flew out again."

"But between here and there. . ." George's voice betrayed his pain.

"We need a diversion."

CHAPTER THREE

At ten in the morning, Bronwen held Frank's office phone to her ear. She seemed to be staring across the street at the whimsical concrete ribbons on the upper stories of the famous Graves Portland Building. Most days, the view from Frank's fourth-floor office made her dizzy. This morning, however, instead of seeing the height outside, she concentrated on the image conjured by the lilting voice of Margaret MacGregor, the image of a gentle, patrician lady.

Mrs. MacGregor said, "I had in mind removing the smell of wet wool and lanolin from the vicinity of the house. My guests have a right to a less odorous welcome."

Bronwen smiled to herself "But you work with lambs. Surely that comes into the house on your clothes."

"Oh yes, but it's worse when the lambs and the ewes are dancing about the front yard and tiptoeing onto the porch."

Bronwen laughed. "Well, we'll see what we can do."

Mrs. MacGregor's voice grew subdued, "I would trust any partner of Frank's," she said. "Of course," she continued, "Douglas will have to approve the plans. Right now, he's out in the hills searching for stolen sheep, but, I'm sure he will come around."

Bronwen didn't like the sound of that. She too often mediated between family members who couldn't agree on what they wanted.

"Mrs. MacGregor," she said, "If you could pick me up at the station, I can come to Eugene on the bus next Tuesday. In the meantime, why don't you talk to your husband? It's easier to do these renovations if your family agrees on general principles from the beginning."

"Oh, my dear, my husband died several years ago. This Douglas is my son. I admit he's as conservative about this ranch as an old man, but I'm sure he won't object."

"You will discuss it with him, though, won't you?"

"Of course, dear, and one of us will pick you up in Eugene. The first express bus gets into Eugene by eleven a.m.. Leaves Portland about eight in the morning. Is that too early?"

At the mention of the express bus, Bronwen felt a tingle of apprehension run up her back. Nevertheless, she said, "That time will be fine. I look forward to meeting you on Tuesday, Mrs. MacGregor."

A moment later, Bronwen called the bus station and made a reservation on the milk run, leaving Tuesday morning at six, arriving in Eugene at ten thirty. It traveled the old highway and Bronwen knew from experience that it crossed fewer high bridges than the express.

As she hung up the phone, she made the mistake of really looking out at the Graves Building. Nausea gripped her stomach. Cold fear ran up her spine and she saw, not the comical concrete blue ribbons, but blue ice – a sheer wall of deep blue ice inching downhill toward Benjamin's frozen limbs.

A voice behind Bronwen turned her cold fear into hot sweat. "Bronwen, did you find Margaret at home?" Frank's care embarrassed her. Bronwen's eyes focused again on the concrete just before she slumped to the desk.

His fatherly grip on her shoulders brought her back to sanity. "Damned windows!" he exclaimed. "I'm getting you a phone of your own again."

He muttered as he lowered the Roman shades, "We'll just keep it unlisted, so you don't have to take calls from Leonard Parr anymore."

Bronwen felt ever more foolish. Frank shouldn't have to baby his partners. She should have been able to get rid of Leonard Parr herself, and she should be over this fear of heights by now.

She pushed herself to a standing position. "Don't bother with me, Frank. I'll get my extension line back and take care of Leonard the way I should have in the first place."

Frank turned around, concern written in his posture and every line of his face. "It's going to be all right," he whispered. "You're going to be all right."

She gave him a wavering grin. "I'm better. Most days I'm better," she said. Then, without looking toward the window, Bronwen turned her back on the Graves Building and marched into her windowless office.

CHAPTER FOUR

George's obvious pain made Douglas even more determined to get them out of this trap.

"Between here and that ravine, I'll have to follow this bank of the stream, but we need a diversion, so there's no chance he'll catch on."

"A diversion . . .," George frowned. "Take off your sweater, lad. Coom! Off wi' it."

Douglas, though puzzled, shucked his sweater and handed it over. The old man studied it. "Good. Top-down knit." He said, then bit a thread at the bottom and began pulling at the yarn while issuing orders.

"Run it out around one spindly trunk to the south of us, then back to me. But tread light – don't want to draw fire too early."

Douglas's faith in George's devious mind had been rewarded. "What'll my mother say?" he joked.

"Margaret will say naught, but you'll have a new sweater out of it, I'll wager."

Douglas ran the strong yarn around three widely separated alder trunks, each time returning toward George, but as he came back from the last alder, he bumped the yarn.

A thump and the whistle of a high-speed bullet made him flatten himself into the salal and ferns. A renewed volley kept him down. He glanced up at George, whose weak wave told him to stay put.

Douglas waggled a finger, put his head down and waited for the fusillade to stop. He found himself staring at the white bell flowers which hung below the leathery leaves of the salal. Too clearly, he recalled a similar intimate acquaintance with the low plants of Central America.

The moment the barrage ended, he brought George the tag end of the yarn.

"Your usual graceful self, MacGregor."

Douglas saw the trembling hand that gave away his friend's fear.

"I s'pose I shouldn't have skipped those dance classes, after all," Douglas said, handing George the last of the yarn. "This should keep him busy. Move the alder just enough to keep him watching."

"I'm teaching you this trick," George huffed.

Douglas grinned, "So you are."

"It'll work, MacGregor, if you don't galumph that long body of yours into things. Now go."

Douglas gave a clinical look at his companion's eyes and skin before he stood. "I'll be up top in fifteen minutes."

He dug into his pack, bringing out a box of bullets and a revolver. "Here. This'll keep you company in case he decides to come down."

George took the gun and slipped his arm back under the cover of the sleeping bag. He stared at Douglas for several moments and then whispered, "Dinnae fash yersel'. I can take care of this end o' the business."

Douglas nodded and slipped through the maple into the afternoon shadow of the cliff. Within thirty seconds, the shooting began behind him. George, the old trickster, worked with his yarn. Resisting the temptation to look back, Douglas moved up the stream. He kept to the cover of alder and cottonwood along the stream until he reached the draw, crossed the water and began climbing.

*   *

On the high ledge, the hidden attacker took off a sweaty baseball cap and mopped his thinning hair.

He'd heard the buzz in his pocket and laughed. "Really desperate this time, aren't you, MacGregor?"

Last time I wear a disguise, he thought. Hat's not only ugly, it's an oven."

Sighting through his telescopic lense, he watched the alder below him for any new signs of movement. Twice now that area had given away MacGregor's location.

Just try to make a break for it, MacGregor. You can't even go for water without I know about it. Even at night, with this infra-red, I can keep you pinned.

He took a pull on his water bag and then scanned up and down the creek bed, grinning over the predicament he'd put MacGregor in.

Thought I might kill him when he went for that pack. Shoulda, maybe, but it's more fun when you let 'em hang on and on.

Like her. Days she begged me to let her go, days – 'til she was too gone to care.

*   *

Achieving the top of the pass took Douglas ten minutes of hard scrambling. Having climbed, he took a deep breath and turned south, shifting his rifle to keep its polished barrel out of the sun.

Straight up the fall line, he moved with speed and no noise. Boyhood games of tracking had taught him never to underestimate his opponent and to take advantage of the other man's smallest mistake. Later, "Peace-keeping" in Central America had drilled into him the deadly seriousness of those lessons.

When the large boulders of the hilltop cut his view of George's location, Douglas worried more than he wanted to admit. He climbed between two boulders at the top of the ridge. On the other side of the boulders, about fifty yards away, he could see the alpine grove which concealed his assailant.

Between his position and those trees, budding red huckleberries and dark green salal bushes covered a steep slope. He sighted down his rifle in the cleft between the rocks and watched the grove for movement.

As his body settled into the rocks, he checked the long wound from the bullet that had grazed his arm. It looked angry, but not infected.

He couldn't afford to let down. Leonard Parr never did.

Ever since young Kenjiro Eguchi had come to him, desperate and sick, Douglas understood that Parr fought dirty. He had no doubt Parr hired this rustler, just as Parr somehow managed to get the county to double his taxes in the last year.

But how did Parr know about his small flock of Blackwatch sheep?

Until now, they'd been a well-guarded secret.

Right now, he had to wait until the other guy made some kind of move. He hoped to God he made it soon. George grew weak. Once he freed them from this trap, he'd have to carry George most of the way back to the ranch.

*   *

In the thick grove, the man put down his rifle long enough to jerk his wooly companion away from a leaf.

Starve you fool beast! Starve. You don't kick me and get away with it. Why'd MacGregor set such stock by a mean mamma like you?

Go out, babe. Let's show him what we got for him.

*   *

Douglas lurched from his stupor. A small motion in the dark needles of the sniper's grove alerted him. A figure moved toward the downhill side of the trees – George's side. Douglas readied the rifle. Through the sight he watched a soft-wooled face nosing aside the fir needles, bleating and reaching for the grass growing in the sun … a Blackwatch ewe, the one with the white ring around her eyes – Specs, a feisty kicker, but mother of half his experimental flock.

She's still alive! But look at those ribs.

He held his breath, noting the rope that kept her from the grass for which she strained. He sighted on the rope then realized that if he shot that taut tether, she'd fall forward, tumbling down the long rocky slope.

The sun moved toward the ridge on which Douglas lay. If he didn't move soon, the shadows of evening would make it harder for him to see the attacker.

An afternoon's first-hand acquaintance with the distance capabilities of the man's weapon left Douglas certain that he held a solid weapon, maybe an M2. Something with velocity, and maybe with the kind of night-seeing equipment Douglas had used often while in the marines. If so, waiting until dark guaranteed no cover for escape.

For George's sake, he had to do something soon, even if it meant he might sacrifice his beautiful ewe. He waited for her motion to give him a better idea of the man's location. He decided on the likely spot and let out his breath.

Suddenly, the rustler yanked her back into the cover of trees. Making a quick decision, Douglas aimed into the grove and pulled on the trigger.

At that moment, a shot rang out from within the grove, followed by the report of his own rifle. The two sounds echoed through the hills. It took Douglas a moment to realize that both of them had shot something at almost the same time.

Fear for George brought Douglas to his feet. A violent motion in the salal and ferns alerted him. His attacker was in flight.

Douglas climbed through the cleft in the boulders which had been his shield. While he ran toward the clump of trees, he saw the other man turn. Douglas hit the ground, rolling toward the nearest cover. Shots from the retreating figure sang over his head.

He rose and zig-zagged as the motion of the underbrush telegraphed the pattern of the other man's flight into the deep woods. Douglas closed the gap, but his man leapt off a ten-foot embankment and ran, gimp legged, down a short path to more underbrush.

Afterward, Douglas tried to forget why he didn't use the easy shot the man's broad back had given him. There was something. . . something about the man . . . he couldn't pull the trigger.

The retreating figure turned again, raising the rifle to his shoulder.

Douglas dove to the right and rolled away. A bullet cut a sizzling path through the salal above him, but he kept rolling until he put a rise of ground between him and the deadly weapon.

A few moments later, a distant truck motor turned over, wheezed and then caught. A truck door slammed, groaning metal indicating a damaged hinge. The door groaned twice before it held.

Douglas closed his eyes, trying to pinpoint the direction of the sound. If his mental map of the ranch served him well, the truck lurched down the road from Ian's Draw toward the north. Douglas clenched his fists in anger. Three days and then this . . . failure.

As he lay on the ground, becoming aware of multiple bruises and rock cuts, Douglas tried to reconstruct what he'd seen of the man. From the top of the embankment, he'd had only a glimpse of the Hawaiian print shirttails and black baseball cap of the big man – nobody he knew, thank God. Yet there'd been something, a familiar way of moving . . .

Urged on by the need to return for George, and disgusted with himself for not taking the shot at his back, he pushed up and grabbed his rifle and saw his phone, lying in the salal. He grabbed it up.

Absently kneading the pain in his wounded arm, he approached the rustler's original hide-out among the trees, hoping to find his ewe.

As he pushed into the undergrowth, the smell of hot blood overwhelmed. A strong ewe with the finest wool and the blackest of soft faces lay on the rocky soil, a bullet hole in her head – his Blackwatch.

He sat hard and pulled out his phone. "Mom, George has been shot. I need you to call an ambulance. Have them meet us where Ian's Creek crosses under the bridge. You stay in the house and lock it. Call Ian and Helen and tell them to watch out for anyone driving past their homes in an old truck. Don't open the door for anyone but me or the medics."

*   *

When he stumbled into the shelter of George's maple, his friend leaned next to a tree, holding the kerchief to his shoulder. The pain on George's face showed sadness as much as physical distress. "Did ye see him, Lad?"

"I saw his back and his gun, but never his face. And you?"

"I saw nothing of him, but he let her walk out before he shot her. His warning to ye, Laddie."

"She's the first one he stole, two weeks ago."

"I know, the fractious one. She's butted me with that strong head of hers. Do you s'pose he's killed all the others too?"

"God, I hope not."

"Help me up, son, I can walk now he's gone. You take my pack, if you can. Let's go home and take care of the sheep that are left. Robbie and Roy'll be needin' our help."

Douglas extended his wounded arm, gritted his teeth and helped George lean on him. "Steady now," Douglas said. "You've lost a lot of blood. Let's take it slow."

George gave a feeble attempt to wave off Douglas's arm. "Keep an eye cocked for that buzzard. He might get it in his head to come wheeling back."

"I'm watching," said Douglas.

He knew then that they'd end up this hike with him carrying George home, as George had often carried him.

*   *

In an old open-bed Ford, heading north, the driver wiped his sleeve across his sweat clouded eyes. He cussed the MacGregor luck.

Damn! He near got me. He was pinned – I know he was! Can't run like I used to. And he gets faster. For MacGregor, everything gets better, always.

Until now! George Conall always took MacGregor's side even against her. The old man deserved to die. He deserved it!

CHAPTER FIVE

Two days later, in the early morning sunlight of their kitchen, Margaret MacGregor watched her son smooth his napkin for the sixth or seventh time.

Douglas seemed to be holding his impatience with a tight rein as he asked, "Why isn't Frank coming down the valley from Portland? At least he'd be worth seeing."

Margaret spoke patiently. "Frank is not the landscape architect. He's into buildings."

"Mother, there's too much happening for us to take on landscaping right now." As he talked, he rubbed the arm, grazed by the sniper's bullet. "George is laid up for at least another week and I want him to work short hours for a week after that."

"Hmph! Good luck."

Douglas raked his hand through his black hair, "I know! Can't stop the old man with less than a chain and manacles . . . But you see my point. It's Ian and me. His collie is still an untrained puppy, but we're left to organize the cottonwood harvest and the first lambs'll come soon."

She nodded in agreement, "And there's the theft of your Blackwatch sheep. That's just it, son. Too much is going on. You work yourself to the nubbin and what do you get? They raise our taxes as if we were mining for gold here."

Douglas kept his voice slow and controlled. "So how is landscaping going to help?"

Margaret's small fist came down hard on the table. "I want Parr Land Development to see that we mean to stay."

Douglas took his mother's hand. "There's more goin' on than you ken, Mother. That bast . . . That buzzard has ruined the lives of more than one neighbor. I'll not have him talking to you again."

Her chin came up proudly. "We are here to stay. Our ranching friends who are afraid of him will see that we won't be bullied."

Douglas throaty laugh caught her by surprise. "Mother, explain why landscaping will be seen as a sign we are here to stay?"

Margaret looked with fondness at her son. There were times, since he'd been alone so much, that he sounded very like his father and his pioneer grandfather.

And he'd grown resourceful as the MacGregors before him as well. The farming of swift growing cottonwoods had been an inspiration. Only seven years from seedling until harvest for the Oregon City and Halsey pulp mills – and he'd seen it early on. Taxes all taken care of for years.

But the loss of his priceless Blackwatch flock, now that could break him. All the time and care given to breeding those lovely. . ..

"Margaret Campbell MacGregor!" Douglas said, "Don't dodge me with your day-dreamy ways. I know you well, and you'd best explain this landscaping scheme to me."

Margaret looked into his blue eyes and explained, partly. "I'm landscaping because this poor beautiful house deserves it. And now that we're sure we can handle this year's taxes . . ."

He looked at her with suspicion. "Come now, Mother. In the midst of all that's going on, you hatch a scheme to bring in some garden club lady . . ."

"Fully accredited Landscape Architect!"

". . . to design a garden? What is really going on? Parr . . .?"

She said, "Parr has nothing to do with it. You said to go ahead and spend Judith's money, so . . ."

"I know you've held onto the money from Aunt Judith's estate in case we needed it."

"I wouldn't spend it at all, "she said, "if the cottonwood weren't ready."

A frown creased his dark brow. "I did tell you to go ahead and spend it." He leaned toward her. "But I said spend it on yourself."

"Landscaping is what I need, what the ranch needs . . ."

His eyes narrowed and his hand on hers stiffened, "Why? We've lived here four generations without landscaping. Who are we landscaping for? The realtor?"

Margaret's eyes flashed as she stood, "What's gotten into you? How can you even think I would sell . . . ?"

"I think about it whenever I see how tired you get."

Margaret eyed her son speculatively, as if seeing him in a new way. She smoothed her apron and said, "Worrying about a son with no family, who spends weeks working alone in the Cascade foothills and shuns his friends – that's what wears me out. The ranch can't make me tired. I love this place as you do."

He tossed the wadded linen on the table. "Then why do you want to change it?"

"I'm doing what the three generations of women before me wished they could do. The house the men built is a gem, but it's a gem set in clay until the land around it is equally beautiful. Your grandmother wanted this. Her mother wanted it, but they could never do it. I'm doing it for them – and for the women after me."

He glared at her. "Janet's not going to move back to the Willamette Valley, Mom. She enjoys ranching east of the Cascade Mountains, so don't get your hopes pinned on . . ."

"I'm not talking about your sister."

"Then there'll be no women after you." His eyes warned her that the subject was closed.

"That remains to be seen. In the meantime, all I ask is that you get Mrs. Llewellyn from the bus station at eleven this morning."

"And I'm going right back out to the hills afterward."

"Mrs. Llewellyn will not be needing your help." Margaret turned and began puttering about the kitchen.

"All right," he relented, trying to soften his mother's ramrod back with a joke. "When I get to the bus station, am I looking for some skinny spinster in a pea green suit?"

His mother laughed. "Pea green with flamingo accents, I believe. Really, I have no idea what she looks like. Nice voice, though." She smiled up at him and waved a fine-veined hand. "Well, there are never very many people in that pit of a bus station. Have her paged or something."

*   *

On the way out the front door, Douglas ducked past the old school bell, hung low enough for his mother to reach. He lunged down the stairs, impatient to talk to Leonard Parr before this garden lady's bus arrived. He was also impatient to get out to Cave Springs where he thought the rustlers might be hiding. The Cave sat on Forest Service land that bordered his, but it would be a good place to hide sheep.

For his own safety, he had to assume that the man who shot George and the Blackwatch ewe last week camped out there somewhere, waiting to harass him further. No doubt Leonard Parr had hired him to make life difficult and push his financial losses beyond repair. Otherwise the one-by-one theft of the valuable Blackwatch made no sense. He could kick himself for not thinking of Cave Springs earlier.

Back before his father became too ill to go out in the woods, they had camped there with friends. He and his school mates had used it a few times during hunting season.

As he strode to the garage, Douglas planned how to get Leonard Parr off his back, once and for all, and to keep him away from his mother.

Margaret had endured phone calls and "friendly" visits from some representative of the Parr Land Development Company ever since Douglas had appealed the recent doubling of their property taxes. Like any vulture, Parr smelled carrion and circled for his piece.

Douglas knew from the sad accounts of neighbors that Parr convinced people it was healthier for them to sell. Could Parr have convinced Margaret MacGregor that she should "make life easier for Douglas by selling a little of all that land" – a technique known as blackmail.

Somehow Parr had found out that only Margaret's name was on the title, a fact that had never bothered Douglas before. He knew they should have had it in joint custody after his father's death, but he hadn't wanted to suggest it when she grieved – when they both grieved the loss of his courageous father.

And then Linda asked for part of the property in the divorce, thinking it had been his outright. At that time, the fact that the ranch wasn't his became a boon.

After Linda had finally divorced him, he hadn't wanted to do anything except work and ignore the world. Now, however, he saw that the world could not be ignored. Parr couldn't be ignored, and neither could the nagging thought that somehow, this garden lady promised to be a problem.

In the garage, Douglas by-passed the old Buick, his father's smooth riding pride and joy. Instead, he opted for the ancient Chevy truck. The shock absorbers in the truck gave a delightful ride, if one enjoyed carnivals.

Douglas' personal devil planned to put the truck to good use for this occasion. It made the ideal chariot for someone he did not care to impress. Anything to encourage this Mrs. Llewellyn to take her Portland Garden Club ideas back to Portland. After lambing, he'd get George and Ian to help him do whatever landscaping his mother wanted.

First, however, he'd make sure his mother got the nice garden, not Parr.

*   *

In the crocus meadow, four hundred feet above the ranch, a large wild ram stood very still. He watched activity at the human place below him. Once, he had lived there, eaten well there and been young there. But the place had been for humans and for followers. He didn't understand following anything, so he had kicked open a gate and left.

Some of his kind had followed him from that place, for a time, but he had not wanted them. After one fight with another ram, the few of his kind who remained alive had returned to the human place for safety and food.

He kept an eye on that place, but only out of curiosity. It held nothing for him.

CHAPTER SIX

Bronwen caught the slow bus to Eugene at six in the morning. She took a seat by the middle aisle. Since the bus appeared almost empty, she propped her backpack full of tools between herself and the window.

All the way to Salem, she practiced the technique her doctor had recommended. "Don't look out. Pretend you are in a house reading a good book or typing a report," she'd said.

But it only worked for short bits of time. Bronwen grew disgusted with her mind. She wondered why a phobia, created at age twenty-six, still controlled her at twenty-eight.

From her psychologist, she knew the cause: guilt over Ben's death.

She knew the effect: she feared hurting others if she drove. And she knew the cure: Get out there and do what you fear.

None of that knowledge seemed adequate to solving the problem.

Moreover, the advice made little sense: practice not panicking? and hope you hurt no one?

In the bus, she felt every rise over the smallest bridge, and she had to hold tight to the seat in order not to bolt down the aisle and ask to be let out at the side of the old highway.

Close her eyes, stare at the ceiling, pretend to read: none of her efforts kept her from the occasional moan, or the feeling that her stomach might empty itself into her lap.

The only thing that came close to helping were her sporadic attempts to draw sheep. Her mind had trouble conjuring the dimensions of the head, the wooly body or the taciturn and ever-suffering facial expressions of the sheep she had known.

But her crowds of morose sheep did not take her mind off the swift rise and dramatic drop of the bus going over a bridge. She imagined that by the time she arrived in Eugene, even her sheep would appear to be sick to their multiple stomachs.

CHAPTER SEVEN

Thirty minutes after he took the truck toward Eugene, Douglas MacGregor jounced into the parking lot which surrounded the three-story Parr Administrative Building. Across a good two acres of cars and trucks, sat a squat building which old timers in Eugene referred to as "Fort Ugly".

Around the proverbial cracker barrel in Porter's Grocery, he'd heard less than complimentary jokes about the new definitions of "land development" Parr's company had brought to the southern Willamette Valley.

As he descended from the truck, the shimmering heat of the asphalt hit him in the face. Just nine in the morning. He could imagine what this parking lot felt like by noon.

In the midst of a long and humorous yarn, one Porter's regular had commented that a stroll across the parking lot at Parr Land Development had sent him to the hospital with third degree burns. On arrival, the admitting nurse had written across the top of his chart "Parr boiled."

The story might be funny, in a sad way, until you remembered that until two years ago this had been Eguchi's Strawberry Farm. Ken Eguchi had been forced to sell due to increased difficulty getting access to water. Parr bought the land surrounding the source of Ken's creek. Ken had taken him to court for his rights, but then Parr also created a sickness in Ken's son, Kenjiro, Douglas's godson.

All too easily, Parr had threatened to expose Kenjiro's drug habit. Easy to buy Ken's farm. The last time Douglas had seen Ken to talk to, the man had not looked him in the eye. He was defeated and ashamed. Douglas intended to do more about that situation this morning, as well.

Inside the building, Douglas endured the elevator music and the claustrophobic, windowless design by concentrating on what he planned to say to Leonard. Once on the third floor, he had no trouble finding Leonard's office, the largest brass plaque on the largest teakwood door.

As he approached the very decorative secretary, he heard Parr's voice in the inner office conversing in not too polite tones.

The svelte young woman looked up from her laborious typing. "May I help you?"

"I have an appointment with Leonard Parr."

"Oh yes, Mr. MacGregor." She giggled.

Douglas lanced her with an ice blue stare, "Mr. Parr is in, I hear."

She reset her mouth into the curl. "He'll be with you in a few minutes. Please be seated." Her mandarin fingernail pointed at the Eames chairs.

"The appointment is for now and I'm very busy." Douglas strode past her desk and opened the door.

An immense and immaculate desk faced the door. On the side table, as if for display, were a few rolled up blueprints and a model of the building in which they were standing. Behind the desk in a black silk suit, sat a handsome young wrestler going to seed. Bulging biceps threatened the sleeve seams, but the shirt buttons were more threatened by last night's beer intake.

Leonard Parr looked up from his vehement phone conversation and scowled.

Douglas spoke first, anticipating the secretary hovering behind him. "Leonard, you often barge into my ranch unannounced, I thought you'd like me to return the favor."

Leonard's face began to twist into an ugly glare when the voice on the phone caught his attention again.

"No Ralph," he said to the phone. "Just find him and then call me back this afternoon. Find him. That's what I pay you for."

He hung up and started to berate the secretary, but she got a word in first.

"He walked past me, Lenny. I asked him to wait, 'cause I knew you was on the phone."

"Never mind, Sophie. I can talk to Mr. MacGregor. Briefly."

"Yes, sir. I've wrote that letter you wanted, sir."

"Fine. I'll look at it later. Close the door, Soph." Parr's patience frayed.

When the door had closed, Douglas chuckled at Parr's discomfort. "Money buys many things, Lenny, but it can't put brains into a chic body."

Parr ignored the barb. "You ready to sign, MacGregor? I can get you a good deal for those fifty acres. We'll throw in moving the house to a new site, build you a modern barn . . ."

"I did not come to sign. The house and the barn stay where they are, and you stay off my land."

"It's Mrs. MacGregor's land and she's never been anything but polite to me."

"That's only because she's a lady and is loath to say to your face what she feels. The answer is no."

"We'll see about that." Leonard halted himself and adjusted his face into the salesman mode. "I understand you've been having trouble with your sheep on top of all the trouble you'll have raising the tax money. You've got a lot of land going to waste over there. I get the feeling your mother is not quite so set against selling some of it as you are."

He waited a moment for that bit of news to sink in before he went on. "Just sell fifty acres close to the freeway and you keep the rest. Live on Easy Street for life."

"I don't like the way you design Easy Street. Everything you touch turns ugly." Douglas gestured toward the parking lot on the other side of the one window he'd seen in this building. "This – this is land going to waste. This used to be the most beautifully cared for strawberry farm in the state of Oregon."

Parr shrugged, "Eguchi got himself into financial trouble because he wouldn't admit it isn't practical to use so much land for strawberries."

"Practical didn't lose this land for him. I know what you did to young Kenjiro."

That seemed to strike fear in Parr. "What are you talking about?"

"You might as well tell Ralph to stop looking for my godson. I have Kenjiro far away. He won't be dependent on Ralph's products anymore, and when Kenjiro comes back, his father will be proud of him again."

Leonard Parr had half risen from his chair, a gray pallor on his face. "You got no proof. I had nothin' to do with it. I warned his father about the boy's habit, but I never sold nothin' to the kid. Never."

"Warned? You insinuated that it might get to the newspapers, maybe even to the schools where he applied for admission. That's not what I'd call a helpful warning. You threatened him."

"Ken senior told you this?" Parr's look of disbelief told Douglas that Kenjiro, had told him the truth.

"Ken senior would keep silent to the day he died rather than soil the Eguchi name. But when Kenji returns, he is going to be one clean and sober kid, and he is going to be very unhappy with what you did to his father and mother."

"What can he do about it?"

Douglas leaned both fists on the desk. Holding Leonard's attention, he explained. "Kenji doesn't have the old-world reticence about talking to the press that his father has. He remembers a certain party where he met you and Ralph and he's not going to forget the connection."

"One kid? His story won't stand up to my reputation for getting things done, bringing money into the economy of burgs like Eugene."

"If you don't stay away from my godson and from my mother, I'll show you what else I know, but I'll show you after I take it to the newspapers and to the sheriff."

Parr's face went from angry red to paper white as he fell back into his chair.

Douglas stood from the desk and turned toward the door, knocking a roll of blueprints off the side table. He reached down to pick it up. The sight of the purple seal stamped on the outside of the last sheet jarred him.

"Bauman, Grant and Llewellyn, Architects and Landscape Architect".

He threw the roll back on the table and left. All the way to the bus station, he planned the quickest way to get Parr's spy back on the bus to Portland. Mrs. Llewellyn would be gone within the hour.

CHAPTER EIGHT

Douglas arrived at the Eugene bus station ten minutes before the eleven o'clock bus. His long legs cramped after the ride, but he looked forward to the confrontation with Parr's landscape designer.

He glanced over the few forlorn travelers, but his attention riveted itself on a slim woman looking out the large window on the far side of the station. Gold-blond hair, plaited into one French braid, draped down her back, partially covering her brown tweed jacket. When she pivoted away from the window, her corduroy skirt twirled around slender legs. The corners of her mouth turned up so slightly that he couldn't be sure if she had responded to his obvious stare. She moved to the newspaper stand.

The minutes dragged until the arrival of the eleven o'clock bus.

Douglas had difficulty controlling the impulse to look at that braid and the dark green eyes of the young woman.

He chided himself and tried to find a logical explanation for his discomfort. "If she were just pretty, I wouldn't be doing this. It's the vitality of her movements, like a mare ready to race. Everyone watches an animal like that."

When the eleven o'clock bus arrived, he watched the passengers disembark and grew puzzled. None of the middle-aged women seemed to be looking for him. As the last of the arrivals departed with their families, the place held only one old fellow, asleep under an old coat and brimmed hat, and the woman in tweed and corduroy who now read something from the dog-eared display of tourist brochures.

He stepped to the ticket desk and asked, "Do you have a computer list of the passengers on the eleven o'clock from Portland?"

"Computer? You pulling my leg, fella? We're lucky to have a building at this stop."

A clear voice at his shoulder startled him. "Are you Douglas MacGregor?"

He turned to the deep green eyes of the face he'd avoided for fifteen minutes. Discomfort grew.

He answered curt and tight. "Yep. MacGregor."

"Mr. MacGregor," she barely emphasized the mister. "I'm Mrs. Llewellyn. I came in on the milk run at ten forty-five. I'm sorry to have confused you."

A gentle rhythm tinted her voice.

"You're Frank Bauman's partner?" he asked.

"Yes." She smiled. "What did you expect?"

At last, he could let his eyes do what they wanted. His gaze swept her proud face, her slim shoulders and the rising curves under her sea green blouse and brown tweed jacket.

"I looked for something a little older." He leveled an innocent gaze at her. "Something in pea green with flamingo accents."

She let her amusement be heard. "Frank's choice of partners has more to do with skill than age. Pea green is not one of my favorite colors. Flamingo deserves no comment."

Under his hat, the old man snorted.

Quick-witted, Douglas had to hand her that. But he didn't want to entertain wit. He said, "You've better taste in clothes than I would have given you credit for, considering what I saw this morning of your taste in landscaping and architecture, Mrs. Llewellyn."

"My taste? This morning? I've designed no gardens near Eugene." Mrs. Llewellyn, her back vaguely familiar in its ramrod straightness, began to move toward the parking lot, but Douglas had no intention of taking her out to the truck.

He stood very still until she realized he didn't follow her. Then, she pivoted back toward him, her brows raised in confusion, and he began his interrogation of her. "Do you design for Parr Land Development?"

"Yes." She hesitated, bewilderment slowing her glib tongue. "We did a couple of their properties outside of Portland last year and we're hoping to do one near Eugene, but I don't think the land purchases have been finished."

"They never will be." Douglas could feel anger tightening his chest.

"I beg your pardon?"

"Did Parr send you here?"

"What? No. Your mother called my partner, Frank. I asked your mother to talk to you. I don't enjoy working with families who disagree over whether I should be here at all."

"I'm not against landscaping," he said. "If my mother wants landscaping, she can have landscaping. But I'll not have some spy for Leonard Parr on the property. He has cheated and hectored my neighbors, but I won't stand for him treating her that way."

"You thought I was a . . ., a spy for Leonard! Oh, that's rich! You've a vivid imagination for a Scot, Mr. MacGregor."

He refused to be baited. "He has your designs in his office."

"He would! I have nothing to do with Leonard outside of professional necessity . . . I avoid the man otherwise."

"You avoid him?"

To his surprise, his question and its insinuating tone had the effect he wanted. She blasted him with more vehemence and information than even he expected.

"Leonard Parr has been thoroughly locked out of my apartment and my life. With two new deadbolts, top of the line, installed in a solid core door, paid for by me. As long as I can help it, Leonard Parr will be no more than a cipher in my operating budget."

Her answer seemed so spontaneous and its odd rhythm so captivating that she nearly convinced him. Then the obvious occurred to him.

"You had to change the locks? Did he have a key at one time?"

Now her deep green anger turned on Douglas MacGregor. "Whose business is it? Did you come to take me to your ranch so that I can meet your mother? Or did you come to rake me over the coals and get rid of me?"

On one level, Douglas recognized that her complexion took on a dark peach tint when cornered. On another level, he knew she had offered him an opening he no longer wanted to take.

Instead, he watched her become quite regal as she spoke.

"If your intention is to send me home, I must ask you to pay the firm for my time and the bus fare. I've been on the bus since six o'clock, but I'll only charge you since eight o'clock. I chose to take the slower bus.

"The ticket, round trip is fifty-three dollars and fifty cents. At seventy-five dollars an hour for six hours plus layover in this lovely bus station . . ."

Douglas held up a restraining hand to stop the flow of angry logic. Her eyes blazed fire at him, her lips parted, as if to go on.

"Mine was a rude question," he said softly.

She blinked and took a deep breath. Looking at his hand, she seemed to get her own anger under control.

"Didn't your firm design the Parr Administration Building in Eugene?" he asked.

"That box? That jail set in a lake of oozing asphalt? That abomination? That . . ."

"I take it the answer is no," he said quietly.

She stopped her analysis of Leonard Parr's headquarters. "No. I had nothing to do with that . . . I've seen pictures of it, but . . ."

Bronwen took a deep breath and seemed to take charge of their impasse. "Would you mind explaining this grilling?"

Douglas became aware of the eyes of the station master on them. On the nearby bench, the old man slouched in a more interested attitude than a few moments ago.

Douglas leaned closer to her and whispered, "Let's go out to the parking lot and I'll tell you all about it."

She took a step back, "Could I see your I.D.?"

"My . . .? Whatever for?" Douglas realized he'd nearly shouted at her.

"Other than the black hair, you don't fit the description of Douglas MacGregor that Frank gave me."

"Oh, for Pete's sake!" Douglas pulled out his wallet and flipped it open for her.

"Face is the same." She looked up at him from the driver's license. "Still . . ."

"What did Frank tell you about me that doesn't fit?" Douglas asked.

"Frank remembered you as a gentleman."

"That's it. I've had enough," he blurted. Even as he reached for his check book, he knew an impulse to laugh at how she'd put him in his place, but his pride wouldn't allow him to admit it. "You said seventy-five dollars an hour for seven hours, and plus . . ."

But Mrs. Llewellyn walked away from him toward the parking lot door. Over her shoulder she said, "Pay me when we're done. That is, if you're satisfied."

Now the old man sat upright on his bench and the stationmaster's eyes all but popped out of his head.

"Seventy-five dollars an hour!" intoned the man. "Have to be powerful satisfied at that rate!"

Douglas slapped his check book shut and strode out after her. He knew the sharp mind behind those green eyes understood just what she'd done to him.

As he followed her, his own eyes finished their perusal. Her tweed coat fit well enough to reveal a slender waist. The corduroy skirt emphasized her grace, and the long line of her legs.

"Powerful satisfied," the man's voice rang in his ears. His discomfort became powerful.

She stopped at the one battered truck still in the parking lot. "Yours?"

"Yes." As he reached for the keys, he took another satisfying look at her, pleased to see her right hand reach up to the button on her jacket. She twisted it around and around.

Lady's not as confident as she appears, he thought.

He allowed himself a gloating smile as his glance arrived at her thin leather shoes. "Did my mother tell you we are a sheep ranch?"

"Yes."

"Have you ever been on the grounds of a sheep ranch?"

She looked at her shoes and back up into his smiling eyes. Her face seemed open and pleasant. "Do you wear your muddy boots when you walk in your mother's house, Douglas MacGregor?" She lifted her tote bag to indicate that her boots were within.

Her shaft hit home. Douglas knew he had it coming. He'd come here with all kinds of unfounded assumptions. Gruffness was not a gentlemanly defense, so he did the next best thing. He changed the subject.

"Please get in, Mrs. Llewellyn."

She accepted the truce with a forgiving smile. He withdrew from that vision to open the door of the truck.

So, she's beautiful, he thought, *as graceful and vital as a filly in the spring, but that doesn't mean she's not on Parr's payroll. Be careful, MacGregor. She's clever. She might even fool Mother.*

Douglas opened the door of the old blue truck and stood back.

Bronwen reached in, flipped the seat forward and dropped her brief case on the floor behind. As she turned to climb in, she noted the surprise on his face.

"We used to have this model truck ourselves," she explained, "so I know all its levers. I had to get rid of ours. The shock absorbers die; then your passengers die as well."

His laughing response puzzled her. "The butt of my own joke!" he chuckled as he handed Bronwen the seat belt. Leaning closer, he raised a warning eyebrow, "Better buckle tightly."

She did.

*   *

They left Eugene in mutual tension, heading north along I-5, with Bronwen Llewellyn aware that this man still didn't trust her. At least he'd conceded defeat in the first skirmish. But Bronwen would just as soon do without other battles. She wanted to get this job done without distraction.

She glanced at the dark curls of the man beside her. Not exactly the features of a country lout, she admitted to herself. Yet, black curls and brilliant blue-eyes did not make up for loutish manners.

She reran their discussion in her mind, trying to understand what her work for Parr Land Development had to do with his anger. Parr's badgering tactics she'd become well aware of, having been a victim of them herself.

Bronwen realized that she searched for a way to placate Mr. MacGregor. She caught herself up short. Here she sat, doing what countless generations of women before her had always done when they met a man's anger; she sought ways to calm, to soothe, to solve his problem.

Let him keep his damned suspicions. Let him stew and fret. Not her problem. His suspicions? Totally irrelevant.

A sharp rise loomed in the freeway, and Bronwen knew she had worse problems than Douglas MacGregor to deal with. She gripped the side of the seat and turned her face toward the door frame, closing her eyes.

He drove fast, every bounce of the truck emphasizing her tenuous connection with firm land. Her heart pounded. Her frantic mind sought something solid to think about. The truck front rose in the air, climbing, climbing.

She braced for the plunge downward and when it came, she felt her whole being rise into her throat and threaten to come out in a moan. She clamped her lips tight.

Hold on! Hold on, it can't be too far. Only twenty miles north. Isn't that what Frank said?

After a few moments, she realized that the truck hurried again on flat ground. She opened her eyes and concentrated on the rye grass and Oregon White Oaks as they flew past. Soon, the beauty of the land took hold of her mind again, absorbing her attention as she renewed her acquaintance with the round hills of the upper Willamette Valley.

She looked for the wetlands near the freeway which she remembered from seven years previous. At dusk, she'd often seen herons stalking the edge of a pool. She found the area, but the long pool had gone dry. She turned a questioning look to Douglas.

"Wasn't there a deep marsh just before that last exit?"

*   *

"Yes. A beautiful place." It surprised Douglas that she knew of it. "The owners of the motel drained it, illegally, several years ago. They ruined the heron habitat."

"The herons were the one reason Ben and I chose to stay there. It certainly wasn't the elegance of the clone rooms and the coffee shop."

He felt himself thaw a little. "A special area, all right. Very few wildlife habitats sit close enough so that even freeway drivers can enjoy them. Why were you on the milk run coming down, Mrs. Llewellyn?"

The suddenness of the question seemed to catch her off guard. She studied the floor of the truck, twisting her coat button again. "I had things to read and . . . I like the old highway best. The rural towns and farms are easier on the eyes."

He would have thought her too busy to indulge such a preference but decided not to pursue the subject. "How do you remember the heron and the waterway?"

"Ben and I both went to graduate school in Eugene. We spent weekends in the hills around here. He liked to fish. I like to sketch. This end of the valley is good . . ."

Her voice seemed to pinch off.

They drove in silence for several minutes. With an occasional glance, Douglas watched her. She grew very still, but, two or three times, a sudden stiffness in her caught his attention. At those moments, her tension carried its vibrations across the truck seat to him. Then twice, she made a sudden motion of her hand toward the floor of the truck. At first, he thought she must have twisted off that coat button, but nothing fell. The last time she reached down, he commented on it.

"That makes three."

"Three what?"

"Three times we've been on an overpass and you've ducked down pretending to get something off the floor. What's the matter?"

He could feel her studying him and coming to some decision. Finally, she leaned back against the seat of the truck and let out a long sigh.

"I've a fear of high places, bridges and overpasses. I know it doesn't make sense, but the falling feeling doesn't go away, so I've learned to live around it."

He glanced at her and added, "So you ride on the old highway when you can, to avoid the new, higher bridges." He slowed the Chevy. "I'm sorry I brought this truck. Very selfish."

"Selfish?" she asked.

". . . because of the lady I expected, the one in the pea green suit. I intended to make her visit uncomfortable. And then after I met Parr this morning and saw that some of his blueprints were from your firm, I drew some conclusions that may have been unwarranted."

"May have been unwarranted?" she asked.

"Yes. `May'. Where my mother and my ranch are concerned, I am very wary."

"That's ridiculous."

"Perhaps, but it's the way of it."

A moment later, he said, "We're coming to the last overpass before our exit. Look out at the farthest hills. That'll be a better view than the floor."

She did look out and up. She appeared to concentrate on the clouds first and then on the hills. He took her forearm in his free hand and felt the tension in her whole body.

"Focus on one thing. That's it. Study that one thing as if you wanted to go home and sketch it. Are you drawing it? Good. That's it. . . You're going to make it."

As they approached the top of the overpass, her tension became small tremors until at the top she pulled her arm away to cover her eyes.

When they were at the bottom, she took a breath. "It did work at first."

"I know." He wasn't sure what else to say.

"I just couldn't keep it going," she said.

He glanced at her pale face and at the darkness under her eyes. Her fear seemed deep and difficult.

He said, "Just practice. A little and then a little more."

His reward became her slight smile. "Want to see my sad drawings of sheep?" she asked.

He laughed. "So, you already were practicing on the way down."

She nodded and then her face tightened, and he realized he'd come to another small hill. Off to the right sat a large old tree.

"The oak," he whispered, and saw that she did study it as they passed it.

"It's all right," he said. "We're off it now. That was a lot better than ducking for the floor."

"Thanks. I'll think about sketching on the return to Portland."

"On the milk run or the express?" His glance challenged.

"We'll see. I have the schedule for both." She looked away.

They took the next exit to the east. As Douglas slowed down on the farm road, he looked at her. Those eyes stopped his breath. He almost gunned the truck up the hill to get rid of her faster. Then he realized how shaken even this simple hill road would make her. She needed a moment to gather her wits, so he pulled over to the side of the road.

"Mrs. Llewellyn, I want you to see the layout of the ranch. This road serves our place, and one elderly neighbor, Helen Smith, whose house is a little north. Our house is up on that hill to your right."

She glanced up toward the house.

"This cottage off to the left is part of the farm," he said.

She turned to look at the cottage. "That's a lovely home. I like the wide front porch."

"Our friends and crofters, Ian and George, live there," he said. They work with me on the ranch."

He watched her study Ian's careful vegetable gardening, then Douglas looked at the grove of trees on the slope below the house. These trees were his sentinels, guarding the entrance to his home.

Because of the sentinel trees, casual freeway drivers could not even guess at the existence of his ranch. Since his divorce, he'd learned to prize his solitude, and the trees made that solitude very safe.

Until lately. Until the theft of his sheep.

He allowed his gaze to shift from the grove of trees to the braid curving at Bronwen's neck. Tendrils escaped the braid to curl around her throat, making her seem vulnerable. In spite of her sharp mind, she was defenseless in some respects. He believed her fear of heights had become debilitating.

How could she live with it, he wondered. Her husband liked to go out in the hills. Could she not hike with him because of this?

And then a blacker thought came to him. Does Parr know? He preys on peoples' weaknesses. Has he found a way to use this fear against her? Is it drug induced? Why has she needed to lock Parr out of her apartment?

Bronwen's soft voice came through his thoughts. "A Silver Maple! It's magnificent! Who planted it there?"

His attention caught at her love of a beautiful thing. "My . . . my grandfather planted it, to celebrate the birth of my father."

"I've never seen one so old and in such good condition," she said, rolling down the truck window and leaning on the sill to look more closely at the tree. "Silver Maples usually suffer from storm damage."

"My father and I thinned it every year before winter to keep it strong," he explained.

Bronwen seemed to shiver before she turned toward him. "I hope you use a safety harness whenever you're up in that mammoth."

"Of course," he answered her, feeling his scalp tighten. *After the way I treated her this morning, why would her fear translate into concern?*

"Are each of these trees a celebration?" she asked.

How did she guess? "Yes," he said. "My father called this The Celebration Grove. He planted the Tulip Tree for mother, the Cherry for my sister Janet, the Copper Beech for me."

Again, the roughness in his voice made her glance at him. Her excitement about the grove had touched an unresolved chord in him, yet as he answered, he tried to sound detached.

"Closer to the house," he continued, "stands the Magnolia that my grandfather planted for my grandmother Mary. The Japanese Red Pine represents my father. The Engelmann Spruce was planted for my grandfather's birth by my great-grandfather."

There followed a silence during which Bronwen studied each tree from the car window. "I'm glad you showed me the grove," she said at last. "I wouldn't have touched the trees in my plan, even if I hadn't known their significance. They're beautiful."

He let out a breath he hadn't realized he'd been holding. His sentinels were safe. His family seemed safe with her. But himself, no longer safe.

His anger at his own thoughts deepened. He began thinking of ways to avoid where his mind took him.

He thought he'd allowed himself to be charmed. He'd have to watch his step with this one. She could get under his armor, and he couldn't know for sure her connection with Parr.

Misinterpreting his apparent hesitation, Bronwen added, "I'm not here to disturb the harmony of your ranch, Mr. MacGregor."

He made himself look away from her, tried to stop imagining the feel of Mr. Llewellyn's wife in his arms. Without answering, he started the truck again and drove the rest of the way to the house in a silence that crackled with self-disgust on his side and puzzled anger on hers.

CHAPTER NINE

Margaret MacGregor stood on the porch. Seeing her, Bronwen felt relief. Though only five-foot-four, Mrs. MacGregor carried herself with pride. Her graying hair, cut short, set off her fine features. She exuded old world elegance and self-control. To Bronwen, she looked quite capable of taking care of her son's moods.

She came to the side of the truck as Bronwen alighted. "Mrs. Llewellyn, I expect you could do with a spot of tea after a ride in that vehicle."

Margaret took Bronwen's briefcase and handed it to Douglas. "Could you take that into the library, son? We'll have tea in there."

Bronwen saw the amused look on Douglas' face. Apparently he often took orders from his mother. Yet, Bronwen had no doubt that when necessary, he also took charge. An air of interdependence and caring between them comforted her. Douglas alone might be difficult, but together they seemed easy.

Ducking past the old school bell on the porch, Bronwen followed Margaret into the house.

* *

From the firs and cedars high above the ranch, a man slammed black binoculars against his knee, unheeding of the pain his anger caused him. The venom in his mind dominated his thoughts.

MacGregor, you arrogant bastard – bring home a beautiful woman in a beat-up truck! Purebred dogs and purebred women, nothin' too good for you, eh, MacGregor?

And purebred sheep, with fleece like silken hair. All lost. Maybe you'll lose another woman, too. The first wasn't good enough for you? Too good for me, though, with her sleek hair – too good to let go.

*   *

In the tall Oregon grape bushes at the edge of the crocus meadow, the wild ram stared upwards another one hundred feet. He watched the human on the bluff above. He knew that man too well, the one who sometimes carried a long stick that killed. Because of that man, the ram had moved south to new pastures.

The wild ram glanced down toward the humans at the buildings. He remembered living there for a time with the gentle man, with small pestering dogs and with dull-brained sheep. But now he lived free, among the dark trees that were his safety and ensured his solitude.

*   *

Margaret MacGregor led the way into their home. As soon as she entered the front door, Bronwen knew great pride had gone into its construction. In the foyer, a gleaming White Oak banister curved up the central stairwell to a landing dominated by leaded and stained-glass windows. A design of delicate branches covered with peach blossoms gave the whole a warm glow. Light through the blossoms filled the foyer.

Douglas followed his mother into the library. As Bronwen neared the door, she overheard him say, "I'm going to call Sheriff Crawley again. Also, David Brock and Phil Smith. None of them have been in the office for several days."

"Sheriff Crawley," Margaret replied, "seems to be about as helpful as ever. We haven't seen David or Phil out here for a long time. Haven't they gotten beyond all that yet?"

"I'm not sure how any of them are now, Mother. It's been a long time since she left."

As Bronwen stepped inside the room, Douglas broke off, then changed the subject. "George wouldn't stay in bed anymore. He and Ian are bringing the other flocks close for lambing. I've locked the Blackwatch rams in the barn. I hate penning them, but they should be safe there while I'm out in the hills."

"You're not going alone again?"

"I've no choice. I have to find them."

"Call Ken, or John Barsoti, if David Brock and Phil Smith can't help you. Any one of those four would go with you rather than have you out there alone."

Douglas glanced toward Bronwen. "I'll be gone just two hours."

"Where?"

Douglas's attention flicked to Bronwen then back to his mother. "I'll let Alice know, when I leave." He started toward the door but turned back. "By the way, I had an interesting meeting in Eugene before the bus arrived. Did you know, Mother, that Bauman, Grant and Llewellyn are the architects for Parr Land Development?"

"Bauman and Llewellyn?"

"The same." He left the library. Margaret's concerned gaze focused on the oak-grain pattern of the door. In the silence that followed, Bronwen could hear Douglas conversing with someone, then his steady footsteps moved down the hall and across the front veranda.

As his truck sputtered into life, Margaret dragged her attention back to Bronwen. "Architects for Parr. How nice for you."

"It's a financially successful arrangement." Although angry at the unspoken accusation she knew Douglas had leveled at her, Bronwen tried to keep her voice even.

Margaret heard the anger. She could guess at least one cause. "Financially successful, but there are some drawbacks?"

Bronwen laughed, feeling mischievous, "Have you met Leonard Parr, Mrs. MacGregor?"

"Yes . . . Ah! I see – after your hand, is he?"

Bron sniffed. "More my knee."

Margaret's laugh brought a welcome warmth. "Well, Mrs. Llewellyn, let's get started. How was your ride to Eugene?"

"The valley is beautiful!" Bronwen's attention turned to the leaded and beveled window of the library. Beyond the glass, creek beds edged with the grey trunks of alder and hazelnut cut crosswise through the rolling hills. The sight lifted her spirits. Despite Douglas MacGregor, she felt glad she had left the city to see this land again.

"The hills are losing their snow," Bronwen said, "but the valley trees are already green, and . . ." She realized what an effusive answer she gave. "I'm sorry. I mean, I had a good ride down."

Margaret smiled. "That's all right, lass. I'm glad to meet someone who appreciates what she has. Too many of us are anxious to have something else and be somewhere better. Now, draw up a chair and let's discuss this project. I saw that Douglas stopped and showed you things from the entry drive. Did he tell you about the Celebration Grove?"

"Yes – a wonderful reason to plant trees! Are there any other special uses we need to plan for? Pets? Grandchildren who need play space?"

"Yes. My daughter, Janet, brings her children three or four times a year from Bend. They love to sled on the hill just outside this window. I'd like the space to be open and safe for them."

The door to the library opened. "Ah, Alice," said Margaret. "Thank you for the sandwiches."

A smiling, round woman in her late fifties carried a tray with teacups and sandwiches. Bronwen brightened, aware of how long ago she'd eaten breakfast.

Turning to Margaret, the woman said, "Young Mr. Douglas took a sandwich to eat on his way out. Said to tell you he'd be back for Mrs. Llewellyn."

"That's fine, Alice. Would you put me through when Deputy Smith returns Douglas's call?"

"Certainly."

As Alice left, Mrs. MacGregor explained to Bronwen. "Douglas has developed a very special breed of fine-wooled sheep. For several sheep generations, he's selectively cross-bred the long, coarse-haired Highland Blackface and the fine-wooled Winninghams from Australia. The Highlanders give the Winninghams length of hair and stamina for our wet climate. The new breed is called `Blackwatch' after the irregular Highland regiments of the seventeen hundreds.

Margaret's forehead puckered in concern. "In the last two weeks, several of the Blackwatch ewes have been stolen. Several days ago, Douglas and old George Conall, our crofter – our farm hand and shepherd, went out in the hills looking for the rustler and nearly got themselves killed by a sniper. The man did kill the original mother of our Blackwatch flock.

"And he wounded George in the chest. George almost died before Douglas scared off the sniper. He had to carry that tough old coot several miles to meet the ambulance."

Bronwen finally understood Douglas's mistrust of her. He had plenty of reasons for being wary.

"After the shooting in the hills," Margaret continued, "Douglas gathered the rams into an area near the house and set the dogs to watch. Then, last night, the dogs set up an awful racket. By the time we got outside, one of the rams was gone. The dogs were frantic to chase, but Douglas is as protective of them as of the sheep."

Bronwen asked, "Is this happening at other ranches?"

"Only our ranch has this breed and it could become very valuable. Very few people know about the experiment."

Security needs would affect the landscape needs, so Bronwen asked, "Is the barn big enough to hold the ewes as well as the rams?"

"It's a big barn, but not that big. And it would be unhealthy to crowd them, especially at lambing." Mrs. MacGregor sighed and straightened her small shoulders. "Well, we can't solve that one now, I suppose."

Bronwen made a mental note to see what changes might make protecting the flock easier. "Shall we go out and look over the grounds, Mrs. MacGregor?"

"Yes, and it's Margaret, please. I'm assuming you brought outdoor clothes and boots in that carry-all?"

Bronwen smiled with warmth at Margaret MacGregor's quickness of mind.

*   *

In a small lava cave, east of the ranch, about seven miles into the mountains, Douglas MacGregor stooped over the remains of a campfire. In his hand lay a tuft of the softest, long-staple wool in the world. On the floor of the cave lay the skeletal remains of a recent meal, a ewe and her unborn lamb.

Douglas's blue eyes glittered with rage.

"Another one . . . Yesterday!" he hissed at himself. "If I had come yesterday!"

Outside, in the bright sun of afternoon, he could see where the rustlers' truck had stood, but beyond the first few yards, the distinctive studded tire design had been obliterated. Something like a heavy log, had been dropped down behind the truck to drag out the tracks, just as they had been wiped out in Ian's Draw.

Douglas's mind seethed. What am I left with now? he thought. I know so little about this rustler aside from the fact that when he pinned us down in Ian's Draw, I heard an old truck with one door that wouldn't close – one door hinge must be broken, studded tires and an engine that doesn't want to start. And the gun he used on George, a high-speed rifle.

He knelt to get a clear memory of the tire tracks, but the image of the bones of lamb filled his mind.

By all the saints! It's almost as if he left these skeletons here, hoping I'd find them. Like the ewe he shot yesterday in the hills, just for vengeance. Who can hate me that much? Parr? Until this morning in his office, not even Leonard Parr hated me enough to shoot George Conall.

Turning on his heel, he strode to his own truck, swung into the cab and headed back toward MacGregor Ranch on the road through Ian's Draw.

CHAPTER TEN

By late afternoon, Douglas MacGregor stood once again on the hill above his home, running over in his mind the ugly scene he'd found at Cave Springs this noon. His two collies watched him, waiting for some word, any word from him. Though deeply angered, he remained quiet. He didn't believe in harrying the sheep.

His body remained quiet, but not his mind. Douglas felt the punishment he'd given his body these last few weeks. He and George had covered most of the mountains and hills of his ranch on foot looking for signs of predators or rustlers. The net result of all their hiking had been the near loss of George.

Parr maneuvered behind this. All of it, including the tax increase smelled of Parr bribery. But the theft of the sheep seemed too niggling, one ewe at a time. Douglas didn't think Parr would have the patience for it. From Parr, he expected something bigger, at least a threat with the facade of legality. The stealing of the Blackwatch devastated him but appeared almost petty for a big corporation. More like vengeance.

Yet Douglas had to believe Parr caused all. Any other explanation was unthinkable. Right now, for a few minutes, he didn't want to think at all. He wanted to stop his whirring mind and enjoy the quiet of his land and his animals. It had been too long since he'd even had time to gaze at the sky for more than a weather report.

"By da me, Robbie," he whispered to one of the two border collies. The dog came near, watching Douglas' face, trying to sense ahead of time what he needed.

*   *

Robbie knew Douglas didn't just stand quietly on the hill. There were many signs that his master had worries. Robbie knew he and Roy were treated well, talked to and fed, exercised and praised, but in some way, the man was not present in his contact with the dogs. Douglas had the right motions and words, but without the normal warmth.

Robbie sat close enough to Douglas to lean, just a little, on the man's leg.

Douglas' suspended contemplations when he felt the dog's nudge. "Good boy," he leaned down to pet Robbie. "You're a patient boy, aren't ye? We haven't had a good game of sticks for some days, have we?"

From farther away, Roy saw the attention that Robbie received. He couldn't leave his post, but his short yap let Douglas know that he, too, had missed their usual companionship.

"Fine boy, Roy. You're a sticker, yes? Coom, Roy," he said. The collie could join in the reunion. Douglas knelt. Roy and Robbie sat next to him, glorying in the attentive hands that knew just where they liked to be scratched. At last they could feel the vibrations in those soft, deep tones of his resonant voice.

*   *

The words he used for the collies he'd learned while watching his grandfather train dogs. Douglas had noticed the musical cadences that Welsh imparted to Bronwen's English, but his own remnants of the family Scots brogue were rarely apparent to him.

With a hand on either dog, he lay back and allowed himself to relax. Nearly lambing time, and already tired.

*   *

Much later, the sound of his mother's laughter wafted up the hill to awaken him. Downhill, on the far side of the house, he could see his mother walking with Mrs. Llewellyn. Margaret seemed to be retelling some anecdote about each tree and hillock.

It had been some time since he'd seen his mother with another woman. His father's last illness had been long, requiring Margaret's and Douglas's near constant attention. Absence from friends had isolated both of them. Perhaps Bronwen's presence might be good for his mother after all. Possibly, nothing connected her with Parr beyond business, but he intended to be guarded.

His reaction to Mrs. Llewellyn puzzled him. More it angered him.

He had no intention of being attracted to any woman, and certainly not to Mr. Llewellyn's wife.

Yet, even now, the sound of Bronwen's voice and the memory of her fresh spring smell brought a strong hunger to his body. Until today, this was a hunger he'd almost suppressed with unremitting hard work.

Douglas grew annoyed to realize how much he'd been watching Bronwen's progress around his front acreage. She looked to be deep in conversation with his mother about the hazelnut at the bottom of the hill. He thought it a shrub worth getting rid of.

With one startling slash of her arm, she indicated her preference. Gone.

Even as he watched his mother collapse onto Bronwen's shoulder in mirth, he felt the heat of his own blood rise. His mind must be tired. It meant nothing – nothing at all that she agreed with him about that stupid nut bush. No omen that her gesture mimicked his very thoughts. Coincidence.

He realized that Bronwen stayed very near his mother, near enough to take her arm if she should need it. Close enough to protect, but not hover. His habit with Margaret was the same, allowing her independence while aware of her fragility.

Margaret pointed out some object far away from them. Bronwen nodded and ran across the field to have a closer look at an old oak that had become overgrown with Virginia Creeper. She pulled back the creeper and stepped inside the cave created by the overgrowth. In a few minutes, she darted back outside, pulling creeper vine out of her hair and shirt collar. Douglas caught himself cleaning out his own shirt collar in empathy.

From her gestures, he gathered that Bronwen believed the tree worth saving. To his amazement, she began to dance around the decrepit old oak. In spite of her boots and the uneven terrain, even overalls couldn't disguise the grace of her movements. She looked at his mother, laughing. Across the field, his regal mother joined in the primitive dance for a short time before they both laughed, and Bronwen danced back to Margaret.

Douglas chuckled with them and then stopped himself. As a boy, the primeval aura of that ancient oak had held him in awe. He might have thought of such primitive rites as Bronwen acted out, but had always held those impulses in check. His mother's spontaneous kinship with the girl's instincts surprised him.

In a few short hours, Bronwen Llewellyn had managed to establish herself in his mother's affections. She'd gotten under his own skin within a few minutes. If she owed Leonard Parr anything, she could be dangerous to have around. He'd have to treat her with great caution. He owed it to his family and to his neighbors whose son's Parr had tried to ruin. He knew the man would stop at nothing to get land he wanted, and he wanted this land very badly indeed.

Douglas heard the bleating of ewes and glanced off to the north.

George and his brother Ian herded their Corriedales into the grass which grew under the cottonwood stand on the lower land, across the entry road from the house. Ian's puppy worked hard to follow Ian's orders.

A sling held George's right arm and shoulder immobile. He seemed to be recovering from the near fatal wound. He waved his good arm at Margaret who took Bronwen across the road to introduce him.

George doffed his cap and talked to them. On the far side of the flock, George's brother, Ian, bowed his head and scuffed his boots in the grass. His small dog leaned on his leg and looked eager.

Douglas, whose father had named parts of the ranch for these loyal friends, felt vaguely betrayed by their deference to the woman who could be working on Parr's behalf. Of course, he reminded himself, they had no way of knowing.

Next to Douglas, the collies had flattened themselves, keeping a vigilance that alternated between the sheep, their master and the voice of their mistress. They felt his cautious mood as he observed the women continue their exploration of the hillside.

After a time, he said to the dogs, "Go away to me, Robbie, Roy."

*   *

Bronwen became aware of Douglas's dark figure the moment they came around the east side of the house. She saw that, at a small gesture from him, the dogs took up positions at the edges of the flock. When she and Margaret entered the field, he rose to greet his mother, but he did not look at Bronwen. Bronwen could feel his wariness and wished the afternoon could have concluded without him. Margaret's open friendliness marked a contrast to his suspicious nature.

She saw the collies watch for strays in the herd. Aware that the arrival of a stranger might cause commotion, Bronwen walked with steady steps up the hill.

As they neared Douglas, his mother gestured toward the large, dark roof which could be seen over the slight rise in the meadow. "I haven't taken Bronwen near the barn yet. I thought she ought to talk to you about how to keep the flocks and the crops safe."

For a moment, Bronwen felt he hesitated to explain his security measures, but after looking at his mother, he let down his guard a little. "I'm going to have to put the Blackwatch ewes in the small corral near the barn this afternoon," he said. "Come with us while we move them."

He indicated the collies as his colleagues. "We can discuss possible solutions to sheep housing as we go."

Margaret excused herself, "I'm going to help Alice put up a supper for your drive back to Eugene, Bronwen. Did you want to catch the seven o'clock bus? I believe there aren't any express after that."

Bronwen hesitated a moment. "Yes," she said slowly, then seemed to gather her courage. "Thank you, Margaret. The express would be fine." She glanced at Douglas who merely watched her.

Margaret turned to her son. "Will you be through with the flock in time for the trip back to Eugene or would you rather I drive Bronwen?"

*   *

Feeling cornered, Douglas said what he knew his mother wanted. "I'll drive her into town, Mother," he said, "I believe it still gets dark about six thirty."

Margaret said, "He's protecting me from my own night blindness. Will Frank meet you at the bus station in Portland? That's a seedy part of town, if I recall correctly."

"Oh no, it's only a short walk to my apartment."

Douglas frowned, "Won't your husband meet you?"

Bronwen turned away from him. "My … my husband died." She seemed unaware of his shocked reaction.

She said to Margaret, "Don't worry. I've walked it many times."

Margaret raised her eyebrows but shrugged. "Well, all right. I'll see you two in a little while." She waved and walked off.

Now, Douglas wished he hadn't volunteered to spend more time near her. Bronwen's worried gaze seemed to understand his reluctance, but she misinterpreted his reason. "I'm sorry to put you out," she said. "I wish I could still drive."

Douglas sought to cling to any reason for keeping a barrier between himself and this woman.

Parr! he thought. Where there is Parr there are drugs.

After a long moment, he turned toward her, his mind probing her features for a reaction. "Are you taking any medicine to help you get around that fear?"

"Medicine? I don't know of any that would help." She said, "I am getting better, and I'd be afraid to ruin the improvement with some pill."

"Good," he said, and turned back to his flock, alarmed that he felt so relieved at her answer. Somehow, the more he knew of Bronwen Llewellyn, the more he felt his hard-won self-protection slipping.

He pushed away his reaction, and spoke to the dog, "Go way to me, Robbie."

The dog raced around the edge of the flock. His motions pushed the flock together. Slowly they became a sea of black faces rather than individual sheep.

Out of the corner of his eye, he saw that the dog's smooth work fascinated Bronwen.

"Come by to me, Roy," he said. The other collie ran a line perpendicular to that of Robbie. The sheep began moving down the hill toward the barn road. Working together, the two dogs watched for any who might stray from the stream. A nip at the hind leg of a wanderer brought it back to the flock.

As they neared the gate to the road, Douglas called, "Coom bye, Robbie." The dog came forward with slow tight steps, through the flock. He nudged the lead sheep past Douglas and Bronwen.

Robbie controlled the lead sheep through the gate, followed her and waited for the rest of the flock.

"Coom bye, Roy."

Roy took over nudging sheep toward the gate and soon had a steady stream entering the road for Robbie to control. After the last ewe, Roy went through the gate.

*   *

"Quite a demonstration," said Bronwen. "Did you train the dogs?"

"No, Border Collies are born talking to sheep." His impassive face hinted amusement. "I only taught them how to make it look as if I were in control."

Bronwen laughed, and with her hand, nudged Douglas through the gate the way Roy would. He let her push him in, and then held the gate open for her. As she came downhill toward him, he glanced up at her, saw that her green eyes reflected the light of the low sun. He decided to try a truce between them, so when she came through, he took her arm.

"Steep terrain," he explained.

"These are hiking boots, not high heels."

He smiled at her barb. "All the same, I'm not sure our liability insurance covers this situation."

A moment later he asked, "What's mother want to do with the grounds?"

As Bronwen answered, she acquiesced to his insistent hold. "Your mother has some favorite plants she'd like to keep. There are some she'd love to consign to the burn pile. She'd like lawn that could be used for entertaining in the spring and summer. She wants to grow bulb flowers without worrying about their effect on the digestive tract of lambs. King George Rhododendrons are a favorite flowering. . ."

Douglas used his hand on her arm to get her to slow down a little in their descent. "Your strides are about twice normal when you're enthusiastic. I like to walk with my ewes not scurry them."

She glanced at Douglas. Seeing no teasing smile on his face, decided to ignore possible double meanings. She looked toward the flock, "I do get carried away. I never expected to find such a beautiful setting. Already, I can imagine the lawn and the narcissus in the spring."

She made herself stop her effusions. Let him be annoyed that she'd come. She enjoyed the beauty of this land. It was his mother's home as well. At least his mother lived at the ranch. From what Bronwen had heard, he lived out in the hills most of the time anyway, so why should he care what they did to the landscape? She looked away from him and out over the house and front meadow, a vision of what would be, already in her head.

*　*

Douglas's hand could feel the warmth of this earnest woman through the sleeve of her turtleneck shirt. He watched the high color of her face as she studied his ranch, imagining how beautiful it could be for his mother.

Perhaps he'd been wrong. She'd shown herself far too interested in life to be in Parr's hip pocket, either for drugs or for money. He had the strong and uncomfortable feeling that his mother and his home might be in good hands.

CHAPTER ELEVEN

As they approached the rise between the barn and the house, Douglas slowed a little. "Mrs. Llewellyn," he said, "My mother needs to entertain friends more often. What you're doing will make that easier for her."

Apparently embarrassed by his oblique thanks, she reached for her coat button and glanced away toward the kitchen light.

"Your mother is a welcoming person," she said, then she gazed at him and added, "Your friends will enjoy the garden as well."

Douglas stopped walking and stared at her. "Sheepherding is done alone," he whispered. "I haven't friends to speak of."

Surprised by the strong emotion behind his simple statement, Bronwen thought there was much more to his reaction than not having time for friends.

She couldn't escape the feeling that she'd ignited a smoldering fire. Not knowing what to say, she cast about for something, anything to help her ignore his burning energy.

Ahead of them, Robbie and Roy herded the sheep over the rise in the farm road. The top of the barn roof loomed beyond. To escape his tension, she walked after the dogs.

Looking at the barn fully for the first time, she exclaimed, "Great Coxwell!"

"What did you say?" He watched her.

"Your barn!" she waved an arm at the massive building. "I saw only the roof from the lower hill. If I'd seen the end wall, I'd have known."

"Known what?" He came uphill toward her.

"It's . . . It's like barns built by the monasteries of England, before King Harry."

"Yes," he chuckled, (remembering that his grandfather would have said 'before Fat Harry.') "I know what type of barn it is, but what did you say, first?"

"Uhm . . ." She stared at it as at a famous work of art. "It's like Great Coxwell in England – a mother hen protecting her children. So simple and beautiful a building . . . I never thought to see another."

Douglas's eyes lit up at her comparison with hens and chicks. He chuckled as he followed her animation. "Would you like to see the rest of it?"

"Please. Of course. Oh yes!"

He laughed out loud, releasing the tension of their previous moment. "I've never seen such a vigorous response to something so mundane as my barn."

"Mundane? Mundane!" She glanced at him. "Utilitarian? Yes. Common? No. Who built it?"

Before he answered her, he opened the gate into a small corral near the barn and let the dogs marshal the flock inside. "My great-grandfather and Frank Bauman's grandfather built it when they first arrived from Scotland in the late eighteen hundreds." He looked the barn over. "It does serve its purpose well."

Bronwen looked askance. "You've lived with this great barn all your life and you can only say, 'It serves its purpose well'?"

"Isn't that the highest praise for any building?"

"You're right," she admitted.

They were now at the bottom of the draw in which the barn stood. Its enormous front gable loomed over them. Looking up at the ridge of the imposing roof, Bronwen became unsteady.

Douglas saw her reel. The heights again, he thought, and held her shoulders. "Breathe," he ordered.

She took in a fresh breath, realized his diagnosis appeared to be correct and, deeply embarrassed, tried to move away from him toward the sheep corral.

Instead, keeping a guiding hand under her elbow, he moved toward the wide, arched wagon entry in the end of the barn.

"You can't live like this the rest of your life, Bron . . . Mrs. Llewellyn."

He studied her pale features before he continued. "As I see it," he said, "this fear of heights comes on you when you're up, and looking down. Or else it comes when you're down, looking up. Wouldn't you say that was a bit overmuch?"

"Put that way, I guess you could say so."

"Bronwen! It's no so little a thing as you pretend."

The color rushed to her face, yet she managed to look him in the eye as she answered. "I'm sorry you had to go out of your way because of it. I know, for a person with no fears or weaknesses, it must be hard to understand."

In the waning light, he felt suddenly cold, and said, "Oh, I have weaknesses, all right, and fears too."

He reached out and removed a twig of creeper vine from her loosened braid.

Startled, Bronwen pulled back.

Douglas watched her with concern, a knot of regret tightened in his stomach. I've made her fear me, he thought.

Mercifully, at that moment Robbie barked. The sharp yap interrupted Douglas's attention. He frowned and followed the dog away from the barn and out to the corral, his gaze scanning the sheep.

"Damn! Rob's right," he muttered, gripping the gate post in silent anger. "Another ewe's been taken, e'en today." He turned on his booted heel. Without a glance at her, he muttered, "Coom. Let's find her."

Even Douglas wasn't sure if he spoke to Robbie or Mrs. Llewellyn, but she followed his swift strides back through the gate and up to the grassy area. He paced the perimeter, looking at the ground.

"Och, there!" He found the sign in the grass and followed it to where the fence passed the edge of a small wooded area on the north.

*   *

Bronwen saw the cut wires before he did and held them open. He looked at her as if he'd just remembered that they barely knew each other. He studied her face a moment, then took the broken ends and motioned her through. Once through, she fell in next to him.

"See these, Bron . . . Mrs. Llewellyn?"

"The foot prints?"

"Aye and the shoe's covered with something, cloth. You see the warp and the woof of it clearly in this one. It hides the print of the sole."

Bronwen, though following his comments, was also aware of the change that had come over him. His anger grew with each sentence, but not thrown up as a wall between them. Instead, he talked to her as an ally.

"Have you seen this print before?" she asked.

"Each time he's taken one. He's so sure of this disguise that he doesn't even hide where he goes. Along here he's had a rough time with her. See, she dropped there and made a try at runnin'. Good girl. Gave the man a hoof in the leg! See there? He's hopping on one foot through this part.

"And here, he's got her down – a bit of a struggle. She's a game 'un, all right! Now, he's got her again. Deeper footprints here. See how much more weight he carries? She's with young. That bas'... I hope he knows what to do for her when she needs it!"

Bronwen followed all this, knowing he let off steam by talking as he followed the trail. In the side light of the low sun, the shadow of the prints showed very clearly. She, too, stooped to study them. When she rose again, Douglas stood a little to one side of her.

A dead branch lay in her path. She reached to move it.

He looked up, ice in the blue of his eyes. She flinched from the cold look of anger just as he flung himself sideways into her. His weight crushed breath from her. His shoulder thudded into her abdomen. His attack threw her into a huckleberry thicket. Her ears rang with the crack of something far too loud to be bone.

He pulled up and looked behind him then back at her, his dark eyes unreadable. Leaning on his arms over her, he closed his eyes as if to fight down rage. She couldn't move, barely began to feel the stab of a twig in her shoulder blade and forced quick shallow breaths.

*　*

The quick rise and fall of her breathing made Douglas more aware. In her face, he saw the eyes of a startled animal and the pain as she tried a deeper breath.

"Bron, I'm . . . where'd I hurt you?" His hand brushed across her forehead and over her cheek before he slipped it behind her head, probing for any sign of a wound. "I couldn't let you take another step. You'd ha' been right in it, sure! The dead branch tripped it."

She still couldn't speak. She seemed to try but couldn't push enough air to make a sound.

His hand found the twig stabbing her back and pulled it from under her. She grimaced.

He recognized again her pain when breathing. But for that pain, he would have lifted her. He wasn't sure of the cause and knew he shouldn't move her until he was.

The instincts of a husbandry-man took over from the reticence of a gentleman. He kneaded the injured muscles of her neck – a healing motion he'd used many times with his animals. He felt her battered body begin to relax, breath returning to her lungs and color to her face.

The sudden heat of his own body warned him against his natural ways. He pulled up, his eyes at once probing her reaction and apologizing for his touch. "I . . . When ye can breathe a bit I'll…"

Bronwen closed her eyes and reached to massage the large muscle under her rib cage. He watched the pulse return to her throat and her breathing become deeper. When she opened her eyes, he forced his gaze from her body.

I should never have touched her.

Her voice seemed just a whistle of air. "What . . .? What . . . cracked?"

He turned back. "Ach! Ye've not seen it. A trap. A big . . . can you sit up?" Douglas slipped a hand under her head again, waiting for her reply. At her nod, he lifted her head, careful of her bruised shoulder and ribs.

When she sat up, Bronwen took a deep breath and blew it out, then took a deeper one still. "I'll be fine . . . just that blow from your shoul. . . Oh, Duw!"

He watched her eyes widen as she saw the rusty tooth of an animal trap stabbed completely through the heavy branch – the jawbone of an enormous shark ripping the limb.

"What if Margaret . . . or Robbie . . . Oh, diafol!" She twisted her head away from the sight. He felt her arms go cold. He rubbed her arms. His own thoughts of what might have happened still knotted his guts. "You're still in a bit of shock from my tackle."

The approaching sunset grayed all around them, but into the dark levels of his consciousness shot a faint first light.

Her thoughts were for others, he realized, for mother and my collie.

Pain and fear slammed her when she saw the trap, yet it wasn't for herself she felt fear.

She looked up at him, her face pale. "Someone hates you very much, Douglas MacGregor," she whispered.

She echoes the very thought I've pushed from my mind all day, he acknowledged. Glancing behind him at the rusty jaw crushing the limb, he felt anguish twist his heart.

"Hates?" he asked, "No. They want me to back off, not to search for them. Greed, yes. Not hate."

Though her voice remained weak, Bronwen persisted. "This was no warning. Nor was the shooting of George and the ewe in the hills last week, this was for you – to maim or to kill. Those tracks were disguised, but far from hidden. He wanted you to follow and . . ."

Afraid to give her idea credence, he forced suspicion to blot out other thoughts. "How do you know about the ewe?" He watched her for any betraying hesitation.

"Your mother told me," she pushed out a tired whisper, "and about George Conall."

Worry and fatigue showed on her features. His shoulder had hurt her more than she let on, he thought. Her arms had grown cold, but at her temple, wet hairs curled tightly like those of a fevered child. His hand brushed her forehead and jerked back as the brief contact burned.

"Who hates you enough to do these things?" she asked, struggling to get up.

He helped her stand and then held her at arms' length. "No one hates me. The Blackwatch are extremely valuable. That alone is enough to explain all of this."

"And how many know of their existence? Your mother, your ranch hands, how many friends . . .?"

"Bron!" He refused to suspect his friends as they had once suspected him. "Stay out of this!"

She looked back at the trap and up at him.

His hands still gripped her upper arms, his gaze remained on the trap as well. "I'll not believe this the work of a friend," he said.

"But who? Who knows enough?"

He blew out a ragged, angry breath and looked at the ground between them. "I'm sorry, Mrs. Llewellyn. I know you're trying to help. But I know no one who would do such an evil thing. No one."

"I'm sorry, too, Mr. MacGregor. I didn't mean to push and interfere. But you might have been killed . . ."

Surprised, he looked at her, fear in his heart.

*   *

Bronwen stepped back, pulling her arms free, she wondered why she cared so much that he not be hurt?

It had to be the fear. Both of them felt it. That godawful trap could have killed him. With adrenaline pumping, both of them were bound to feel an abnormal need to comfort and be comforted. She had to walk away from this man before she made a fool of herself.

"Your sheep!" she remembered. "We didn't close the corral. Only the dogs are keeping them from your mother's vegetables."

When she brushed the back of her overalls, a sharp pain reminded her of his sharp shoulder bone. She straightened, saw that he noticed and tried to laugh it off. "That was some tackle. Did you play football as a boy?'

"No, ma'am. Basketball."

"Must have been a rough-house league. I'm not complaining, mind you, I'm just wondering which would have been less permanent, the tackle or the trap."

His laugh seemed forced. "Young lady, according to my split-second calculations, gangrene of the leg seemed more permanent than a broken rib."

"Oes. 'tis true."

She followed him back through the fence and across the meadow with the dogs and the sheep. The fearful image of the trap wouldn't leave her mind. The lingering memory of his hand on her neck and shoulders grew strong.

Marching with his long-legged strides across the grass, Bronwen felt drawn into his dark thoughts. As in the truck this morning, he became alternately solicitous and curt. Such moodiness was understandable, given the recent occurrences on his ranch.

The trap appeared to be just one of many vicious things that had happened to him lately. She couldn't blame him for being suspicious of her or of anybody, but he seemed unwilling to consider the possibility that anyone besides Parr was involved. She didn't like Parr, knew he had great greed for land, yet she didn't believe him interested in the kind of personal vengeance represented by the trap and by last week's murderous sniper.

As she saw it, the rustlers, whoever they were, had raised the ante with the injury of his friend and shepherd, George. With this trap, they had tipped their hand. They were after more than sheep or land. They meant to hurt Douglas MacGregor as deeply as possible, and he didn't want to believe it.

Not only did he avoid the hurt of truth, he'd grown angry with her for pointing it out. His silence, as they walked, exuded eloquent disdain, telling her to stay out of his problems. If she worked for his mother during the weeks it would take to install the plan they'd sketched out, she wasn't sure she could stay out. She didn't care much for Douglas MacGregor, but if anything hurt him, it would hurt his mother. Bronwen had come to like his mother very much.

In fact, she felt the need to be with Margaret MacGregor again, to put some distance between herself and Douglas. She needed to regain a balanced perspective.

"I'm going to say good-bye to your mother," she said, "but I'll let you tell her about the trap. I don't want to frighten her."

"Tonight, when you're gone," he answered.

*   *

For Douglas MacGregor, it had been a long time since a woman had surprised him as thoroughly as Bronwen Llewellyn. She seemed so at home tramping around his ranch with his mother, so easy around his sheep and his dogs. And when danger had threatened her life, her fear was for his mother, his animals, even himself. Her own pain and danger were dismissed with humor.

He worried. The strong physical attraction he'd felt in the truck this morning compounded now by deeper knowledge of her. He'd better watch his step.

He watched Bronwen until she entered the kitchen door, telling himself that he would avoid contact with her after tonight.

Yet images of her crowded his mind, replacing resolve with desire: Bronwen pivoting toward him from the bus station window, leaning out of the truck to admire the grove, dancing with his mother before the oak tree, staring, transfixed by the light of the sun on his barn, lying beneath him in the woods . . .

His anger at himself lay deep. Wanting her, wanting any woman was wrong. He had learned that lesson well.

*   *

Atop the low hill east of the barn, the sun set angled a golden light through the binocular's magnifying lenses, but the heavy man saw his own dark hatred.

MacGregor doesn't deserve her, not her or any woman.

When I heard the trap, it felt so good, so good . . . but the sound lied.

They came out of the woods touching each other, as if nothing had happened but their touching.

MacGregor's gonna lose something he loves – everything he loves, and then before he dies, he's gonna know why.

CHAPTER TWELVE

At seven o'clock in Eugene, Douglas watched Bronwen's bus disappear. The soft spring rain coated his hair and stood in beads on his sweater.

He returned to the old Buick. Folding his long frame into the driver's seat, he rested his head on his arms over the steering wheel, exhausted with the effort of the silence which had enveloped their drive to Eugene.

Before they left the ranch, he knew Margaret had been aware of the heavy atmosphere, yet she'd puttered about the warm kitchen, making sandwiches and making plans with Bronwen for a subsequent visit.

Like a recording, his mind played over and over Bronwen's bald statement, "My … my husband died. My husband died."

He sensed the bleakness behind the brief phrase and wanted to know more. But the more he knew, the more he cared, and he couldn't let himself care.

And then there was that other odd statement, Great Coxwell – a mother hen protecting her children. He sensed a deep significance to her of that moment, his barn, her reaction to it.

And she'd said children, not chicks.

He analyzed too much. She bothered him too much. Douglas vowed to absent himself two days from now when Bronwen returned to work on the landscape.

Getting his mind back to the problem of the lost sheep would save him from being so gut-wrenched by her. He must be tired or stupid to have allowed her to . . .

To what? Well, what had she done?

Nothing except be totally alive, and for him, totally inappropriate.

The rest – his fault. His awareness of Bronwen, the memory of her so close to the springing trap – a day's worth of indelible memories of a warm and beautiful woman, coupled with his helpless anger this afternoon in the cave with the bones of his ewe and her lamb – all these images crowded into his mind and seemed to separate him from humanity, making polite discourse impossible.

Douglas sat up, smacking his hands on the steering wheel. His reaction to her had proven nothing more than that he was overworked and needed to see old friends. He should make himself get out with people.

"Sheepherding is done alone," he told himself again. Until today he'd loved the solitude. Hiding beyond his sentinel grove, listening to the sounds of the hills, smelling the wet wool, the grass and the rocks, he knew a peace he'd longed for all the years of his schooling and of his pleasureless marriage.

But today, `being alone' had taken on the taint of `loneliness'.

As he looked back, he saw that three things had become obstacles in his friendships. A few friends still believed the lies spread by his ex-wife, Linda. Others, in an effort to make up for the pain she'd caused were always fixing him up with some friend of a friend.

But the most important obstacle of all had been his own withdrawal from the world. He had turned his back on anyone who might disappoint him. That decision had cut him off from most people who had known and cared for both him and Linda. He needed to reach out again and see which were his real friends.

As long as he was in Eugene tonight, he ought to pay a call on one old acquaintance – Gerald Crawley, the sheriff. Something big must be happening in Lane County to keep Gerald away from the office for so many days. In all the years Douglas had known Crawley, the man had never been far from a chair. Even when they'd both been serving in Central America, Crawley had managed to be sitting in the quartermasters' office while Douglas spent two months in the mountains as a prisoner of the opposition.

Douglas started his car, flipped on the windshield wipers and eased out of the bus station lot onto Pearl Street and headed toward Eighth Avenue for the short drive to the sheriff's office. Within minutes, he parked in the lot with three brand new Fords bearing the county seal.

The slick cars were to be expected. Ever since running for the office of sheriff, Gerald Crawley had aped every western hero on celluloid film. Speedy cars, western boots and an Andy Divine accent had been adopted as soon as Crawley had been sworn in.

Entering the building, Douglas spotted Gerald in the expected position: feet crossed on the desk, swivel chair tilted back, hat shielding his eyes from the ceiling light.

Douglas reached across the desk and lifted the bottom boot, tilting the sheriff and the sheriff's chair to a precarious angle.

Crawley shouted, "Damn you, Phil Smith!"

He caught at his falling Stetson and glared. As soon as he saw who faced him, Crawley rearranged his jowly features toward pleasant. "Oh, MacGregor – I was just cogitatin' on your problem. You didn' have to come all the way into town."

"Crawley, this is how you cogitated your way through high school. Any reports of missing sheep on other ranches?" Douglas let the heavy feet slap back to the desk.

Crawley jammed his hat down tight. "There ain't no unusual losses. There is some varmint, maybe cougar, around the east valley, ya know."

"Cougar? No, I don't know. I've been all over my place and seen nothing to indicate cougar. What evidence have you for that hypothesis?"

"Hypothesis! MacGregor, did ya ever use anything less than tuxedo-type words your whole life?"

Douglas ignored Gerald's red herring. "What evidence?"

"Ranchers talk. Phil heard it up by Coburg. I don't go crawlin' through the woods lookin' for varmints, ya know."

"Which ranchers?"

"I don't know, just talk." Crawley sounded testy.

"Well, here's some rancher talk I hope you'll keep in mind. I am missing five ewes and one ram, all from the same flock, the flock I keep closest to home. I have a lot of less valuable, but very tasty sheep out in the hills with the crofters – easier prey for cougar. This is not cougar. The signs are all wrong. When we were boys, I saw the ritual way they open their kill."

Gerald sputtered, "I don't know nothin' about all that ritual stuff, but some animal is the most likely explanation."

"No, Gerald, it's the most convenient explanation for you. You even chose to believe the shooting of George was a hunting accident – out of season. But this varmint, which chooses my most valuable sheep, leaves footprints not dead carcasses behind as evidence. He cooked and ate my ewe and her lamb at Cave Springs. He shot another ewe the same day he shot George. The varmint is human."

"Well," drawled Gerald, "You might ought to talk to John Barsoti over to the Sheep Ranchers' Association. Seems like, as chairman, he'd know about other ranches with "human cougar" troubles."

"Barsoti is also running for state senator right now. He's hardly ever home. You know that."

"Cain't do much fer ya then, MacGregor."

"No man can do much while sitting on his center of gravity," said Douglas.

Gerald started to talk, but Douglas held up his hand to halt the excuses. "I invite you to the ranch, any day, to see whether you can find evidence of cougar or coyote or anything other than human hand in the disappearance of these sheep. In the meantime, unless you've good reason to treat it otherwise, I'd appreciate it if you'd treat this as the theft I told you about."

"Sure, MacGregor. I've got your report filed right here." Crawley tapped the file cabinet behind him. "Why don't you just go ahead and make your insurance claim."

"Because, I don't want money. I want the sheep and the thief."

"You could use the money on those property taxes."

Douglas's blue eyes bored into Crawley, making him squirm. "What do you know about my taxes?"

"Just rumor. I make it my business to listen to rumor."

"Who passed it on to you?"

"I don't rightly recollect."

It wasn't work that brought out that sweat on Crawley's forehead. "If you should happen to remember," Douglas said, "I'd like to know."

Gerald leaned forward in what he must have assumed appeared a friendly attitude. "It was just one of those talks, you know. Fella says to Phil, `MacGregor's losin' sheep just for the insurance. Got a big tax assessment comin' due.' You know how it goes. Makes sense to me and I don't do dirt to my friends, so I file your reports and keep quiet."

"Gerald, it makes no sense to me. You've known me all our lives. Have I ever operated by subterfuge?"

"Who knows what a fella might do when his back's against the wall. And besides," his small eyes narrowed as he leaned back, "I been led to understand you'd changed considerable during your little stint as prisoner of war in Central America."

Douglas felt his scalp tighten and his skin go cold. He stood straight, holding himself in check. So, it was always going to be this. Linda had been gone from his home almost four years, gone from the state a year, but her accusations left a permanent wound festering in his life.

He stared at Crawley and pretended to ignore the comment. "Right now, I'd like to have the help of the sheriff's investigative department. Is David Brock here?"

"I've had to let David go this winter. He got a little loose with the accounting for travel funds."

Douglas could not believe this. "Are you accusing David of dishonesty, too?"

"Not dishonesty exactly, just loose accounting. I could let ya take my deputy, Phil Smith, out to your ranch to look for evidence."

"Fine, may I call him here, tomorrow morning?"

"Sure thing. He'll be lookin' forward to it."

"In the meantime," said Douglas in as even a tone as he could maintain, "unless you have specific accusations to make, I suggest you keep your loose tongue off David's reputation. My lawyer is David's lawyer."

While Crawley sputtered, Douglas considered his next move. The sound of things here didn't encourage him. David Brock had been the one person in this office with any real knowledge of investigative procedure.

Deputy Phil Smith recently joined the force and had relied on David's judgement. Still, Phil was a good man.

Crawley's bored voice put a stop to Douglas's thoughts. "Y'all through makin' loud, edjicated noises in my office, MacGregor? Ain't it time to go home to Mamma?"

Disgusted with Crawley, Douglas moved toward the door, but swiveled back for one last question. "Speaking of tuxedo-type words, Gerald," Douglas drawled, "how come ya never did talk this bad before ya was sheriff. Ya don' even sound like yur own kin no more."

"Git off it, MacGregor!" Gerald already slapped his feet back up on the desk.

*   *

A distracted David Brock answered the door with two toddlers hanging on his legs. His face brightened as he recognized his caller.

"Doug! What's up, old man?"

"Hi Dave. I visited Crawley's office, looking for you. Crawley gave me his line about travel money, and how sorry he was."

"Yeah," David lifted his daughter to his hip. "I should have cut out of that joint long ago." He shrugged and stepped back. "Come on in, Doug. Can I get you some tea and ask you to set a spell while I read to the troops? Angie gets home from the hospital soon."

"I'd be glad to relax after this day."

David pointed Douglas to the couch near the fireplace. Douglas felt his tension begin to release in the cheerful warmth of his friends' house. David and the little ones started toward the kitchen. As Douglas sat down on the couch, the older boy, rosy cheeked and blond like his dad, returned to climb on the couch, too.

David made re-introductions over his shoulder as he left. "Oh, 'Uncle' Doug, you remember little John."

"Sure, little buddy."

"I go to kindergarten," John said. "Today we went to a farm. I got to milk a cow. You smell like a farmer, too. Do you grow cows?"

Douglas laughed, "I do smell like a farmer. I raise sheep."

David returned from the kitchen carrying a tea pot and some mugs. "Doug, pour yourself some tea. I'll be down in about twenty minutes, after teeth, story and tucking in time."

"Thanks, David. Good night, Sarah, John. Come see my sheep sometime soon."

Douglas leaned back with the tea mug against his chest, the smoked-herb steam rising to warm his face. Listening to the sound of giggles and splashing water upstairs, his mind drifted.

With Bronwen bussing, back to Portland, he could at least allow himself to savor the warmth he'd found in her. At this distance, it should be safe. Douglas felt his neck and shoulders relax as he watched the fire tongues flicker up toward the chimney.

A few minutes later, when Angie came home from work, she found her husband's friend asleep on their couch with a mug full of tea lightly held on his chest. She loosened the mug from his grip, put it on the coffee table and went upstairs to see her family.

By the time David and Angie came downstairs, Douglas's head had found the pillows at the end of the sofa. David hugged Angie's waist and chuckled to himself. "I think we are his port in a storm."

"I'm glad, Honey. He looks like he could use one. Why don't you put his feet up, while I get a blanket."

After they had made Douglas comfortable for the night, David called Margaret at the ranch.

CHAPTER THIRTEEN

Wednesday morning in Portland bloomed glorious and sunny. The soft rain of the night before had cleared the air. Bronwen took the changes in the atmosphere as a sign that yesterday's meeting with Douglas MacGregor had been a mild storm she could weather.

There had been two positive outcomes from her visit to MacGregor Ranch. First, Margaret MacGregor delighted Bronwen. Next best, despite the tension caused by his obvious distrust of her, Bronwen had benefited from Douglas's suggestion. All the way home on the bus, when she felt fear of heights, she pretended to be studying the scenery for a detailed sketch.

As a result, she'd ridden the express back to Portland without overwhelming terror. She'd stayed up late, sketching one scene after another, until she realized that MacGregor's medieval barn kept thrusting itself into each drawing.

She did one final sketch of the enormous trap and fell asleep to nightmares. In each dream, she stood with her back to the edge of a precipice and tried to pry the trap off Douglas MacGregor's leg.

She'd awakened a bit groggy but decided to test herself. Using the sketching technique, she drove from her apartment across the Willamette River over the Steel Bridge. She felt so good about driving at last, that she re-crossed the river on the Broadway Bridge and drove a short distance into the west hills of Portland.

After two more Willamette River bridges, she thought about trying Portland's two tallest bridges. Into her head came a familiar voice, one she heard sometimes as the protector he had been in their childhood.

"Bron, enough for one day."

"Not the Fremont Bridge, Ben?"

"Nope. Not yet. That guy is right, though. You can get over this fear by drawing."

"Okay," she thought. "What's with that guy?"

Ben's voice chuckled. "Awkward as hell."

"How come?"

Ben didn't answer.

She decided he was right, though. Play it safe and turn back to the apartment in the city.

*   *

Bronwen parked her old Peugeot in the tight garage space and called Ben's mother on her cell.

"Mom?"

"Bron, good to hear your voice, Honey."

Bronwen loved that greeting from Mora Llewellyn and had loved it since she was ten years old.

"I've got a brag," she said, a line she had learned from Ben when they were kids.

"Brag away, Sparrow."

"I can drive again."

"Wow. Cariad, that's wonderful."

Her foster mom dropped into loving Welsh words when excited. So, for honesty's sake, Bronwen added, "All the bridges except the Fremont and the Marquam."

"I don't like those hulks myself," Mora said. "What caused this improvement?

"I've a job in Eugene. Nice lady on a sheep ranch. Her son suggested while I drive that I pretend I'm looking at things to draw them. I practiced and it works."

"You love to draw," Mora said. "Going to have a showing of those drawings anytime soon?"

Bronwen laughed, "Sure. Big gallery up in the Pearl District."

"Bron, I'm proud of you. Can I kiss the kid who made that suggestion?"

Bronwen smiled at the phone but didn't enlighten her mom. "Oh, he might sit still for it."

"Give him a hug for me," Mora said.

A tick of silence went by, and then Bron could talk again, hoping Mom hadn't noticed. "I'll tell him thanks for you."

After they signed off, Bronwen left on foot for the downtown area. She made several promises to herself as she jostled along in the familiar workday crowd.

"After I stop at the Oregon Outdoor Store about that trap, maybe I'll step into Frank's office and take a good look at the Graves' Portland Building," she pledged. "I'll even look at the tops of the library elms."

Her world began to feel a little more under control. She enjoyed the spring air and the camaraderie of morning pedestrians. She crossed Burnside and entered the brick building which housed the biggest sports, hunting and fishing outlet in Oregon.

*   *

Wednesday morning, Frank Bauman perched on his drafting stool, doodling nervously in the margins of a design while he talked on the phone. A rose in full bloom took shape under his pencil. Inside the rose sat a soft white pearl.

"Yes, Margaret, I think Bronwen has a good idea there. That kind of barn often does have large side rooms called transept porches. You'd have improved circulation and there'd be almost double the storage capacity."

Margaret said, "She mentioned this to me after she realized what a safety problem we had for the Blackwatch, but I haven't brought it up with Douglas yet."

"A little conservative, is he?"

"Stuck in honoring what his father and grandfather always did, but he'll soon see the value of change. He prizes his sheep more than tradition."

Frank chuckled. "I know the type," he said. "I am the type."

Margaret laughed, and then her soft, clear voice asked, "When he agrees, could you design the transept porches, Frank? I know you're very busy, but I just wouldn't trust anyone else to keep the beauty of our barn intact."

Frank took a deep breath before he spoke. "I wouldn't let anyone else touch that barn either. It's a part of our lives . . . I mean, it's without a doubt the one medieval barn west of the Atlantic. Where else could you find hand hewn timbers and the play of light? "

Margaret's musical laughter brought him up short. "Frank, stop! You don't have to sell me on this barn. Just say you'll come down and look it over. You could stay in our guest room while Bronwen is here."

Frank had been waiting for that invitation. When it came, he lost words. "Good idea" he forced out. It sounded too stiff.

Margaret seemed not to notice. She plunged on. "The two of you could give it a going over – she's a real find that girl!"

Frank lowered his voice, "Yes, she's a gem. I knew you'd love her."

Margaret's whisper was conspiratorial, "But you were right about Bronwen's effect on Douglas's mental fortress. They got off on the wrong foot right at the start. She's open, wise and fun with me, but puzzled by his barrier-building heart. By the end of the day, in this kitchen, you could cut the tension with a knife."

Frank had allowed his fatherly instincts to tune in to Bronwen's changing moods and became acutely aware of the young woman unhappily wadding paper in the office opposite his wall.

"In their case, Margaret, tension isn't all that bad. With their history, we should be glad they reacted at all."

*   *

Later, as Frank hung up, Bronwen appeared in his doorway, a box of drawing tools in her hand. He noticed the tinge of blue under her eyes and felt satisfied that Douglas MacGregor had bothered her sleep patterns. She needed somebody to wake her up from guilty grief.

"Could we talk?" she asked.

"Of course. What's up?" Frank lay down his pencil.

"Did you know Parr Land Development is after the MacGregor ranch?"

"That's too far from Eugene," he frowned. "Why would they want that?"

"I get the feeling there's no love lost between Leonard Parr and Douglas MacGregor," Bronwen said. "Maybe Leonard wants it for spite."

"Margaret's never mentioned that. How did you find out?"

"He attacked me with it right from the first. Mr. MacGregor thought I was a spy for Parr, and he was ready to pack me back on the next bus."

"A spy!?" Frank registered shock for a moment before the grin took over. "Ah! But then Mata Hari Llewellyn batted her eyelashes, and all was ... "

"Frank! Your age is showing."

"You mean the new generation of men can't be placated by those eyes? I don't believe ... "

"Mr. Bauman, for your chauvinist information, I batted no eyelashes. Instead, I stopped him cold with a list of the costs of sending me home."

"Ah . . . Yes, the sight of you angry would be almost as good as the batted eyelash ploy. Stopped him dead in his tracks, eh?"

Bron saw the twinkle and the itch to laugh. He baited her. She tossed her Eberhard eraser at him and followed with a second one as he dodged.

A grin wreathed his face, "I'm delighted that your business-like logic forced him to see the error of his ways,"

She treated him to a very wry face.

"No, really, I am," he said. "I'm sure you pointed out to him that Parr doesn't operate along those lines. That you would never do anything of the kind for Leonard, etcetera."

Bronwen sighed. "Frankly, Frank, I couldn't swear that Leonard Parr never operates in that manner."

"Oh, come now. One invasion of your apartment and you're willing to believe Leonard's able to stoop to spying?"

"Right." Bronwen could feel her usual frustration rising.

Frank went on, oblivious to her silence. "Bronwen, I've done business with Parr for years. They have always been above-board."

"You've done business with the senior Parr. I've had to deal with the junior."

"You and Leonard junior have your differences, it's true, but he can't be that unlike his father. As soon as he sees you're not his for the asking, he'll treat you like a business colleague. I have faith you can handle it."

"Frank, the point is I shouldn't have to handle it."

"That's true, Bronwen, but the reality is you're a good-looking young lady, and it is almost inevitable that he should notice. Just because he put the moves on you after the last meeting doesn't mean ..."

"After? After! He was putting the moves on during the meeting, under the table."

"During? Under?" Then the light dawned.

"Oh my . . . You took care of it all right – that's why he doubled up and looked so green, isn't it?"

She nodded.

"What did you use? A shoe?"

"A briefcase. It weighs more."

Frank sat back, wiping his face with his hand, and rethinking some old accepted ideas. After a few moments, he looked up at her, "I'm sorry, Bronwen. I guess I've not really backed you all the way, have I."

She smiled and looked down at her pencils for a moment before trusting her voice. "You back me a lot. But I'd like Leonard to stop being a source of humor at the office."

"Sure, Bron." Frank leaned on his drafting table, rethinking some other things he'd been doing to ignore this topic for women all his life.

After a moment's silence, Frank said, "I'll stop it, and if I hear it, I'll squash it. I'm sorry."

"Thank you, Frank."

He fiddled with his empty mechanical pencil and finally asked, "This trap you told me about, do you think there might be others like it set to go off?"

"Not like that one. I did some checking – took a sketch I made of it to the Oregon Outdoor Store. It's rare. They couldn't believe I'd seen one. It hasn't been manufactured since 1937. They had a picture of one in an old catalogue – a Zivner Bear Trap. It's considered extremely cruel because it has saw-like teeth running backwards along the edge of each major tooth. There's no way to get it open without doing even more damage to the animal than was done when the trap closed."

Frank paled. "What if . . . You could have . . . She . . . "

For the first time, Bronwen was aware of his unspoken care for Margaret MacGregor. Perhaps her own care for Margaret alerted her to his.

She touched his sleeve and whispered, "But I didn't step in the trap. And Margaret didn't, and now Douglas has the trap locked away in his barn. When I called her, Margaret said that he's checked all around the house and outbuildings for other traps."

"Where could it have come from?"

"I called the four major outlets in the valley that sell traps now," she said. "One old man in the Albany store used to work in an outlet that folded in 1950. He remembered that they once sold a Zivner to the Sheep Rancher's Association. That's the only trap any of them remembered."

"Bronwen, I don't like this. You get too close to whoever did this and they might know of your search before you know who they are. Tell your story about the trap to the sheriff or Douglas and let them handle it. You could get hurt while trying to help."

"I'll be careful, Frank. So far, even the stores don't know my name. They think they were talking to a Mrs. Cleveland."

He arched an eyebrow, "Let's keep it that way. Stay two steps removed from the front lines, my dear. We can't run our partnership without a partner."

"I'm playing it safe. Don't worry. By the way, I'm expected in Eugene tomorrow, but I want to go back down today instead. Is that going to throw off our schedule too much?"

Frank wondered why he felt uneasy with her interest in the MacGregor project. After all, he'd wanted her to meet the MacGregors. For her own good.

Well, and his, also.

Frank made a show of looking through his calendar – a play for time while he tried to figure out the reasons for his worry.

"Uhm … looks like today is pretty free, except for the park design review tonight."

"Weren't you going to handle that, Frank?"

He glanced up. She didn't let go of a pet project so easily. "Why are you going a day early?"

Bronwen shrugged her shoulders and looked off at his drafting board. "Oh, I want to look into the local nurseries and find some local labor. There's a backhoe to rent. I want to clear up some things with Parr on his Eugene project … I figure it will take the extra day just to be able to do all that."

If she had maintained eye contact with him, Frank wouldn't have paid much attention to the comment about Parr. The rest made sense, but he knew she disliked Parr. So, why was she looking shifty?

"Uh, I get the bit about the nurseries and the backhoe," he said, "but I can't imagine you looking for time to spend with Parr. I told you I'd handle him."

She straightened and smiled at him. "That's great Frank. I'll just go down and take care of the rest."

She seemed about to dart out of his office, but Frank asked, "What did you think of Douglas MacGregor?"

Bronwen's hand reached automatically to twist the cuff on her shirt.

Frank leaned his chin onto his hand to hide a small smile.

"I think he likes to be left alone," she said.

"All right, I'll leave that one alone."

"He's very moody. I don't understand it; he was so thoughtful to his mother and in such a dark mood every time he spoke to me."

"Needs explanation, all right," Frank said.

"Oh, he's no doubt tired from investigating the theft of his sheep." she continued.

"No doubt that explains it," he said.

"But he came to the bus station with all kinds of negative expectations of me," she went on.

"That didn't put things on a good footing," he speculated.

"And he was so angry about something I said, (I don't even know what), that he hardly spoke to me all the way back to Eugene."

"Must have been a difficult ride," he observed.

"Frank, why are you asking me all these questions? I can handle this, myself."

"I'm sure you can. I'll back out."

There was a long silence as Frank refilled his mechanical pencil.

Bronwen began to laugh, softly. She looked over at Frank who began to chuckle, too. She reached out and took his hand.

"You're too good to me, Frank."

"I know."

*   *

Frank sat very still while he listened to her pack drafting tools. He pondered the strange elusiveness of their conversation and decided it had to do with the very outcome he'd wanted for her. He had loved Benjamin Llewellyn as he would have loved a son. But two years after his death, Bronwen could rediscover love. Frank couldn't think of a better man than young Douglas MacGregor.

If the thought seemed new and gave him a twinge of regret now and then, how much more uncomfortable would it be for her? Her emotions must be very confused right now. "Tension you could cut with a knife." That's how Margaret put it this morning.

*   *

Bronwen capped her fine point pen and laid it in the briefcase with the T-square and the templates.

The old man at the Outdoor Store had been very helpful. He recognized the trap from her sketch right away. Bronwen wanted to know more about it, especially if there was any way to tie Parr to it. At the same time, she would be looking for any acquaintances of the MacGregors who might be involved.

Bronwen liked Margaret MacGregor very much. It could have been Margaret instead of Bronwen who nearly stepped in the trap yesterday.

Furthermore, Douglas MacGregor clearly had pinned all his suspicions on Parr and wouldn't look beyond him for a culprit.

Someone with a fresh perspective might see the truth which Douglas seemed to overlook on purpose.

That someone was Bronwen Llewellyn.

She snapped her briefcase shut and headed for the elevators. One other thing, she meant not to let Frank know, just yet. She intended to drive her car down to Eugene. If he knew, he'd just worry for the whole two hours and want her to call him when she arrived.

She had to be able to get around Eugene, and there wasn't much of a call for taxis in the small town. Probably out of her mind to try it. But her experience driving during recent days had convinced her that she should just get in the Peugeot, turn on the ignition and think a lot about sketching what she saw. She hoped it would work.

*   *

Two hours later, Bronwen entered a teakwood office door and came face to face with a secretary. This was the kind of secretary she'd always known Leonard would choose – wild hair, pouty mouth and minuscule waist.

"May I help you?"

Bronwen wondered how a person could learn to speak without moving her pout. "Is Leonard Parr in?"

"Do you have an appointment?"

"Yes. Mrs. Llewellyn."

The elegant fingers began to point at the Eames chairs, but just then, the door to the inner office flung open.

"Sophie! We never keep Bronwen Llewellyn waiting." Leonard's silk suit rustled as he advanced on her, hands out to grab her shoulders.

Bronwen stepped aside and reached to shake his hand instead. "How do you do, Leonard. I hope you have a few minutes to show me the maps I asked you about."

"Anything. Anything for you, Bronwen. Let's go into my office for some privacy." He shot her an appreciative glance and followed her into his office.

She acknowledged but didn't sit in the chair Leonard indicated. "I have two minutes," she said. "I need to get to my small-house village project in Springfield soon. May I see the maps of the land you want to acquire for the shopping center?"

"Sure. Sure. Right over here."

He led the way to a large table on which there was a model of the ugly building in which they stood, and several rolled up blueprints. Bronwen flinched when she saw the seal of her own company stamped on the outside of one print.

Leonard pushed the model and prints aside and rolled out a map of Lane County. On it, marked in red ink, she saw a corridor following Interstate 5 north from Eugene. There were parcels of land that were skipped over and others that were marked with question marks. One piece of land he had marked with an exclamation point – the most northern piece – the MacGregor Ranch.

"Why so far north?"

"Prime land. It's close to the Harrisburg exit and getting close enough to the Corvallis-Albany crowd. It will someday be an ideal shopping center – you know, movies, clothes store. People would flock to this location."

Bronwen shook her head. "It would be just as easy to attract them to a mall in Eugene and another within Corvallis. Why bring them all the way out to the freeway when you can add to the economic base of a town?"

"The Valley Mall will become a new town."

Bronwen could not contain her disdain for this idea. "Leonard, you'll have to convince the state to build an overpass just to get shoppers to the mall. In Eugene and Corvallis, the access would be simple."

"I got friends in the transportation department. I got investments in the right people all over the state. No mere overpass is going to be a difficulty. You got to think big, Bronwen."

Bronwen bit down on her retort. She wanted to ask for a list of people he'd 'invested' in. Instead she moved to her next question. "Leonard, I tried to call you yesterday afternoon. Where were you?"

Parr turned his bright smile on her. "Yesterday afternoon? Tuesday? Oh, I was at the Golf and Tennis Club having lunch with some new state candidates." He moved closer, nudging her hand on the map with his bronzed fingers. "I wish I'd known you wanted to see me. I could have postponed that lunch and shown you around Eugene."

"I just called to make today's appointment. How much of this land is purchased?" Bronwen pointed at MacGregor Ranch.

"That one's not quite ready to sell, but I think he'll come around pretty fast. He's got a big tax assessment coming due and he's got a cash flow problem. All his money's tied up in breeding some fancy sheep. He'll sell a little to keep the rest."

"What if he doesn't?"

Parr smiled as if at a private joke. "Oh, he will. Come May, we'll have that property. Then we just need to remove the house and barn and we're ready to go."

Bronwen almost lost it. "Tear down the barn? Why that's . . ." she caught herself. "That's expensive. Barns cost a lot to build."

"Well, maybe we can leave it. Use it somehow in the scheme of things – Old Barn Shoppes or Big Red Barn Mall or . . . "

At that idea, she knew she couldn't stand here much longer without showing her hand. "Leonard. I've got to go. I'll see you when you've finished the land purchases."

Leonard sidled closer, looking at her pleadingly. "I meant to take you to lunch, Bronwen. I cleared a corner window table at the Golf and Tennis Club just for us."

Bronwen had learned long ago to resist his guilt inducing tactics. "Sorry, Leonard. I'm down here on a project. I'll bet your secretary would enjoy the lunch."

"Sophie? She never eats, so far as I can figure."

"Well call and cancel then." Bronwen whipped out the door as fast as she could. Leonard started after her.

"Bronwen, I'd could introduce you to lots of potential clients at the . . ."

Having spotted the location of the stairwell on her way in, she used it now. Nothing stopped Leonard Parr so fast as the thought of climbing up or down. Working up a sweat in his expensive suit was anathema to him.

Yet, on the way down, Bronwen regretted her haste. She hadn't given much thought to how climbing affected her. After her success with driving the Peugeot all the way down I-5, it didn't seem fair to get hung up in an ugly stairwell. Clammy and tense, she hung onto the rail on the wall side, studied the texture of porous concrete very closely and made herself take each step.

CHAPTER FOURTEEN

Thursday morning brought a beautiful day for the drive from her bed and breakfast near Eugene to MacGregor Ranch. Before she drove north, she called Mora Llewellyn. When her foster mother didn't pick up, she left a message.

"Mom, I made it to Eugene. Lots of drawings of sheep and fir trees. Talk to you when I come back through Beavercreek."

This morning, Bronwen knew a lot more than she had the day before, but it was too early to tell anyone. She needed details and specifics.

Yesterday, the Golf and Tennis Club had confirmed Leonard Parr's claim to have been there on Tuesday, the day of the trap. Leonard could have hired someone else to set the trap, but it had to have been someone who knew the MacGregor habits. It had been set when the dogs were somewhere away from the sheep for a short time.

Yesterday, Bronwen also had been to the Sheep Ranchers Association to ask about the trap. What she found there gave her an unbelievable suspect. It had been stolen during the sheriff's investigation of a previous theft at the association's museum. According to the secretary who helped Bronwen, there had been no forced entry. She knew she'd have to find more evidence before even hinting that such an important member of the community would risk his reputation for a deranged form of vengeance.

John Barsoti, president of the association, and candidate for state senator, had opportunity, but what his motive might be, Bronwen couldn't figure out. Still, his ranch lay next to MacGregor's. A startling coincidence?

That bit of information she wouldn't be able to use until she had more to back it up. Douglas and Margaret would dismiss it out of hand. And well they should – flimsy. She'd just have to keep the knowledge under her hat and remain alert to other hints which might point to Barsoti or any other suspects.

Though she hadn't had time to unpack, Bronwen had stayed the night at the B and B because she refused to be subject to the changeable moods of Douglas MacGregor.

However, she did look forward to seeing Margaret MacGregor again. So, her spirits rose as she took the exit north of Eugene. A few moments later, she turned onto MacGregor Road and came to a halt. A black truck blocked her way, its cab empty.

At the right side of the road, two burly men held a four-by-four post upright in wet concrete. A third bent over, nailing temporary supports to the post.

One of the two men leaned over to tap the third on the shoulder. The third man jerked a look over his shoulder, long enough for her to recognize Douglas MacGregor, and long enough to notice him slump as if defeated in some plan.

Douglas stood up, glanced at her, frowned and glanced at his watch before coming to the side of her car.

Disappointed at this cool reception, Bronwen rolled down her window.

"Should I just park until you finish up?" she asked.

Douglas's hand strayed to his flapping shirt tail as he stared at her.

Absently, he tucked the shirt into his levis and looked over her old green Peugeot. His gaze focused again on her face and he broke into a blaze of smile.

"You drove!"

She tried not to be too happy about the smile. "I tried your suggestion. I've got reams of drawings at home. Sheep, fir trees, and bridges."

"Cured?"

"Can't do the Fremont or the Marquam Bridges yet."

"Bad, huh?"

Bronwen raised her hand in a sweeping arc, shuddered and dropped her hand in her lap. "Very bad." She could feel the color rise in her cheeks.

Douglas looked at her warmly and then shifted his attention to the two men at the post who watched their conversation with avid interest. One smiled with a boyish grin framed by cherubic black curls. The other man watched Bronwen with open interest and touched the tip of his hat when she looked toward him.

"Let her out of that little bitty car, MacGregor?" he joked. "Don't want to introduce us?"

Douglas laughter seemed forced. He bent toward Bronwen. "I guess you might as well park and meet Phil and John. We'll just be a little while setting this post." He opened the door and held it for her.

As she stepped out, he explained. "We're putting a gate here to discourage trespassers. If our thief wants to visit, he'll have to walk the last mile."

Bronwen looked up toward the road beyond the house. "Are you going to close off the road to the north as well?"

"No, that road goes to Phil's mother, and beyond that it connects to my logging spurs. The thieves have to use this entry or slog through the marsh to the south."

Douglas shifted his hammer and took her elbow. "Might as well meet these guys." His voice rose, "Their curiosity has to be satisfied."

The curly-haired man wiped his hand on his levis and reached to shake with her. "John Barsoti," he said, "friend of Douglas's, next ranch over." John nodded his head toward the south.

"Next ranch," said Bronwen, "and next senator from the state of Oregon."

Her recognition elicited a brilliant grin. She felt chagrined to suspect him, but somebody had set that trap.

Douglas's grip on her elbow tightened. "And this is Phil Smith."

Bronwen reached for his hand. He hastily wiped it and shook with her. "The Deputy Sheriff," he said.

"Oh yes," remembered Bronwen. "Mr. MacGregor looked for your help last Tuesday."

Phil glanced up at Douglas and then back at Bronwen with interest. "You were here Tuesday as well?"

Douglas interrupted. "Mrs. Llewellyn came to design landscaping around the house. She's working with mother."

Bronwen could feel his hand telegraphing some message to her elbow.

Since she couldn't read the message, she decided to say nothing more. Instead, she started back toward the car, saying, "I'll let you gentlemen get back to work."

Douglas hand dropped as he followed her back.

When they arrived at the driver's side, she asked, "What was that all about? You didn't want them to know I worked here before."

"Sorry. It's just that any time they see me with a lady, they tend to take it too seriously." He looked at her with a cool blue gaze, as if challenging her not to take seriously anything that had happened between them two days ago.

"Landscaping is important to me, Mr. MacGregor. And that's all." She began to roll up her window, but he put a hand on it.

"I appreciate your work," he said. "I'll move John's truck."

"Thank you."

She started to close the window again but stopped because he kept his fingers over the glass as he spoke. "Mother's gone to help Phil's mother, Helen Smith, but I can leave the house open for you when we go."

"Thank you. I'll be working outdoors until I need to leave for the Bed and Breakfast where I'm staying."

"B and B down toward Coburg Junction?"

"Yes, they're expecting me for the week."

"I'm sure Mother intended . . ." he broke off, seemed to think better of what he might have said, and began anew. "I'm sure that's a good place."

Bronwen began rolling the window up. He leaned down one last time. "After we work on the corral with the ewes, Phil, John and I are heading south for a while. See you tomorrow, if I'm around."

She knew he planned not to be around tomorrow – indeed had planned to be gone when she arrived today. Fine with her. She didn't like his challenging presence – attracting and repelling at the same time.

"By the way," he said, "Don't go near the ewe corral when you come back. We're booby-trapping it."

"Nowhere near," she answered and hesitated until he took his fingers off her window.

What an unreadable man. All I want to do is survey his property.

*   *

An hour later, the men left the ewe corral and walked away on a dirt path toward the south. Bronwen had been surveying the land farthest from them. When they were gone, she walked down the road toward the highway, she turned her back to the new gate posts and sketched the spruce. "Engelmann Spruce smells wonderful," Bronwen thought. "A great place for a playhouse."

She circled the hill, stopping often to write notes, sketch and measure. Occasionally she reached into her backpack for a small hooked garden fork and a shovel. With these, she collected soil samples to be tested later.

Bronwen found the dogs with the Blackwatch ewes. Robbie and Roy seemed to recognize her. They wagged their tails but stayed at their posts near the ewe corral.

By noon, Bronwen decided to get a view of the property from the mountain which rose northeast of the ranch. She had control of her fear of heights. Her renewed self-confidence proved that Douglas was right.

Keeping her mind on sketching what she saw, she could ignore the learned fear until it no longer controlled any part of her. Her efforts had begun to work in the car. Now she wanted to make it work in the mountains.

As she left, she heard the dogs barking. Bronwen turned back to see what aroused them and found they were barking at her.

"Good boyos," she called and got back to hiking. For some reason Roy left the sheep and followed her part way up the trail, sniffing the air around him with every step, which puzzled her. He didn't menace her. If he protected her, she couldn't tell why. After half a mile, he turned back to the ranch and Bronwen continued.

Hiking through the lower meadows, she remembered the pleasure of solitude with grass, rocks and trees. It seemed to her that, except for certain moments with Benjamin, all her life she'd been alone. At a very young age, she'd spent night after night alone in her mother's dank house. Even her fostering by Ben's family at age ten couldn't make up for the terror of being shut away from love when she was small.

Outdoors, she felt no fear when alone. Outdoors, she experienced a solitude she had cherished before Ben's death.

* *

John Barsoti paced the confines of the small cave. "Damn it, MacGregor!" he said. "Whoever did this has got to be crazy-mean!"

"Not crazy," said Phil Smith, "Clever. These sheep are your greatest asset. He's planning to drive you crazy, one ewe at a time."

Douglas no longer could bear to look at the drying bones of his ewe and her lamb. "I left them here so you could see what I saw. Pure spite. No man can eat that much meat just for hunger."

Phil looked sympathetic. "The ewe he shot near Ian's Draw last week was one of your best breeders, wasn't she?"

"George tell you about her?"

"Yeah," Phil nodded. He came in the tavern last Saturday, babying his injured arm. Kind of blew your predicament all out of proportion, but I think we got the basic story."

Barsoti stalked to the truck and grabbed a shovel. Over his shoulder he said, "It'd be hard to exaggerate nearly gettin' killed, Phil." He started digging a grave in the sandy soil outside the cave.

Phil grabbed a canvas tarp and began gathering the bones. "Our hot-headed friend, Barsoti, is blowing off steam," he said to Douglas. "But I think you ought to be real worried about this guy. Be extra careful of the people and things you care about. Looks like he means to get at you where it hurts the most."

Douglas bent to help gather the tiny lamb bones. "Leonard Parr is greedy, but until he got Kenjiro on cocaine, I didn't think him evil."

"Parr'll stop at nothing to get his way," said Phil. "And he knows each man's weakest point."

John Barsoti's shadow blotted out what little light there was in the cave. "If the sheriff's department knows so much about Parr," he asked, "When's the arrest?"

"When we have enough evidence," Phil said.

"With Crawley on the case, we can wait till doomsday for action," John huffed.

Douglas gathered the corners of the tarp and carried the bones to the shallow grave. As he laid them in the hole, he looked up at his friends. "I'd like you to climb up to the meadow with me. I'm not going back to the ranch right away and your company would be welcome."

"Side-stepping the little lady, are you?" asked John.

"Mrs. Llewellyn's got a job to do and so do I. Are you coming with me?"

Phil took John's shovel and began filling in the grave, saying, "Since she's Mrs. Llewellyn, I guess I might as well follow your tush up the hill. But it won't be as rewarding as watching hers."

Douglas yanked the keys out of his pocket and strode toward the truck.

John glanced at Douglas's taut back and bent close to Phil. "No jokes about her, Phil," he whispered.

Phil looked up at Douglas's receding back and chuckled. "You think the granite man is eroding? I'll have to investigate this a little further."

"Leave it," said John. "Let what happens, happen."

"You think she'll be safe with him? His temper got to be something fierce there toward the end with Linda."

John straightened, "He didn't do it, I tell you. I mean that last night in the tavern, we asked for that fight . . . But before that night, we never saw him raise a hand toward anybody."

"Calm down, Barsoti," said Phil, raising his hands as if to give in. "All right, I don't know what to believe. You got to admit, Linda was in bad shape sometimes. I just think maybe MacGregor's not the saint we've made him out to be."

"He's no saint. But he's been my friend for a long time. Yours too. I'd think you'd remember all the times he's gone to bat for you when things were rough . . ."

"Barsoti," said Phil hoarsely. "My old man's dead. I'd like to keep him buried."

"Sorry, Phil," John looked chagrined at blundering into the taboo subject of Phil's drunken father. "Let's forget this and go for a hike for old time's sake.

*   *

"John Barsoti sweats a lot," joked Phil Smith. "Have you noticed?"

"That's not sweat, Phil, that's lanolin." John groaned as he climbed the hill. "Years of sheep herding brings it out in a man. It's what keeps me looking so young and handsome."

Phil snorted, but John continued joking with him "You lawmen, on the other hand, you sweat tin and salt water. Very bad for the skin."

Douglas looked back and noticed that John had lost the hardness to his muscles. But his dark hair still seemed as thick and his face as full of wry humor.

Phil's ailing mother worried Phil and all her friends. Douglas knew that, once in a while, Phil needed some form of release from his responsibilities. Douglas hoped this hike would renew their old friendship and help both Phil and himself find some joy in life. He felt pretty sure John's life was in good shape.

He said, "Phil, we can see your mom's house from up here."

The Smith ranch had adjoined MacGregor's on the north. Helen Smith still lived in the house, though the rest of the ranch now belonged to Douglas.

Phil gazed north. "Mom sure loves those fool roses," he commented.

John whistled, "Green already! Heck of a show they'll make in the summer."

Phil said, "The one nice thing Dad ever did for her – a driveway lined with brambly roses that bloom their hearts out."

Douglas felt the buried embarrassment in Phil's comment. Phil had turned away from ranching. Instead, he worked for Lane County and proved a far greater asset to the sheriff's force than the lazy Gerald Crawley.

Phil turned from the view of his mother's home and studied the ranch to the south, shading his eyes from the spring sun. "Your Mary's out feeding chickens, John."

From up here, they could make out the image of dark-haired Mary Barsoti. They saw only her gesture of sowing seed in the fowl yard, but Douglas could imagine the song Mary would be singing as she worked. She'd given up a career in San Francisco opera to marry John, but she hadn't given up singing when happy.

John had met Mary at a concert. As far as Douglas knew, they were still doing well.

After a moment of watching, John and Phil followed Douglas uphill for another hundred yards where they stopped in an alpine meadow.

Douglas decided to broach the one subject that seemed to keep them apart. "Either of you heard from Linda since she went to San Francisco?"

John's surprise seemed genuine. "Not since that night in the tavern . . . I mean . . ."

"It's all right, John. I know the night we all won't talk about." Douglas said, and glanced at Phil. Phil had dated Linda for a time after the jerk from the tavern disappeared.

Phil cleared his throat, took off his hat and slapped dust off on his pants. "I got a letter from her," he said. "'Bout a month after she left for Frisco. Seemed happy enough."

"Good," said Douglas. "She always liked bright lights. I'll bet that would be her kind of town. We're all too tied to the land to be exciting enough."

Phil sighed. "She wanted me to go to Frisco with her. I wouldn't be any good down there, so I told her to just go if that was what she wanted."

"Glad you stayed, Phil," Douglas said. "We need you here."

John fidgeted, casting about for a less sensitive subject. "This place always had a lot of wild crocus."

"Great view of the whole barn and lower meadow," Phil seemed to make an effort to rejoin the present. "From up here, you can see the size of the marsh behind your barn."

"A lot of wasted land, all right," Douglas said. "Thought about draining it, but I'm not sure how I'd do it. Right now, I'm glad I have it. It acts like a moat to protect us from intruders in that direction."

John shaded his eyes for a longer view of the roads. "You should hire a security guard." John plopped down on the turf. "That's what we ended up doing at the Sheep Ranchers Association."

"Why?" Douglas asked.

"Two break-ins in a week – happened about a month ago. First a big heist from the safe, and the second time, just historical stuff – tools and the like."

"Nothing ever turned up," added Phil.

"No," John said.

Phil said, "David had a lead on some of it, but then he got himself fired."

Douglas' voice cut through Phil. "David was not fired. He was let go because of Crawley's stupid claim that he embezzled."

John looked surprised. "I thought Crawley let him go for lack of funds. Isn't that what Crawley said the day you took over the investigation, Phil?"

"Technically," said Phil, " 'not rehired'. But the truth is, quite a lot of money went missing from his travel fund."

Douglas snorted, "I'd never believe David stole. It's more believable that Crawley put it into sheepskin covers for his cars."

Phil laughed, "A distinct possibility."

"At any rate, Doug," John said. "I think you need manpower to help you guard for the next few weeks." Frowning, John tossed a rock across the meadow. "Your Blackwatch are . . . well, soon they'll be a major international breed."

Pushing his hat back to rub at his sunburnt forehead, Phil agreed, "They really are something. Mom goes on and on about Blackwatch yarn."

"I don't suppose . . .," said John, his eyes twinkling, "I don't suppose you'd know if my old Lincoln ram has been into your flock since he decided to go wild?"

"No, John," Douglas laughed, "you can't take credit for this breed improvement. I wish I'd never bought that bullying ram from you. I believe you knew he had the wild-eye and wander-lust when you sold him to me."

Phil asked, "What you guys talking about?"

Douglas answered, "I bought a cute little Lincoln ram from John about five years ago. He weighs at least three hundred pounds now, and that's with living off the land, wintering himself. I hate to think what he'd weigh if I fed him.

"Yep," John said, "That cute little ram took off for the high country, up north beyond your old house – believes himself to be the king of the mountains.

"If I find him with my flock," Douglas said, "he's minutes away from the freezer. A visit to the Blackwatch could kill my ewes. His offspring would be far too large."

"He's a tough old guy," John said. He tightened his paunch into a poor imitation of the well-muscled man. "Phil, you and I have got to do something about the shape we're in," said John. "Remember how we all used to hop in your old trucks after a B-Ball game and go attract the ladies."

Douglas hooted at John's distorted memory. "Among the ladies, Phil's Ford and my old Chevy truck were the butt of laughter. We just didn't notice 'cause we were having too good a time celebrating the slaughter of some team of city boys."

Phil smiled, "At least I got smart enough to let some poor joker bash up the Ford. I got the insurance money. You've still got the Chevy."

After a little reminiscing about their team days, John turned to a more sober subject. "MacGregor," John said, "You need more sleep. We ought to start taking turns guarding that flock."

"Isn't that the truth? I'll finish that gate and then sleep well tonight," Douglas promised.

"I better take off," said Phil. "I'm gonna hike down to Mom's from here. Keep in touch about this."

After Phil started down, Douglas asked John. "Want to join me? I think I'll go on up this trail to where I planted some beautiful Noble Fir and Grand Fir. Someday, your children will come up here on Christmas tree hunts."

"You plant Noble Fir for my children?"

"Yours and my sister Janet's. David and Angie have great kids, too."

John decided to chance a rebuff, "How about your children, MacGregor?"

"Not likely." Douglas said.

But John persisted. "You never let a woman get beyond those defenses, do you? It's been a long time since Linda left. You can't be happy with occasional dates. You're not that kind of man."

"John, I don't want to defend myself to you." Douglas pinned him with an ice blue glare.

"Have it your way." John's black eyes held his without flinching. "Believe me, what seems safe to you is contrary to your nature. That's never safe in the long run. When you finally lose this cold self-control, I hope to heaven the woman is strong and caring."

Douglas looked down at the ranch. The lines of his face hardened.

"Thanks for the hike," John said, "but I think I better get back to the ranch and get some work done before I hit the campaign trail this weekend. Thought I'd gotten into good shape until this little outing."

"A little less campaign eating, and you'll be as good as new."

John made a belching face. "About the one part of me in good shape now is my jaw – chewing rubber chicken and jawing with Parr all week."

"Leonard Parr been calling you?"

"Sure. Isn't he trying to get all of us to sell him the few acres along the road?" asked John.

Douglas' disgust surfaced. "He's after enough of mine to have to move the house and tear down the barn if he gets it."

John's eyes widened. "Tear down your barn? That's like tearing down Westminster Abbey."

Douglas nodded, "You selling him anything?"

"Hell no."

"Not even after he contributed to your campaign?" Douglas studied John's reaction.

"He what?"

The surprise seemed genuine. Douglas said, "You mean my lawyer, Lloyd Jones, knows more about your campaign chest than you do?"

"Lloyd told you? I didn't want money from Parr."

"Well, you've got it. Where're you going?"

"To give it back. No wonder he's been acting like I owe him a big favor."

As Douglas watched his friend descend the hill, he regretted having asked his lawyer, Lloyd Jones, to have Parr investigated. He had a feeling he wasn't going to like everything Jones's man turned up. Barsoti's campaign contribution might be the mildest surprise. Douglas couldn't help wondering if the money would go back to Parr or return to the Barsoti coffers under a disguise. Reluctantly, Douglas admitted that John's surprise could be, not that Parr had donated, but that others knew about it.

Allowing his suspicions of John to surface also dredged up other forbidden thoughts. Douglas glanced down at the ranch.

As they'd climbed this morning, Douglas had looked for Bronwen on his own ranch. He forced himself to admit he wanted to see her. At the same time, he was wary of her exuberant gracefulness and wanted to be miles away from it. An occasional glance had left him puzzled. If she were down there, he couldn't see where.

Some unbidden pride had come to him when he realized that she'd driven herself all the way from Portland. He wanted to be with her, to congratulate her on conquering the bridges, but he did not want the inner turmoil her presence had given him last Tuesday. Nor did he want to lay himself open to the insatiable longing the memory of her had brought him since.

So, at high noon, he turned to the northeastern mountains and climbed as far as he could.

CHAPTER FIFTEEN

By one o'clock in the afternoon, among the wild crocus in a meadow some four hundred feet above the ranch, Bronwen saw the entire house and barn complex. After an hour of thoughtful watching she had a good plan to meet Margaret MacGregor's needs. From here, she could see the one problem area. The MacGregor's had lived with it so long that they probably didn't even think of it anymore.

A natural spring had created a shallow marsh out of an area about a quarter of a mile behind the barn, a breeding place for mosquitoes and a waste of about four acres. A deeper marsh could have been a breeding ground for heron and other waterfowl. If brought under control, the spring could be used to create a stream and pond for wildlife in another part of the property. The old marsh could become another cottonwood field. Cottonwood needed a source of water nearby.

Chill in the mountain air made Bronwen put on her red wool coat and her pack. As she looked around her, she realized some other animal often visited this meadow. There were places where the crocus had been trampled or slept on. She thought this could be a deer hangout. Not a bad life for a wild animal.

When she had her landscape plan in mind, she decided to continue up what appeared to be a deer path through the tall Oregon Grape bushes toward the forest of firs and hemlocks. She celebrated being able to climb, and moved in silence for another hour.

*   *

As the sun reached two o'clock, Bronwen stopped to decide how much longer she could hike before turning back.

The moment she looked back she knew she'd made a mistake. She looked up in order not to sway with the tops of trees far below. She tried to take a step forward, but her feet seemed rooted to the narrow trail.

Not here. Oh please, not way out here! I've come so far. One more step. That's it. Now, the other foot. I can just watch each foot, concentrate on each foot. Why did I look down?

The memory of a newer voice came to her. "Breathe. Pretend you're going home to sketch. Breathe, Bron. Breathe."

Bronwen made herself take a deep breath, and then another and another. Years of glacial weight had grooved the rock to her left – an interesting subject – time, and change. She sighed and took in another deep gulp of air.

Breathe and think of drawing the next rock or pinecone. Walk, keep walking.

A thud. Several thumps.

She held her breath, listening. Listening.

Again, the sharp, fast thud of hooves.

The sound came from somewhere farther up the trail. Again, she heard it. The hooves thumped, followed by scuffling and snorting.

Two animals fighting.

She didn't want to meet an animal as large as these two seemed to be, but the tight curve of the trail behind made retreat frightening. She remembered a long stretch of about a mile beyond that curve where the trail became extremely narrow. Yet, she had to figure out how to get out of the animals' path.

Ahead loomed an outcropping of rock, a sheer wall intruding into the trail. The path veered around the outcrop.

Beyond it, she couldn't see the path until it curved back into view, up and to the right.

The hoof beats sounded again, as if the animals rushed forward, stopped, then rushed forward. That fight would continue down this trail until one of the animals knocked the other into the ravine below.

Get out of the way, she thought. But where?

She admitted she'd been able to climb because she'd gone up. Going down, looking down, she could freeze the way she had on the Morrison Bridge in Portland. Here, no Frank could rescue her.

She searched for safety and called on her lifelong friend.

Ben, help me think. No more dizziness! Please!

Jutting out into the trail in front of her, the granite outcrop offered a few handholds, maybe enough footholds to get her out of the action.

Since the climb hung over the ravine, this was a solution of last resort. Be prepared.

She swung her pack down to get out the rope she used when she climbed and pruned tall trees – climbing she never did these days.

The approaching sound of hooves again brought her attention to the switch-back. Twenty feet beyond the rock that obstructed her view, the trail turned right, so she could see that area from where she stood.

From there, the trail crossed an area of fallen boulders, empty of all vegetation. About a hundred yards beyond the boulders, several scrub pines grew next to the trail. The gnarled trees swayed with the weight of combatants who could not yet be seen.

Two jays scurried out of the nearest pine, screaming their fear. Their motion drew Bron's attention to the Cooper's hawk circling far above.

Bronwen pulled her mind back to the narrow trail and more realistic solutions.

Having found the rope, she tried to think. The gleam of steel from her gardener's fork caught her eye. An idea leapt into her mind – an idea that might be useless, even dangerous, depending on the quality of the fork's metal. She had to take the chance.

Bronwen shed her wool coat and began tying the rope to the hooked soil fork, creating a grapple.

She glanced up the trail. Near the open part of the upper switchback, trees and shrubs shook. The animal on the upper ground evidently forced the lower one closer and closer to Bronwen's part of the trail. By the sound of it, they'd covered several yards in the time it had taken her to rid herself of the pack and add a grapple to the rope.

Act fast.

Holding the grappling-fork end of her rope, Bronwen made sure the rope coils were untangled, lifting the grapple with her left hand. She picked out a boulder at the top of the thirty-foot outcrop.

She swung the rope. The grapple flew up in an arc that aimed too far to the right.

It fell toward the empty space over the ravine. She steadied herself on the wall to her left, trying not to watch the fall of the rope.

Vertigo threatened to control her mind. She forced herself to concentrate on re-coiling the rope. Standing with her back to the void, she breathed deeply to clear her head.

"Look up," she commanded herself. "This is a baseball. There's the runner. The first baseman's mitt is to the left. Throw!"

The grapple wrapped around the left side of the rock and held. Bron tugged, then pulled harder. It still held. She tested it with her weight.

Still okay.

Bron looked around the rock wall, up the trail ahead of her, trying to see the fight. Perhaps an invasion of territory, a battle between males caused this ruckus.

What she saw next laid all her speculation to rest. Above and to her right, Douglas MacGregor strode out of the pine trees and turned to face his opponent. He chose his place, set his feet with quick care, ready for the onslaught.

Sweat blackened the back of his red shirt. The dust of a long fight covered his boots and the lower half of his levis. His face and arms glowed slick with sweat. His gaze took in his surroundings, calculating his next move.

He seemed not to see Bronwen, but looked down at the ravine and then up toward the pines. The closest pines waved in the breeze. Too spindly. He shook his head, gave up on escape and readjusted to the coming moments.

Ripping out of the trees came the largest ram Bronwen had ever seen.

His powerful shoulders lowered his huge head as he charged down the path toward his quarry. Blood red eyes held those of his enemy as he gained speed.

Douglas crouched to meet him, one boot on a rock at the side of the cliff. If the rock held, he had a chance.

Bronwen knew a succession of charges like this had already worn Douglas out. Something had to distract this ram.

The ram's head hit Douglas' outstretched hands, pivoting him off his free foot and pinning him against the cliff. Douglas, a hand grasping each side of the head, wrestled from as low a position as the ram would allow. The ram worked hard to wear Douglas down and shove him into the ravine.

She knew Douglas couldn't last through many more such encounters. Sweat and labored breath already showed the strain of the long fight.

Bronwen pushed fear to the back of her mind as she cast about for a way out of this for them both. The red of her jacket caught her eye. She stooped to pick it up – a distracting ruse.

Down the trail, a small pine tree hung over the path. She covered the few feet to it and hung the jacket over the pine. The tree bowed under the weight and dropped the jacket onto the path. Bronwen glanced at the battle above her. The ram had backed off from the stalemate.

Douglas kept the animal's mind occupied with continuous eye contact while he retreated to a new position.

Bron tore at a dead branch off the little pine, aware of the deep ravine at her back. The pine branch snapped off. She forked it under the parent tree and propped the lower end of the branch against the rocky wall creating a buttress. Again, she tried the weight of the coat on it.

It stayed!

"Don't let the wind blow," she prayed. The slightest breeze would tumble her hasty plan.

Trying not to see the drop-off on her right, Bronwen ran back to the rope on the outcropping of rock. Her body tensed at what she saw.

Douglas and the ram had turned the corner and the ram seemed to be coming straight at her. From her side of the steep wall of the outcrop, Bron could see only Douglas' right boot. He'd braced himself on the other side.

Her gaze held the glaring eyes of the ram who faced Douglas on the far side of the wall that intruded into the trail.

Bronwen, too, crouched in the low, ready position. Instinct thrust her right hand out to ward off the coming blow. She grabbed at the rocks between them.

The enraged animal lowered his massive head and charged. When he hit Douglas, she could feel the shocking blow through the rock. A wave of the ram's body heat hit her, along with the smell, the years of dirt and lanolin and rage.

Bronwen knew the pattern. The ram must back off soon, to get new momentum, but he continued to push and shove at Douglas.

Perhaps he sensed the slowing down of his opponent and hoped to finish him soon. Bronwen felt Douglas' weariness in heavy, slowed responses. She tried to breathe for both of them.

At last the ram snorted. He backed a step, weighing the merits of a renewed charge or more wrestling. He picked his feet up, slowly moving away as Douglas maintained an alert crouch. The ram stepped back a little faster, seeming to have made a decision to prepare for another charge.

When the ram turned his head, Douglas began to slide his body around the outcrop. Bronwen took his leading hand in hers and whispered. "It's Bronwen. I have a rope and a way up, around here."

His hot hand gripped hers in response. He kept his attention on the retreating ram and slid toward her. Once behind the rock he leaned over her onto the wall. His breath deepened in relief.

"Where's the rope?" he whispered.

His dark eyes were drained of emotion. She handed him the tail of the rope. "The grapple is around the rock above. I tested it with my full weight."

"Your weight?" He took it in his strong hands and tugged, looking up at the rock to see if it moved. "What's he doing?"

"Still backing, and puzzled about where you went."

"Let me test the rope with my weight," he said. "Then I'll pull you up. While I'm climbing, you tie a sling around you with the other end."

He looked at her for the first time. "You know how, don't you?" His jaw tensed. His eyes willed her to answer him truthfully.

"Yes, I know how. He's pawing the ground, now."

"Check your knots." He reached up over her head, grabbed the rope and planted a foot on the first perch. He pulled steadily and climbed, trying not to cause any change in the angle of purchase afforded by the grapple. Even as she heard the ram snort, she tied as fast as she could, creating a rope sling around her legs and torso. Her hands trembled. The knots seemed to take forever. She finished and tested them as Douglas arrived on the ledge above her.

A glance around the outcrop showed the ram had picked out her red coat as his enemy. He would thunder past her in seconds. She tugged her ready signal on the rope and braced for the effort.

Douglas already took up the slack. He pulled smoothly. She rose in the air, steadying herself with one hand and her feet as she came up the face of the cliff. Looking at the cliff, she willed herself to imagine the path wider and her assent shorter. Despite her efforts, the prickles of terror swept up her back. She had to force herself to concentrate on keeping a distance between herself and the cliff so that the rope would not hang up.

On Douglas's third pull she heard the ram pass inches beneath her feet. The rope and the cliff took all her attention. Up and up she rose for twenty more feet. Then his hands pulled her onto the knoll at the top of the cliff.

They both fell back on the grass, exhausted. His breath came hard and fast. She could feel the tension leave him as her head rested on the grasses. His chest rose more and more slowly. She had nothing left. Her hands and feet floated free of her mind. She tried but could not rise or move.

"Don't even try," he whispered, hoarsely. "That coat? a stroke of genius."

The smell of pine needles and dust mingled with his sweat and the smells of earth. Safety and peace made her aware of the minute details of whatever was near — a red shirt button, the rise and fall of his shirt-print of wet, red geese. The grass between them smelled soft and new.

He groaned, "We're too close to the edge for this much relaxing. Let's move inland a bit. Then we can see about recouping our strength."

"Is he dead? Did he make it around the next turn?" she asked. Douglas sat up, looking down on the path. "He's as healthy as ever, which is more than I can say for his enemy, the red coat."

Bronwen assessed Douglas's own health while he watched the ram trample her coat. His dark curls showed the highlight of a fine dust from the trail. Dust caught in the shadow of his afternoon beard. Only his eyes retained their blue brilliance. The rest of Douglas MacGregor appeared to be softened by the covering of mountain soil and the sweat of his battle.

He glanced at her, chuckling, "Don't worry. Your ram will live."

"Good. He didn't pick this fight on purpose, did he?"

"Neither of us chose to be playing that way today. We took each other by surprise in a cul-de-sac about three miles up the hill."

"Three miles of battering?"

He nodded. "Usually he is north of here about five miles."

"Something must have scared him away from his normal hang-outs," Bronwen said.

Douglas looked down on the ram. "You could be right about that. And he wouldn't have attacked if he could avoid it."

Standing, he offered her a hand. She rose, and then saw again the horrifying depths of the ravine into which they might have fallen. She glanced up.

His eyes darkened. The grim set of his jaw baffled her. Roughly, he turned her around and with his hands on her shoulders, forced her uphill into the forest.

She tried to turn toward him, but his grip on her wouldn't allow it.

When they were well into the trees, he twisted her toward him. The dark anger in his face astonished her. She had no idea what drove him.

"What were you doing up here!" he asked. His glowering gaze bore into her. "Why, Bron? You could have been killed."

Now she understood. He'd been afraid for her, not angry at her. He held her arms and stood before her, breathing hard, but his head bowed suddenly.

"What's hurting you?" she asked.

He looked up, his face tight. He said nothing, but the depth of his breathing told her something pained him.

"We need to get you home," she whispered.

His hands on her arms tightened, but he looked up at the treetops and closed his eyes.

"Please," he seemed to gasp, "God, please." And then he looked at her. "How could I ever have found you?"

The depth of his fear surprised her. "I …" she started, "Thoughtless. I wanted to prove to myself …"

He held her very still, watching her twist the cuff of her turtleneck. "I climbed because at last I could, but when I tried to go down … I just kept going up."

Douglas' bit his lower lip, his eyes opaque. "Don't ever come up without me," he whispered.

"No," she said.

He let go of her arms and stepped back looking at her. At first, he appeared perplexed by his own actions, and then looked away, a martial tightness in his shoulders. For a few moments, neither of them moved.

Bronwen felt caught again between his hard silence and his fear for her. She didn't know what caused the war taking place in him.

Her own emotions puzzled her. She never intended to care as much as she did. His danger with the ram, the trap, the shooting of George, everything seemed to be her danger – and for no reason. What was he to her? Margaret's beloved son, a suspicious and taut man, a man whose fear for her seemed to come from a depth she didn't understand.

At this moment, it became more important to find a way back to Douglas's home. She looked up through the spiral of spruce and fir boughs and stepped away from Douglas.

"We'll have to find a new way down, away from the ram," she said. "I don't want to meet that fellow out here again." She succeeded in sounding almost nonchalant as she asked, "Where did he come from?"

"From my ranch, but went wild early." Douglas answered, and seemed to be getting himself back under control. "I never expected to see him this far south."

At last, he took a deep breath and began to lead the way to an almost invisible path through the forest. She followed. He reached back, holding brambles and branches so they wouldn't hit her.

"Where does he usually graze?" Bronwen asked, determined to sound as if their near death and his confusing emotions were forgotten nothings.

"He lives north of here on what used to be the Smith ranch.

"He belongs to the Smith's?" she asked.

"No. I bought the ram from a friend, but he chose to go it alone in the mountains." Douglas slowed as he continued to speak. "Occasionally a ram will do that, just as do solo men. The ones who've not inherited the flocking instinct won't learn it either."

*   *

Douglas grew certain she pretended not to notice his pointed comment about solo men.

She plucked at a thimbleberry leaf. "Does he attract other sheep away from your flocks?" she asked.

"You mean like wild stallions attracting mares?" Sweet Jesu, why did I say that to this filly? he thought, but he plunged on. "He has an occasional dalliance, but they don't seem to stick by him for long."

"So, he's been isolated for all that time. How lonely he must be."

Douglas looked quickly at Bronwen, but she seemed to have only concern for the ram.

"Have you named him?" she asked.

"Named him? Very few of my Blackwatch sheep have names. Why would I name a wild ram?" He looked down at her, and saw a faint sparkle of amusement in her eyes, so he asked, "Would you choose a name for him?"

She looked up, seeming to check his mood. "Ah," she laughed, "How about Samson?"

"Samson? Why Samson?"

"Because he's wild, strong and unshorn."

Douglas let loose a ringing laugh, a surprise even to himself.

In her soft humor, Douglas recognized what he'd been missing for so long. He could ignore her suspicions of the wrong people. He could control her well-meaning interference in his problems. But he wanted to know what made this woman so strong, smart and yet so vulnerable.

He decided to start by learning about the problem she worked to conquer.

As they came to a meadow and began following a path through crocus and ferns, he asked, "Bronwen, do you know why you are afraid of heights?"

This time, unlike in the truck on their first meeting, he heard no deep sigh before she spoke, and she didn't twist a button or a cuff. This time, for sure, she would tell him all of it.

She looked at her hands and began. "Ben and I used to climb mountains," she said. "We'd climbed most of the major peaks in the Cascade Range. About two years ago, Ben and a friend who was something of a daredevil, went up Saw Tooth Mountain, in Washington. That weekend I had a big project that was breaking ground. So, I stayed down."

She stopped just long enough that Douglas knew 'staying down' had become her deep regret. Then she continued.

"During the climb, they went up an unusual route that involved climbing some loose rock. Ice lay under the snow. An avalanche started. They both fell.

"Our friend died of his head injuries. Ben died, hours later, from exposure. Ben's injuries prevented him from getting to his pack, his phone, his sleeping bag and extra clothing. Those things were only thirty feet below him when I found him."

Deep in his gut, Douglas felt a cold horror at the idea that she'd had to find her husband's body. He imagined her searching, hoping, dreading – and (he knew) blaming herself. He stopped walking and watched her, gazing at the ground as she came toward him.

"If I'd been along," she said, "Ben would never have agreed to try that route. When I climbed with him, he was much more conservative. He knew the difference in our arm and shoulder strength. He hadn't as much evidence for gauging Terry's skill."

Bronwen stopped close to him, but her voice grew softer and more distant. Douglas could see that her eyes looked at pictures inside her mind. He bent his head to hear her more clearly.

His own emotions shouted at him. Empathy, guilt, jealousy – all battered themselves at the gate of his consciousness like a flock with no dog to guide them through. He didn't want to be drawn to her but could not deny her powerful pull. For her sake, he knew he should push her away, as he had all others since Linda.

But he touched her arm.

She turned her face up to his. As she spoke, her breath warmed his throat. He closed his eyes and listened, feeling that warmth enter him.

"Every night," she murmured, "I dreamt of falling with them. In my dreams, I would do incredible somersaults, while falling down an endless cliff. I would land on my feet and try to save Ben. Yet, every dream ended in his death."

Douglas moved a hand up her arm to the back of her neck. The tension there mirrored the tension in her voice. He said, "You couldn't have been with him every time he climbed."

Her head bowed, either in response to his words or to hide tears. After a moment, she continued her story. "The falling parts of the dreams began happening to me as I drove across bridges. I stopped driving and they happened while I walked, on bridges, on stairs, in elevators. Frank had to come, twice, to pull me off some place where I was unable to move. For a time, I became useless to Frank, but I've gotten much better. I've been able to function better for two years now. Until you and I met, I only drove in my neighborhood."

Douglas chuckled, "Let me guess. It's a flat neighborhood."

Bronwen gave a small laugh and lifted her glistening eyes to him. "So right! But you convinced me I could do better than that. When I returned to Portland, I drove very early in the mornings. I crossed most of the ten bridges of the Willamette River in Portland."

He imitated her earlier gesture, outlining a steep curve. "Except those two big ones," he said.

She nodded, a slight smile on her face. "I even crossed the nearest bridge over the Columbia into Washington State. I drove down here, and I climbed this sheep's path."

Douglas smiled down at her. "And, you saved my life."

She looked at him for a long moment. "Yes, I did, didn't I," she said, and he hoped her guilt over Ben began to find a cure.

For himself, he felt apprehensive of his desires.

Yet, at that moment, he felt his needs lay safely in her heart. He bent to kiss her, a long, warm, searching kiss that was not hungry, nor apologetic.

Neither was it pure gratitude.

CHAPTER SIXTEEN

Margaret MacGregor wiped her hands on her apron, shielded her eyes and gazed from her porch up the hill behind her house. "He should be back by now, Robbie. Unless he's found something. I wish he had taken you and Roy with him."

The dog lowered his head between his paws and whined. Margaret reached down and patted them both. "I would have to be gone when Bronwen arrived, and on Alice's day off! Och, it can't be helped," she explained to Robbie as he nudged her hand. "You can feel it too, can't you boy? They're both out too late and no sign of either of them. I don't like it at all."

Roy nodded as he watched her mood. He seemed to be dividing his attention between her worry and the scent in the cool wind.

As she watched the roads and paths, the dogs sat up, pointing their noses toward the maple at the top of the hill. Both broke into a run. After a few moments, even Margaret could see Bronwen and Douglas coming down the slope, greeting the dogs.

It pleased her that her son's arm hung around Bronwen's shoulders.

But she puzzled over Bronwen wearing Douglas's wool shirt, and Douglas in a t-shirt.

As they came up to the porch, Douglas, pointed toward Bronwen. "Mother, you should have seen her . . . brave! fearless! clever!"

Bronwen pulled a wry face at Margaret, "Not to mention tolerant and forbearing!"

Margaret stepped down to her son. She felt the sweat and dirt on his face, and saw the tinge of blue under the normal cream of Bronwen's complexion. She passed a testing hand over Bronwen's forehead. "Bronwen is shivering. Where is your coat, young lady?"

Douglas hugged Bronwen, teasing, "No coat? Where is your good sense?"

Margaret shooed them up the stairs. "I'm sure there's a story but come in by the wood stove and have some soup before you regale me.

As they climbed the steps, Bronwen let Douglas tell Margaret about the coat and the ram, and then said, "I'm not sure who rescued whom, in the last analysis. I might not have had strength to climb the cliff."

He interrupted, "But you provided a way to do it."

At the kitchen table, during his tale, Douglas kept urging Bronwen to eat the soup. Margaret watched with amazement as her son took possessive care of Bronwen.

There must be more to this afternoon's tale than I'll ever hear, she thought.

Bronwen seemed as surprised at Douglas as Margaret as she shivered and hugged the soup bowl to her. Douglas hovered near her and kept pulling his mother's loaned sweater closer around her shoulders. Finally, he took the bowl from her and set it down on the table.

Holding the sweater clasped near her throat, he turned to his mother and asked, "Is Janet's room available?

Bron said, "I'm already . . ."

Douglas interrupted her. "Bronwen has checked herself into the Bed and Breakfast near Coburg," he said, "but her things are still in the car and I want her in a hot shower, right now."

He studied Bronwen with concern. "This shivering's gone on long enough."

She tried to come to life. "I'm fine. Really, it's not far . . ."

Margaret, equally unconvinced by Bronwen's effort to look energetic, hurried her toward the stairs. "I've been assuming you'd stay in Janet's room. No, young lady, it's not an imposition. Now, no shilly-shallying. Get upstairs with you. Second room on the right."

Bronwen cast a questioning glance at Douglas. Shrugging his shoulders, he smiled. "Better mind her. She's mighty tough for such a little mother."

* *

From a hill north of the ranch, the man watched the lights in the house. Yanking at a nearby branch, he spat out his venom.

His mother waits for him – waits for him and wrings her apron. His dogs – even his dogs wait and sniff the air for his return. Who does that for me? Who is left to do that for me?

The new woman even – she goes into the hills looking for him. I should have done it. It's just the dogs followin' her that stopped me. I should have, when I saw her near the barn, I should have made sure he never saw her again.

* *

While Bronwen showered, Margaret took her things out of the car and hung them in Janet's closet. Then she and Douglas worked together in the kitchen.

And Douglas made use of the time to get control over his errant emotions. To himself, he admitted concern for Bronwen. But his concern was no different from the worry he'd felt when his sister Janet was in danger – he'd paced the floor the whole night when Janet had given birth to her first son.

Margaret's voice interrupted his rationalization. "I'm sorry I wasn't home when Bronwen came. Helen Smith had called."

"Uh, Helen? How is she?" He worked to make small talk.

"She's kind of bad today and Phil was on duty over at Mary's Peak, so he couldn't help her."

"No, Mom. Early this morning, Phil came with John Barsoti and me to Cave Springs. He left us to go by his mother's on the way home."

"Oh? Well, you know how Helen mixes things up, lately," Margaret said as she eyed her son with a maternal concern.

Douglas puttered around the sink for a few minutes, doing next to nothing. Margaret noticed he didn't seem as alert as usual.

Well, they had a close call with that ram.

"Douglas?" He seemed far away. "Douglas? Please, wash your hands and knead the oat bread while you wait your turn in the shower."

He appeared to awaken abruptly. A slow, mischievous smile spread across his dark features. "Why wash my hands? Don't you think a little sweat and salt might improve the dough?"

"Really, young man!" Margaret pretended shock, though she remembered how quick to have fun he used to be, before his father's death – before Linda.

"How about an experiment?" he teased. "I divide the dough, knead the first half with sweat. Wash, and then knead the second half without."

"Wash." She lifted an imperious eyebrow.

"Yes, ma'am." He bowed and headed for the sink.

Margaret laughed to herself, recalling how unmercifully he used to tease his sister. "You're feeling pretty good for one who was almost murdered by a poor sheep."

Douglas grinned over his shoulder at her. "I think I could have taken that bully ram. I was wearing him down pretty fast."

"Sure is lucky for him that Bronwen came to haul you off," Margaret joked. "Still, I want you in that shower as soon as Bronwen is out. I don't want two cases of pneumonia here."

*   *

Douglas turned off the tap at the kitchen sink and could hear the water running up the pipes to the bathroom. He dried his hands, listening. His eyes stared out the window, but his mind dwelt in the shower, watching the water run over Bronwen's soft gold hair, down over her shoulders and breasts . . .

"Douglas! The bread, please."

"What?" Douglas couldn't believe how far he'd changed in one afternoon. He'd intended to be more brotherly toward Bronwen. But his fear for her … and that kiss … Too late.

"The bread dough is cooling off. Are you sure you're warm enough?"

"I'm warm enough, thanks." Douglas forced his mind return to the kitchen.

He tried to recapture their joking mood. "Let me tell you the rest of the story of the ram and Bronwen. Where was I?"

"You had your back to the wall when a Welsh queen of great beauty and supernatural powers took your hand."

"Is that what I said?"

"Not exactly. I paraphrased it for you."

"Och, ever helpful. Well, Bronwen managed to lodge a gardener's fork, like a grapple hook, around a rock at the top of the cliff. I climbed the rope and pulled her up."

Margaret interjected, "This was a supernatural fork, too, I take it. I've had a lot of gardener's forks that would come out of their handles at the first sign of hard work."

He looked at her, "I'm glad you weren't there to mention that fact.

Anyway," he said, " I got Bronwen about four feet above the ground just as Samson charged down the trail at her coat."

"Samson?"

"The ram, newly christened."

She chuckled. "Samson, then. I hope he didn't fall. What a waste of fine animal that would be."

"No, he's perfectly healthy." Douglas laughed. "Why is it that my mother and Bronwen both asked after the health of my near murderer?"

Margaret said, "Women who care." Then she asked. "Isn't he usually up by Ben Mor or Turkey Vulture Mountain?"

"He may have followed the Corriedales down closer to the ranch," replied Douglas.

"Or, he could have been scared out of his usual haunts," Margaret suggested.

"Bron thought of that, too, but George and Ian were up that way last week and saw no sign of rustlers."

"Well, he has been attracted to the Corries before, so perhaps that's it," Margaret said.

While he kneaded, Douglas grew ever more aware of the water running upstairs. It stopped. He stared at the Oregon mountains calendar in front of him, thinking, *she's reaching for a towel.*

"I hope Bronwen got warmed up, enough." Margaret said.

"Umm" Douglas said.

Margaret said, "Gerald Crawley called, asking if he could come by in the morning. I hope he can help."

That brought Douglas's mind back with a slam. "At this point I'm putting my confidence in Phil Smith, John Barsoti and David Brock."

"It's criminal that Gerald Crawley didn't take George's wound more seriously," she said.

"Gerald's never taken anything seriously."

"Now, son – people can change."

Douglas attention sharpened. He saw that his mother didn't realize the implications of her assertion for his own case. Not surprising that she didn't understand, he admitted. After all, it was he who kept her from knowing all the accusations which had been levelled at him by Linda. People change, all right. Linda's accusations had changed him a lot.

Margaret went on, dropping dumplings into the stew as if no bitterness had ever touched their lives.

"I heard Bronwen go into Janet's room," she said, "so off with you to the showers. I'll have supper ready by the time you're dressed again."

*   *

As Douglas arrived at the top of the stairs, he heard her footsteps in Janet's room. He headed into the bathroom. A lightweight blouse hung in the shower. She'd probably been trying to steam out the wrinkles and then forgot to retrieve it. He unhooked its hanger from the shower rail and started to take it to hang on the bedroom doorknob.

The lace on the blouse front caught his attention. The very idea that she owned such a feminine fabric made him thoughtful. In two days, he'd learned to enjoy her laughter, the way she acted with his mother, how she listened, how she watched, how decisively she reacted in a crisis.

I guess I've given up seeing her as an annoyance.

His thought contained just the touch of self-mockery he needed. But what about safe solitude?

And how will I make it through dinner next to this woman? And then there'll be the rest of the week . . .

He hung the blouse on Janet's bedroom doorknob and hurried into the shower.

CHAPTER SEVENTEEN

During dinner, Margaret's curiosity rose with Douglas and Bronwen's transparent attempts to ignore each other. After dinner, they each retreated into work. Douglas went out to check on the Blackwatch ewes. Despite Margaret's concern about putting a guest to work, Bronwen took over the twice-risen oat bread.

"I've not made bread since my husband died, Margaret," she explained. "I love to cook and have no one to cook for."

Margaret understood.

Clearing the table and setting up the sink for dish washing, Margaret kept looking out the window. She could see her son talking to his dogs and going through the ewes in the corral. She liked to watch the soothing way he dealt with skitterish mothers-to-be in his flocks.

She had great pride in this young man; he'd always gone at life with an enormous honesty. When eight-year-old Douglas took out the garbage, she remembered, he chased down the last little slip of paper and put the lids on the cans tightly.

Now, as an adult, that pride and honesty accounted for his success with the breeding of the new flock. It galled her that high taxes and blatant theft might ruin years of his work.

* *

Bronwen joined her at the sink. Following Margaret's gaze, she too watched Douglas, wondering what the other woman remembered about him.

Margaret said, "That young man thinks he's got things under control – He doesn't know he's lit a match near the kindling pile."

Bronwen's attention shifted to the wood stacked in the south yard. "What do you mean? I don't see ... "

Margaret laughed, "An expression, lass. I mean when my son spends the whole of dinner feigning indifference to the woman who saved his life, I know he's trying to ignore the one thing that frightens him."

"I frighten him?"

"Not you – his own emotions. You'd do him a world of good. You're just the woman to move him beyond his lonely work into the rest of life's pleasures."

Bronwen's balked at such assumptions. "My business in life is designing," she said. "If he wants to learn about life's pleasures, he'll have to tackle it on his own."

Margaret looked up at Bronwen, a mischievous gleam in her eyes. "Bronwen Llewellyn, I'm aware that you are an outstanding landscape architect. I've read of your work in several widely distributed publications. Your designs for the Portland Zoo and for the Pioneer Memorial are incredible.

"Still," Margaret raised both hands in a gesture of fatalism, "I think it fair to warn you what it's like, loving a sheep rancher."

Bronwen certainly didn't think this was love. She remembered how confused she'd felt whenever in Douglas' presence. Attracted, yet as afraid of his touch as he seemed afraid to touch her. At least Douglas feared his ability to hurt her. Ben had never even been aware of it.

She could tell that some deep wound from the past made Douglas distrust himself. Had she been drawn to him because he needed healing?

Or to fill her own emptiness? It could be the family warmth she felt when they were with Margaret, a warmth of the kind she'd craved since childhood, and that Ben's mother and father had provided after she was ten.

Margaret began washing dishes again as she talked. "Ranching's hard work of course, and lonely when he's gone for any length of time. You get exhausted, but there's a satisfaction in being exhausted.

"And for some there are deep disappointments. My neighbor, Helen, married a fine man. But Helen should have run the ranch while Ken taught school or did something with people. Loneliness sent him to the bottle.

"Luckily, the humor of ranching kept me from cracking. During the Vietnam War, when Douglas senior was gone, Helen Smith helped me, and I helped her. We couldn't afford to hire anyone to castrate the lambs and dock their tails. We did it ourselves.

"Afterward, I was pretty sick, I'll tell you, but it got done. I've never eaten Rocky Mountain Oysters since."

"Rocky Mountain Oysters?" Bronwen asked.

"I used to think they were a great delicacy when pan fried. Used to even do the frying."

Bronwen decided to look them up later. Right now, she didn't want to stop the flow of reminiscences. Margaret regaled Bronwen with tales of lambing time.

A half hour later, Douglas returned to the kitchen. While washing his hands, he listened to the end of his mother's tale. As he made tea, he bragged about his mother.

"You should see this delicate little lady at shearing time. She can keep up with the biggest of them."

Margaret chuckled. "I can keep up for the first few sheep. After that, Ian or George can have my spot any day."

"The wool of the Blackwatch is hers to knit or weave," he said. "She's a tough one when it comes to shearing her sheep. Watches us, very closely."

Margaret laughed and grabbed a towel to dry dishes.

As they talked, Bronwen allowed Douglas to take over one third of the bread dough. He molded it into the pan and took all three pans in his large hands. Bronwen opened the oven door and helped him place them on the shelves.

All this time, he stood back whenever she approached the stove, and gave her at least three feet of blank personal space at the sink and at the dining table. The room seemed almost too large with him in it.

*   *

All the time they worked with his mother in the kitchen, Douglas felt buoyant, almost whimsical, and impulsive in Bronwen's presence.

Warning bells gonged all around him, but he seemed unable to stop himself from thinking about how close she stood when they were at the stove.

As he worked, he kept up a running banter with his mother about how the Blackwatch ewes should be penned during lambing time. All the time he talked, he mentally gave himself unwelcome advice.

For Pete's sake, MacGregor, he lectured, if she had pigtails, you'd be dunking them in ink wells.

And he stepped further away from her at the sink.

During dessert, Douglas became quiet and thoughtful, glancing at Bronwen.

Then he noticed that, during dessert, Margaret asked several questions designed to know more about Frank Bauman's life in Portland than about Bron's. Bronwen seemed not to wonder about that, even seemed eager to tell Margaret what a fine man her senior partner was.

Douglas began to rethink his mother's interest in this project and listened even more carefully.

At nine-thirty, Margaret bid a taciturn Douglas and a very quiet Bronwen, good night. As soon as she left them alone, the warm mood of Margaret's kitchen evaporated into no talk. In heavy silence, Douglas went into the library and laid a fire.

* *

Bronwen went out to her car to get her briefcase. When she returned, he'd already set up a desk for her on an old oak table in the corner of the room. She enjoyed this room with its heavy furniture and its walls lined with leather volumes. She started to comment on the room when he turned to her. "After designing all those tech parks, how well do you know Leonard Parr?"

Bronwen smothered a laugh. "I don't design his ugly tech and asphalt plantations. I know him well enough to say you've a right to be suspicious of anybody who works for him."

"Including you?" His dark blue eyes watched her.

"I don't work for Leonard Parr. I work around him. Frank works with Parr senior who is an entirely different and better person

"Of course, Parr and Standard Investments account for a large part of our company's income, but I'm not a spy for Leonard."

After a moment, Douglas gaze softened. "I want to believe that."

Bronwen picked up her pencils with one hand, and, as usual, reached for her shirt cuff with the other. In spite of his sudden softness she said exactly what she thought. "You can't go through life wary of everyone, and isolated from humanity. Somewhere along the way, you'll have to start believing in something again, even if it's just your own instincts."

Douglas jerked. He turned away from her, feeding the fire the logs it didn't need.

Bronwen ignored his reaction and set about mapping out the grounds according to her measurements from this morning. She drew her vision for his ranch. After noting the areas where contour surveys were going to be necessary, she played with various arrangements of an automatic sprinkler for the large gardens.

*   *

Douglas sat in front of the fire, perusing a collection of Robert Frost for some recognition of his turbulent emotions. Her mention of instincts set him on edge. She'd said nothing suggestive, yet her very presence suggested.

He stopped reading and watched Bronwen concentrate. She focused on what she did, yet she rubbed the ears of Robbie, who had put his head in her lap. Roy's head warmed her feet.

Roy and Robbie trusted her. Douglas believed he could trust Bronwen, even if he could hardly trust himself with her.

He relaxed on the hearth rug, basking in her quiet presence. When he thought of her without reference to Parr, she seemed to be a source of strength and comfort, a foil for the noisy world. He closed his eyes and listened to the peace of his home.

An hour later, Douglas roused himself, put away the poetry and took the prancing dogs on an inspection tour of the barn full of fine-fleeced rams and the corral of ewes.

Yesterday afternoon, John and Phil had helped booby-trap the corral so that the dogs didn't have to be out all night. Douglas went out to get away from his own stupid thoughts.

With his night vision, he could have an element of surprise if some fool did try to get beyond the clanging bells and barbed wire. So, he'd left all the lights off outside and in the barn.

As he neared the corral, Robbie barked once and raced around to the far side. Perplexed, Douglas followed the shadow of the collie as he dashed around the fence. A dark shape rose, arms raised. Douglas saw the large stick.

"By to me, Robbie!" he shouted. The dog whirled to return just as the blow fell.

The shrieking howls ripped at Douglas' heart. He raced to the dog, who whined and pawed toward him as the shadow-man disappeared down the road. The screen door of the house slammed.

"Mother, get back in the house and lock it! And call the vet! Robbie's been hit!"

"It's Bron. I'll get the number."

"On the frig," he shouted.

Down the entry road, Douglas heard a familiar truck engine trying to turn over. He left the dog to run after the truck. The motor caught and jammed into gear before Douglas could even reach the junction to the road – the truck he'd heard when the sniper escaped from Ian's Draw.

Too fearful and frustrated even to swear, he watched the truck drive away at top speed, none of its running lights were visible as it drove through the open gate.

And he hadn't finished building the gate because the concrete wasn't ready for the weight.

He returned quickly to care for his collie. Bronwen had covered Robbie with a blanket from the den. As he knelt, he realized she crooned to calm the dog.

"I told you to get back in the house and lock it."

"I locked it. Your mother's safe. Here's the key. The vet's on his way."

He took the key, muttered something about her safety and knelt by the stricken Robbie. Bronwen looked up at Douglas with tears hovering on her lids. Roy lay down beside his brother to warm him, while Douglas checked Robbie's body for signs of injury.

By the time the vet arrived, Robbie had grown weak.

"The hip is broken, Jeff," Douglas said to the vet, "but I'm not sure about the backbone. I didn't want to move him at all until you could check that out."

The vet knelt on the ground beside Robbie. Bronwen held the lantern over the dog and noticed his eyes glazing over. The vet noticed it, too. Shock could kill the dog as soon as any blow. He reached into his bag and began fixing an injection.

Soon, Robbie's whining stopped, and his body lay quiet. Moments later, the vet said, "Only the hip bone. But it's bad."

*   *

In the dark cover of the oak by the highway, the man heard the dog's painful whining cease.

I killed him! I killed poor Robbie! Poor Robbie, Poor Robbie. I'll rock you to sleep here. Rock you, rock you ... She liked that. I could hold her and rock her and make her forget the hurt. Rocking and rocking and sometimes kiss her hair – just her hair. It hurt to have her and never have her.

Oh, Robbie, Robbie. You wagged your tail for me, but you always went back to him if he called.

That's why I had to do it, you know. You wanted to go back to him.

And I couldn't touch anything but your beautiful hair, just your hair, this lock of silk in my pocket.

*   *

While the vet worked on Robbie, Douglas and Bronwen left Roy with his brother and worked to herd the rest of the sheep into the barn. The pens were small for the large flock. Bronwen could see why Douglas hadn't thought to keep them in here before.

"Douglas," Bronwen said, "This type of barn often has side rooms called transept porches. They once were used to drive a hay wagon straight through from one side to the other, so they could also provide plenty of room for the Blackwatch."

He glanced up at her. "More room would help, but we make do with what we have."

She didn't say any more, knowing he was right, but hoping he might think about such a change for the future. She also realized that Margaret hadn't mentioned the idea to him, but now he might see the usefulness of the idea.

From now on, her plans would assume transept porches existed, just in case.

* *

Hours later, Bronwen and Douglas carried Robbie home from the veterinary hospital. They met Ian and George, who had volunteered to make sure Margaret slept safely.

"Nary a sound out of the ewes, or Margaret," George said. "Roy just paced the whole time you were gone."

The brothers moved from playing cards in the den back to sleeping in their own home.

Bronwen and Douglas carried Robbie on a blanket-stretcher up to Douglas's room where Robbie slept off the effects of the anesthetic, his left hind leg sticking out in a cast. Roy slept on the floor next to him.

As Bronwen rose from the dogs' bed, Douglas's arm circled her waist. "You must be exhausted, Bronwen. My shoulder muscles are beginning to remind me of Samson."

"Samson!" Bronwen said. "That seems like years ago."

"This afternoon." Douglas's lips brushed her forehead. He seemed too tired to remember his fear of himself. She felt too tired to sidestep his desire.

He walked her to her room. As she pushed open the door, he looked at her out of eyes veiled with dark fatigue. One hand moved up and down her back while the other played absently with her loosened hairs. Her body responded with sensations she'd become too sleepy to analyze.

Clearly, he'd suspended his suspicions of her as a spy. Right now, Douglas seemed to be a worn man who'd been through hell twice in one day. She admitted to herself that Margaret had been right. She did care for him.

She was equally sure he cared for her, but he sent mixed signals. He tried to hide his own feelings in playful teasing and when that didn't work, he hid it by withdrawing into himself. At this moment, though worn out, he seemed almost at ease with his affection for the first time.

"I'll be going in a minute," he whispered, leaning back against the door jamb and pulling her as close to his body as he could. A long shudder ran through him.

"Are you hurt?" Worried, she glanced up at his taut mouth and closed eyelids.

"Hurt? No. My defenses are down."

"Defenses against me?"

"Against myself. In two harrowing days, I've come to care for you more than I should."

"Should? Where did `Should' come from?" She shifted in his arms, but held very still when she saw his jaw tighten.

After a moment, he sighed, "'Should' comes from knowledge of myself." His solemn gaze willed her to hear him out. "Do you recognize how closely love is related to hate, Bronwen?"

She stared at him. "What do you mean?"

"I lived with both emotions at once for a long time. One day, I looked in the mirror and saw a malignant hate that had grown ugly."

"What made you so afraid of yourself?"

Surprised by her choice of words, he studied her before deciding to go on. "My last year with my wife. She wanted out. To preserve her own dignity, she accused me of vicious crimes."

"You? How could she?"

"Too easily, it turns out." The dark angles of his face became sharper, his features taut. "She just had to say it and even my closest friends believed."

"Unjustly!"

Douglas lips softened. "Thank you. But not altogether unjustly. By the time she got through with me, I walked a fine line between thinking and actually doing a great deal of violence."

"Thinking and doing are not the same."

He let his gaze descend to her mouth. "Maybe not the same, but thought and action are this close to each other."

Douglas lifted her, her toes brushing the floor. His head bent and his lips moved over hers, gently at first, and then with more intensity as he awakened her pent-up desire. He traced the curve of her lower lip with his tongue, teasing her with its roughness.

She moaned. His insistent mouth aroused her in a way Ben had never done. Each stroke of his tongue coaxed responses deep in her body over and over until a sharp emptiness racked her.

*   *

Douglas heard her moan. Lifting his head, he saw her skin had gone pale and tight over her cheek bones. Remorse hit him like a sledgehammer.

"Bron?" He lowered her to the floor, where she stood wavering for a second.

"I'm all right." She looked at him from beneath fatigue-heavy lids.

He whispered, "I didn't mean to let go like that."

"What did you mean?"

He reached out, laying one finger on her lip for a breath before dropping his hand at his side. "To show you how close thought and action are . . . never to frighten you."

"That wasn't fear . . ."

"Don't placate me, Bronwen." Douglas pushed from the door jamb and groped his way into his room.

*   *

She stood in the hall, realizing that his fear of hurting her had some powerful significance, but she didn't understand why. She wouldn't ask Margaret, but soon, she had to ask him.

Entering her own room, Bronwen felt drained. She sank onto the bed. After near disaster with a wild ram and the frightening attack on Robbie, she couldn't think. Why did the powerful magnetism between them swing so wildly, repelling and attracting?

Love? She responded to Douglas MacGregor. His touch made her feel cherished. His reaction to her touch made her feel powerful. But she had no experience other than a lifetime with Ben to use for comparison, and this was not the same . . .

This was so different from the long, slow-growing relationship she'd had with Ben. Douglas's touch was much gentler than the urgent passion of her husband, and she didn't know how to react to it.

Yet, how could something that blossoms so fast last very long? She thought this emotion seemed like the bloom of a Colchicum and would hold up for the same three days. Perhaps Douglas is right to distrust it.

Bronwen lay down on top of the comforter, still in her dress, wanting to sort it all out before she looked for her night gown.

CHAPTER EIGHTEEN

The warmth of the morning sun woke Bronwen. Stretching languorously, she enjoyed the sensation of comfortable laziness. However, a glance at her arms told her she was still wearing her knit dress. Sitting up, she realized that she'd never awakened last night, yet her shoes were lined up near the door and she lay under the comforter.

"Sleepy people do the oddest things," she mused.

She could hear Margaret working in the kitchen, so she hurried into the shower and changed to her overalls for a day of surveying.

Coming downstairs, Roy's thumping tail and Margaret's warm smile greeted her. "Good to see you," said Margaret. "I'm sorry I slept through the ruckus last night. I expect you're exhausted."

"I'm fine. It's just as well you were asleep, Margaret. There wasn't much to be done after he hit Robbie. The vet came pretty fast and Roy here helped to keep Robbie warm, didn't you boyo?" She knelt to pet the collie. "How is Robbie this morning?"

"Douglas says he's still under the effect of the drug," Margaret answered. "During the night, Douglas checked on all the animals two or three times. I even heard him open my door once to see if I was all right. The attack on Robbie must have made him more concerned than usual about everyone he loves."

Suddenly, the image of her shoes lined up by the bedroom door made Bronwen uncomfortable. But Margaret continued, "Ah, here's Douglas, come in from his barn chores."

The back door opened. Douglas stepped into the kitchen, his dark eyes taking in both Bronwen and the dog. Roy ran to greet him, licking his hands. Douglas's somber glance held Bronwen as he bent to hug the collie. An awkward silence fell over the kitchen.

After a moment's hesitation, Margaret said, "Wash up, you two dog lovers. Waffles are ready."

About two waffles into breakfast, Roy's barking sent Douglas out to the back porch. A police siren blipped on, stopped and then shrieked up its scale several times. By the time Margaret and Bronwen came out, Douglas's laughter allayed their fears.

Roy growled at the wheels of a brand-new sheriff's car. Inside, working the horns and the lights sat a red-faced Gerald Crawley.

"Coom, Roy. Sit!" Douglas said.

The dog sat by Douglas's leg. The sheriff turned off all the parts to his new car and climbed out. His passengers, laughing, extricated themselves from the inconvenient and small, but sporty seats. Roy gave low rumbles of protest until Douglas shook hands with each man. At that, the collie lay down, his head between his paws, and gave one final whine.

Crawley looked anxious about the dog. Roy growled under his breath.

"Had that dog checked for rabies, MacGregor?"

"Every year, Gerald, and you?"

"Is he gonna stay there?"

"He'll stay."

Sheriff Crawley turned to the other men, "It's okay, fellows." To Margaret, he grinned, "Mornin', Mizz MacGregor. Long time, no see."

As the men climbed out of the car, Roy growled once more, but stayed by Douglas.

Margaret said, "Good morning, Gerald."

The sheriff's gaze came to rest on Bronwen. "Good mornin', little lady. MacGregor, whyn't ya introduce us to your lady friend?"

Margaret stepped in front of Crawley again. "Mrs. Llewellyn is my lady friend, Gerald. Perhaps you would be so kind as to introduce Mrs. Llewellyn to these gentlemen."

"Why sure, Ma'am." The sheriff huffed. "This here's John Barsoti of the Sheep Ranchers Association. This is Arne Alverson, rancher from across the highway over there. And this here is Phil Smith, my deputy sheriff.

As Bronwen shook hands with the men, Roy kept up a low growl until Douglas put a hand in front of his muzzle.

Bronwen recalled meeting John and Phil yesterday morning at the gate posts. She knew that the Zivner trap had come from the Sheep Ranchers Association Museum, so she paid close attention to John Barsoti. He was tall and sturdy built, and had an open and friendly- seeming face.

The fact was that each man with the sheriff seemed large enough to wrestle sheep to the ground or set that huge trap into position.

Crawley's glance kept returning to Bronwen as he spoke to Douglas. "These gentlemen was curious about your missing sheep, MacGregor. Thought I'd bring 'em right along, sorta to see fer they-selves. You bein' so close to the mountains and the wild varmints an' all, why you is just got yourself set up to be losin' the occasional sheep."

John Barsoti glared at Crawley, then said, "I wanted to offer the association's help doing guard duty, Doug."

"Thanks, John," Douglas said. "I'll need it, now. Someone attacked my other collie last night. His hip is broken."

"Did you get a look at the animal what attacked your dog, MacGregor?" asked Gerald.

"No, it was dark and the human was on the far side of the corral," Douglas said, "but I'm sure Roy will recognize the guy with his nose."

Roy barked again, but Douglas raised a palm to tell him to stop.

"That's a rough go," said Arne Alverson. "My man and I can spell you a couple of nights between now and lambing time. My man'd be a good 'un to set up nights with."

"Thank you, Arne," said Douglas. "I know Ole, and like him."

Phil Smith stepped up, "How'd he get around the gate?"

"The post concrete hadn't dried, so we haven't put the gates into its hinges yet. The gate was sitting across the space, just leaning. He moved the whole gate to one side."

"Dry now," John said, poking at the concrete around the metal stirrup of one post.

"Let's fix that, then," Arne said. "And bury the stirrup, so it's not obvious."

John said, "Did the alarm around the ewe corral go off?"

Douglas shook his head. "I don't think he'd gotten close enough to set it off by the time we came out."

"By the way, MacGregor," Crawley chimed in, "Phil here heard rumors of some sort of disease what's killin' sheep down near Cottage Grove. You know anythin' about that?"

"No. I guess I haven't been out much to hear. Whose ranch is it, Phil?"

"So far it's just rumor." Phil said. "I haven't been able to trace it down. You heard anything at the association, John?"

"Nothing," said John. "And we'd get word pretty fast about disease."

"Did anyone say what the disease was?"

Phil's glance surveyed the flock on the hill above them. "Nobody's willing to give it a name. But the sheep die hard, they say, and there's a lot of blood."

John drew in a sharp breath, "Anthrax! Not in our valley. . ."

Bronwen interrupted, "What is anthrax?"

"A disease – very contagious. It's picked up through contaminated water or feed." John explained. "It can be passed to all mammals, even humans. The death is pretty ugly."

"Isn't there a cure?" Bronwen asked.

"No. There's a preventive vaccine," said John Barsoti, "but it's only used where anthrax is known to occur. Oregon has never been one of those areas."

Phil added, "It's the kind of vaccine you want to save until you really need it."

"And if you need it," Crawley added. "You're in deep shit."

"Gerald!" Margaret cut in.

Douglas and John exchanged winks. Bronwen guessed they'd received that tone of voice from Margaret MacGregor in their more juvenile years.

Douglas frowned. "Gerald, a rumor about anthrax could ruin everyone in the valley whether it's true or not. We can help you check it out, but let's not just talk about it without knowing more."

Phil tried to move the group back to the problem at hand. "We came here to help MacGregor's. Let's get on it, and then Barsoti and I can work on tracing this anthrax business later."

Roy began growling again, but Douglas signaled him to stop.

When the men left for the barn, Douglas said, "Mom, Roy's pretty upset. I think he should stay in the house with Robbie while we work."

Margaret nodded and said, "Coom, Roy."

The dog stood, his back hairs standing straight up, but he came to Margaret.

After the men left, Bronwen turned to Margaret. "Are all these men on good terms with Douglas?"

"Of course. John and Phil have been friends since boyhood. Arne is a little older, but he's always been a solid man."

"And the sheriff?"

"The sheriff's kind of lazy, but otherwise okay. He and Douglas were in the Marines together."

"That's good to hear! By the way, Margaret, where's the sheriff from?"

Margaret scoffed, "Crawley grew up in Eugene. His speech mannerisms and his low-slung britches are recent additions to his character. Before he ran for sheriff, he spoke like an Oregonian, and had a waist."

Bronwen laughed. "I suppose he's got to live up to his idea of a sheriff. Me? I'd better get to hustling my survey equipment."

"May I help you?"

Bronwen said, "Wouldn't you like to help the men? As part-owner, you may have some ideas yourself about this affair of the sheep."

"I sure do. See you later, 'little lady'." Margaret chuckled, "but first, I need to take some things up to Phil's mother. She left a message about being out of food in her house. Phil usually shops for her, but he's been pretty busy."

The collie growled again, even though Margaret had a hand on his head. Bronwen saw his hair rise again as he stared at the men together.

"Roy doesn't seem to like Sheriff Crawley," Bronwen said.

"I expect he's pretty on edge after last night," Margaret said. "I'll take him in the house while Crawley's here."

Bronwen watched Roy give the group one last short bark. When he was inside, she hoisted her surveying transit and struck off first up to the ewe corral. In the daylight, as she followed the electric wires and barbed wire she came to one post on the far side from the house where things hung loose. She bent down and found that the alarm bell wire had been unscrewed from its electrical connection. And, someone had made a good start on cutting the barbed wire in the same area.

She looked up, wanting to point the cut out to Douglas, but saw that he and his friends had moved to the far side of the house. Margaret had taken her car toward the north.

So, Bronwen closed the gap in the barbed wire and re-hooked the bell to its electric wires. Then, she left a note in the house about the wire break and then started down the entry road.

Outside again, the warm air, combined with the relief that Douglas would have help, made her sing to herself. She stopped abruptly when she realized she hummed the old Elizabethan tune, "Sweet Lovers Love the Spring".

Bronwen made herself stop thinking about Douglas's startling kiss and reluctant declarations of the night before. She did care about Douglas MacGregor, but she wasn't about to give him the physical intimacy which his kiss suggested. For one thing, except when extremely tired, Douglas had been on guard against his attraction.

For another thing, she had become reluctant to allow any man to need as much from her as Ben had. Instead, she would concentrate on her work.

To begin with, she ought to be surveying, and concentrating on the plants in the fields. This field had very rich soil, able to support an abundance of life. The field to her right had a large plantation of cottonwood trees.

During her climb to Samson's ridge yesterday, she'd noticed, several cottonwood fields of this type in varying stages of growth and remembered Margaret saying that the sale of cottonwood for paper pulp would pay their property taxes.

Just as she set up her survey base, Sheriff Crawley ambled around the side of the house and down the field toward her. Clearly, he intended to speak to her. Given his earlier curiosity about her, Bronwen grew concerned about his intentions.

"Mornin' Mizz Llewellyn." He touched his Stetson.

"Good morning, sheriff."

"I understand y'all staying here for a week or two."

I'm taking my vacation time to work on Mrs. MacGregor's landscape. I believe it will take two weeks."

Crawley looked up toward the house then back at her. "That's a long time to be living in the same house with a man you don't hardly know, don't ya think?"

Bronwen felt the blood drain from her cheeks. She kept her voice even. "May I ask why that is your business?"

"As the sheriff, it's my bounden duty to warn you. I've known MacGregor a long time, through high school. We was in a little action in Central America. He got captured by the other guys and beat up, a lot – changed him, they say. Now, MacGregor has a kind of a reputation for violence. Don't want you to be caught by surprise."

With a sudden flush of anger, Bronwen rounded on him. "As I hear it, Mr. Crawley, you have a reputation yourself. Now, if you'll get out of my line of sight, I'll get back to work."

"At least I don't go beatin' on women," Crawley spat out. "You don't never want to be alone with him."

For a moment, Bronwen couldn't breathe for the control she exerted over her anger. "I can't believe you're saying these things. Do you understand the laws of libel?"

Crawley backed up three steps, sneering, "Don't come crawlin' to me when he turns on you."

He climbed the front field with more speed than he'd used coming down.

Bronwen leaned on her transit, her stomach roiling. She'd put no credence in Crawley's accusations.

But why take the trouble to make them? What could he gain?

And he'd said, 'We're concerned about you'. Who is 'we'?

She turned back to her instruments and worked for half an hour, non-stop. After making two major errors and having to repeat readings several times, Bronwen had to admit it wasn't possible to put Crawley out of her mind, so she went for a walk toward the cottonwood stand.

Bronwen's peripheral vision picked up something unusual in the road which nudged at her subconscious. There were tire tracks off to the right side which were very unusual. The tread looked like a deep chevron pattern with small indentations in the center of each portion – snow tires with lugs. East of the Cascade mountain range, they were a common sight, but not here where the snow became only an occasional problem.

Bronwen walked back to where the truck had made a u-turn. From there, she looked up and realized the house couldn't be seen because of the grove. By the same token, from the house, no one could have seen the truck.

The track in the road didn't look old, little of it had been covered with other tire marks. In fact, just one car, maybe the sheriff's slick sport's car, had come up the road since the snow tires. She glanced on over the hill near the house and felt a chill run up her spine.

A tall man, standing in the shadow of the big maple, stared down the long road at her. With the sun behind him, she couldn't see who it was, but she recognized the menace in his quiet stance. He'd watched her discover the tracks, so she began to walk toward him.

He turned into the woods behind him.

By the time she reached the top of the road, all of Douglas' companions were gathered in front of the barn, and all were laughing like old friends. Bronwen gave up, angry at herself for allowing the man to know she recognized his role in last night's events. At least she could find out later from Douglas who had left the group for any length of time. That would help identify the man. Meanwhile, she'd keep a constant look over her shoulder. She didn't want him coming up on her back.

And she knew Roy was right to be hackled about one man. But which?

*   *

After the friends left, Douglas trotted up the hill toward her. When he arrived, she told him about the cut in the ewe corral and the loosened alarm connection.

After they looked over her repairs, he said, "Let me help you survey. This goes a lot faster with two of us."

She smiled and handed him her notebook.

An hour later, as they finished surveying the lower hill, Douglas hoisted her transit and started to hike toward the house. Bronwen again brought up the subject of last night's invader.

"Was that man last night waiting for Robbie? Or was he taken by surprise?"

"I think we took him by surprise. I'm usually out there about an hour earlier, closing up."

"So, you think it's someone who knows your routine?"

"Bron, please don't get that bit in your teeth. Parr doesn't hire my friends to harass me. How would he know who he could trust?"

"Maybe he knows who you can't trust. How close have you been with these men?"

"Very close. Every one of them."

"Let me show you something." She marched off to the road and stopped at the tracks.

He came up to her and stared at the marks.

She said, "These were not here yesterday when I worked. I found them this morning, and the moment I found them, I looked up at the big leaf Maple and saw a man, one of your friends, tall, big-built, staring at me as if he knew what I had found and wanted to see what I would do about it."

"Or merely enjoyed watching you," he said.

Her voice went icy. "Don't you think I could tell the difference by now? He wanted to know what I would do, but when I began walking toward him, he went back into the woods."

"I'll no have you slurring men who came to help me."

"I think Roy knows who the man is. His reaction this morning…"

"Stop yersel'. It was no friend."

She heard the Scots burr thicken and said nothing more.

Douglas said, "It's simpler than that. One of Leonard's henchmen hangs around, learns my ways, sees that these sheep are important to me and he takes off with a few just to get a reaction."

"No one but Parr has a grudge," she said, "Big business is after fifty acres of your ranch, so they take helpless ewes, one at a time. Now there's patience for you . . ."

"Leonard's a bit particular in his dislike of me."

"I see that. He's so particular that he hangs around shooting your crofter instead of attending board meetings? Why would he risk a murder charge for fifty acres?"

Douglas set the transit down and stopped walking. "Why are you trying to deflect me from Parr?"

"Because I'm his spy, remember?" She turned on him. "In truth it's . . . it's because I want you to open your eyes. As long as you think this is all Parr's doing, you're going to treat it with less respect. You'll get careless." In her frustration, she felt her voice break. The threat of tears made her even angrier.

*   *

Douglas saw the glimmer in her eyes. He swallowed hard around his own emotions. Almost without thought, he moved closer and whispered, "Don't worry Bronwen. Believe me, I'm careful. I know he's plenty capable of fighting dirty. However, now that I've some help, this'll all come clear in a few days. Parr will have to give it up."

"You're in more danger than you admit," she said. "Guarding the flock won't make the rustlers go for easier prey. It's you they're after, not your flock, valuable as it is."

The almost loving worry in her soft voice sent an ache through him. "Why do you think it's vengeance aimed at me and not harassment to get my land?"

"Several things, but let's start with the trap," she suggested. "That vicious plan makes this look like a vendetta. I've checked around. The only known sale of that trap was in 1937 to the Sheep Ranchers Association, of which your friend Mr. Barsoti is president. It's part of their historical display – that is, it was until a month ago when they had a break-in. They assume that the trap had been taken during the break-in, but they didn't discover it gone until sometime during the sheriff's investigation."

Douglas felt his eyes widen with fear as she spoke, but she plunged on. "I stopped at the museum on the way to your ranch Wednesday and asked about it. They thought I was an insurance investigator, so they gave me a list of all the items that were stolen."

Douglas grew stiff with denial as she explained. He said, "John Barsoti had nothing to do with setting the trap, stealing my sheep or bludgeoning my dog. He's a good friend."

"Maybe he is," she said, "but the two break-ins at the association were done by someone with a key."

"That's very circumstantial evidence, Bronwen. John is not your culprit." He waved the thought away from him. "You said there were other things I should know."

"The electrical wire and barb wire around the ewe corral?"

"Anyone with a screwdriver and wire cutters could have done that."

"A screwdriver, wire cutters and the knowledge that the new alarm was there and where to find the connection."

"A good flashlight told him that. And what else have you got?"

"The man who beat Robbie last night must have driven in here," she said, "And he turned his truck face out for a quick escape."

He studied what was left of the marks. "I've seen those tracks other places where I know the rustler's been, at Ian's Draw and Cave Springs." It took a moment for him to return from bitter thoughts. "But I'm confused, Bron. Who are you accusing?"

"That's the problem. All your friends are tall."

"Yep," he chuckled. "Bunch of farm boys who won the state basketball championships together in high school. You're making the wrong assumptions. None of those guys would do any of this."

"Maybe not, but at least you can tell me who left your conference, even to go to the bathroom."

"Unfortunately, I can't. We divided up the area and scoured it separately for an hour or so, looking for more traps, or footprints or any clue we could come up with."

"Oh, great! And what did you get?"

"Nothing."

"Whose idea was this scouting exercise?"

"John's. And he does not hate me." Douglas looked at her until she met his gaze.

Then he said, "You take too many chances. That was dangerous, fishing for information about the trap. Knowing my friends as I do, my conclusions may not be the same as yours. And I want you to stop, because it isn't safe for you and I ...."

She ignored his order and said. "Someone has wiped the tracks out after this first little bit."

Douglas stared at the place. "Yes. He's used this method to wipe it out before, in other places."

"Looks like he dragged a log behind something – maybe the same truck."

He stood up and leaned toward her. "Did you hear me? Stop searching. I want you safe. Thanks for finding this. When we've fixed the gate, it will keep him off this road."

"But not all your roads."

Douglas started to say something but glanced up and stopped. A few yards away, George Conall stood, hat rolled in his solid hands, his eyes on the stand of cottonwood trees. Douglas wondered how long he'd been there. It must have been quite some time, for their conversation to have embarrassed him this much.

Bronwen strode toward George.

CHAPTER NINETEEN

Douglas caught up to Bronwen and approached George. "Did you need to talk to me?" he asked.

"I've a message from Mrs. MacGregor. She asks could you go over to Mrs. Smith's and see about the electricity? It seems to have gone off. Phil Smith already left here before she called." He plunged his hat back on his head.

Sure. Please tell Mother that I've taken Mrs. Llewellyn with me to meet Helen Smith."

"Yes, Laddie. I'll tell her."

Once in the truck, Bronwen teased Douglas. "Well, Laddie, how'm I going to finish your mother's design if you take me off on excursions?"

Douglas liked the "Laddie" teasing, but he concentrated on shifting gears and didn't quite look at her. "Spending some time with Helen Smith is important for you and for me. The design can wait."

"Would you mind telling me why?"

"Yes, I mind. I'd rather you see why for yourself."

He shifted into low gear and slowed down. "I forgot what this truck does to you."

"Not anymore. I'm getting better."

He shot her a quick smile and just drove for a few minutes. She watched the fir trees and Big Leaf Maple float past. Her stomach threatened to make a liar out of her. She thought she'd licked the dizziness, but this felt like riding a log jam down the Rogue River.

Douglas rested a steadying hand on her arm.

Bronwen took a deep breath and then another before she could mask her illness with common conversation.

"Who is Helen Smith?" she asked.

His hand loosened. "She's Phil's mother, the deputy sheriff. He was here today."

"Do they ranch too?"

"No. Helen's lived alone since her husband died. She owns the five acres around her house. The rest is MacGregor land now. Phil prefers police work to raising sheep."

He glanced at her pallid features and removed his hand while he pulled over to the side of the road.

He opened his door and started to climb out. "Bron, slide over. It'll be better if you drive. You'll have the steering wheel to hold."

Two miles later, Douglas directed her to turn into a long driveway lined with a profusion of wild roses. She drove past a small barn and tool shed before pulling into the turn-around. They parked in front of a two- story house which had once been white with green trim, but now needed a scraping and new paint. As she turned off the motor, an elderly woman shuffled onto the porch, pulling her tattered sweater across her chest.

Bronwen climbed down from the truck and let Douglas greet the woman.

"Philip? That you, Honey? I thought you were thinning trees today, dear."

"It's Douglas, Mrs. Smith. Phil is at the sheriff's office and I came to help with the electricity."

The old woman patted her graying brown hair and labored toward her visitor, trying to step down her stairs. "Oh my, Douglas. What's the matter with me? Silly not to recognize you right off."

Douglas moved toward the stairs and took her arm as she came down. "I'll just have to come by more often, so you can remember me better. I want you to meet . . . "

"Oh, that's Linda, you brought." She patted Bronwen on the arm and looked her up and down. "Linda Beloit! You get prettier all the time. Haven't seen you since you took off for San Francisco."

Bronwen watched the skin tighten over Douglas' cheek bones. She hastened to interrupt the flow of the woman's cracked voice. "Mrs. Smith, I'm Bronwen Llewellyn, a friend of Margaret MacGregor."

Mrs. Smith looked up at Douglas, perplexed. "Not Linda?" She looked back at Bronwen, "A friend of Margaret's. Margaret doesn't get old, you know. She never gets old. Will you have some tea? Oh … I can't make tea without electricity, now can I?"

Bronwen took Mrs. Smith's arm and walked down the drive with her, leaving Douglas free to work on the house.

"Douglas will see what's wrong in the house," Bronwen explained. "Would you show me your wild roses?"

Helen Smith ambled, pointing out peonies sprouting up and tangled thickets of mock orange leafing out. Bronwen couldn't help thinking how much more energetic her own foster mother was. She figured that Mora Llewellyn was about the same age as Helen. What had made Helen this frail?

"You know, Margaret," Helen said, "I planted this area with narcissus. But I haven't gotten any flowers here these last few years. Something must have et the bulbs, don't you think?"

"My name is Bronwen, Mrs. Smith."

Bronwen studied the pattern of tire tracks in the mud and recognized it as the same she'd seen in the road to MacGregor Ranch.

"Bonnie, huh?" said Mrs. Smith. "Nice name. What do you think's eatin' at my bulbs?"

"It looks to me as if someone is driving over the bed. See these leaves have tried to come up, but something heavy is shredding them."

"Driving over them? Must be those sheep shearers. My Philip asked them several times to park out by the barn, but they don't listen too well, you know. Drive in here and ruin my bulbs like that!"

"Maybe we could put a stop to that by planting something big right here, to direct traffic away." Bronwen stood in a critical location, arms extended to show how the planting would work.

"Mighty good idea, Bonnie. How about moving that Spiraea that's over there in that field? It's just a start offen the one in the hedge."

"Should be easy to dig up and transplant right now. Do you have a shovel?"

"Right there in the tool shed." Helen Smith directed her toward the small weathered building.

The tool shed had been left unlocked and Bronwen had little trouble finding the shovel even in the darkness, but she snagged her overalls on the leftover barbed wire which had been rolled into the corner.

"Bonnie?" Helen Smith sounded anxious.

"I'm here," Bronwen called stooping down to disentangle the pant leg. She grew annoyed with herself for being as clumsy as the sheep who'd left white tufts of wool in the barbs.

"Found the shovel." Bronwen emerged from the shed, brandishing the shovel for Mrs. Smith to see before she hopped the old split-rail fence and began digging out the Spiraea. As she did this, she marveled at how interested in gardening the older woman seemed to be.

* *

Bronwen smacked a boot to push out pocketed air, and just finished the transplant when Douglas came out of the house. "I unplugged the television and radio in Phil's old room, Helen. Why were they on all the time? They were blowing fuses."

"Oh, Phil must forget. He comes and goes to work so fast. Those lambs can't wait you know . . ." Her voice trailed off.

Douglas grew uncomfortable. He glanced at Bronwen and shook his head before turning back to his neighbor. "We can leave them unplugged now, since Phil lives in town. I'll call him and explain."

"Oh, he'll be home soon. I'll have him call you."

"Good. We need to update your wiring, put in circuit breakers. Tell Phil, I'll come help him do that."

"Course, he's got lambing and such coming up."

Bronwen watched the color deepen in Douglas's face and knew he hadn't been aware of the extent of Helen Smith's forgetfulness.

However, he rallied and played along with her world view. "Helen, whenever Phil gets through with lambing, that'll be soon enough. Just don't plug in anymore appliances."

"Thank you, Douglas." Helen brightened. "Could I treat you to a spot of tea, now that you've both done good jobs for me?" The woman looked with hope toward Bronwen.

"Sure," she answered. "Love some tea. I'll put away this shovel while you and Douglas go on into the kitchen."

Behind Helen's back, Bronwen made a small motion to Douglas. He looked where she pointed at the tire tracks in the narcissus bed. He glanced up at her, worry plain on his face.

"Helen, did you see the truck . . ."

Afraid he might frighten the older woman, Bronwen motioned him to silence. He understood right away, took Mrs. Smith's arm and, with shortened steps, returned to the porch.

*   *

During the next hour, it seemed to Bronwen that Helen Smith wafted in and out of calling her Margaret or Bonnie several times, so many times in fact that it became difficult to tell when she lived in the present and when she talked to her friend of the past.

Douglas seemed to take it as a matter of course that Helen would be confused. He tried on occasion to set her on the course of reality, but backed off when pressing the point worried her. Helen Smith didn't seem to notice the discontinuity in her tales, nor the carefulness of Douglas's answers to her questions.

"Well, Douglas. When are you and Phil going to be harvesting those wood lots up in the mountains?"

"Helen, I don't think Phil has wood lots to harvest."

"Oh sure. He's always out checking on them."

"Helen. Phil is a sheriff now. He's out catching criminals and breaking up brawls."

"Oh, I know that. But he has these wood lots too, you see. He never gave up on ranching the way Kenneth did."

"I'm glad he's spending more time at your house these days."

"It is nice to have him around, but then he has to worry about the sheep and all."

"Sheep? What sheep?" Douglas asked.

"Oh, he's been raising sheep ever since college. Has them fenced in where Kenneth used to have ours. I can't walk that far anymore, so I never get to see the lambs. That would be fun . . . to see the lambs."

Douglas rose, taking his teacup toward the kitchen. "It is fun to see lambs," he said. "Would you like to come see some of our lambs this year? They should start coming any day now. George says his Corriedales are about ready."

"I'd love to see yours," Helen said. "Maybe visit with Margaret for a while and help with the lambing. I love to work at lambing time."

As soon as Douglas went into the kitchen, Helen leaned toward Bronwen. "I know you're not Linda."

Bronwen smiled, "Right."

Helen went on, leaning closer and whispering. "You shouldn't be with him, you know."

Bronwen thought she saw the train of thought. "Linda is gone, Helen."

"Linda had to leave, Honey. He's vicious. You watch out."

Bronwen sat, so stunned, she couldn't say a word. Just how sick was this woman?

Helen forgot to whisper as her warnings became more urgent. "Linda, she was bad hurt sometimes when she came here. You be careful of him."

At that, Bronwen found her tongue. "You misunderstand, Mrs. Smith. He's not capable of hurting . . . "

She became aware of Douglas standing in the doorway. Glancing at him, she saw the quick tightening of his scalp and the flash of pain in his eyes just before he stepped toward them.

"Could I take your cup, Helen?"

He was going to pretend he hadn't heard them. He bent over the old lady and lifted her fine china.

Bronwen followed Douglas to the sink and watched him washing Helen's cup, over and over. She nudged his arm and looked up at him. He looked at her bleakly, taking her cup and washing it too.

In the other room, Helen continued reminiscing about ranching even though her audience had disappeared. Douglas refused to say anything, but turned away from Bronwen to comment on something Helen had said, as if no accusation had been made, no blight upon the visit was allowed.

Bronwen wandered back into the living room.

Helen rambled on, remembered the delivery of one unusual set of triplets. One of the lambs was smaller and had a black face like the Highland flock. She said her Cheviots had nothing to do with the MacGregor Highlanders.

"That birth stumped us all," said Helen. Very unusual for a mother to deliver children of two fathers in the same spring."

Douglas listened to the end of his neighbor's tale, then began to nudge her memory.

"Do you remember," he asked, "when you taught me how to get a balky ewe to adopt an orphaned lamb?"

"Oh, yes. That was the cutest little fellow. The ewe's own lamb had died. This other little fellow had been a difficult birth and his mother died. Douglas helped me skin the dead baby and make a coat for the orphan, so he'd smell just like her lamb. The orphan kept after her until her resistance wore down. After that, she was an adequate mother, but just barely."

Bronwen felt open mouthed. Except when discussing the garden, the woman had seemed old and helpless. She'd suddenly become lucid, and talked about having been a very capable person. Bronwen watched Douglas smile and laugh with Helen, his own manner to all appearances more carefree than it had been since they came.

"Helen," he said, "after lambing, I'm coming to pick you up and show you every lamb on the place. You can help me pick the best future rams out of the new bunch."

"Be delighted, young Douglas. Give my regards to your parents. And take care of Linda there. She's nice to plant Spiraea for me. She might make it on the ranch after all."

*   *

In the truck, Douglas let go of the breath he'd been holding ever since Helen's last remark. He leaned on the steering wheel, his jaw muscles clenching and unclenching, then sat up and yanked the truck into gear. At the end of Helen's long driveway, he stopped.

After a moment of silence, he asked, "Worried?"

She gave him a quizzical look, so he filled in the gap. "Helen's little warning worry you?"

"About being with you?" At his somber nod, she laughed. "Never. You're the one who tackled me into the huckleberries and hoisted me over a cliff with a rope. Heck, life with you is one big adventure."

His laugh sounded perfunctory. "I forgot" he said, turning off the motor. "You need to drive."

She got out and moved around to the driver's side.

"Now," said Bronwen. "You need to sit still and tell me about it all."

*   *

As she pulled up the emergency brake, he stared at the windshield. "I don't know where to start, Bronwen."

She thought back over all she had heard, and said, "Start with Linda." Douglas' looked at her, his face unreadable. He struggled to begin.

She figured he had never had a chance to lay out events in a rational way.

"I should have known better than to get married," he said. "She'd never wanted to be at the ranch for more than three hours. Within six months of our marriage, she was gone from the ranch most of the time, whole days at first, then weekends. She visited friends all the time – or so I thought.

"One evening when she had left, my friend David Brock came to the ranch. He confronted me with evidence that I had been beating Linda. She'd told his wife, Angie that I tried to keep her at the ranch and in – and in bed all the time.

"I knew she had bruises on her arms, but she always explained them away and I . . . well we weren't intimate any more by then, so I hadn't known the extent of it all."

Douglas' glance caressed Bronwen's face, a bitter pain darkened his eyes. "For the next year and a half, she elicited help from each of my old friends. She made them need to take care of her. She made them believe I was the one who …"

Bronwen grew indignant. "But who was beating her?"

He closed his eyes, sick at the memory, "Her lover. I never knew about him before the divorce, but he became pretty evident right after. One night, he took her to Harry's bar in Eugene. By ten o'clock he'd gotten very drunk, picked a fight with her and beat her senseless before anyone else realized what happened."

"Then everyone knows it wasn't you."

A sad smile came to his eyes, but he shook his head. "Some read it as proof of my innocence. Others say she just found another man to beat her after I divorced her – that she's a victim type and I was her first …"

For a moment, he couldn't go on. Bronwen wanted to reach out to him, but he'd wrapped himself in a brittle armor of tension.

"Bronwen, she was so convincing! It never leaves me. I see it in faces on the street, in questioning looks from my friends, even Parr uses it to get at me."

This time Bronwen did reach out, taking his strong hand in hers. "I've known you in the most telling circumstances. Having seen how you treat Margaret and Helen Smith, I won't believe there is anything violent about you."

He looked down at their hands. Removing his, he said, "Bronwen, don't believe in me too strongly." His blue-eyed gaze traveled up to her face. "The worst of it is, I'm a hairs' breadth from being everything she accused me of. The anger and jealousy she built in me became real and volatile."

Bronwen smacked the dash in front of her. "Damn it, Douglas MacGregor, don't let her continue to ruin your life. Don't you understand? All human beings are a hairs' breadth from being inhuman. Me, Frank, even your little mother could be pushed to the wall and come out spitting fire, I'll wager."

That image brought a little amusement to his eyes. He smiled, for a brief moment when she stopped ranting. His eyes were less opaque, his jaw less tight, but he still had that air of resignation to loss when he spoke. "You are a lot like my 'little mother', and like Helen, too, in her better times."

Almost without thought, his arm rested on her shoulder as he spoke, "I've seen both Helen and Mother pushed to the wall and come out fighting in defense of their family. For Helen, her defense of Ken was futile. He drank even more when she stuck up for him than when she didn't."

"Why was my meeting Helen important to you?" she asked.

He frowned, his hand tightening on her shoulder while he tried to dredge up the right words. "You saw how she is. She used to be strong. She knew a lot about ranching, about sheep and the land. But it's asking too much of anyone to share this. I should never have brought Linda to this isolation. Since she left, I've built a life for myself, a life of solitude. Except for an occasional foray into town to test friendships, I got along until last Tuesday."

He turned his full attention on her. "Last Tuesday I felt how much I'd been denying myself. When you came – when I first saw you at the window of the bus station, I knew. You were a magnet, drawing me."

Bronwen smiled, remembering the bus station confrontation very differently. "Frankly, I thought my magnetic powers seemed to be on the wane that day."

Laugh, darn you! she thought.

But Douglas seemed unable to feel anything more than the wound that had been laid open by Helen Smith's whispered warnings.

He said, "Wanting you, I'll try to convince you that life with me would be wonderful. The truth is, I've seen ranching wives wither in the heat of the ridiculous demands. Some become vacant, withdrawn, some bitter, and some like Linda just – they just – in the long run they leave."

"Your mother isn't too vacant or withered." Bronwen said. She herself thrived on the quiet, felt more creative when isolated. Being alone was not loneliness. Loneliness was loving someone and having their life snuffed out while you were looking the other way.

"Bronwen," he whispered, "I can't trust myself as you try to. Through my time with Linda, I came face to face with a Douglas MacGregor whose capacity for jealous anger is frightening."

"You are the only person frightened by your emotions, Douglas."

"I'm the only person who knows me," he said.

At that moment, Bronwen knew he truly believed that about himself. So, she shook her head at him, turned on the motor and drove back to the ranch.

CHAPTER TWENTY

When they returned to the ranch, Douglas confirmed that the tracks in the entry road were the same ones he'd seen at Cave Springs and on the road to Ian's Draw where the thief shot George. They were also like the muddy pattern Bronwen had pointed out to him near Helen's house, and that worried them even more – Helen had little protection. He worried that someone came through telling her he was a sheep shearer but would become a danger to her if she questioned him.

As he stood up, still staring at the tracks, Bronwen watched him. His shoulders were as straight as ever. The slight tilt to his head and the deep shadows under his eyes gave away his need for rest – mental and physical. Hoping to get him to go into the house and relax, she handed him the keys to his truck.

"Go ahead and tell your mother about Helen," she suggested. "I have a little surveying to do, but I'll come in the house in half an hour."

Douglas absent-mindedly jingled his keys while he watched her walk away from him. To Bronwen, it seemed clear he'd lost the drive that kept him working from dawn to dusk. Perhaps he would take the time to catch up on some sleep. She didn't have high hopes for that, but there might be a slim possibility.

As she walked past his truck in the entry road, Bronwen heard the clamor of a bell. Alarmed, she turned toward the house. On the front veranda, Margaret stood, pulling on the clapper of the old school bell. Her other arm extended, pointing toward the bottom land near the highway. Bronwen jerked around, her glance taking in several things at once. Douglas ran toward the cottonwood stand. Smoke rose from the far side of that field of trees. Corriedale sheep streamed out of the field toward the road, Ian and his collie prodding to hurry their exit.

Even as Bronwen watched, the smoke turned to dark gray and then black. A faint orange glow joined the peach of the late afternoon sun. Bronwen ran back to the truck and climbed into the bed. Among boxes of bud capping supplies, saws and axes, she found two shovels, one a root pruner and the other for snow. They'd have to do.

She grabbed the shovels, clambered down from the truck and ran, skirting the sea of sheep and dogs.

The distinctive yapping of Roy seemed to follow her toward the trees. She'd lost track of Douglas, but her goal was the fire area, feeling sure he would need help.

As she neared the far side of the stand of trees, the heat surprised her and the thick, shifting smoke. Inside the stand, she heard the crackle of dry wood and another sound, the purposeful hacking of an axe blade.

"Douglas!" As she called, she dropped the short-handled snow shovel and, using the root pruning shovel, began digging a trench between the fire and the next line of trees.

Thank God it's spring and the grass is new, she thought. Where's Douglas?

"Douglas?" She called again as she threw dirt toward the nearest flames. They sputtered a moment but were replaced by new licks of orange climbing toward the precious cottonwood. She shoveled faster and deeper between the rows of trees.

The axe-like sound had stopped. Wondering where it was, she continued digging. In front of her, the fire moved toward the next rank of trees. She angled left to surround it and bent faster in her rhythm.

Shovel, bend-lift, throw. Shovel, bend-lift, throw.

Behind her, she heard the ring of metal on rock. She whirled to find George following her with the second shovel, widening the small defense she had built up.

"Right idea," said George. "Just covering your retreat." He didn't even stop shoveling to look at her.

Bronwen bent to the task again. "That your axe I heard?"

"Yep. A slower way than trenching though. Watch that over your head." Dropping his shovel, he took out his axe and in three stokes removed a low branch that invited the flames to climb. Without comment, the axe went back into his belt and the snow shovel flashed in the light of sun and fire.

Bronwen didn't know how long they dug together, building up a steady rhythm with grim concentration. The heat to their right billowed, intense. The cotton of her sleeves seemed to melt into the flesh of her arms. The buckles and snaps on her overalls grew hot to the touch.

Sometimes, George turned and shoveled a new wider trench behind them because the fire had breached the first line. The smoke shifted, becoming unbearable for a few moments and then for no apparent reason billowing straight up. After one bout with the thick blackness, George dragged Bronwen away from the fire, waited until her cough subsided and handed her his neckerchief. She tied it over her face and headed back toward the line of fire, but he grabbed her arm and shook his head.

"We have to dig farther away. You've slowed the fire, but we're too close. We'll do a second line about four ranks of trees to the south and dig back toward the east edge of the plantation."

"Where's Douglas?"

"Dunno. Never saw him. Volunteer firemen'll be along soon. Just got to slow it down without gettin' killed. MacGregor'll have my hide if you get hurt."

George turned and resumed the rhythm of his digging, making a new trench going in the opposite direction from their original line. Bronwen frowned a moment before she shoveled again.

*   *

Douglas MacGregor crawled on his hands and knees in the irrigation ditch near the highway. Roy slunk forward on his belly, glancing at Douglas for a sign to charge. Both had an eye on the figure behind the White Oak in the next field. This ditch ran directly behind the man. If he continued to watch the progress of the fire, they had a chance of surprising him.

Douglas recognized the wiry, gray-haired man as Parr's henchman, Ralph. This was just the chance he'd been waiting for, an opportunity to connect Parr to the harassment at his ranch and to the shooting of George. To his right and behind him, his tax money was going up in flames. He had to catch this man or lose everything.

Douglas signaled the dog forward. Roy had astounding speed on his belly, a trick Douglas now wished he'd perfected during the war. Ralph seemed fascinated by the havoc he'd begun and didn't even look around him.

Douglas thought he'd heard Bronwen yell his name twice, but the voice had been very far away and muffled by the wind of the hot air in the cottonwoods. Douglas had a deep fear that she did something heroically stupid. Wishing he'd yelled orders at her as he ran, he also admitted to himself that she wouldn't have followed those orders if she saw something more vital needed doing.

In truth, he hadn't thought about anything that first moment except the thin form of this man running away from the cottonwoods. He'd known that with everything so wet and green, no fire would start spontaneously. Ralph had to have set it with something pretty volatile. If Douglas captured him, David Brock could figure how it had been done. David was an expert at tracking down the method.

Right now, Douglas's job was to get Ralph in custody and then he could find Bronwen.

Don't let her be in the trees. There has to be a can of gas in there somewhere. He started this with something!

Douglas crouched and ran down the ditch from Alder to Hazelnut. Keeping an eye on the figure at the White Oak, Douglas took care not to splash into the water at the bottom of the ditch. Roy had stopped directly in line with the White Oak and waited for Douglas. He nodded as his master came into line with him.

Still Ralph seemed unaware of anything but the flames and smoke.

Douglas sent the dog ahead a few yards, then pulled himself out of the ditch and noticed Roy following suit to his left. They began running across the fifty feet of open ground that separated them.

At that moment, the wind shifted. For the first time, black smoke whooshed toward the White Oak and the man, realizing that the fire could come his way, turned to check his lines of retreat. He reacted to the tall, dark figure roaring towards him.

Douglas had crossed all but ten feet when Ralph raised his right hand to his holster. Without thinking, Douglas dove and rolled toward the man. A flash of black and tan fur flew through air above him. The boom of the revolver deafened him.

*   *

At first, Bronwen's arms and back felt strong, but at some point, her hands began to tire, letting the shovel flip sideways.

"Use your upper leg to help lift it," came George's terse advice. She watched him and returned to her digging, using his technique. They seemed to have been digging for hours. The section of the trees near their first trench held in some places, but the fire breached the trench in others. Where they had not trenched, the fire moved much more quickly down the ranks of trees from north to south. At least the trench had some effect, but unless the fire trucks came soon, the trench would be worthless. She listened in vain for some siren to announce deliverance.

Instead, a loud crack startled her. Her spine stiffened in fear. She saw George react in the same way and then glance at her.

"Gun." he said.

"Douglas," she whispered.

"Bronwen!" Margaret's voice called from the east. "Bronwen, George, come out of there. Helicopters are . . ."

George gripped her arm and started running, yelling at the same time, "Coming Misses. She's with me. Stay out. We're coming."

Another loud blast sounded behind them. A sharp pain shot through Bronwen's arm which George gripped, but his urgency was so great that she had no time to figure out what caused the stabbing. They ran across the fifty yards to the weed Alders at the edge of the stand. As they crashed out of the trees, another explosion cracked behind them.

Bronwen felt George jerk, but he ran faster. A fourth explosion followed. The fire leapt into the area between their two trenches.

"What was . . .?"

"Metal," he grunted. "Cans of gasoline, maybe." He still pushed her away from the trees.

Margaret spotted them and pointed into the sky where two helicopters approached, dragging heavy water bags below their bellies.

"Firefighters." she shouted.

George propelled Bronwen away from the cottonwoods. "Run. Water's heavy." He turned to Margaret and lifted Mrs. MacGregor by the elbows to get her away from the trees as fast as he could.

Sure enough, the first drop went astray, a rocklike wall of water crashing near their retreat, breaking the alders it landed on and coating the three of them with a backsplash of mud. The next pilot found his bearings from the mistake of the first and dropped on the heart of the fire. The first already swung back toward the Fern Lake Reservoir for a refill.

The sirens of two pumper trucks wailed in the distance. Ground and air crew would work together now. Bronwen let out a sigh of relief and turned to Margaret.

Bronwen remembered the sound of the gun. "Where's Douglas?"

"I don't know," said Margaret. "Ian saw him running toward the highway. No one's seen him since."

"Toward the highway?" asked George, "or toward the irrigation ditch? Is he pumping water from the ditch?"

"The pump isn't that direction," Margaret said, pointing further north.

Bronwen closed her eyes, trying to remember the map of the area that she had sketched on the first day. This football field stand of cottonwoods had an irrigation ditch surrounding it, and then the ditch turned to cross the ryegrass field. Between rye grass and cottonwood, a small rise contained a round headed and gnarled Oregon White Oak.

The sound of the gun had come from the area near the oak.

Bronwen ran around the burning cottonwoods toward the White Oak in the north field.

After several yards, George caught up with her, gasping. "Get down. You want to get shot too?"

She kept running. "Get down where? and what if he's bleeding to death while we crawl . . . "

She didn't need to finish her sentence. Around the White Oak trotted Roy, tongue lolling, tail wagging. Douglas followed Roy. He pushed a wiry man in front of him. Douglas held the man's left arm up behind his back in a hold that Ben had often used on opponents in his playground wrestling matches. The man's right arm hung limp in a ragged sleeve.

Douglas grinned at Bronwen in relief. "Hello Beauty. Mud good for the complexion?"

"What happened to you?"

Douglas nodded in the man's direction. "Arsonist. Name's Ralph – works for our friend Leonard Parr. Wonder if Parr is going to let him take the attempted murder rap by himself."

"Attempted murder?" Bronwen looked Douglas over.

"No actual holes, thanks to Roy. He knows how to set up a pincer movement."

Ralph shuffled along, sullen and silent, but his small black eyes glanced at Bronwen and George. His most venomous look he reserved for the collie who seemed to feel the hatred and turned to growl him into submission.

As George and Bronwen came close to Margaret, the fire trucks pulled into the entry drive and headed for the cottonwoods. A sleek white sports car followed. The sheriff's office. Deputy Phil Smith pulled up at the truck and stepped out. Douglas waved at him and turned his prisoner toward justice.

"I want a lawyer. I don't say a word until I get a lawyer, you hear?"

That was the last Bronwen heard Ralph say. She took Margaret by the arm, felt the trembling in the older woman's body and knew she should get her away from the heat of the fire.

"Douglas is all right, Margaret. Roy chewed the man's shooting arm and the shot went wild. Let's get inside and make something for all these men to eat when they get this mopped up."

Margaret seemed to relate to that kind of necessity and allowed Bronwen to walk her uphill to the back porch. Bronwen's arm stabbed once more with pain and she saw blood running down her sleeve.

Behind them, the helicopters took turns dumping water on the hissing anger of fire, while down by the sheriff's car, the angry set of the arsonist's jaw created a mask fitting to the whole afternoon.

CHAPTER TWENTY-ONE

"**T**hat has to come out, young lady. But I can do it if you hold very still for a minute or two."

Margaret's gentle hands swept Bronwen's sleeve away from her painful upper arm. "That's a nasty piece of business. What if you'd still been in the trees?"

"I think that was the idea, Margaret." Bronwen tilted her head away from the exposed shoulder. "This metal can, or whatever it was, was left in there in the hopes of its exploding near someone."

"I heard three explosions." Margaret, aggravated, banged the pan in which she boiled water to sterilize a small knife. "What kind of devil does that – set fire to our tax crop and leave bombs in the midst of it all?"

Bronwen shifted on the kitchen chair and drew her kimono close around her other shoulder and tied it tightly. She'd grown cold and wished she'd dried her hair before asking Margaret to look at her arm.

Margaret returned to her, carrying the bandages and the sterilized knife. "This is going to hurt a lot, but only for two flicks of a lamb's tail. I perfected this technique on sheep injuries, so I'm sure I'll do you no harm."

"I believe you, Margaret," Bronwen glanced over her shoulder and smiled at the older woman, who rewarded her with a look of approval that meant everything.

At that moment, the back door opened, bringing in a gust of cool evening air. Bronwen shuddered. Douglas's deep voice filled the kitchen.

"Phil has read him his rights and taken him off in hand-cuffs. The fire's nearly out and about half the trees are going to be salvageable. It's not great, but maybe the bank . . . What's this?"

His shadow loomed over Bronwen. "Where did this come from?"

Margaret answered, "Piece of metal. She was hit when something exploded in the fire."

Douglas's shadow reached to stop his mother's knife. "I want a doctor to take this out."

Bronwen pulled the kimono close about her and turned, "I trust your mother. She cares about my arm a lot more than some doctor I don't know, and she's done this sort of thing before."

"On sheep."

Margaret went back to her preparations, "She's had her tetanus shot. Sheep don't sit still for this. Bronwen will. Easier to do her."

Bronwen laughed at that comparison. "I'm more of a dumb animal even than the Corriedales."

Douglas loosened up a bit. He knelt in front of Bronwen. "Where were you?"

"Northeast section of the cottonwoods. George and I were trenching in front of the fire."

"Damn! Was George hit too?"

"He did kind of flinch at about the same time that I felt this. He may have been."

"You saved half my crop and nearly got killed." His eyes darkened blue-black for a second. Then awareness of his mother and the knife returned. "Give me your hand, Bronwen." Douglas took the hand in her lap. "You ready?"

"As ever." She steeled herself to the effect of his warm grip and the coming surgery.

He nodded to his mother. Bronwen felt the pressure of the knife more than the incision. It was when Margaret took hold of the metal with the tweezers that Bronwen's hand tightened around Douglas fingers. His gaze held hers with a strengthening power as Margaret removed the jagged piece from her flesh. Fire coursed down her arm and across her back. She felt sweat run down the edges of her hair and onto her neck just as Douglas's other hand steadied her.

Margaret held a compress to her wound. She heard Margaret's voice behind her. "Now the antiseptic and the bandages."

Douglas stood, adjusted Bronwen's kimono across her thigh again and stepped to the sink. "Mother, I'll wash up and finish her bandages. Would you see if the explosion wounded George, too? I don't want him to let it fester."

"I'm worrying about that myself."

To Bronwen, it seemed that Margaret turned over her care to Douglas a little breezily. She would have said so if she hadn't been feeling so disoriented by pain. She put a shaky hand to her head for a moment. When she tried to open her eyes and focus, he offered a glass of water and two pain pills. She took them.

He enfolded her hair in a towel and dropped an afghan across her lap, tucking it in behind her. With no clear idea how he had gotten these items, she accepted their warmth. When he washed her wound with the antiseptic, she felt enough better just to grit her teeth. He dabbed it dry with a fresh towel and began to apply butterfly bandages as sutures. In silence, he wrapped her arm in cotton.

As he finished, he knelt in front of her again. His gaze ran over her pale face and unfocused eyes. One finger trailed down her neck and across her shoulder.

"You should never have been there," he whispered. "I can't keep you out of their traps if you insist on being there."

"I thought you had run in there," she blurted and then regretted it as a grimace of regret tightened his features.

"First the bear trap," he said, his voice unsteady, "now this fire and shrapnel. I couldn't bear it if . . . I want you to go home until we get Parr behind bars."

"It's not just Parr."

"It has to be."

"Are you never going to believe me? Someone is telling him what is important to you and when you will be vulnerable."

"Bronwen, I know what it is to be accused and judged without proof. I won't do that to my friends."

"But if you had proof that someone was involved . . .?"

"I'd take it into account."

She bowed her head, exhausted by the smoke and the pain. His finger trailed down her arm and she heard him whisper, "A sweet disorder in the dress . . ."

The man's quoting poetry again, she thought. He really does read those books in his library. She tried to make a joke with him but couldn't get up enough energy to speak.

Then he lifted her in his arms and carried her upstairs.

CHAPTER TWENTY-TWO

The next day, Douglas and George left the doctor's office in Eugene. All the time in the waiting room, Douglas had been fretting about how close they'd come to losing both George and Bronwen.

And all that time in the waiting room, an image kept intruding into his mind.

Last night, as he put her in the bed, her right leg had become exposed. For a long moment, he'd imagined how it would feel to lay his hand on that taut muscle just above her knee.

But he'd yanked the covers over her and up to her chin, stood back and watched her sleep while he forced himself to breathe again.

Now, outside Doc's office, that picture came back. He yanked the keys from his pocket and strode toward the old truck.

Beside him, George scrambled to keep up, even while talking. "The lassie may be right, you know," George said. "Somebody's feeding information to Parr."

"Don't get on me, George Conall," said Douglas. "Not my friends."

"But who else knew the value of the Blackwatch and the cottonwood?"

"Parr seems able to find out everything else. Why not this as well?" Douglas unlocked the truck door and held it open, waiting for George to climb in.

George glanced down the streets of Eugene as if looking for something.

Douglas wanted to call Portland to make sure Bronwen had arrived home. He'd put her in the Peugeot this morning as soon as he thought she'd recovered enough to drive. He wanted her far away from his ranch until Phil or Crawley locked up Parr.

George hesitated, moving his arm in its sling to ease its pain. Last night, Margaret had found a little shrapnel in George's arm, but worse, his wound from the shooting in Ian's Draw had become infected.

"As long as it's Friday afternoon," George said glibly, "and seein' we're in town, why not stop off at Harry's. You could do with a bit of a drink. Ever since that Welsh charmer came, you've been . . ."

"George! The doctor said to get you and your meds home to bed. Damn! I should have checked your dressings myself instead of leaving it up to you and Ian."

George snorted. "Ian's idea of cleaning a wound is to pour something greater than eighty proof all over it and cover it up again."

His glance slid over Douglas' shoulder. "Would ya lookit that? Young Hargert's father and that theatrical lawyer o' yourn, steppin' into Harry's."

George had caught him in a weakness, knowing Douglas had business to discuss with those very men. A quick visit would save a lot of time.

"All right, George. One beer, then to bed with you."

George gave a sly glance at him. "Do your attitude a world of good."

Douglas glowered, but his interfering old friend already marched off toward the swinging door of Harry's bar.

While locking up George's side of the truck, Douglas admitted to himself that he hadn't been at his best since last Tuesday. The truth was, Bronwen Llewellyn's coming had brought up the two things he most wanted to avoid thinking about – loneliness and betrayal.

And he wouldn't think about them, not the aching memory of her warmth, and certainly not her belief that a vindictive friend rustled his sheep.

Parr had hired someone to harass him. That simple. Somehow, in spite of his appalling ignorance of animals, Parr had found out the value of the Blackwatch sheep and realized he had hold of Douglas's Achilles' heel.

After Douglas's return from military service, as he recuperated from captivity, David Brock, John Barsoti and Phil Smith had helped him fence the new flock separately from the others. Their interest had remained strong and supportive right up until Linda's accusations had made their loyalty waver. Even then, it had been concern for Linda, not disloyalty to him that had made them withdraw from him. He couldn't accept the idea that one of them might have told Parr.

So, instead of thinking about Bronwen or her beliefs now, he'd spend an hour in Harry's with his lawyer and find out about progress on the appeal of his property taxes.

Douglas pushed away from his truck and from his thoughts and wandered toward Harry's. Once in the bar, he squinted into the darkness.

"Over here, MacGregor." A voice from the vicinity of the corner booth guided him through the gloom. He could almost make out George. Across from George, sipping dark ale, were Michael Hargert, rye grass farmer, and Lloyd Jones, attorney-at-law.

Jones' deep voice cut through the darkness. "I found something very interesting pertaining to your taxes, MacGregor."

Douglas sat down, accepting the beer poured for him. "Keep it down, Jones," he whispered. "God knows who else is in the bar."

"Dinnae sweat it, laddie," chimed in George. "I e'en kicked open the ladies' room. Not a soul besides ourselves and the bar-keep, and he's into the top o' the ninth, no runs, no hits."

"Your tax assessor," intoned Jones as if George had said nothing. "took a liking to your barn. Said it had been undervalued in previous assessments and that it, plus numerous road improvements, accounted for the doubling of your tax."

"Jacked up our taxes, too," Mike Hargert said.

"And who is this assessor?" Douglas asked.

"A new man. Moved here from Chico, California last year. Worked up and down the ranches of the Chico canyon area for several years before that. Belongs to the Willamette Golf and Tennis Club where he keeps his sipping arm exercised."

"The Golf and Tennis Club is one of Parr's favorite business lunches," Douglas said.

"Yes, indeed," Jones said. "Unfortunately, Parr's lunched nearly everyone in town there. So, that doesn't tie your exorbitant assessment to Parr or bribery."

Douglas felt sure there was a connection. Parr had come after him too soon after the assessment had been made. There had to be collusion. The three-cocktail business-lunch could explain much of Parr's knowledge about him. A man's sheep weren't normally insured for something close to the price of gold, and his insurance agent might have chosen to impress potential clients. The Blackwatch could have been the topic of some lunch-table entertainment.

Douglas considered their options for a minute and then asked Lloyd Jones, "Your private eye still following Parr?"

"Yes, best in the busi. . ." Jones began expansively.

"Put him on this assessor," interrupted Douglas. "There has to be some connection with Parr. Neither Mike here, nor I can afford these new taxes."

Jones puffed up. "Let me tell you, this is costing you ranching fellows money. It might be cheaper to pay the assessments than to prove that Parr and this assessor are colluding in running you off your land."

Douglas put his glass down hard. "I think I speak for Hargert."

Mike Hargert nodded.

"And for several others who've joined us. I won't pay. I'll appeal and delay until someone slips up and reveals his hand. The assessment is wrong."

"Then we'll keep looking under rocks until the lizard crawls out," said Jones, pouring himself another beer.

"What have you turned up about Parr?" Douglas asked.

"Looks like the sheriff's department is after Parr, too. They've been to his house several times in the last two weeks."

"Which officer?" Douglas voice grew tense.

"David Brock once, before he was fired, then Phil Smith."

"Just visiting or really after something?" Douglas pursued. "Fishing would be my guess," said Jones. "Both men are closed mouthed about it."

Douglas pushed a nagging thought to the back of his mind. "I'll ask Phil and David when they come guard my sheep."

At that, Lloyd Jones bristled. "David Brock? Is he a friend of yours?"

"Yes . . ."

"Basketball and huntin' laddies, they were," chimed in George.

Lloyd Jones coughed, wiped his face with his linen handkerchief and finally said what was on his mind. "Brock seems to have embezzled money from the sheriff's office."

"Can't be!" scoffed George.

Outside the tavern, an engine started up. George had to raise his voice over the sputtering noise. "David would have nothing to do with cheatin'!"

"I do not make mistakes." Jones raised one beetle brow at George before turning back to Douglas. "I don't like to cast aspersions on your acquaintances, but in this case . . . not only is Crawley sure the money's gone, but the Eugene Police have held off hiring Brock because of it. "

The noisy engine outside finally caught, but its racing motor made Douglas shout. "Crawley can't count. He wouldn't know whether he's been embezzled or misplaced a column in his books."

Beyond the tavern walls, a metal door hinge groaned twice as its owner tried to shut it.

Lloyd Jones shrugged his massive shoulders. "Just be aware, there are times when a man's ambition changes his morals." He looked at George and Mike as if to impress them with this aphorism, then turned back to Douglas.

But Douglas had bounded out of his chair and headed for the door. He'd finally recognized the sound of that truck – the same truck he'd heard after the shots at George in Ian's Draw. He reached the tavern door as the motor jerked into gear. By the time he ran onto the sidewalk, he looked at the receding back of a very rusty vehicle with no license plate. He raced for his own truck, hoping to follow, but glanced up the road to see the other driver head into the mass of concrete spaghetti that would take him in any of three directions out of Eugene.

Discouraged, Douglas started to wander back inside Harry's, but made an about turn back to his own truck because his mind replayed the memory of an explosion rending the dark of night in a Central American mountain range, leaving two good men dead and himself a prisoner.

Cold sweat slid down his back.

He must not have locked the driver's side of the truck. Gingerly, he pulled the latch and lifted the hood. Inside he found what he dreaded – plastique – ignition would have set it off, killing him and anybody nearby. He reached in, pulled the wires and took out the bomb and its detonator. In a daze, he walked to the back of the truck, climbed in the bed and buried the mass in a bucket of sand he kept for grass fires.

By this time, George rolled out of Harry's to figure out what had happened to Douglas.

When he saw the bomb in the sand bucket, George said. "This is hate."

Douglas couldn't say anything. His memory filled with the moments after the death of his companions.

George ducked down under the truck. Douglas joined him in a search for any other signs of tampering.

Finding none, they started back into Harry's.

At the last moment, Douglas looked up the street one more time.

Driving down Franklin Boulevard toward the city center, he saw a dark green Peugeot. The distinctive square body couldn't be missed.

Bronwen's car disappeared into the Friday afternoon traffic.

Douglas froze.

George said, "What's she doing here? You sent that lassie off hours ago."

Hustling into Harry's, Douglas pulled his cell phone from one pocket and Bronwen's business card from another. He dialed her cell. Her home. Nothing.

At the Portland offices, the secretary told him Bronwen had not come in and that Frank was out, expected back next week. A call to Margaret confirmed that Bronwen hadn't returned to the ranch.

George stood at his elbow as he got off the phone. "She's not arrived home, Lad?"

"No. Not at the office and not at the ranch."

George shuddered. "You're not suspecting her are ye?"

"Never. But she could be in danger, doing something foolish."

"Like digging trenches in a forest fire," suggested George.

"We've got to search," Douglas said and turned to explain to Hargert and Jones. "Her car drove east on Franklin Boulevard."

Jones' baritone boomed through Hargert's offers of help. "If Mrs. Llewellyn turns up missing, there's something I think you ought to be aware of, MacGregor. There are many in town who remember certain rumors about you being violent. And they know you were the last one to see Kenjiro Eguchi."

George knocked his beer into the wall. The glass pieces flew over the table. "Damn!" he blasted out. "Linda Beloit can't still be hounding us. She showed the whole world what she was the night her slick gent beat her up – right here in this bar. After that, sure everybody knew that Douglas never beat her!"

Douglas pulled out his truck keys and picked the pieces of glass from his sweater. He looked at neither man as he spoke. "And what reason would they say I have for harming the boy, or Mrs. Llewellyn?"

"They don't need a reason." said Hargert.

"You've got to tell them the truth about the boys, Douglas." George blurted.

"No!" Hargert's voice hissed of fear. "Parr will do something to them while they're helpless and sick like that."

"Don't worry, Mike," said Douglas. "I won't tell. People talk all the time. They can't prove anything and I'm not running for office, so I've nothin' to lose just keeping the boys' situation to myself."

Jones stood, dropping a bill on the table. "Drinks on me gentlemen." He turned to Douglas. "I thought you ought to know how people feel, especially if the lady doesn't reach home soon. What you do is up to you."

Douglas's mind dwelled on the bomb in the back of his truck. Someone pushed him pretty hard toward death. He had to hope Bronwen and his mother were far away when it came.

"GBS 059" Douglas said. "Easy to spot. And I'm afraid Parr will recognize it as well."

The men in the bar split up. Each man going a different way to scan the local roads, and call if they spotted Bronwen's green Peugeot.

CHAPTER TWENTY-THREE

Early that same Friday morning, Bronwen had pretended to follow Douglas's firm directives. After his mother left for Helen Smith's, Douglas had put Bronwen's packed suitcase in the car and ordered her back to Portland. He'd been too busy playing the peremptory laird of the manor to notice the humble grocery sack containing the borrowed phone book. He'd taken the sack, plunked it into the car with the rest, checked the bandages on her arm and sent her off to safety.

She had no intention of returning to Portland while he refused to think that someone besides Parr might be victimizing him. So, she would look for the truck with the studded tires, the ill-fitting door and bad motor that he'd heard in Ian's Draw and after someone hit Robbie.

As he'd ordered, she'd driven away from MacGregor Ranch.

However, instead of taking the entrance to the freeway, Bronwen turned south, parked her Peugeot and pulled the copy of the phone book into her lap.

The directory for "Eugene and Environs" gave her addresses. The map of Lane County provided directions. Douglas had told her he would pay attention if she had proof that one of his friends was responsible. If she found the truck, they'd know who caused the shootings, the trap and the beating of Robbie.

If none of his friends owned such a truck, she would at least know who to trust. Well, maybe.

Glancing around, she assured herself that this little dirt road wasn't visible from the MacGregor house. She smiled when she realized his sentinels, his celebration trees kept him from seeing her car.

So much for the usefulness of isolation. Isolation creates blind spots.

She lifted the directory and began making notes. Comparing the four addresses with the map, she decided on the order in which to visit Douglas' friends.

Because the bear trap had come from John Barsoti's museum, Bronwen decided to start with him. Her information was scant, but she could work with it. She eased the car out onto the old road and headed south of MacGregor's.

*   *

From where Bronwen crouched beside the Barsoti barn, it didn't sound as if Mary Barsoti was one of those vacant and withered ranch wives Douglas referred to. Her rich contralto voice was wasted on the fat sheep and high stepping hens, but Bronwen enjoyed it.

"John and Mary Barsoti, Box fifty-four, East Hills Road," owned a new John Deere tractor. All this and a campaign chest for the senatorial race to finance – could be testy times in the Barsoti bank account. What might debt do to friendship and loyalty?

The beautiful voice hummed its way back to the house, leaving behind the cluck of well-fed hens. Bronwen slipped around to the front of the barn and eased inside. Hay, sheep, roosting chickens and no truck.

Getting a peek at the garage would be harder.

Bronwen retreated to the wood lot behind the barn. It appeared that Douglas had shared his cottonwood idea with John some years back.

This stand seemed almost as old as the stand which had burned yesterday. And the Barsotis must know how vital cottonwood had become to Douglas.

At the far end of the cottonwood stand sat the garage. The back of the garage had a window, high in the wall. Stacking two discarded apple crates gave Bronwen access to the window.

She stood for a minute kneading her shoulder to cut the pain from her arm wound. Contemplating the height of the two apple crates, she felt her ridiculous sickness returning. She took one giant step onto the stack and grabbed the sill, closed her eyes and waited for the initial wave of dizziness to pass before she pulled herself up and looked through the window.

The front door of the garage sat open, giving plenty of light.

Bronwen was disappointed to find a Willys Overland Jeep facing her, but in the empty space next to it, she saw the stain of an oil spill. The stain could be from an old truck.

Beyond the oil stain lay a stack of four tires.

Her eyes widened. The tires seemed to have those distinctive chevron shaped ridges. Once she got into the garage, she might find fresh dirt or some other sign that the tires had been in use recently.

While easing herself toward the safety of earth, she heard a low growl. The pain in her arm grew as she clutched the sill and turned to face the beast.

Two brown eyes framed by twitching dark brows stared. A wet black nose pointed at her.

"Boyo?" she tried.

The collie tilted his head to one side but growled once more. Her grip on the sill couldn't last much longer. She'd better make friends fast.

"Boyo, you're a fine puppy, neh?"

The growl stopped, the head tilted to the other side. Bronwen decided to talk to him as Douglas would, on the off chance that everyone in the county talked that way to their Border Collies.

"Go way to me, Boyo, way to me."

The dog moved to the right a step or two, brown doggy eyebrows twitching in an effort to figure out this wall crawler.

"Atta Boyo. Sit, now, Puppy."

He sat. Her fingers cramped. "Good 'un. Now stay."

His bottom wiggled itself deeper into the dirt.

Bronwen stepped down and put out her hand in the "stay" sign she'd seen Margaret use with Roy. She walked into the woods, hoping the bluff would work. No chance to sneak a peek at the tires now.

The boyo rose and followed her at a safe distance. Bronwen walked as calmly as possible toward her car on the woods' road. He didn't growl, merely saw her politely off his property. When she reached the car, he sat, watching. As she pulled away, he charged a few feet in her direction, barking. He barked two more times and turned back toward the farmhouse, prancing proudly.

* *

By late in the morning, she came up empty handed and very sore in the arm. At David Brock's, she'd watched a pretty blond with two preschoolers get in the family car and leave for errands. There was a truck out front, but it had no studded tires.

She straightened her sun-glasses and covered her hair with her tweed hat, climbed to the porch and rang the doorbell. A handsome young man with receding blond hair answered.

"I'm with the city forester," she said, flashing her old I.D. card from Portland's city forest crew. "We're going to prune the street trees along your block soon. We would like you to move your truck."

"I didn't know we had a city forester," David frowned.

Rallying fast, she ad-libbed. "Eugene city council adopted the idea just recently. We don't yet have the budget to send warning postcards to residents of streets that will be pruned or sprayed. Could you move your truck, sir?"

"Sure. Thanks."

Bronwen went to the next house, prepared to do the same song and dance. In the meantime, she listened to the well-oiled door and the smooth-running engine of David Brock's truck and knew it wasn't his vehicle that had been involved in the shooting of George.

Back in her car, she doffed her disguise and drove to the address for Gerald Crawley where the grass grew high, the garage door splayed open and no vehicle sat in sight.

Driving through the apartment parking lot at the address for Philip Smith, she found one pick-up truck, shiny red, riding high on enormous un-studded tires and with doors that looked to be in spiff condition.

Even the lot at the sheriff's office yielded no truck. She parked, donned her disguise and went in the building.

Gerald Crawley looked at his reflection in her sunglasses and adjusted his gaping shirt front. "What kin ah do fer you, young thing?"

"I'm looking for Deputy Philip Smith."

"He's out on the road, up to Harrisburg."

"Oh, I thought I saw his truck parked in the lot."

"He wouldn't drive that new red truck of his on the job, Honey. He's in the car I bought for his official use."

"He's got a new truck?"

"New as your shiny face, Sweetheart. That Harley Hog near to killed him one night when he was a bit under the weather."

"Drunk?"

"He can't hold the stuff anymore'n his old man used to. Now me, I can drink all night and still cut up the dance floor somethin' fierce."

"I'll bet you can. This Harley Hog surprises me. I thought he had an old beat up truck."

"Oh no. He had one back in high school. That'd be ancient by now, but I ain't seen him in it for a good ten year."

"Well, maybe I've got the wrong man. You don't own an old truck do you?"

"Not me, Honey. I like my cars fast."

"Well, tell Philip that Shirley Anne was by, would ya. He's got my number."

"He'll be delighted. You wasn't lookin' for company for tonight was ya?"

"If Phil is free. Have him call me, okay, Honey?"

*   *

Bronwen hopped in her car and pulled off her old tweed roll-up hat.

She ignored the pain in her upper arm and thought about what she'd learned. Barsoti might have an old truck. He had studded tires, which on closer inspection might prove to be *the* studded tires. Everybody else had ordinary cars or, as in the case of Phil, a new truck replacing a Harley. She'd narrowed down the field considerably. Now to eliminate the possibility that Parr had the truck in question.

*   *

The doorbell chimes played the theme from Star Wars. Bronwen steeled herself to be polite.

When the door opened, Bronwen recognized that Leonard in a t-shirt appeared even further removed from 'suave' than Leonard in a suit.

"Bronwen! This is a surprise." He opened the door wide and beckoned her in.

She stayed on the porch. "Not here to visit, Leonard. I'm down here doing a design for a small village project and Frank asked me to check about your truck. There's an old truck at your tech park in Beaverton. We're about to have it towed, but some of the guys thought it might be yours."

"I don't own a truck – hate the things. Come on in, Bronwen. I'll make us some iced tea."

"I can't stay, Leonard. I have to get back to the design."

"We both know that if you didn't want to see me, you could have called, Bronwen. I won't mention to Frank that you were here."

Bronwen shook her head, "I came about the truck, Leonard. Just the truck. Is it yours?"

He smiled and opened the door wider, "Come on in while I wrack my brain about this truck."

"I'm not here to visit. You should have gotten that message when I invited you out of my apartment."

"All right! All right! I admit I made a mistake where you're concerned. It's just that I thought after so many years without a husband you might be getting kind of. . ."

"I am. I'm getting real tired of your type and their assumptions." Bronwen turned on her heel and strode off the porch to her car.

*   *

She stopped in the center of Eugene near Franklin Boulevard to call her foster parents.

Evan Llewellyn answered. "'Lo?"

"Dad, Bronwen."

"Hi, Little Sparrow. Mom said you were working in Eugene and drove yourself down there."

"All fact," Bron said. "Could you tell Mom I won't be up to Beavercreek for a week or so?"

"Getting muddy in the Eugene hills, eh?"

"Yep. Nice ranch and a house you'd love to see, Dad. Good woodwork. Oak and maple."

"Take photos," he said.

"Will do. See you soon."

"We love you, Little Bird. Be careful."

After she hung up, Bronwen thought about her foster family. They'd been taken aback when she and Ben wanted to get married, after long friendship and then living in the same house as kids. The folks had pushed the idea of looking at others, dating others before they decided, but had realized how strongly they wanted to be together.

She knew their hesitancy hadn't been lack of love for her, but a feeling that she and Ben had no way to compare their love to the bigger world of men and women. Bron was glad they'd had those few years together, but she also knew their isolation as a couple had made her grief harder to bear. She had only ever known Ben as a friend, companion and then lover. The wider world had seemed unnecessary back then.

She decided next to call Frank. If he should happen to call the ranch and find that Douglas thought she was in Portland, Frank would be very worried about her. Relief flooded her on hearing that Frank didn't expect her. In fact, he'd already left for Albany and then would drive on down to Eugene to begin work on the MacGregor barn.

Then, Eliza, their secretary said a Mr. MacGregor had called wanting to talk to her.

Best get to the ranch, she thought. Douglas will be frantic.

She hoped Frank might be able to encourage Douglas to look at the evidence against John that she'd gathered today.

As Bronwen finished up her call to Portland, she realized that she'd been passed by an ancient truck with no license plates.

The truck had passed her car blowing black smoke, and headed off into the freeway clover-leaf. Frustrated that she'd missed the only suspect truck she'd been close to all day, Bronwen pulled out onto Franklin Boulevard.

Her arm was a pain. It aggravated her to be angry, stymied and in pain all at once. After she tried for half an hour to follow the old truck, she had to admit that it was impossible to catch it and see who drove it.

She drove back to the MacGregor's ranch, hoping to find Margaret at home and Douglas gone. He'd been planning to take George to the doctor in Eugene and then visit his godson, wherever he might be. With luck, he'd still be gone.

As she drove into the ranch, she heard a large flock of sheep moving on the road. Ian, George's brother, herded their Corriedales onto the hill above the house. Almost their lambing time. The sea of white wool seemed endless and kept the shepherds so busy that they didn't see her drive in.

On finding that Douglas's truck was not parked at the ranch, Bronwen breathed a sigh of relief.

Bronwen entered the kitchen where Alice and Margaret put up early fruit and spring vegetables. Peas and spinach awaited cleaning in the sink.

Margaret's eyebrows went up, but she had spinach in her mouth, so Bronwen answered the question she thought Margaret wanted answered.

"Did Douglas tell you I had business in Portland?"

Margaret nodded.

"He just wanted to get rid of me because he thinks I'm a magnet for shrapnel and bear traps. I go nowhere 'till we find out who's behind all this."

Margaret frowned.

Belatedly, Bronwen asked, "May I stay?"

After a moment's consideration, Margaret shrugged and nodded, swallowed her spinach leaf and said, "He saw your car in Eugene and called here, very worried about you. I don't think it's safe for you around here, myself."

"It's no more dangerous for me than you," Bronwen pointed out.

Alice grunted, "Yep to that."

Margaret ignored Alice, saying, "Sure seems more dangerous for you. I don't have the wound in my arm."

"At least let me stay long enough to plead my case. If I can't convince him, I'll go."

Margaret gave that considerable thought. "I agree with you. There's more than Parr behind this, but Douglas has strong reasons for avoiding suspicion of his friends, and he's right to want you away from here."

Bronwen's frustration asserted itself. "It's so obvious that whoever began taking the Blackwatch knew their value. Who knew but you and the friends who helped him when he first fenced off their pasture?"

"Well, Linda could have known," Margaret said.

Alice nodded and harrumphed.

Margaret went on, "but Linda was too busy flitting to wonder what Douglas was trying to do. And there weren't but a few lambs by the time of the divorce."

"So," Bronwen said "it has to be John, Gerald, Phil or David Brock."

Margaret shook her head. For the first time, Bronwen saw age creep into the other woman's posture. "Bronwen, those boys are like nephews to me. I don't want to believe it any more than he does. Stay. Argue it out with him, but don't be surprised if he just packs you off again for your own safety."

Bronwen had just set her suitcase in Janet's room again when she heard his truck barreling up the drive. A moment later, the kitchen door slammed.

"Where is she?" boomed his deep voice.

"In her room," Margaret answered.

He bounded up the steps and met her coming down.

"What the hell are you doing?" His angry eyes glared up at her. "I thought I made myself clear this morning . . ."

She stayed on the step above him and steeled herself for the fight. "I've been out looking for that truck."

"What? You've been . . ." The color drained from his face, but his blue eyes had become lightning silver.

"There wasn't any danger," she said. "I just made myself look different – sun glasses and a funky hat – and talked to David Brock and Gerald Crawley. David's truck nearly sings when he starts it up. Gerald doesn't like trucks and he says Phil has a brand-new red truck, after trading in his Harley. I saw Phil's new truck – enormous tires, no studs. And Parr claims to own no trucks at all."

"Parr? You went to see Parr?"

"Don't worry, I stayed on the front porch. He thinks I came down to check on a low-income housing development. I did go over to the small house site. It's at the ground-breaking stage."

"I don't want you anywhere near that man, you hear me? First, you're around looking for the owner of the trap, and now you bust off in some half-baked disguise asking about trucks. You're going to get killed just for being nosey."

"Ah, but the question is who will kill me?"

Douglas stepped up to her level and lifted her by the waist. Striding into Janet's room he said, "Kill you? You'll do that for them. Don't you know your shrapnel wound is bleeding again?"

Held off the floor and a little above him, it became hard to look down at her arm, so she closed her eyes and just kept arguing. "John Barsoti has studded tires and a Willys jeep that could sound like an old truck. I bet the car or truck he drove today doesn't sound too good either, it has a big oil leak."

Douglas placed her on the bed and straightened to hold up her arm.

What she'd said did not seem to sink in at all. He stared at her arm. Down her sleeve there ran a bright red streak of blood.

"Take off your blouse."

"I can take care of this."

"I'll turn around if you like, but I nearly lost George by letting him take care of a wound like that. I'm not going to lose. . ." He seemed to realize what he lay claim to and stopped cold.

"Right! You're not going to lose me," said Bronwen. "Don't you worry about that, Douglas MacGregor."

His eyes lost their angry flash and his whole face became softer. "Damn, Bronwen, how'm I to keep you safe?"

"Why should that be your responsibility?"

"You're on my ranch! and your damned arm is bleeding!"

"Are you afraid people will think you did this to me?"

He stepped back as if she'd hit him. "They'll believe that anyway," he said dully.

"Without evidence!"

"Oh, they've plenty of evidence of my temper. I went to jail for displaying it publicly – very publicly." He leaned against the wall.

Bronwen sat up. "You? Even at Helen's, when the woman insinuated the worst about you, I never saw any reaction from you but stoic frustration."

He continued to stare at her, letting his bald statement sink in. "Why jail?" she asked.

"Get your robe on."

She hauled the robe out of her suitcase and stepped into the closet, saying again, "Why jail?"

Douglas paced to the window, drew back the curtain and stared out at the hills as if he could no longer face her.

"One night after the divorce finalized, I decided to meet some friends at Harry's Bar. I hadn't been with them for a long time. David, John, Phil, Ken Eguchi, Mike Hargert – all there celebrating God knows what, and David called me to come on down and join them."

Bronwen came out of the closet and watched his profile as he spoke.

His features and his voice displayed no emotion.

"I hadn't been there an hour when Linda came in with the guy I knew by then was her lover. She laughed and leaned on him when she spotted me and waved. I walked out. It made me sick to see her hanging on this guy who treated her like shit."

Douglas swallowed hard before he turned toward Bronwen. "As I left, I heard her call my name, but I just kept walking. I wasn't even a block away when all hell broke loose in the bar.

"The shouting grew pretty loud, but what made me run back were the two shots I heard. By the time I got back inside, Linda lay on the floor, her face all bloody. Hargert and Barsoti had her lover up against the wall. He had a gun in his hand. There were holes in the ceiling. Phil took the gun as I came in.

"I thought he'd killed her, but Eguchi said she would be all right, that guy had just punched her in the face for wanting to talk to me. The guy had pulled the gun trying to scare away the men who surrounded him in the tavern."

Douglas stopped and stared at his clenched fists. Bronwen had a feeling he'd spent the last four years trying to put this night from his mind. She held very still, not wanting to interrupt until he'd gotten it all out.

"When I got up from checking on her, I lunged at him. And I got my hands on his throat. All I could think about were those times when he'd beaten her, and she'd dragged herself to my friends – all the accusations and the news stories about my treatment of her, the lies and the martyred refusal to take me to court – she'd done all that to me for this bastard."

Douglas wouldn't look at Bronwen as he continued, but she could see his eyelids darken with remembered pain and anger. "I heard the ambulance sirens as my friends pulled me off him. The medics came in and took her away while everyone yelled at once, telling me the guy wasn't worth it and neither was she.

"Then something brought the whole thing crashing in on me.

"Phil pulled my arm behind me and I heard him yell, 'Why kill him? He's done no more than you've done yourself, when she was yours.'"

Bronwen gasped. Douglas's glance jerked up at her. His gaze held hers as he bore in on the heart of it all. "I stopped then and looked around at each of them for a moment. I saw it in their eyes. At that moment, every one of them still believed I had done it.

"Something in me broke and I swung on them with everything I had. Twenty minutes later, the ambulance returned to take Phil and John off to the hospital. The Eugene Police took me to jail for disturbing the peace and assaulting an officer of the law. The headlines in the Register Guard were sensational."

Bronwen took a deep breath and let it out before she could trust her voice. "You'd every right to be angered."

"This was more than anger," he said, walking toward her. "Linda had it right all along. I could have killed any one of them if he'd fought me alone in those few minutes. And if I'd gotten my hands on her just then, I would have . . ."

"Stop it!" Bronwen was on him in a breath, unclenching his fist with her hand. "Stop blaming yourself for finally reacting. She had ruined you, and in spite of all the evidence, your friends believed her!"

Her own body's angry trembling surprised her. "I don't know why you still speak to any of them . . . the way they treated you. . ."

Douglas shook his head, a sad smile shone for a second. "My friends have each made a separate peace with me. As they realized what had happened, most of them have made public and private statements defending me. It's over. But I can't forget that there were times – many times, when I was close to showing my anger even before that night in the bar, even with Linda. My temper is dangerous."

"So, you're going to stay away from emotion – live in solitude the rest of your life?" she asked.

He nodded.

"What a dull way to get to heaven," she said.

For the space of a wink, Bronwen thought he was going to smile.

Instead, he reached out to caress her cheek. "At least I won't be hurting anyone."

And then let his hand slide down her throat to the top of her robe. "I'm going to take care of that arm. And then I want you to take some pain killer and get into bed. We'll talk later about whether you'll stay."

"You have a lot of ewes and lambs to take care of, I'll get this."

"No." The simple word came out so quietly and with such force that she stared at him. "Get that arm out," he said.

She reached up to do the button, but couldn't get it off. His fingers took over. When the twisted button fell off in his palm, he looked at its broken halves, then at her, and they both gave a start of laughter.

As his glance caressed her smiling face, he sighed heavily. "You'd distract the most determined of men."

His eyes flickered downward over her robe. "I'll go get the bandages. You get your arm out." He strode out of the room.

CHAPTER TWENTY-FOUR

After Douglas bandaged her arm, Bronwen napped for an hour and felt refreshed. As soon as she had dressed, (quite a feat considering the size of bandage Douglas had put around her arm), she checked on Robbie who limped around Douglas' room. Even in the sling Douglas had been using, Robbie weighed almost more than she could carry outside with one arm.

She used the sling to hold his back legs off the ground as he stumbled around the outside of the house. As she neared the back porch, Douglas waved his thanks to her from the hill meadow and got down on his knees to help a ewe who had some trouble.

Maybe he's reconsidered, she thought. I'd hate to be banished now, when I'm close to figuring out who did it.

The dog licked her forearm. She rubbed under his chin and then carried the drooping collie to his bed.

"Good boyo," she crooned, and then remembered the collie at John and Mary's. "Is Barsoti's little collie your brother?" Robbie licked her hand.

She smoothed Robbie's coat and went outside to work. If Douglas might force her to leave, at least she wanted to have all the information necessary to finish the landscape design from the desk in the Bed and

Breakfast at Coburg. For certain, she intended to go no farther away from here than that.

She surveyed behind the barn and then worked in the den, drawing what she had in mind for draining the marsh. As she cleared her desk, Margaret called her to the phone in the kitchen.

"Bronwen!" Over the line came Frank's voice, anxious.

"Frank, I understand you're on your way down here."

"I am. But I called the office. They said Douglas believed you were in Portland. They also told me that you had called from Eugene looking for me, so I thought maybe something had happened to you."

Bronwen rubbed her bandaged arm. "No, I'm fine. Just a bit of a mix-up in communications here." She tried to ignore Margaret's raised eyebrow.

Frank's voice softened, "Is everyone else there all right? Douglas? Margaret?"

"She's fine. Looking forward to your visit." Bronwen smiled at Margaret's embarrassed frown.

"Great! See you tomorrow then. Stay put till I get there, huh?"

"Scout's honor," Bronwen said.

Margaret's hands sat on her hips as Bronwen hung up. "Slight communication mix-up, my foot . . . Scout's honor, indeed. If you hadn't come up the driveway when you did, Douglas would have called Phil Smith and Gerald Crawley with a missing person's report."

"Why so worried?"

"He saw your car right after he found a bomb planted in his truck motor."

"Bomb!" Waves of cold flashed through Bronwen. "Who? Oh! He thought I did it?"

"Certainly not. He thought you might become the next victim." Margaret, seeing how pale Bronwen had become, gestured her toward a chair as she continued to explain. "I've been thinking about your theory – that our suspect might be a friend." Margaret poured tea into a fine china cup and set it in front of Bronwen. "Drink. You're about to faint."

Startled, Bronwen reached for the cup and found the warmth on her hands brought back her sense. "My theory?"

"I don't like your theory," Margaret said, "but I can't bury my head in the sand when someone is trying to kill my son." She picked up a piece of paper, wet from the lettuce and covered with pencil jottings. "These are the men who knew about the sheep.

This column lists what I know of their experience with explosives and this column, firearms."

Bronwen took the list from Margaret's shaky hand.

"Several of these men are near sons to me," Margaret whispered. Bronwen glanced up at her. Tears hovered in the older woman's eyes. "But whoever it is has got to be stopped before he kills," Margaret said.

"I'm sorry," Bronwen said, then dropped her gaze from the sight of the other woman's sadness. She studied the list.

'David Brock, construction/demolition during college, owns shot gun, sheriff's revolver

Gerald Crawley, munitions distribution in armed service, sheriff's revolver, medal for sharp shooting, no known experience with explosives

Phil Smith, used dynamite in road construction, owns hunting gun of some kind

Ken Eguchi, Douglas's godson is his son, hunts with Douglas with ? kind of rifle. No known experience with explosives

John Barsoti, dug wells with dynamite, hunting gun – same brand as Douglas's gun.'

Mike Hargert, neighbor to Ken, part of hunting friends, ? type of rifle, worked on roads with Phil Smith, so has used dynamite.

The inclusion of Gerald Crawley puzzled Bronwen. He wasn't one of Douglas's close friends. "Margaret, how does Gerald know about the sheep?"

"General nosiness and working with Phil Smith and David Brock," said Margaret. "I expect he spends most of his sheriffing energy pretending to be asleep but listening from under his hat."

"Would he have a reason to take that information to Parr?"

"Money, maybe. I can't think of a better reason for some men."

Out of her pocket, Bronwen drew her list of vehicles for some of these same men. Margaret took a look.

"Parr! No wonder Douglas got so worked up when he found out what you'd been doing."

"But I stayed on the porch, in plain sight of the street and perfectly safe."

Margaret sighed. "You wouldn't know how to be perfectly safe in an old-folks home. Come help me put up these early peas, young lady. At least I know the vegetables won't kill you."

Bronwen helped Margaret with the preserving. An hour later, Douglas looked in and asked her to come outside. Bronwen felt certain he planned to order her off to Portland. With any luck, she might convince him to let her stay until Frank arrived. Frank knew the families of his friends better than she did. Perhaps he'd recognize a motive where an outsider like herself would not.

She joined Douglas on the back lawn. "The one time I'm doing something safe and useful and you have to interrupt," she joked.

He smiled. "Mother can manage. I realized that, with all your 'investigating', you've probably eaten nothing since breakfast. It's gone four o'clock already. I certainly need the break. Let me show you what I stowed under the Engelmann Spruce while you were asleep."

Seeing her hesitation, he smiled. "We need to talk. Bron, come." He began walking downhill.

"Douglas MacGregor, you've sure got me confused."

"No more confused than I am," he said. When he turned to look back at her, his glance took her in from head to toe. A mischievous gleam shone in his eye. "Whenas in silks my Julia goes," he said. "Ah, then methinks how sweetly flows, the liquefaction of her clothes."

Bronwen glanced down at her work-worn overalls and laughed. "Are you letting the poet Herrick make fun of my Osh-Koshes?"

"No. Your overalls are just as high fashion as silks, only less," his long fingers gestured a certain sensuous flow. "less . . . liquid."

He chuckled at her embarrassment and ducked under the ground-sweeping branches of the Engelmann Spruce, holding them apart for her to enter. After she sat on a worn boulder, he pulled a tablecloth and food containers out of a picnic basket and watched her pleasure.

Bronwen rested under the tree, leaning back against the trunk. She looked up into the dizzying spiral of ascending branches. The needles showed new green, touched with the light of warm spring sun. The sun lit the cave under the low-hanging branches as if with a skylight, yet the branches protected the space from wind and rain.

Looking up brought on her vertigo. Bronwen closed her eyes to regain her equilibrium, pretending to rest, because she felt Douglas watching.

As she relaxed, he relaxed. Handing her a sandwich and taking one for himself, he leaned against the tree trunk and against her shoulder. They ate for a time, without talking.

After a while, he produced a thermos of tea and handed her a steaming cup. They both settled back. Douglas began musing. "Janet, my sister, and I used to play under here. You're sitting on the sofa of our living room. I, bad boy as usual, am sitting on the dining table.

"Sometimes, this was our caveman home. We were fearless hunters. The sheep were mammoths, dinosaurs, what have you."

"Someone has been playing here recently," said Bronwen.

"Yes, Janet's children. They don't know that their mother and I used to hide here, too."

"I imagine your father played here, himself." Bronwen thought of the generations represented in this playhouse. Her hand trembled as she put her cup of tea down on the tablecloth.

Douglas slipped his arm around her shoulders as she leaned back again. "I owe you an explanation, Bronwen, or at least I owe you as much as I understand myself. You make me feel alive in a way I haven't for years. When I'm not with you, I steel myself against your impact on my senses. I prepare my part and then whamo, enter Bronwen and all my well-learned lines are of no use.

"It's not in the play for me to touch you, but when you are near, I reach out. You come to me as if it were in your script, natural, unrehearsed, compelling. And yet, beneath your warmth, I feel an odd reluctance toward my touch. I feel as if we are in two simultaneous and vastly different plays."

*   *

Even as he spoke of her reluctance, Bronwen made herself relax against his arm. He retreated, obviously alert to subtle signals.

She swallowed hard, angry at her involuntary tension. Douglas had always been gentle, never moving fast or insistently as she had come to expect with Ben. She moved back into the curve of his arm.

Douglas inhaled. "I care," he went on, "and I'm afraid to care. I'm not the man you deserve nor is this the kind of life you need. Yet, whenever I'm near you, I feel full. . . I don't know . . . full of..." His brow knitted.

Bronwen surprised herself, prompting him, "Full of vinegar?"

His somber face transformed into the soft humor she'd so often found in him when he talked to others. She laughed and tried to duck as his arm trapped her shoulders.

"Witch!" he laughed. "When will you take me seriously?"

"Never!" she gasped, between attempts to wrestle free. "Never. As long as you laugh, you can't take yourself too seriously either."

His arms tightened around her. Bronwen heard him mutter, "Sweet Jesu!" His hand held her shoulder, but he leaned his head back against the trees. At last, he turned his gaze toward her.

"You see what happens? I shouldn't even begin to touch you."

She ducked her head, then brought it up. Somewhere, along with worrying about him and his sheep, Bronwen realized she had learned to trust Douglas MacGregor to be thoughtful and gentle. "Perhaps it would be better for both of us," she said, "if you did touch me."

A sad longing grayed his eyes. "I wish that were true," he said. After a tense moment, he looked away. "Bronwen, I've told you about Linda. Tell me about Ben."

All motion in her stopped.

*   *

His glance took in her worried features, her disheveled braid, the curve of the hip that had been close to his. He tried to regain some semblance of calm, but the images that intruded were far from restful. He took her hand in his and turned her around to face him. His knee came up to support her back.

When he could see that she breathed again, he added, "I need to know."

He waited while she gathered her thoughts. Her hand rotated the buckle of her overalls. The color in her cheeks faded from a warm pink to a creamy white.

"We came to Beavercreek when I was five," she began. "My father had emphysema. He'd been a miner in the mountains back east. Mother had a friend who offered to help us – her friend was Ben's mother. We rented a small house from them, for next to nothing. My father lay in the hospital most of the time. The hospital allowed no child visitors. I don't remember much except his sadness. At my age, I knew he feared death. I never got to comfort him."

Douglas imagined that heartbreak. He caressed her cheek and found it wet. Bronwen shivered and turned her gaze up to the branches. His fingers slid to her shoulder and rested there.

She took up her story again.

"Mother worked in a restaurant. Ben and I were in school together. We walked home from school. I would go into our little house, lock the doors and stay by myself until after midnight when Mother came home from . . . from work. I imagined ghosts and ghouls in the basement. I was afraid of falling through the floor to the cellar because of the ghosts, so I walked around the edges of the rooms."

Douglas's hands tensed on her shoulders. "That was the real beginning of it," he whispered.

Puzzled, Bronwen glanced at him. "Beginning of what?" she asked.

His jaw set hard. "Of your fear of falling. Damn! You were so young . . . a child who knows her dying father is afraid of death, and then to come home to that emptiness? No wonder you conjured demons in the basement. You had no protection from any of it."

"My mother was just as hurt and frightened . . . "

His hand moved up her throat, forcing her chin up. His angry gaze held hers. "Your mother had a child, a responsibility. She could have done something, asked someone to care for you after school, brought you to the restaurant, anything. She abandoned you."

"No!" Bronwen choked back a sob. "No, she just couldn't face …"

"You? She couldn't face you?"

Bronwen held back threatening tears and tried to look away from him. "I guess I looked like Dad. I know I did; I've seen the pictures."

Douglas's hand relaxed under her chin and began its slow stroking of the back of her neck again. "And Ben? How did he figure in all this?"

"He found out I feared our house." Through her tears, Bronwen laughed. "When we were eight, he read a book about vampires and witches and got the idea of doing an exorcism with garlic and burning crosses and stakes – the whole show. Nearly burned the house down."

Douglas's inner heart cheered for her eight-year-old gallant knight. "And after the smoke cleared?"

"By the time the fire trucks pulled out, Ben had told his mother all about the ghosts and the hours alone. She talked my mother into letting me stay with their family after school. By age ten, I became their foster daughter because my mother disappeared soon after my father died."

Douglas throat and chest ached. Bronwen had been tossed away so callously. He knew she still felt the effects of the lonely house and the loss of her mother. He listened to the effort it took to control her voice.

"Ben and I were very close from the beginning. We both loved the woods and the streams of their property. We played with the other children, but most often, we played by ourselves in their woods, building things – dams, lakes, houses, bridges, whatever can be built with sticks and mud. By the time we reached fifteen, we'd decided to become an architect and a landscape architect and to get married someday. We never fell in love; always, we were in some stage of being in love. It wasn't like this at all."

*   *

Her last sentence made him tighten his hand on hers. She could hear his heart hammer. When she looked up at him, she saw his hope and fear.

At last he spoke, "Are we falling in love? Is that what this is for you, too?"

"Yes. At least I think so." She studied him as she answered. "I want to be with you, doing whatever it is we're doing. And when Helen Smith began accusing . . ."

He reached for her. "Hush. I won't think about that." he whispered. His hands slipped inside the sides of her stiff overalls, felt the warmth of her flannel shirt and pulled her to him. His lips caressed her lashes and the wisps of loose hair before he sought her mouth.

The gentleness of his touch confused Bronwen. The almost reverent caress of his lips and hands called forth all her senses in a way she had never known. When his hand pushed inside the overalls and brushed down her waist, she grew aware of a new kind of desire in her own body – not the desire to give shelter that Ben had aroused, but a hunger to be touched and filled with Douglas' loving.

Douglas wrapped his arms around her. He held her close to his sweatered chest, and with a great effort, he seemed to force his breathing to a slower tempo.

*   *

The closeness of her made it difficult to know what he ought to do.

He tried twice to speak before he was able to say, "Bronwen, I love you. There is no question that I want you here, now. I don't understand how this love came to us, but I can't deny it." He closed his eyes, fighting down his desire, groping for the right words.

"I didn't want to love you," she whispered. "When we first met, I was ready to leave rather than put up with your suspicions. I should have gone then. This is too hard, caring for you and not being allowed to care."

His voice became husky with self-disgust. "It was pure selfishness for me to risk this happening."

"Why are you allowed to listen and care about me, but I'm not allowed to trust you, or comfort you?"

"Comfort me?" Distress hardened the sound of his voice.

Bronwen said, "I know you've spent a long time building your defenses against all that Linda did," she said, "but I refuse to believe your anger ever could cause you to hurt me. Linda recreated you as a beast in front of so many audiences that even you began to believe it."

"And that night at the bar, I was forced to recognize it in myself." She sat up. He let his arms drop from around her waist.

She whispered, "Neither of us intended to encourage love, but it has happened to us. If your mother, Robbie and Roy can trust you, why can't I?"

* *

As she hoped, Douglas looked sharply at her, and then, he smiled. "Mother and my collies?"

"Well, and George and Ian."

He laughed and took her hands in his. "That's my short list?"

"There are others who trust you, I'm certain, but I've not known them long enough to be sure."

He kissed her fingers and caressed her cheek. "This is what I love in you," he whispered. "Courage and humor."

She held his hand at her cheek. "And in you," she said, "Not yet certain, but I think you are courageous enough to shun the definitions that others have put upon you."

"A warning, Lassie. Trust but verify."

She touched his lips. "Been doing that."

His startled expression made her smile. She began repacking the picnic basket. As he watched her, a puzzlement raised his eyebrows.

"Wait," he said. "Kissing me was a method of verifying?"

"And eating your sandwiches. Pretty creative, what with water cress and bay leaf in with the beef."

He glanced at her bandaged arm and chuckled. "You are a witch. Let me help you, my one-handed beauty."

They lifted the basket and moved out into the late afternoon sun and climbed the hill to the house.

Bronwen tried unsuccessfully to get her mind back to work.

An ominous breeze whipped at her pant-legs. On the horizon, dark clouds approached the valley from north.

CHAPTER TWENTY-FIVE

Margaret seemed unaware of Bronwen's bemused mood as she re-entered the kitchen. Closing the door against the chill wind, Bronwen walked to the sink and began washing more Snow Peas to freeze.

Douglas couldn't have been far behind her. Within minutes, he poked his head around the back door and asked his mother to put together the temporary lambing pens.

After he ducked out again, Bronwen asked, "May I help?" Margaret looked a bit reluctant. Bronwen leaned forward and whispered. "You wanted me to know what it is like, Margaret. No time like the present."

Margaret brightened. "Well, if you're willing, lass. Coom bye to me." She led the way to the barn. The evening breeze ruffled the fur on Roy's back as he greeted the women. They stooped to pet him before heading on into the barn. The collie licked Bronwen's hand, barked and then ran around the side of the barn to nip at the heels of a straying ewe.

Bronwen learned from Margaret how to set up the pre-built walls to make extra stalls in the barn. In one of these, they installed an incubator light for any premature lambs. The fence-like walls were heavy, but easily fit together, even for one-armed Bronwen. Douglas and his father had built them, years before.

She stood a moment after creating one stall, and she looked up at the pattern of sunlight from the doorway as it warmed the interior structure. Above, the rafters, side bracing and beams all down the length of the barn created beautiful shadows and light in a work of symmetry and strength. She smiled and turned to watch Margaret working on the next stall. Another pattern of beauty and strength. She loved Margaret McGregor and her son.

Near sunset, a gust of wind and soft thudding on the barn roof announced the coming of rain. Douglas strode around the corner of a stall. Bronwen greeted him with apprehension. His presence brought up the unmet needs he'd created in her.

"How's the arm?" he asked.

"Fine. Not bleeding."

He said, "You and Mother should quit now."

"Are you quitting?" she asked.

He ignored her question. "Mother, I'm going back up to the field in a few minutes. David is coming to act as a guard for the night. Would you greet him?"

"I'll greet him with a brass band if he's coming so that you can get some sleep, son."

Douglas laughed, "Coffee would be as welcoming as music." His laugh ended in a cough.

Bronwen turned sharply, realizing that she'd been hearing that cough all the time they worked in the barn.

Shrugging off her concern for him, Douglas bent toward Bronwen's ear. His face felt warm to her as he whispered, "I'm fine. Just worried about you. Tomorrow you must go home."

A car changed gears to climb the entry road. Margaret left to greet David.

Bronwen faced Douglas. As the rain and wind pelted the roof high overhead, the smell of hay and ancient wood filled her nostrils. The silence of the barn and the gray peach of the wet afternoon light made the wordless moment heavy with promise. A moment of peace held them in thrall, aware but not touching.

"I do love you, Bronwen," he whispered at last.

"Then let me stay and finish what we've begun together," she pleaded. The indecision in his eyes gave her hope.

"It's too dangerous," he said.

At that moment, the back door to the barn blew open onto the marsh. Bronwen saw a dark body lying in the wet grasses, lank fur blowing in the rising breeze.

Douglas ran out the back doorway, followed by Bronwen. In the dull gray of the setting sun, they found the body of Roy – his throat clawed open.

Nearby lay the body of a Blackwatch ewe. Cloth covered footprints fouled the mud, the same disguised prints they had followed into the meadow the afternoon the Zivner trap had sprung.

Margaret and David came upon Douglas, down on his knees in the wet marsh, next to his dead collie, painful anguish twisted his face. He became visibly knotted up.

"Cougar!" David exclaimed pointing at the gaping wound.

Margaret dropped down in the mud to help Bronwen deliver a premature lamb from the dead Blackwatch ewe. She whispered to Bronwen, "Don't touch him."

It took Bronwen a moment to realize that Margaret referred to Douglas.

"Here," Margaret said. "Take this poor lamb into the barn and sit with it in the incubator pen until I get there."

Bronwen sat in the pen, crying and warming the lamb, when she heard Douglas' anger burst through his grief. "This was no cougar! A human killed them. The signs are wrong! Oh, Roy!"

Ian came into the barn, not seeing Bronwen. His big fist knotted.

When he hit the post, she felt reverberations in the pen. "I'll kill 'em for ye, MacGregor. I'll . . ." Ian hit the post over and over until he heard a ewe bleating nearby. He went to her aid, muttering about how sorry he was to have frightened his old girl.

Margaret came into the barn carrying a baby bottle. She sat next to Bronwen and took the lamb. Bronwen rose numbly.

Margaret looked up at her. "Bronwen . . . my son . . . He's worn out, already. If he doesn't sleep, he . . . He's ill now."

"I know, Margaret. But how can we get him to sleep after what has happened? He'll be working until the work is done and then he'll be looking for Roy's murderer."

*   *

From the woods south of the barn, the man watched through the heavy rains. Across the marsh he could see Douglas MacGregor lift the dead dog in his arms.

I know where you bury the dead, MacGregor. I've buried the dead, myself, you know. Bury Roy and you'll see what I left for you. You'll find the evidence, and you'll understand you're alone. No one to trust – helpless and dying – alone. She was alone when I buried . . . I bury the dead alone.

*   *

An hour later, Roy had been buried under the Big Leaf Maple and the Blackwatch ewes were crowded into the temporary pens and locked into the barn. David Brock stationed himself in the loft over the western doorway. As George and Ian urged Douglas to stop working, Margaret asked Bronwen to go upstairs and leave some sherry next to Douglas's bed, while he was in the shower.

After leaving the sherry, Bronwen changed into her nightgown and robe. She heard, the shower and thought it must be Douglas.

She returned to the room to give Robbie his pain medicine, urging him to get well. Douglas needed him more than ever, now.

At the sound of a footstep, Bronwen turned to see a haggard, dark-faced Douglas, back in his work clothes and leaning against the doorjamb. "It isn't just Robbie that I need. I don't think I can do another thing."

Guiding him down onto his bed, she could feel the fever through his shirt. "I'll be right back." She left for the bathroom, warmed a washcloth and grabbed a towel and some Ibeprophen.

Returning she found him in a troubled sleep. Fever dampened his shirt and face. His dark, wet hair formed small curls. Several weeks of little sleep, the two nights of exposure, worry over his sheep and Robbie, and grief for Roy had left him wrung out, susceptible to anything.

"Why didn't I see this coming?" she berated herself. "I could at least have gotten him a sweater and tea to keep him warm. He was so exhausted. I should have expected this!"

Bronwen dismissed the nagging thought that caring for Douglas MacGregor was not her job. He needed care.

She lifted him long enough to get the anti-inflammatory taken. Then she washed his face and throat, unbuttoned his shirt and washed his arms and chest to cool him. He sort of smiled at her and slept again while she took off his shoes and socks. Even his feet were hot with the fever. The cloth cooled them, but she could feel the heat in them again in a few moments.

Struggling with his length and dead-tired weight, she pulled off his levis, his strong legs almost too much for her to handle. She knew his small mother would have been unable to help him. Bruskly efficient in the face of his high fever, she cooled his chest with a freshened cloth. Every few minutes throughout the night, she wet his curling hair and washed his heated chest. For several hours, the heat returned almost as soon as she dispelled it.

Nearby, Robbie whined a little, glancing at her and at the bed.

"He will get well," she assured Robbie, and herself.

At three in the morning, his temperature began to fall. Exhausted, she sat at the edge of the bed, aware that she drank in the sight of his shoulders and tanned skin, but unable to tear herself away. Dark wet lashes rested on his high cheekbones. In contrast to his broad forehead and thick black brows, his lips seemed almost vulnerable.

Bronwen knew he was vulnerable, deep inside where wounds are hardest to cure, he'd been flayed raw by the slashing hate of his ex-wife and the doubt of his friends. This man who showed care for others, who loved and who sometimes teased with joy, had struggled to keep her at arm's length and maintain his hard-won solitude.

He might never allow her to care for the wound in his soul as she had cared for his body this night.

She covered him with the sheet and blankets. Rousing, he reached up and tangled his hand in her braid as she bent over him. When he returned to sleep, the trapped hand fell, pulling her head to his chest.

She lay there, listening to the slowing beat of his heart, holding his body close. Bronwen wanted to rest with him but knew he was still far from well.

"Stay, Bron," his hoarse voice agitated.

"I'm staying, Douglas."

"Stay, please."

"I'm right here." She freed her hair from his icy fingers.

He sat up in bed, eyes glazed. Then, just as suddenly, he fell back, shivering.

She made up her mind, pulled up the quilt and climbed into the bed.

Once in her arms under the comforter, he began to grow quiet, his hands warmer against her body. He fell into a deep sleep. Finally, Bronwen slept as well.

CHAPTER TWENTY-SIX

Douglas awoke, savoring the warmth of the woman in his dreams. She'd dispelled his fever and then warmed his body. He wanted to linger in the memory. His lips moved against a smooth shoulder. The beautiful eidolon shuddered in his arms. His eyes flicked open.

Her open robe revealed a light cotton gown which clung to the contours of her body. Tilting his head back he let his gaze linger on her mouth and gold lashes. She was no apparition, no fantasy.

Her hair had been loosened and lay framing her face. Reaching up, he ran his fingers through it. It felt just as thick and soft as he'd imagined. Softer.

What had he done after he saw her taking care of Robbie? He couldn't remember. He didn't feel any remorse, only very much better. His eyes were no longer hot. His throat was not raw. The warmth he felt, emanated from her body not from a fevered self. And her presence brought wonder. He closed his eyes and let his body feel the sleep stirrings of hers.

When he awoke again, she had turned on her side with her back to him. Her body lay full against his, his arm around her waist. She still slept, but this new position woke him fully at last. She felt safe with him, her unconscious self sought his nearness when she slept.

The implications of this sleeping gesture aroused his protective instincts. He lifted his hand from her waist and backed to the far side of the bed.

Whatever had happened between them last night had exhausted her. Watching her, he began to remember pulling Bronwen to him, the cool cloth, the cool hands.

He almost knocked over the glass of sherry and the note she'd left with it the night before.

"Douglas, Margaret sends you this sherry as a sleeping potion. Please use it and sleep well. I've taken care of Robbie. Love, Bronwen"

He put the note in his dresser drawer and drained the sherry, feeling its fire and warmth. It might be early in the day for an elixir, but he felt the need to toast the young woman in his bed.

He dressed to the rhythmic thumping of Robbie's tail and then lifted his collie in his arms.

In the kitchen, his mother looked up as he took Robbie out the back door.

He tried to ignore her study of him and continued outside. Later, he returned to the kitchen with the limping dog. "Good Robbie. You're starting to make a bit o' progress." Scooping Robbie up in his arms again, he began to ascend the stairs. "I'll be down in a few minutes, Mother."

"Is Bronwen stirring at all?"

"No, I don't want to awaken her. She's very tired." He started up the stairs, then turned back, about to say something, thought better of it and continued up the stairs.

After bedding Robbie, Douglas stood over Bronwen's sleeping form. The faint blue shadows under her lashes reawakened his vague memories of the night. He knew she'd been with him a long time, had sat by him through the darkest hours after Roy's murder, had put up with his vengeful dreams and delirious thrashings. The shadow of blue became the badge of a hard-earned exhaustion.

Last night's events had proven her correct. In the meadow under the Big Leaf Maple, near where he'd buried Roy, he'd turned up a skillfully carved shepherd's staff. Set in the curve of the crook he'd found the forepaw of a cougar with the hairs of Roy's coat tangled in the bloodied claws.

Years ago, Douglas's father had made the staff for a twelve-year-old John Barsoti.

Douglas's heart weighed heavy at the evidence of John's betrayal. He bit back hot tears, remembering young John's wide-eyed admiration for Douglas senior. It didn't make sense. They'd been such good friends – near brothers until those few months when Linda's accusations had turned everyone he loved away from him.

Douglas eased his sorrow with a few moments' unhurried gazing at Bronwen's gentle face. The tangled hairs of her braid had fallen over one shoulder. A tress wrapped her throat. With one tentative finger, he attempted to pull the curl back. She stirred at his touch, pulling her head back to free the strand. Her hand brushed away his offending finger, making their hands fall together on her soft breast. Her body pressed against his hand as she whispered in her sleep, "Bore da, fy 'nghariad."

Her gesture seemed so sensual and her greeting so loving that Douglas was inches from kissing her before he realized she'd spoken in Welsh.

He ached at the knowledge that her loving greeting was for her Welsh husband. "I live!" he whispered and stumbled from the room.

The aura of anger and despair reached into Bronwen's sleep. She awoke to see the bedroom door swing closed after him. She wanted to follow him, to see for herself if he felt better, but the feeling that he'd left in anger stopped her halfway out of the covers.

She looked down at her open robe and thin nightgown and felt a slow heat creep up her cheeks. She grew ashamed at what he must think. He'd been very sick last night, and he had no reason to remember why she'd stayed in his bed. What she'd done probably seemed like brazen wantonness to him. In truth, her dreams of him had been embarrassingly so.

She could hope, since she dreamt in Welsh, that he'd not understood anything she might have said. She pulled herself from the bed and prepared to meet whatever cold disapproval he would be dishing up at breakfast.

*   *

David, George and Ian rose as she came in. Douglas flipped two pancakes onto her plate, flicked his eyes down her overalls and pulled the chair out for her. He did look much healthier. Bronwen's relief equaled her embarrassment, though she could detect in him no overt sign of disgust with her. The hand he lay on her shoulder startled her. She couldn't reconcile such a gesture with the anger she'd sensed upstairs a few minutes ago.

He felt her body flinch and removed his hand.

David, trying to break the heavy silence, announced, "I hear Robbie upstairs trying to walk."

Douglas growled, "Soon Robbie will realize that Roy is not around." Another long silence followed.

Bronwen broke through their gloom with an invitation. "I'll make soup this morning. If you'll take a minute from lambing to eat soup and biscuits, you won't get as drained as you were yesterday."

They knew she talked to Douglas. He knew it. He looked at her and heard the thoughts they could not say to each other.

Then he said, "I'll be back at one o'clock. I won't forget to eat, Bron."

David watched their eyes. My lucky, friend, he thought and then whispered to George, "At last."

George raised his grizzled eyebrows.

A red-faced Ian scraped his chair back from the table and thanked Mrs. MacGregor for a fine meal.

George wiped his mouth and allowed as how he'd better see to the sheep. Neither brother had ever been so keenly aware of how lonely their young MacGregor had been.

*   *

After breakfast, Bronwen began to clear the table. Douglas took her elbow. "Leave these."

Margaret, smiling, took the plates from her. "You're the designer, not the dishwasher."

Douglas guided her into the library and closed the door. "I need to ask you something before you get started."

Bronwen was hopeful. Perhaps he would give her a chance to explain before he judged her actions.

Douglas kept his hands at his sides and spoke in clipped, cold tones. "You said the Sheep Ranchers Association had given you a list of the items taken from their historical collection. Do you still have it?"

Disappointment and embarrassment made her unsure of her voice. She said nothing but stepped to the desk and found the list. Avoiding contact with her hand, he took the list and scanned it. "Yes! There it is." He pointed to the item on line 19. "Shepherd's Crook with Cougar paw, carved by Douglas MacGregor."

"You carved it?"

"No, my father. He gave it to John Barsoti years ago. Last night it was used to kill Roy and the ewe."

Bronwen felt a chill invade her. She got no pleasure from being proven right. She wanted to salve the wound of his friend's duplicity.

"Maybe it wasn't John," she said, "Those items were stolen."

"Yes. As you said, stolen by someone with a key to the museum. This morning, Mother gave me her list concerning explosives and yours about the trucks. With this crook and the trap, it all adds up. If it isn't John, I don't see who else it points to."

"Someone who knows and hates John?"

"Bronwen, you make me look at the truth and then you want to blur what I see. Don't try to make me feel less betrayed. You were right that I should suspect him. He's one of the friends that Linda… she convinced him of my guilt for a while. Maybe he never got over it. I don't know. I'm going to Eugene this morning to see what else I can find."

"Who else did she convince, Douglas?"

He leaned both hands on her desk. "Her champions were legion. David and Angie believed her, at least for a time. John took her part against me just before our divorce. Even last year, Phil was taken in by her. She got him to take her to San Francisco . . . I guess I should be wary of all of them.

"But who knows who it might be?" she said. "Who even knows if she is the reason for this vendetta."

He glared at her. "Yes, I'm admitting it looks like a vendetta."

Bronwen reached out to comfort him. He slumped and then he circled her waist with his hands. "Bron. . . Bron, I don't know what I did last night after I found you with Robbie."

She felt her color rise but looked boldly at him. "You were very sick, that's all. I chose to be in your bed. I'm sorry that made you angry."

He pulled her to him. "You think I was angry because you fell asleep next to me? I know why you chose to be there. After such a night, I awoke to the most healing warmth – awoke to find that the best dreams of my fever were very real." Douglas whispered, "Now, I know that when I really need you, you're not afraid of my touch."

As his lips moved over her cheeks and eyelids, Bronwen believed at last that he felt trusting acceptance of his feelings and of her. "It's not your touch I fear . . ." she began, but his lips found hers again.

He caressed her ear whispering, "This morning came so peacefully, so . . ."

He stopped, his face hard. "But when you stirred and spoke in your husband's tongue, I knew what you dreamt! All that sleeping sensuousness had been his not mine!"

A dark distress veiled the blue of his eyes. "But no more. I'll make you put aside the past and choose the present – my bed, my body, my love."

She was too surprised to find voice for her protests and then could not have spoken. He left the den and the house in ten long strides.

Staring at the closed door, Bronwen found a smile creeping across her face. "I think what this means," she said to herself, "is that he's decided to take a chance on love but is giving himself one last reason to doubt his wisdom."

*   *

Amid the clatter of kitchen pans, Bronwen prepared chicken soup with rice. There was more clatter than she usually caused. She knew her tension was obvious when she caught Margaret staring at her.

"You want some help, dear?"

"I need to do this. Really, I just need to cook . . ."

Margaret smiled, "I understand dear. Leave the pans for me. I need to wash, when I'm worried."

Bronwen glanced at the gentle lady. "Thank you, Margaret."

"Anytime. You know, George and Ian have the lambing under control, so when I go outside, I'll be in the flower beds." Margaret pushed at her hair and straightened her dress before she slipped out the back door.

As Bronwen cut vegetables, she considered the challenge Douglas had issued as he left the den. It was clear that, as she'd hoped, Douglas had not understood what she was dreaming about this morning. The dream content must have been shamefully obvious, but he'd totally misconstrued the choice of protagonists. The ensuing misunderstanding was what she richly deserved.

Yes, she loved Ben – always would think of Ben with love. But this love that she felt for Douglas was different, less physically hurtful, yet in some way more frightening. Something about him demanded more risk-taking, perhaps because he'd been so hurt. He needed her to reach out and convince him that she wouldn't misuse his love.

*   *

Outside, Margaret stood from her weeding and straightened her dress again as she watched the dust trail of an old Volvo approach her home. She could not keep the pleasure of anticipation from her eyes, so Frank Bauman received a very warm greeting. Even as she reached out to hug her old friend, Margaret chided herself for being so transparent and happy to see him.

Frank beamed. "My goodness, Margaret, you get more beautiful every time I visit."

Margaret laughed and linked arms with him. "You may be spreading honey, but I confess to liking honey."

He pretended indignation. "I'm very sparing with my honey. I only spread it for quality tastes."

"Franklin Bauman," she laughed, "you know how to make me feel good again."

Frank grinned, "Feeling good enough to go dancing with me tonight?"

"Dancing sounds like a fine idea," said Margaret. "We can leave these children to their own devices for a while."

"Is the Waltz Emporium still in business?" he asked.

"Not since Janet was a baby."

"What happened? Did you and Douglas senior take her dancing with you? She cried the musicians into a route?"

"No sir, we took her in the baby seat, but she stood up and taught everybody how to do the Boogaloo."

"And that was the end of waltzing, I suppose."

"It was out."

"Well, then I guess renovating the barn will have to be our entertainment for this trip. I can hardly wait. I've dreamed about putting transept porches on that barn ever since I was a kid. By the way, where's Bronwen?"

"In the kitchen, banging pots and pans, very loudly."

"Sparks, huh?"

"Flame, but not steady flame."

"Think we made a mistake?" Frank tucked Margaret's hand in his arm.

"Our timing was off. What with the rustlers still harassing the Black watch flock, the poor dogs and the fire two days ago."

"Dogs? What's happened?"

Margaret explained, ending, "Douglas is exhausted."

"Not at his best, eh?"

"Volatile. Both of them. He sent her off to safety yesterday and what did she do? Disguised herself and went looking for clues."

"Lord! She promised me she'd play it safe down here." Frank said.

"Do you think she knows what safe looks like?" asked Margaret.

"If she cares about him as much as it sounds like, 'safe' may get short shrift. We'll have to keep close tabs on her."

Margaret chuckled. "I intend to. She's the best thing to come down the pike in a long time. I'd hate to lose her."

"What next, do you think?" he asked.

"I think I'm going to get a beautiful garden and a much larger barn out of all this. The rest is unpredictable."

"And I'm going to get to spend time with one of my best friends," he said.

*   *

Twenty minutes later, as Frank and Margaret emerged from the barn, they saw Douglas's truck pull up the drive. Douglas leapt from the cab and ran up the steps to the house.

Margaret put a restraining hand on Frank's arm. "He looks to be in high dudgeon. Let's wait a few minutes and see what happens."

Frank slipped a hand over the slight fingers on his arm. "Do you think either of them will need rescue?"

"Douglas will, perhaps, but she can't do too much damage in five or ten minutes."

* *

Douglas strode into the kitchen, filling the atmosphere with tension. "You were right, Bronwen. It could be John or David doing all of this."

Bronwen felt as if she'd been punched. "I'm sorry, Douglas."

"Sorry? I tell you you're right and you are sorry?"

"I know how much it hurts you."

"Hurts?" He glared at her. "It makes me raging mad."

"I hope you're not jumping to conclusions, as you did this morning," she said.

"I've evidence that both of them are up to something. David is embezzling. John is accepting campaign funds from a snake ..." Her previous words finally penetrated his anger. "What conclusions did I jump to this morning?"

She lifted the lid on the soup pan and stirred, keeping her back to him. Impatient, he took the lid from her, placed it on the pan and said. "What conclusions?"

She looked down, straightening the lace on the edge of the apron as she talked. "In my home valley, isolated in the Appalachians, all the communicants spoke an archaic Welsh – you can't even hear it in Wales, they say. Even our English was heavily laced with Celtic words. Ben's mother spoke it, but Ben's father grew up in more worldly surroundings. Ben understood very little Welsh."

Douglas stood stock still. He drew in a deep breath. "Are you telling me Ben wouldn't have understood you? You weren't dreaming of Ben this morning?"

Bronwen felt the blood rush to her face, yet she looked at him. "I'm not telling you anything about my dreams. I'm telling you not to jump to conclusions based on incomplete evidence."

He caressed her cheek and held her chin tilted up so that he could watch the blush tint her skin and her eyes smolder with anticipation of his kiss.

* *

Frank and Margaret circumnavigated the barn twice. When they thought it safe, they went in the back door.

In the kitchen, they discovered Douglas stabbing a pencil at a list and gesturing angrily. Bronwen stood poised at the stove, a half-filled soup bowl in hand, her concentration on the jabbing pencil.

"It doesn't add up," said Douglas. "Neither of them has much reason to do this. They don't gain anything except vengeance for something I didn't do."

"Who is they?" queried Margaret.

Douglas and Bronwen started out of their intense conversation. "Frank!" Bronwen rushed at her partner. Margaret rescued the soup bowl at the very last moment.

Frank swung her around. "Hi, Kid. Did you think I forgot to come?"

Douglas and Margaret MacGregor winked at each other because the parent role seemed so natural for their bachelor friend.

Frank set Bronwen down and kept her in the crook of his arm as he extended a hand to Douglas. "Douglas, I'm appalled about Roy. I hope the additions to the barn will keep these murderers from your animals."

Douglas dropped his list and shook hands with Frank. "Bron drew me a sketch of the expanded barn. I think it's needed. I'm just worried about the process."

"We'll build the rooms and then open the side of the barn when we're ready to finish," said Frank. "With careful planning, we'll only have openings in the barn for one day. I'll bring down my best crew for that."

Margaret picked up the pencil-stabbed list and looked it over. "David embezzle? That's impossible!"

Douglas' eyes were dark with sadness. "Not impossible. There's a lot of evidence. Crawley's going to have to haul him into court soon and the Eugene police have put off hiring him."

Margaret scoffed and turned back to the list. "And what's this about John Barsoti? Steal? Why most of this stuff in the sheep rancher's museum either belonged to his father or yours any way. Why would he steal that?"

"I can't figure it either. But that's what the insurance detective believes. And there's other evidence. They all could have known how to make the bomb. Phil, David, Mike, Crawley, John, but not Ken. They know enough about guns and explosives to have done everything. We know Ralph set the fire. But someone had to have told Parr how important the cottonwood was to us."

Douglas's glance at Bronwen held a trace of apology. "And someone had to tell him about the Blackwatch."

Coming into the situation in mid-stream, Frank had to ask, "Am I to understand that you suspect a close friend of sabotage?"

"The evidence indicates one or more of these four," Douglas said, jabbing a finger at the list. "David, Phil, John and Crawley. Right now, there's a great deal of evidence pointing to John. I found a rusty, abandoned truck in his north pasture and Bronwen found the studded tires in his garage. Yet Mary Barsoti seemed surprised to see both the truck and the tires – didn't recognize either of them. I couldn't talk to John. This morning, he flew to eastern Oregon on a speaking tour."

In the last few sentences, a growing heartache replaced Douglas's anger. Bronwen saw his dejection and left Frank's hug to go to his side.

"Sit down," she ordered. "The soup is hot and the biscuits are fresh. Once we've all eaten lunch, we can look at the evidence and see how to help your friends."

Douglas sat. "Help my friends? You pointed out that a friend must have done all this. Why help them?"

"Because you love them. And because the things that we've turned up don't make sense. How stupid is John Barsoti? Not very, from what I've seen. Why would he use something so closely connected to him when he kills your dog?"

Margaret began setting out bowls and silver. "And what would David be using the embezzled money for?" she asked. "He's risking a promising career in law enforcement to steal your sheep?"

"All this makes it look as if John and David are in cahoots together," said Frank.

"There's one more thing about John," said Douglas. "He never showed up at home last night. When Roy was killed, John had gone 'out somewhere'."

"Who told you that?" asked Margaret.

"Mary, but he'd given her an explanation of sorts. Do you remember that rumor about sheep dying of an unknown disease down near Creswell? I heard that story twice more in town – guys in the hardware store were discussing it. In Skinner's Feed and Seed the owner asked me if I'd heard about distemper, or anthrax."

"What's anthrax got to do with John's absence last night?" Bronwen asked.

"He was supposed to be out tracking down that rumor last night. However, he hasn't even turned up one case of distemper."

"So, he might have been here." Margaret paced the floor. "John kill Roy? like that? What possible reason could he have?"

Frank took over ladling up the soup while he joined the think tank. "Seems either somebody hopes to make a bundle on your flock, or somebody hopes to ruin you. Why would you have enemies?"

The room went silent. Frank looked around, puzzled by the knowing looks and reticence on each face. Finally, Douglas broke the hush. "My ex-wife accused me of beating her. She hung around even after our divorce, convincing my friends to protect her. I could never be sure of any of them after that."

Margaret sagged against the counter. Frank watched her.

Bronwen jabbed a knife into the butter and slathered it on a biscuit.

She put the biscuit on Douglas' plate and angrily went after another biscuit. When she spoke at last, she almost controlled the tremors in her voice. "How could anyone believe what she said? How could they?"

Douglas stared at her. Straightening up in his chair, he reached for her knife wielding hand, took her wrist in his grip and stilled her attack on the jam. "Thank you, Bron."

Douglas's situation overwhelmed her. His life's work was being systematically stolen, as his friendships had been poisoned for years. Tears hovered behind her lids. She swallowed hard around the rock of injustice that clogged her throat. Douglas watching her, took the knife from her hand and pulled her hand to his lips.

"My friends had no choice. They had known her all their lives, too. And someone beat her." He glanced up at her. "Your belief in me helps. I wish I'd had you then."

CHAPTER TWENTY-SEVEN

For several days, peace seemed to reign over the emptiness that had been Roy's place in their lives. Robbie hobbled about, looking for his brother, and shunned attention from Ian's collie until the puppy became insistent. Then Robbie tolerated him.

But the sun shone. George and Ian helped a few late Corriedale lambs into the world. The Corriedale sheep suckled their new lambs to the envy of the Blackwatch mothers-to-be, whose lambs tended always to arrive a little later.

Douglas worked on the barn as he recovered from exhaustion and overexposure.

Frank's crew poured foundations for the transept porches. The framing timbers went up. Douglas knew he had no conclusive proof against either David or John, so he held his tongue and watched for overt action on their part. His friends, unaware of his suspicions, came to the ranch to help.

* *

Twice that week, Douglas disappeared to the hospital where his godson recovered from cocaine addiction.

"How's it coming, son?" Douglas asked.

"Dad won't come near this place," Kenjiro said.

Douglas sat down in the chair next to the bed. "Your father will come around. He's in shock at this point."

"Mother comes."

"I know. And she'll keep talking until your father understands addiction. He still thinks it all has to do with will-power. He wasn't here to see how sick getting off of it makes a man."

Kenjiro turned his face away. "I wish I had been a man."

Douglas took his hand. "If even now, you think it was weakness and not sickness that did this to you, how can we expect your dad to understand?"

Kenjiro stared at Douglas's hand on his. "That first time…"

"Yes, that was childish curiosity. Once he got you to try it, the rest was the sickness of the drug."

"Roger Hargert still wants to get out and find some more stuff. He talks like there's no way he'll ever please his dad, so why try."

"That's how he talks in group?"

"Yeah, but Jimmy Macklin just tells him to stop posturing."

"Jimmy's got the picture, now, huh?" Douglas prompted.

Kenjiro looked at him straight. "Yeah. Jimmy tells Roger it takes time to earn the old man's trust again, and he might as well start working on it now."

Douglas smiled at Kenjiro. "You're on the right road. I'm glad. Your mom is deeply glad, and she'll bring your father to understand one day. You keep working on being your better self, and even if he doesn't see it, you will know."

"I know. Earn respect, even if you never get it."

Douglas nodded. He knew all about loss of respect and the long road back to it.

"Well, I've got someone else to visit. I'd best go."

"Here in the drug unit?"

"No, in the Alzheimer's unit."

"Oh, the other end of life, eh?"

Douglas smiled. "You are at the beginning. That's the truth."

*   *

At the other end of the hospital, Douglas looked in on Linda's mother. He thanked the Gods that Mrs. Beloit had never understood all that Linda had done to him. She thought they were happily married, still, and that Linda would come and visit her any minute now.

In her world, each minute became a new day.

"Linda called me just an hour ago. She out shopping?" Mrs. Beloit asked.

"No. I bet she's at work. That's nice that she called you." Douglas straightened the flowers he had brought from the gift shop. He kicked himself for not taking the time to find flowers on the farm. Mrs. Beloit had always loved chickory and other meadow flowers.

"Linda calls every day. She comes to visit right after you."

Douglas knew the visits were not real, but maybe the phone calls were. San Francisco was in the same time zone. How hard could that be?

But he wondered. None of his friends ever mentioned calls from Linda.

In fact, why would they? They'd know it would hurt him, or they would not want to talk about what Linda was doing these days.

He said, "It's good to see you looking so well, Mrs. Beloit. I'm on my way back to the ranch."

"Give Linda my love," she said.

"I will do that when I see her," he said.

That send-off still had the power to batter his gut, but it didn't touch his heart.

*   *

Toward the end of the week, John Barsoti came over to lend a hand.

He seemed guileless when asked about the abandoned truck and the snow tires.

"I found the tires in the garage," he admitted, "but I sure as Hell don't know where they came from. And none o' my hired people know anything about that old beat up truck."

There seemed to be no way Douglas could prove his friend's innocence. And now that suspicion had reared its ugly head, there was no way to ignore it either. With a heavy heart, Douglas accepted John's help. They framed in the west transept porch together.

While working with John, Douglas kept a watchful eye on Bronwen, who worked at the bottom of the hill. She perched on a short ladder, so she could prune the Virginia Creeper vine off the lowest branches of the old oak.

John teased Douglas. "Why don't you take up landscaping, old man?"

"I barely have talent for sheep; I couldn't herd plants at all."

"I wasn't thinking you'd want to herd plants, but it looks like you've taken an interest in herding the plants-woman there."

Douglas became curt. "She'll be going back to the city soon."

"She's different, Douglas. Looks like she enjoys animals and farm dirt. You ought to test that."

Douglas's glare got John back on task.

*   *

Yet, on Friday night, Douglas did his daily climb up the scaffolding to the roof beam of the west porch. Thirty-five feet up, straddling the highest timber, he watched the sun set over the Willamette Valley. From this height, he also watched Bronwen, working as usual, right up to last light.

In her landscaping, he could see how efficient and hard-working she was. Her encouragement and her own willingness to sweat kept her temporary crew inspired. Bronwen took her turn at every mucky job that the new landscape called for. She enjoyed herself.

This evening, from the roof, Douglas watched Bronwen backhoeing a ditch for the new creek bed. Below Douglas, Frank figured how much rock he needed to face the additions.

Stretching his stiff back, Frank looked up at Douglas. The younger man became aware that Frank watched him. He glanced down.

"She always drive things like that?" he asked Frank.

"She tries not to," shouted Frank. "It embarrasses the fellas on the crew."

"Looks to me like she knows what she's doing."defended Douglas.

"That's the problem. Makes the guys feel inadequate."

Douglas laughed and scrambled down from the roof. When he jumped next to Frank, he turned again to watch the sun as it back-lit her hair, which hard work had loosened from her braid.

"About the only thing Bronwen can't do," Douglas said, "is climb anything over three feet off the ground."

"But even that is getting better," said Frank. "I understand you got her to drive across bridges again."

"I think she was ready to try, I just got her to take the first step."

"I'm glad you did," said Frank. "I saw her out here test climbing on the scaffolding this morning."

"I wish she wouldn't do that alone." Douglas remembered something about Bronwen's being paralyzed on a bridge over the Willamette River.

"I wouldn't worry," said Frank. "Down here she's become herself again. She used to prune Portland's tallest elm trees near the library. And you should have seen her clamber over Ben's office towers. They designed a roof-top garden once, and she was the main installer."

"They worked pretty closely together, did they?" Douglas stared off into space, keeping his face devoid of emotion.

Frank studied his companion a moment before he answered. "Bronwen and Ben complemented each other," he said. "Ben's runaway imagination spurred her to even more exciting design. Bronwen's practical instincts kept him from bankrupting us with crazy ideas."

A loneliness in the older man's voice made Douglas uncomfortably aware of what losing Ben had meant to Frank. "Did Ben appreciate her?" he asked.

"He was young and impetuous, but Bronwen was very important to him, always. He loved her."

"And well he should have." Douglas hit the door post of the new structure. The wood rang with bell-like clarity, mocking, and reminding him of the solid edifice of Bronwen's marriage to her dashing and brilliant architect. His own experience with love had been as ill-constructed as Helen Smith's house.

Douglas grabbed up his tool belt and took a quick leave from Frank.

His recognition of Frank's long, carefully correct love for Margaret MacGregor was a chill reminder to Douglas of how lonely he too could be someday.

All the way to the barn door, he fought the feeling of losing a battle with his emotions. He fed the Blackwatch, aching because his evening hunger for Bronwen grew. Each night this week, his desire had been staved off by what he characterized as his sense of propriety.

Propriety be damned! Every evening his mother and Frank went into town, to visit friends or to go dancing. There was no one at the ranch to be proper for. What he did or did not do had to be a decision between himself and Bronwen. Yet, each evening, when he would have swept her into his arms and carried her to his room, he either pulled down another book to stare at, or he took Robbie for a walk.

He'd begun to see that his life of solitude had become as distorted as the Pine of the poet Sefiriades "which keeps the shape of the wind, even when the wind has fled and is no longer there."

Ever since the night of his ugly street brawl, Douglas's passions had been under a tight control. Nevertheless, under the gentle influence of Bronwen, he wanted to resist the twisting influence of his past. His need for intimacy with her grew powerful. His fear of hurting her receded in the face of her steady trust.

After locking up the barn, Douglas glanced up at the dark firs on his mountain, their broken tops bobbing in the sunset winds – firs, broken by ice and the weight of winter snows, yet straight of trunk and strong through life's struggles.

He glanced toward the marsh where Roy had been killed and missed the way Roy often leaned on his leg, or played games of tug with Robbie.

Douglas squared his shoulders and headed for the house.

At the back door, he met Bronwen, who removed her muddy boots.

He waited while she bared her feet.

*   *

When Bronwen stood and saw the warmth in his eyes, she reached out her hand and entered the kitchen in the circle of his arm.

Margaret's apron bow disappeared from the kitchen into the dining room as they came in. Douglas took advantage of the empty room to pull Bron further into his embrace.

"I'm very muddy," she whispered.

"And I'm full of saw dust, but I like the smell of mud." He nuzzled her temple and kissed her eyelids. She shivered.

He pulled up. "You're cold again."

"I'm not cold. Stop running from . . ."

"You are. Look at those bare feet! Now march."

He turned her toward the stairs and marched lock step with her up to the second floor.

Bronwen knew he pulled back again – using her shiver as an excuse.

This man still feared himself.

She marched upstairs with him, turned at the bathroom door and said, "I love you, ready or not. Please get my robe."

He blinked and stepped back. "I'll hang it on the doorknob." She smiled and stepped inside.

*   *

In her closet, Douglas grabbed her robe and held it to his face a moment. He berated his timing once again. Why did he hold his impulses in check for so long only to unleash them when she least expected? He wanted her so desperately that a smooth approach had become impossible.

Disgusted with himself, he grabbed her slippers and took them back to the door, hanging the robe on the knob.

Dashing down the stairs to the kitchen, he passed his mother and gave a hasty explanation. "I'm taking a shower outside. Bron is cold. I put her in the shower upstairs."

After the door slammed, Margaret glanced at Frank whose perplexed gaze trained on the back-door window, as if expecting the glass to shatter.

"What do you think, Frank? Another night at the movies? or a moonlight drive to the Coburg hills?"

Frank laughed. "I wish I thought he was enjoying our absences as much as I am. I must admit, I'm beginning to despair of him."

"Once bitten. . ."

"Bitten? He acts like a man who was badly mauled."

"That pretty accurately describes what Linda did to him," said Margaret.

Frank stood silent for a time, mulling over their situation. "At least the sheep rustling has been stopped for a week now."

"I'm not sure I take comfort in that," Margaret murmured.

Frank folded the newspaper he'd been reading and checked the casserole in the oven. "Mmm. This smells great. Alice off today?"

"You don't like Alice's cooking?"

"Love it, but there's a difference," he glanced up at her. "Yours smells like you, Marget, all herbal and fresh."

"Marget?" she blushed. "No one has called me Marget since my mother died."

Frank straightened up to watch her. "How would you like someone to call you Marget for the rest of your life?"

Margaret stopped stirring the pudding and stared at him. "What are you saying, Frank?"

"I'm asking you to marry me." He took her spoon and stirred with deep concentration while she stood stock still. "Well?" he prodded gently.

"Well!" She sat down suddenly. "Well, yes."

Frank left the pudding and bent to take her face between his hands. "Oh, my beautiful Marget!" he whispered as he kissed her.

Margaret's hands clasped his forearms, prolonging the kiss. Both of them were blind to the shadow of Douglas's surprised face as he passed by the back-door window.

When Frank came up for air, Margaret stood and threw her arms around him. "Oh Frank, I thought you had forgotten."

"How could I forget? I've loved you for forty years!"

"Franklin Bauman, when did you think of this – this being married?"

"Just now, when I smelled your cooking. Could we have this once a week?"

"I only cook once a week," she joked.

"Oh. Is there a chance of negotiating that up a few days?"

"No. Want to retract?" She raised her eyebrows, daring him.

Frank's arms tightened around her. "Not on your life. Your acceptance was a pledge – as good as a signed contract. Will you come up to Portland and see our home next week?"

"Our home?"

"I built it for you."

"Since when?"

Frank looked off at the back-door window and up at the ceiling fan. "Oh, over a number of years." He looked back at her. "Forty, to be exact, but I didn't admit that to myself until this month."

"Why not until this month?"

"Because a few weeks ago, when you called about landscaping and then began sharing your concerns about your young lone wolf out there, I had to admit to myself that Douglas wasn't the only hermit we had a chance of curing down here."

Frank bent his head to kiss Margaret once more, adding, "I want to be well and truly cured."

"I think I have herbs for fighting loneliness." Margaret hugged Frank, enjoying the wonderful feeling. As she leaned her head on his chest, she thought of all the years of loyal friendship Frank had given Douglas senior, never letting on that they had both asked for Margaret's hand on the same night.

Margaret roused herself and stepped back a little. "What about Douglas and Bronwen? How will we tell them?"

"Bronwen's already guessed. Douglas will see it as soon as he emerges from the personal hell he's found himself in."

"And when he does – when we tell them, do you think they'll feel we've gone beyond the pale? – overdone it somehow?"

Frank sniffed and looked at the stove top. "They'll think we've overdone the pudding at any rate!"

He stepped around Margaret and grabbed the pan, immediately dropping it and dashing for the kitchen sink where he couldn't get the cold water on fast enough. Margaret reached over his burned hand for the faucet.

Douglas, smiling, came in the back door, hair dripping wet from the shower. Bronwen came down the stairs, shiny clean and bewildered.

"What happened?" Bronwen leapt down the last stairs.

"Frank is cooking," Margaret said, running back to the sink with a towel to wet for his hand.

Douglas turned off the burner under the pudding and grabbed a hot pad.

"Are you all right?" asked Bron, hovering near Frank.

"Never better! Feel wonderful!" wheezed Frank around his elbow as his head sunk to his arm.

"What's going on here?" Bronwen grew anxious.

Douglas shoved a chair under Frank and pressed him down into it. "Frank's been kissing my mother and got lightheaded."

Margaret straightened. "He got burned!"

Douglas put a hand on her shoulder and shook his head in mock astonishment. "That good, was it?"

CHAPTER TWENTY-EIGHT

In the library, late in the evening, mellowed by laughter and the joy of sharing Frank and Margaret's happiness, Bronwen tucked her feet under her and watched contentedly as Douglas knelt by the fire. Margaret's hand sought Frank's bandaged palm for the umpteenth time in the last hour. Their love, now that it had been announced, surfaced in many small gestures of touching, looking, caring. Bronwen felt as happy as she had ever been. Frank's long loneliness was over.

How many nights had she and Ben speculated on the reason for Frank's terminated relationships with several suitable and lovely women?

Margaret had been the cause they had never known about. Frank Bauman, supremely honest, had never been able to fool himself into accepting affection as a substitute for the love he had for Margaret Campbell MacGregor

Almost as if they had come to silent agreement, Frank and Margaret rose from the love seat. Bronwen rose as well, planning to go to bed when they left.

"Bronwen," Frank said, leaning over the landscaping plans on the table, "Correct me if I'm wrong, but I believe you have too many heads on this one line of sprinklers. There won't be enough water pressure."

Concerned, Bronwen came to the table to check. Frank's finger lingered near the longest row of sprinklers. "Let me know in the morning," he said. "Good night, you two."

While she puzzled out the pressure needed per head, Frank disappeared from the library. When Bronwen looked up, Margaret had slipped out. She heard the front door close and then the engine sounds of Frank's car. She turned to Douglas who knelt by the fire, watching her.

She flushed and shrugged. "I think he's wrong."

"Of course, he's wrong. He maneuvered you into staying here." Douglas' dark eyes followed her back to the sofa.

"Wants to kiss her somewhere away from the pudding pan?" Bronwen joked.

"Probably." Douglas' body tensed, his long fingers lay still on the small log he held. "Come sit by the fire Bronwen."

An order, not a request. What had pushed him to brave closeness between them? Bronwen slipped down beside him without touching.

*   *

Douglas's breath caught. She moved with such grace . . . The mere act of lowering herself to the floor made him aware. Her cotton blouse was finely woven and fell softly over her curves. Her corduroy skirt hugged her waist and hips before its circle spread around her on the hearth rug. He knew it would take great control to keep from pulling Bronwen to the floor beneath him.

He also knew he couldn't continue damming up his emotions only to have them burst forth and frighten her as he was certain they had in the kitchen earlier this evening. He needed her, a support, a companion and later, perhaps, a lover.

How to begin? How could he move her step by step toward him, accepting his love in spite of his damned awkward ways?

Boldly, he struck out on the path. "The love between my mother and my father was strong, but she'll learn to love Frank, I think."

"She loves him now. Can't you see that?"

"I see signs of affection. Her affection will grow into love." He reached out carefully, touching the hair that had fallen in front of her ear.

Bronwen leaned toward him, faintly smiling. "Feeling the pinch of jealousy, perhaps?"

"What do you mean?" His attention focused.

"Is it hard to see your mother love a second time as she loved your father?"

His gaze probed her thoughts. "Could you love as deeply a second time, Bron?"

"I didn't think so at first. I do now."

"What's changed?" His voice rang rough in his ears.

"I love you," she said.

There was a moment's silence as he tried to digest this leap.

Incredible, he thought. "You believe you love me."

"I know I do."

He saw that she held silent, waiting for him to collect his thoughts.

"I believed I would never let this happen to me again," he said. "Before, I loved a mirage, a woman I thought I knew because I'd known her all my life. But in two short weeks, I know more about you than I ever knew about any woman. I know the deepest truths about Bronwen Llewellyn, and I love the brave and loyal woman you are."

He watched the green of her eyes mist over, and he made the risky leap himself. "I want you tonight, Bronwen."

"– and have for many nights," she whispered. "Why do you hide your need in a book or try to outwalk it with Robbie?"

"My feelings for you are frightening."

"It's not me they frighten." Bronwen touched his arm. "Love me, Douglas. Love me and set aside your disbelief."

He'd planned to walk her this way a step at a time, but she'd danced to it before he'd even begun.

Fool, he was, but he would take her for as long as he could. And when she left . . . he would deal with consequences later.

His kiss began tentatively, but her response grew tender, gentle, coaxing. Bronwen's hands ran lightly up his shirt front, feeling the tension in the muscles of his chest. She reached inside his collar.

His right arm pulled her firmly toward him. She turned in his arm, pressing her body to his and holding him tight. Her arms and fingers kneaded his back.

The amazing realization came to him that the more he took, the more she gave. Her body begged him to enjoy it, to release his long-pent need. Even as his hand fumbled with her buttons, she kissed him with a heat that fired his. He tugged her blouse from the skirt band. She stood up and released the skirt button. The blouse fell open. Bronwen drew it off her shoulders and let it drop to the floor with the skirt.

Only a soft cotton petticoat covered her body.

He stood, and with care approaching reverence, he slipped the lace ribbons from her shoulders and held himself in check as she drew the petticoat down her body.

He anticipated pleasure at the sight of her honey sweet skin, but in the flickering firelight it was her slender curves and the upward turn of her breasts that pushed him to the edge. He reached again for her, caressing her face and throat with his thumbs and then moving his hands gently over the smooth warmth of her shoulders and arms.

"Oh, Bronwen! If you have doubts . . ."

"No doubts. Love me, Douglas."

He shuddered, whispering, "I do." His hands slid across her arms to caress her breasts as he leaned forward. The yielding softness of her body brought a moan from the back of his throat. Her hands reached for him. His body waited as her hands touched his chest arousing his breasts as he aroused hers.

His thoughts whirled.

Let me do this slowly, he prayed. Let me take time for her.

He felt her hands at the top button of his jeans, and he whispered hoarsely, "Bron you're making this so hard."

"I'm sorry, Douglas. I didn't mean to be so clumsy and slow."

"Slow? Lass, you drive me."

She reached again for his waistband.

"No. Let me do this." He stepped back, unbuttoned his pants and slid them off his legs, swallowing hard as he saw her gaze stop a moment on the front of his briefs. He felt himself grow suddenly tight. Her eyelids flickered with what he thought must have been fear.

He stepped closer and tried to reassure her with gentle kisses.

Her arms wrapped around his back, pulling him toward her. His last logical thought told him she was the most generous woman he had ever been with – a potent aphrodisiac.

At that moment, she knelt on the hearth rug, her arms reaching up to him, "Come to me now. Douglas, Please!"

He yanked off his briefs and covered her warm body with his. His lips teased her breasts and his hand trembled as he reached between her thighs. Her legs tightened, momentarily barring his caress. When he pushed his knee between her legs, she sucked in a sharp breath and twisted away from him.

He had enough awareness to wonder why she expected his mere touch to hurt her, but not enough control to keep from caressing her. His fingers sought the softness of her and reveled in the sudden intake of breath his stroking brought from her. Her legs parted, her hips reached up to his and he entered her quickly.

Her hands moved over his back and buttocks, down his thighs. The more she touched him, the sharper his desire became until he was driven only by the need to know her more and more deeply. When his passion exploded within her, he cried out.

"Ach, Bron!"

The torment his body had known so long, shattered, leaving him heavily tired and spent above her. Conscious thought returned to him, beginning with the feel of her hair across his face and the soothing caress of her hands across his back. Their bodies were still joined. He moved greedily inside her, recapturing for a moment the pleasure of her moist warmth.

He felt her body flinch and then push against his.

Doubt nagged him, and he raised up on his elbows, pushing into her as he watched her face. Her eyes were closed. Not knowing what she revealed, her brow furrowed, and her lips tightened at his thrust. She quickly smoothed her brow and hugged him to her. Nevertheless, he knew he'd hurt her.

*   *

For the first time in her life, Bronwen understood a little of what drove men sexually. With Douglas, she had begun to experience that same tension and need herself. She had been afraid of the powerful sensations and had wanted to stop them by giving her body to his needs before his touch aroused more than she could handle. Now she wanted to lie here holding him and think out what was happening to her.

She'd been tense, as she always was with Ben, expecting pain. The tension in her had made his entry hard to bear, but the desire to have Douglas inside of her had been strong.

With Ben, she had known that he needed something and could take it only from her. His need had been reason enough. She loved him and so gave to him. He'd always taken her swiftly, driving hard into her body in the same way he drove himself into everything.

Douglas' caresses and gentleness had begun to open a new world of sensations for Bronwen and she wanted time to sort them out.

Until this moment, she hadn't been aware that hurt didn't need to be a part of it.

She should have talked to Ben. Her silence had been unfair to him.

Douglas' sudden withdrawal awoke Bronwen from her reverie. She opened her eyes to see him drawing on his jeans, his jaw clenched.

She sat up. "What?"

He turned on her, icy fury in his eyes, "You let me take you like some drugged beast. I hurt you and you were going to say nothing!"

And then truth came. Love making did not have to be giving only, as it had been with Ben.

*   *

Douglas dragged his attention away from her body, but the warm memory of her softness pulled him back. Lips compressed, his gaze lingered a moment on the curve of her hip and the thrust of her breasts before he looked into her eyes. Tears stood ready to spill from their dark green depths. Her lips were swollen from the pressure of his. Everything about her increased his guilt.

"Damn it, Bronwen. You let me treat you like this because you felt sorry for me."

"No!"

He began gathering her clothes. "Put this on." He ordered, handing her the chaste petticoat.

She held it to her, staring at him. "Why do you think I pity you?"

"Put it on before I come at you again." He stood and walked away from her, grabbing his own shirt. When he turned back, the slip was taut across her breasts. She faced him, standing tall, but her hand, winding the ribbon at the top of the petticoat, and the deep rise and fall of her breathing telegraphed her turmoil.

"Why?" she asked.

He bit his lip, looking away. When her hand touched his arm, he started, violently pushing her from him. "I wanted to give you so much," he said, "to make love with you, not at you."

He turned, pinning her against the wall. "But you knew how close to the edge I was. You made me take you hard and fast. What were you thinking? – that if I hurt you, I couldn't touch that inner heart where you keep him enshrined?"

The import of his words hit Bronwen like a shaft. All those years together with Ben and something more had been just out of their reach – something greater.

How could she tell Douglas what she'd discovered without betraying Ben's youthful lusts to his disgust? A low keen of bereavement escaped her.

*   *

He barely heard her smothered moan, "Perhaps . . ." She began again with more strength, "Perhaps I need you to teach me how to accept your caresses."

"How can I do that if I can only hurt you? That's not love. That's abuse."

She sucked in sharply as if punched. He glanced at the pain showing in her face.

I have done this to the one I love, he thought.

Rough voiced, he said, "I wanted to give you as much pleasure as you give me, but I have only hurt you. I can't … I won't keep doing that."

It hurt him to see Bronwen stare up at him, wide eyed and despairing. God he wanted to have her, just once more – maybe once more would cure him.

Her hand made a small helpless gesture and fell to his chest. "You're a courageous man in most things," she said, "but with other human beings, you're a coward."

He wrenched his hand back from her and paced the den floor. "I'm not afraid of others, but of myself. I would shatter you."

"I'm not that breakable. And I don't run away."

He closed his eyes to escape the sight of her wet lashes and lips. "Bronwen, I would know my power was between us – in our most intimate moments, this cold fear would gnaw at me."

Douglas ran a hand over his face. Afraid any longer to be next to her, he gathered his clothes and left the room.

Bronwen collapsed to the hearth rug. There was no way Douglas could know how, in a few passionate moments, he'd exposed Ben's raw inexperience.

CHAPTER TWENTY-NINE

In Eugene, Douglas found himself at a loss. He'd left the house early this morning to get away from the memory of the night in the den.

He'd tried, with increasing frustration, to get in the drug recovery center to see Kenjiro Eguchi. Puzzled at the sudden obstructions thrown up by the hospital, he'd driven on into town and bought all the electrical equipment he needed for the barn. He'd stalled most of the morning and still couldn't go back to the ranch and face Bronwen. Instead, he leaned against the side of his truck, folded his arms across his chest and idly watched the comings and goings at Porter's Grocery while his thoughts whirled.

There was no denying that he loved Bronwen Llewellyn. As much as he'd tried to fight it, her attraction was too powerful. Ironically, the moment he gave in, the very emotion he feared most had reared up and attacked him.

There was no denying that jealousy had stabbed him last night as soon as he realized he couldn't love her without causing pain. Benjamin Llewellyn had been in the back of his mind from that first day, but last night, the specter of Ben had come to the forefront.

It wasn't that Douglas wanted her to deny having loved before. He'd just hoped they could share a love that was uniquely their own.

After finding the courage to acknowledge his feelings, he'd been surprised by her unhesitating response. Then, his hope had been shattered. His love making was painful for her. He would never be able to touch her again.

*   *

"You taking up sidewalk statue for a living?"

Douglas awoke at the familiar booming voice and came face to face with the shirt buttons on his pompous, but effective lawyer, Lloyd Jones.

"Actually, I'm doing an imitation of Rodin's Thinker." Douglas said, uncrossing his legs and pushing away from the side of the truck.

"Thinker?" scoffed Jones. "Too hard for your first impersonation." Jones shifted with impatience, "Seen young Eguchi lately?"

"I stopped at the hospital on the way into town," Douglas said. "They wouldn't let me see him – kept telling me it wasn't a good time in his treatment to have visitors outside the family. By God! I was the only family he had there until his mother braved papa's wrath to visit him."

"That's the rigamarol I got, too," said Jones. "I represent his legal interests and can't get past the receptionist!" Jones was always shocked when his Legal Self was not the object of obeisance.

"When were you at the hospital?" asked Douglas with a growing sense of foreboding.

"Yesterday afternoon. I got this hint that something is "going down", as they say. Rumor has it that Kenji is out of the home. Putting the evidence in a certain perspect . . ."

"Kenjiro may be in sheep dip up to his nose." Douglas interrupted. "This is Parr's doing." Douglas yanked open the truck door. "Let's beard the lion in his den." He jumped inside his truck in no time. Lloyd Jones hurried as much as a guy of his size and dignity can, but by the time he got the door closed, the truck ran the next stop light.

"We could have made a quieter approach in my Mazarati," complained Jones as they swung up Orchard Street on the climb toward Parr's art nouveau mansion.

"Our approach will be on foot."

"Your feet, maybe. My size fifteens are an early warning device." Jones' grim face and tight grip on the dashboard were an eloquent plea for new shock absorbers.

Douglas relented. "When we get within a block, I'll let you take charge of the truck while I brave the fence and the dogs. Wait at most an hour. If you see me wave my arms, or you hear shots, get the police."

"Police and ambulance?"

"And ambulance. If your informants are correct . . ."

"My information is always . . ."

"If. Then, we won't have long to wait. I hope we're not too late to stop Kenji." Douglas pulled over just out of sight of Parr's.

"I'd no plans outside of a few court appearances today," huffed Jones.

"Great!" Douglas left the keys in the ignition and slipped out.

*   *

Within three breaths, Lloyd Jones could no longer see Douglas among the plantings surrounding the mansion. Within six minutes, four unmarked police cars had pulled up to the approaches to Parr's and a polite, but burly sergeant ordered Jones out of the truck.

"This is not my truck," intoned Jones as the officer propelled him toward the city police captain's car. "I own a blue Mazerati, actually. This is just . . ."

Police Captain Jules Wilson climbed out of his car. "This is not MacGregor. Jones, what the hell did you do with MacGregor?"

Jones pointed at Parr's shrubbery. The captains' voice behind him sounded strained. "Not in Parr's house! Ohhh chicken droppings! Is he trying to stop the buy?"

Jones nodded.

"How'd he find out?"

Jones shrugged his shoulders.

The captain was in too much of a hurry to wait for an answer. "Boyce! You and Pearsals get in there over the fence. The dogs are drugged. All you gotta worry about is flattening MacGregor without hurting him or the kid. And do it before he interferes with this buy."

"Piece o' cake, Cap," said Boyce, checking his holster as he ran across the street toward the same shrubs Douglas had just penetrated.

*   *

On the Parr grounds, Douglas had quite a forest in which to hide. He had a momentary twinge, wondering if Bronwen had designed this garden. Then there was no time for speculation. Kenjiro Eguchi, tall and lithe, sauntered out the patio doors with Leonard Parr. Douglas sucked in his breath. His godson seemed such a tadpole next to the shark that Parr had become.

What was Kenji thinking? He'd been so clearly devastated by the dishonor he'd brought on his father and mother – so frightened, but so sure he wanted to be free of cocaine. When he came to Douglas for help, it had been because he'd learned that the public disclosure of his addiction had been held over his parents to coerce them out of their farm.

And recovery drew so close for him. How could he ruin it this way?

Parr had become careless. Two German shepherds usually guarded the house, but they were nowhere. Neither were the lady-friends and the yes-men who normally populated Parr's life.

"MacGregor is a funny man," Kenji said. "So easy to convince your godfather you want to go straight. It is, after all, what he wants to hear."

"Yeah Kid. Ya had me goin' some too, I'll tell you."

"Truth is, I did want to kick the crack habit because I saw where that leads. But making money selling for you is a habit I could enjoy."

"I always thought you were smarter than those other two," said Parr. Douglas went cold. How could Kenji have taken him in so deeply?

Together they'd convinced the Macklin and Hargert families to force their boys into recovery. Douglas had watched Kenji sweat to live without the stuff for those hours until he knew his friends were safe, too. He couldn't have been doing an acting job in the grip of pain and the shakes.

Parr faced toward Douglas now, lighting a cigarette and offering one to Kenji. As he raised his hand to light Kenji's cigarette, Douglas could see an odd bulge in the sleeve of Parr's suitcoat. Parr glanced down at his arm and dropped it to his side. Douglas' blood froze at what he glimpsed – a gun!

To his left, a Stellar Jay flashed out of the shrubbery and squawked!

Douglas held very still. Parr and Kenji turned toward the sound and then Parr laughed.

"Damn bird's after my strawberries. Everybody wants somethin' for nothin'. You want to sell my stuff, but you don't like the percentages. Who do you think invests all the money? takes all the risks gettin' it here? Sixty-forty seems generous."

"I take risks on the street," said Kenjiro. "Now that they're watching Ralph, this stuff just sits in your china cupboard and makes no money if you don't have me."

Don't get greedy, thought Douglas. Make your deal and get out.

The jay sat on the ground hopping and cocking his head. With one more squawk, he took off over the house. His actions made Douglas aware of the dark shadows that moved in the shrubs to his left – two policemen!

Between himself and Eugene's finest stood the foliage of a King George Rhododendron – very big and very dense leaves. Douglas held still and thanked his stars that today his Pendleton shirt was brown and green.

Parr held forth on the relative risks of being the man at the top and didn't notice the subtle changes in his garden.

"Take it or leave it, Kid. For your health, I'd take it."

"All right, Lenny. I've saved up two hundred."

"That won't get you much, especially if you sample it."

"I want the wholesale rate, and powder – The police are forgettin' to look for powder. They think everybody's doin' crack."

"Two hundred won't get you no more'n what's in my pocket right now."

Douglas had trouble keeping an eye on the two policemen to his left and on the gun in Parr's sleeve. These guys in blue knew little about silence. What were they after? If they were here to watch this sale, they ought to sit still. Instead, they were constantly looking everywhere, except at the action.

At that moment, Douglas realized that the police were here because they'd set up this whole thing with Kenjiro. Nothing else made sense. He wouldn't believe that the boy had lied to him about his remorse. The hospital staff knew about this situation and had been told to keep everyone else in the dark.

Douglas didn't like the little gun. It indicated a degree of nervous distrust on Parr's part. If Parr thought Kenjiro pulled a fast one, he would shoot first and ask questions later.

Parr had the baggie out of his pocket and let Kenji check it when one of the policemen stepped on something. Douglas watched Parr's minute reaction to the sound. Only his eyes came up, glancing over the shrubbery, coming to rest on an azalea where the Stellar Jay bounced up and down on a leggy branch.

Leonard Parr relaxed.

"Fine," said Kenjiro. "It's good stuff. Maybe I should test a little this afternoon."

"You do that, Kid. Where's the money?"

Kenji pulled a wad of fives and tens out of his pocket. As he counted the bills out-loud, Douglas realized he took his sweet time.

They must be filming this. But where? He glanced around and noticed a tall White Oak in the neighbor's yard. Last year's leather brown leaves were hanging on until the new leaves pushed them off. They created enough coverage to make that an ideal camera angle. Kenjiro had maneuvered so that their transaction played out in full view of the oak.

Parr pocketed the boy's money when the jay made one last complaint against the invaders and flew into the White Oak. This time, Parr's eyes caught the movement in the foliage. He reached inside his sleeve as Kenjiro turned to follow his gaze.

"Move it Kenji!" Douglas charged across the lawn.

In that moment, Douglas saw Parr's thoughts as plainly as he'd ever seen any man's. Drawing out the small pistol, Parr smiled. His eyes gleamed with hatred. The weapon turned toward Kenjiro whose attention was on his godfather. Despair and fear filled Kenji's eyes.

"The knees!" Douglas shouted. With remarkable speed, Kenji dove for Parr's knees, throwing the man off balance just as the shot rang out.

Douglas heard a cry, but his attention stayed on Parr's arm with the gun. When Douglas's boot slammed down on the flailing arm, Parr's hatred found a renewed energy. Rolling, he threw Kenji off his body and into Douglas' knees. To counteract the force, Douglas dove over Kenji, landing on Parr and grabbing at the gun arm again.

Kenji rolled away, moaning and holding his stomach. Douglas had only a moment to see the blood spread in a growing blot across the boy's tee shirt.

Parr's anger and fear made him strong and all those years on the wrestling team gave him the right moves.

Douglas called, "Medic! Medic!" even as Parr's gun arm came up, threatening anyone foolish enough to be close.

Douglas grabbed the arm. He had landed high on the man's chest. Parr heaved his bulk up into the air, throwing Douglas like a buckaroo. Douglas splayed his legs as he felt himself flying. When he landed, more of the weight of his long thighs leaned near Parr's center of gravity. His grip on the flailing arm held firm. No telling how long they could keep this up. Parr's legs were still under him, his feet planted flat, but this time when he heaved upward, he didn't have so easy a time of it.

Douglas slid his free hand under Parr's nearest thigh and grabbed for the other leg. He knew he risked a broken arm, but the locked position would keep the man from turning over.

In Parr's frustration, he fired the pistol once more. The bullet sang across the ground, burying itself in the turf two feet from Kenji's head.

"Police!" Douglas yelled. "Get the kid away from here. He's hit."

With all his strength, Douglas pulled the gun arm down, down, until it aimed at Parr's own leg. "Get Kenji, now!"

The two policemen converged on the thrashing bodies. A black shoe came down on the gun hand. As Douglas watched through sweat clouded eyes, a blue jacketed arm reached down, took the gun and handcuffed the burly arm.

*   *

After two hours in the waiting room, doctors told Douglas that Kenji would make it. The bullet had entered his back, collapsed one lung and exited from his upper abdomen. Surgery was successful. The boy slept in recovery.

Relieved, Douglas put his head back against the wall and closed his eyes. Patrolman Boyce found Douglas outside Kenjiro's room, asleep in the chair.

"Mr. MacGregor, sir?"

"Uhh!" Douglas sat bolt upright out of a dream in which Bronwen fell from a White Oak.

"He's confessed." Seeing that Douglas was groggy, Boyce retraced his story. "Leonard Parr confessed. Told us who his accomplices were too."

"Accomplices? Well, Ralph, of course."

"And John Barsoti – you know, the one that's running for senator."

Douglas' senses reeled. "John? You got to be kidding me. John?"

"Barsoti. Yes, sir. The studded tires that were in his garage fit those marks we made plasters of, in Ian's Draw where you showed us. And the truck they come off of was in his north woods not a mile from your house."

"John." He moaned. "Why?"

"Covering a drug habit, Parr says. And there was Parr's money in the campaign fund. Barsoti had pretended to give it back, but it got returned under the name of three other Parr land developments – not a very clever disguise."

Douglas mumbled. "John's not the drug type . . . "

"I don't think there is a type. You get addicted and that's it. Anyway, he's been picked up for questioning. Cap says for you to go on home. Your ranch should be safe now. And Eguchi's parents are in the room with him."

"Parents?"

"Father, too. We had to have the parent's permission to send him into Parr's."

"Who talked them into the stupid sting?"

"Kenjiro. He said it was that or Seppuku – suicide for disgracing his family."

"He doesn't even know how to perform Seppuku." whispered Douglas.

"That's what his father pointed out. So Kenjiro said, `Well, it's gotta be the drug bust then, Dad.'"

For the first time in days, Douglas felt like laughing. As he laughed, the tears began coursing down his face. He stood and strode away from Boyce, feeling everything: the evident betrayal of John Barsoti, the near death of his godson, the loneliness of never having Bronwen. When he reached the truck, he had no tears, only a cold emptiness and fatigue.

Against all his losses, Douglas MacGregor was not sure it mattered anymore that his ranch might be safe. At least he could be sure that now Bronwen and his mother would not be in danger.

CHAPTER THIRTY

Somehow Bronwen's presence lingered in his truck. Douglas didn't even question the strong sense of her as he turned the ignition. He glanced at the empty passenger seat and knew what she would want him to do.

He pulled out of the hospital parking and headed for the police station to give John a fair hearing before accepting Parr's confession at face value. Perhaps John hid a drug habit, as Parr claimed, but Douglas owed his friend a chance to tell it his way.

Ten minutes later, he leapt up the steps of Eugene's western gothic police station, forcing himself to hurry toward the painful encounter with John. He expected the worst, but he wanted to be convinced of John's innocence.

In the front hall of the station, two T.V. camera crews and several reporters swiveled their attention toward Douglas. As he strode through the door, Greg Simms of the Eugene Register-Guard recognized him right away.

"MacGregor, we understand you were instrumental in saving young Kenny's life during the bust this morning. Would you tell us how it happened?"

"Kenjiro Eguchi handled himself very well in the situation. And the hospital staff says he's showing progress this afternoon. The rest will have to wait. I wouldn't want to jeopardize the prosecution's case against the defendant."

"Could you tell us how you happened to be in Leonard Parr's garden at the time?"

"Yes." Douglas saw Police Captain Jules Wilson shake his head. "I could, but that's one of those things that will have to wait. Now if you'll excuse me, I need to talk to someone."

"Who are you here to see?"

"Could you let me in Captain?" Douglas ignored the clamor of questions.

Careful not to say anything in front of the news reporters, Captain Wilson took Douglas into his office and out the office back door to the interrogation rooms.

"You want to see Barsoti?"

"Yes, Jules. I should have talked to him before this broke."

"The way I hear it, you were busy saving the Eguchi kid."

"Sorry about interfering in that set-up,"

"Frankly, I'm glad you were there. With the crowd we had at that party, you were the only one who knew about Parr's gun."

"Does the press know about John?" asked Douglas.

"No. So far they think the drug bust is the big story."

"Eugene's a regular Sleepy Hollow, isn't it?" said Douglas.

"Your ranch alone has accounted for half the action in the county this month. That's a fact."

Jules gestured toward the end of the hall. "I told John about your Mrs. Llewellyn nearly getting bombed during the cottonwood fire. Kind of a test. I'd swear he didn't know about it until that moment."

Douglas had a moment of hope for John and then dashed it with a hard thought. "You don't suppose he was surprised that I wasn't the one near the exploding cans?"

"I thought of that. 'Course there's no way to be sure."

"Where is he?"

"We're about done with him – about to let him out on bail. You can take him home out the back way when you're done. Mary said she'd stay at the ranch, so the press wouldn't get on to him." Captain Wilson opened a door in the end of the corridor and stepped aside for Douglas to enter.

A guard stood to one side of the small room, arms across his chest. Bleary-eyed, John Barsoti stood up from behind a table when Douglas entered. "How's Mrs. Llewellyn?" he asked.

Douglas stood stiffly quiet. "She'll be fine."

John ran a hand over his weary face and sat back down. "Great. That's great." His head drooped. "I didn't know she was injured in your fire. Mary knew about George, not Mrs. Llewellyn. I've been on the road campaigning so long . . . I keep thinkin' about her, ever since Jules told me, I keep seeing her in the flames."

He looked up. Douglas' still figure stopped him in mid-sentence. John started to speak again, but bone tiredness hit him hard. His hand dropped at his side. "You don't know what to believe do you?"

Douglas, his eyes intense and watching, shook his head slowly.

John let out a long sigh, closed his eyes and slumped against the chair back. "I can't blame you. Linda's tale hit me that way – I wanted to shout that she had to be wrong, had to be wrong, dreamed it all or something. But there was too much evidence. I had to take her seriously or be responsible for her death if the beatings kept on like that."

Douglas toyed with the papers left on the table, trying to see his way clear to believing John. Finally, he asked, "Why would Parr point the finger at you?"

"I won't sell. I won't accept his money . . ."

Jules interrupted, "You've still got his money, John. It's disguised, but it's still in your campaign account."

John said nothing, closed his eyes and seemed to shrivel up. "Nobody . . . Nobody is going to believe me now . . ."

Captain Wilson said, "Your drug test will tell us something."

"It'll be aspirin and coffee," John said, "and a tainted reputation."

Douglas cut him short. "John."

John's head came up, his black eyes fixed on his friend.

Douglas leaned on the table and whispered, "Is it you? Have you been doing these things to us?"

John met his unwavering gaze for a long time before his tired eyes closed. He answered, "No." and then opened his eyes, his posture the very image of dejection. "No, I'm not. But you'll never know whether to believe that."

"Help me believe you."

"I can't prove I didn't set the trap. I can't even prove I didn't shoot at George. On that day, I worked out in the fields by myself. I don't know where the truck or the studded tires came from. But I didn't kill Roy, and I think I can prove that."

Douglas' eyes narrowed, "How?"

"That afternoon I visited several farms and ranches around Goshen, looking for that anthrax or anything like it. I stayed the night with friends – went to a barn dance. Those people will remember."

"I want a list," said Douglas.

That stung John, but he rallied. "And I had nothin' to do with the cottonwood fire or the bomb in your truck the next day."

"Where were you the morning of the bomb?"

"On the day of the fire I made a speech in La Grande. Then I stayed with friends while I campaigned around the Idaho border for most of the week. I'd just come home the day I helped you work on the barn."

"We already knew the fire was set by someone else," Douglas pointed out.

Captain Jules broke in. "You know who set the fire?"

His question startled Douglas. "Of course – Ralph Birch, Parr's henchman. Sheriff Crawley's got him for arson and attempted murder."

Jules grabbed the door handle and snapped over his shoulder as he left, "Don't leave. I'm going to have it out with that lazy Crawley for not keeping me informed."

Douglas and John looked at each other, mutually surprised at the extent of Crawley's inept methods. Douglas sat down, disgusted and exhausted.

John looked down at his hands, up at his friend and back at his hands. "You know, even the arrest of Ralph doesn't let me off the hook with Jules about the fire. Even before you told him about Ralph's arrest, he had a theory that keeps me in the hot seat."

"What's that?"

"I hired someone to do it and left town for an alibi." John's voice was stoically flat.

Douglas wanted to shake the complaisance and defeat out of his friend. He leaned into his face. "Did you hire Ralph? Did you hire anybody to burn my fields and leave those gas cans?"

John winced. For a long tense moment, he made no move, then rubbed his hands on his face as he whispered. "You love that lady. I couldn't hurt you that way."

Douglas straightened and took his keys from his pocket. "Yes, I love that lady."

John glanced up as Douglas continued talking.

"It's because of her that I'm here," said Douglas. "She would insist I hear your side of this. I want to believe you, but for the sake of a lot of people, I can't."

"It wasn't friendship that made you come here? It was her?" John's hurt was clear.

"I'm sorry, John," said Douglas. "With Kenjiro in the hospital and Bronwen nearly killed, I'm not sure what to believe. It's crazy though. All along, Bronwen's been telling me this has to be the work of someone who knows me better than Parr, but the minute the evidence began pointing to you, she stood on your side."

John mustered a sad smile. "Keep her, MacGregor. I like her."

Douglas studied his keys as he answered, "I'd keep her. But I doubt she'd stay at MacGregor Ranch for very long."

Scoffing, John rose. "One thing I've noticed about her ..."

"What?"

"She's not Linda. She's no weak and pampered thing."

"I know she's different, but I'm the same man, the man who came close to violence over Linda. Anger can hurt and kill. Even my love can hurt, and I'll not subject Bronwen to that."

"You never laid a hand on Linda, no matter how much provocation she offered."

"God, I came so near!" whispered Douglas.

But John went on, "and that night in the streets – we asked for that. Every blow of it, we asked for. We all should have been in jail with you that night."

Douglas stared at John.

Jules burst into the room. "Crawley says he's had Ralph Birch in for drunk driving a time or two, but he knows nothing about arson or attempted murder."

"Sweet Jesu!" Douglas spit out. "How can any man be so stupid? I went in there to fill out papers. Phil put them in plain sight on Crawley's desk, for Pete's sake! The creep sat in a jail cell at the time."

Jules seemed just as disgusted as Douglas. "Crawley can't do anything right. You wouldn't believe the mix-ups – but this beats 'em all – I swear."

"Now what?" Douglas asked.

"Now," Jules said, "I call Phil Smith and get him to try to make the arrest all over again. In the meantime, you two get on home."

Embarrassed, John asked, "Doug, would you mind giving me a ride? My Mary's worried."

"Out the back," Douglas pointed. "And I'll not tell the press anything. It'll come out sometime, but not from me."

A weary John strolled toward daylight. He said, "When the police picked me up from the airport, Jules was good enough to make it look like a VIP escort."

Jules came out to the door with them. "John, you have to stay in touch, you know."

"Can't go anywhere, anyway. It's lambing time." His smile dragged up, then vanished.

* *

From the driveway of the Barsoti ranch, Douglas had an uncomfortable view of life, watching Mary run out the door and fold John into her arms gave Douglas a twinge. He pulled out of their driveway, careful not to run over the prancing collie, Prince Charlie, who seemed to remember that Douglas had been his trainer.

"Go way to me, Charlie. Sit, now."

The collie sat, staying. Douglas wished he could get Bronwen to mind his commands as well as Charlie. The one time he'd tried to send Bronwen back to Portland, she'd gone to Barsoti's instead, and God knew where else, looking for that damned truck. Charlie should have scared her off. He'd been trained to do just that to strangers.

* *

To avoid home and the mess of feelings there, Douglas took himself to the hospital. He visited Mrs. Beloit first and found he now had to remind her of who he was. After he explained, she chattered as if he were an old friend. She still believed Linda visited her every day.

Saddened by her situation, he dragged himself to the Intensive Care Unit. Kenjiro opened his eyes as Douglas came in.

"Dad visited me."

"Great!"

"He said Seppuku is easier."

"What?"

"He joked." Kenjiro smiled. "Dad can joke, you know."

"I'd forgotten."

"Pissed at Parr, but proud of me."

"I'm glad. You are a man to be proud of."

"Thanks for tackling him. Sure it wasn't football you played?"

"Wrestling move."

Kenjiro smiled. "Don't make me laugh. It hurts."

"Yeah. It'll hurt. That lung is going to take some time, the doc said."

"It's the back and the stomach muscles that hurt when I talk."

Douglas nodded. "Time to take up reading. Can I start getting your school assignments?"

"Mom's been bringing them, even to drug recovery. But you could bring me some shoot-'em-ups and mysteries."

"By shoot-em ups I hope you mean westerns."

"Oh yeah. Not druggee stories. But not Brit lit either."

"Why not? Bobby Burns, …"

"The Brit lit at our school is too much philosophy."

Douglas laughed. "Well, that's the accepted literary canon. There's other Brit literature that would lift your hat."

Douglas left the hospital very pleased with the progress Kenjiro had made, disheartened by young Roger Hargert's continued anger and hopeful about the third boy, James Macklin's prospects.

After dark, he got into his car and drove toward home. Douglas turned toward the entry to his ranch. He intended to pack Bronwen in the car and drive her back to Portland as soon as possible for her own safety. He half believed in John's innocence, but if John were on the up and up, then someone else hid out there looking for ways to get at him and those he loved.

As he pulled in, Robbie bounded toward his car.

Douglas stopped, opened the door to let the dog and his cast jump in and asked, "What's been going on, Boyo?"

CHAPTER THIRTY-ONE

Earlier that day, Bronwen had worked with her crew in the MacGregor garden, all the time mourning the misunderstanding that had created an insurmountable mountain between herself and Douglas.

She knew there was no way to explain to him without betraying Ben.

So, she had watched him leave this morning, and she'd determined to finish this project as fast as possible.

The temporary crew she had hired worked hard, efficient and willing, so the project drew near its goals. Her foreman, Jose Villa, had the plan in mind and deployed his fellows effectively, leaving Bronwen to the job of resurrecting the ancient oak tree.

She watched from up in the oak as several of the men planted ninebark, oakleaf viburnum and Mock orange along the downhill edges of the meadow. Margaret would be able to watch the succession of blooms from every room at the back of the house.

Farther away, Jose and his friend Karl smoothed the creek bed. Jose became the first garden contractor in many years to believe Bronwen about the need to use a curve in the creek bed that related mathematically to the length and steepness of flow. Thus, without the usual 'guy questioning', he swung this creek wide away from behind the barn, running a small way into the forest south of the garden and then swinging lazily back to cross the lawn. At the northern edge of the lawn, he let it widen and slow into a good-sized swimming hole for Janet and Jim's children, and then to a small duck pond just uphill from the oak. From the pond, the creek would run into the area downhill from the celebration grove, watering a new cottonwood stand and then filling a small reservoir. Most of the water would be used on the ranch in some way, even in heavy storms.

Up in the oak, Bronwen cut out the vestiges of the ivy. The old tree already thanked her for last week's work by putting out new leaves on every branch she'd been able to open to air and sunlight. Many of the branches had been smothered by years of ivy.

George had explained that this neglect resulted from the troubled years. During that time, Douglas and his mother were the main caretakers for his father as he grew ever more incapacitated by ALS.

George said, "That Mr. Douglas senior, he was a man of strength and wit who couldn't talk or sit up on his own anymore. It's a mean disease, but he kept his mind on love and care that whole time. Got my brother Ian to take him fishing when Mr. Douglas couldn't hold a rod. Made my brother important, when few others did that for Ian."

Ever since George had said that, Bronwen had noticed how often Douglas or Margaret consulted Ian on matters of ranching. It made her remember how Frank always acted toward his student architects and toward her. And she had watched Frank be as open about decisions with his contractors. To Frank, every job became a team effort, and all contributed to the success.

Bronwen climbed a little higher in the oak to cut off another dead branch. Below her, Robbie and his cast limped about. He chased bugs and then studied what Bronwen did for a time before barking and galumphing across the meadow to chase the backhoe as if it were Bronwen's enemy.

When Douglas left this morning, he had turned to her and said, "You're not safe here. You stay close to the house and Frank."

Then, he had pointed at her and said to Robbie, "Guard!"

Robbie had herded her about the garden all the time she consulted with Jose and the men. He'd given up herding when she climbed.

About three in the afternoon, Jose came to the bottom of the tree and said, "We're done for the day, Bronwen. Back tomorrow to finish the reservoir and get some more plants in."

She knew the men had a long drive to get home, so she wasn't surprised at the stopping time.

"When does the sod arrive?" she asked.

"Oregon Turf is laying that next week as soon as we get all of the gardens outlined and the plants in the ground."

"Will we be doing the underlayment of sand and soil?"

"No, they bring all that and roll it tight before they lay their sod down. They've got the process down pretty good."

"That's great. See you tomorrow, Jose."

"Ummm…" he started and then stopped.

"Something the matter?"

"You wanna come down before I go? I think George and Ian are in town with Mrs. McGregor at the docs."

She waved her belay rope at him. "Got my back-up plan right here," she said. "I've got a lot more daylight to get this thing cleaned up."

"Okay, Bronwen. I know you're a climber. Just be careful up there."

"Thanks, Jose. I'll be down before dark."

He nodded. "Good. See you tomorrow."

She smiled as he and his crew strolled off. Robbie followed them to their truck and then came back to sit in the dirt away from the tree.

He'd learned that branches and ivy clattered down from the tree, so he watched her from a safe distance.

Bronwen tried to work. But the silence of the oak seemed to accuse her as Douglas had accused last night.

Her mind fought back.

"Douglas MacGregor, you are a coward," Bronwen whispered to herself. "Late afternoon already, and you've managed to make yourself scarce all day."

Last night, she'd been appalled at his accusations. Barely aware that physical love would be so different with Douglas than it had been with Ben, she'd spent a sleepless night trying to understand what had made Douglas so condemning. Even today, nothing but the vague outlines of his fear were apparent to her. He'd grown afraid of his own anger and jealousy – afraid because he'd been branded as violent for so long, and because deep inside he recognized a slow burning rage.

His anger seemed justified, but no less appalling to him.

With Bronwen, he'd finally given in to passion, and then believed he'd hurt her. To him, that proved that his emotions were too strong to be indulged.

And now he'd escaped, not to the forested mountains which were his usual escape, but into town on the pretext of following up his lawyer's investigation of Parr.

Bronwen wiped her sleeve across her face and looked across the marsh where Roy had been killed. If she hadn't made herself so tired with digging trenches, and planting shrubs, she would have cried for all that had happened to Douglas. Whoever did this harbored deep hatred.

And Douglas's own self-doubts, on top of grief and fear had brought them to this misunderstanding. How could she tell him that she had never made love without feeling pain?

The outstanding characteristic of Ben's genius had been to do everything very quickly. His lightning mind had flashed from idea to idea, from creation to creation, leaving in his wake a studio strewn with smashed models, wadded paper. And although Bronwen had not recognized it at the time, he'd also left a wounded wife in the bedroom.

In the lowering sun, Robbie, whined and pawed the bottom of the oak, then lay down, his face between his paws.

"You miss Roy all the time, don't you?"

Robbie's body wiggled. His tail flogged the ground, but when the mention of his buddy produced no Roy, he lay still and whined again.

"I'm sorry, puppy. I shouldn't have said his name and given you hope." Bronwen whispered from the oak.

His dark eyes followed her. She could tell he puzzled over her. He'd grown uncomfortable, even nervous today, but he'd stuck with her at every turn.

Frank came down from his work on the barn. "I'm off to the kitchen to make dinner because Margaret is still at the doctor's with Ian and George."

"You want help?"

"No. You're making progress here."

She laughed and looked at the tangle of oak. "Enjoy the kitchen."

"Got your belay rope?

She waved it at him.

Frank smiled and went off to the house.

Today, the clouds sailed away from the sun, reflecting all the colors of a beneficent sky. The roof of the barn caught and held the day's heat and promised protection.

Robbie still pranced and pawed down below the tree, more jealous of human freedoms than usual, she thought.

"Rob, I wish you could see from up here, too."

She worked for another hour, and then thought she heard a chain saw at the barn. She hadn't been aware that Frank had returned to the barn.

Rob barked several times. The chain saw stopped.

Bronwen belayed herself down from the oak and walked up to the barn's new side porch.

Frank was not there. And from the barn she could see that he worked at the kitchen sink. Had that been a chain saw? a neighbor's chain saw?

Her legs were jittery from being in the oak, so she decided not to stay out much longer. No climbing the barn this evening.

But Robbie pranced about the corner posts, whining.

Bronwen stared at the nearest corner post. The grain was tight, making beautiful patterns. For some reason, the tree from which it came had one wide band of dark color running at an angle. Bronwen wondered what caused that coloring – a patch of pitch? An injury from deer antlers? Or the year its neighbor was logged off and its part of the forest enjoyed too much sunshine on that side?

Bronwen put down her tools, but her loppers whacked the near post with a dull thud.

When Bronwen looked up again, today's sunset turned deep orange and lit the crags of the coast range.

Robbie began barking rapidly, fiercely. Bronwen jerked to attention. She felt, more than heard the groan of the wood next to her. Landslide?

No! Collapse!

She scrambled backwards as fast as instinct would carry her. Wood cracked and split in front of her face, spewing out splinters as the addition's beam fell away. The collapse of the new structure threw her back as if she were in the saddle of a bucking horse. One of the beams bounced on the concrete floor and fell sideways, striking her on the back as she scrambled.

When she landed on the floor, she lay motionless. Somewhere in the outside world she heard the sound of timber twisting against nails, joints popping and heavy posts splitting.

"Robbie! Oh God, don't let Robbie be underneath." Bronwen struggled with lethargy opening her eyes to the sky.

"You move and you're dead meat," quipped the voice from her past.

"Ben?" she thought.

"Hang in there, Baby. Beams on you. Don't even wiggle your toes."

"What about . . .?"

"Hear him barking?"

She did.

Bronwen felt the weight of a round post on her leg and another over her chest. The clouds overhead turned gray. How long had she been unconscious? One star shone through the clearing sky. Night, cold night. How would Douglas find her?

"Listen to that racket. Think the dog's gonna let anybody miss you?"

"He was barking at me to move away, wasn't he?"

"He knows the smell of the one who does these things – the one who broke his hip."

"Who is it?

"I only know what you know. Careful. I felt you move."

"How can I get out from under?"

"No, please! Your feet – can you feel 'em?"

"They're under boards, aren't they?"

"Pick-up Sticks. Lie still. Don't lift your head."

"Frank's work doesn't collapse!" thought Bronwen.

"Remember the corner post?"

Bronwen tried to remember what she'd seen on the corner post – the beautiful grain, the one wide dark patch.

"Did it sound right to you?"

"What? Oh, my loppers hit the wood, didn't they?"

"And?"

"The post was dull . . . Frank's special oak made a dull thud. Cut!"

"Yep, cut."

"Who would get more sunshine if Douglas were cut down?"

"Bron, you're wandering. Do I have to sing bawdy songs to clear your head?"

"Who would benefit?"

"Oh, we make some sense after all."

"Parr Land Development," she thought.

"They'd benefit, maybe," he said.

"But why kill Douglas? Margaret would fight, too."

"Someone crazy with anger – jealousy maybe," he suggested.

"Crazy for sure."

"Who knew Douglas climbed here each evening?" he asked.

"Everyone who's been here to help – David, Crawley, Phil, John . . . . Bronwen felt her thoughts wander away from the present – remembering Douglas's friends.

"Jealousy maybe?"

"Jealous of Linda?"

Bronwen's body jerked back to alertness. She had nearly fallen asleep.

Or had she fallen asleep? "Has it been long?" she asked Ben.

"No."

She heard the back-door slam. "Frank is running up here. Don't let him get hurt."

Ben's voice said, "Hear that car?"

"Can't hear it," she whispered.

"Stay with us."

"Why did they love her?" she asked.

"She needed to be taken care of. Men think they love that."

"It makes them feel important?"

"For a while."

"Did I do that to you?"

"Only when you were afraid of falling into the cellar of your mother's house. Later, I loved you because you were brave, and you liked mud."

Bronwen laughed, but Ben continued. "At first you needed me but later, you were my ballast, and my peace in a frenzy of creation."

Between them there was a long silence broken by Ben's quiet voice. "About the other – the bedroom – I'm sorry. I didn't know making love could be like that for you."

"I knew less than you did."

"Regrets, Bronwen?"

"None. I loved you."

"I love you, so stay awake and think."

She heard Frank's voice. "Bron. Lie still. Lie very still."

"My back is one big charley horse." She whispered.

"Breathe and think each muscle loose," Frank said. "That's it. In, out, in. Slow and loose. Concentrate."

Suddenly she heard Douglas. "Frank, not that board. Wait till we have light."

*   *

Douglas swallowed the pain and fear, and turned on the barn's outdoor light. He saw the difficulty of lifting one log. Another would fall on her. There might not be much time.

"Bron, It's Douglas. I'm coming." As smoothly as possible, he lifted a piece that looked safely unattached to others. That piece led him to another. But a piece of the puzzle twitched.

His mind raced ahead of fear and heartache. "Don't move, Bron."

Frank said, "Hand them to me. I'll put them out of the way."

Douglas saw her eyes begin to close. She moaned.

"No!" he shouted. "Don't move! I'm not close enough."

She seemed to work her fingers against the nearest beam, trying to feel her way out from under.

"Let me untangle it."

He and Frank removed one piece at a time, and then had to study the next move. Finally, Douglas had the beams near her body rolled aside. "Can you reach your arms up to me?"

He saw the flexing in her shoulders, but no movement in her arms.

No control over her muscles. How long has she been here?

With great care, so as not to move the rest of the pile at all, he pulled her over his shoulder. The nearest dowel-nail cracked, and the attached part of the fascia board began to fall from the barn toward them.

"Move back, Frank!" he shouted.

He turned his back on the falling pieces. They hit his shoulder but not her head. He felt the blow, but continued walking, breathing deeply to overcome fear.

A car entered the drive.

He carried her down the road toward his mother, George and Ian.

Behind him, Frank stood over the wreckage and tried to see how this had happened.

CHAPTER THIRTY-TWO

From the stained-glass windows on the landing, the gray light of morning followed Douglas up the stair well. He tapped on Bronwen's door and shifted the breakfast tray. Hearing no answer, he opened the door and stepped in.

After clearing space on the bedside table, he stopped to look at her, noticing Bronwen's hair, the golden-brown tresses fanned out over her pillow.

Remembering how close she'd come to dying among the mangled timbers, Douglas trembled and set the tray down more noisily than he intended. Bronwen's eyes fluttered open. A smile lit her face and the hand that had been under her cheek stretched out toward him.

He stepped back. Her smile faded.

Bronwen brushed her hand over her face as if to hide her chagrin at his retreat. "What were you and Frank arguing about this morning?" she asked.

He blinked. "About you. About John. What were you doing up there?"

"I thought Frank was working at the barn. I heard a saw."

"God. You would have run into the one . . ."

"One who cut the post?"

"You figured it out."

"I had a lot of time."

He looked away. "I should have come home sooner."

"What's been going on. I heard the word 'blame' several times."

"I thought you were going to be safe," Douglas blurted out. "Even though nothing else was going right, I thought at least you would be out of danger when you we here with Frank and Jose."

"I was safe."

"Frank called to tell me he was in the kitchen and you were working the oak. But I was at the hospital. Didn't get his message until I was driving home. Then I drove up the driveway to find Robbie yipping wildly."

Bronwen answered, "I worked in the garden with Jose and his crew. I thought Frank had come back from the kitchen and was at the barn."

Douglas glanced at his hands, at her, at the window. After a moment, he spoke. "When I came, you were asking Ben to wait for you . . . I know . . . I know something important happened – it meant something to you and Ben, this other barn you saw in BeauLieu."

"I was checking on the MacGregor barn last night, which is not the barn at BeauLieu."

"But why?"

"I was waiting for you, and the sunset."

His eyes widened.

"And Douglas," she turned earnest eyes up to him, "the barn at Beaulieu – Ben was there, and Frank, but it was my feelings that made it important. I loved that barn and it's warm, safe spaciousness. Ben liked it, but he didn't need it as I did."

Douglas thought, Yes, a mother hen protecting her children.

After a long silence, Douglas sat gingerly, at the edge of the bed and looked at her. "Then why Ben last night?"

"He came . . . I don't know how, I needed someone telling me to lie still until you got there, telling me how to stay alive."

Douglas throat felt raw. When he swallowed, cold spread across his shoulders and down his back. He knew this sensation – knew it too well and hated it in himself. Jealousy.

Once before jealousy had turned him into a possessive jackal. Wasn't his brutal love-making in the den just another manifestation of that flaw? And now, questioning her about Ben's presence in her thoughts . . . She was right. Who else could she talk to when he'd gone off to town to hide? He'd left because he couldn't face having hurt her. He'd left her, prey to the man who'd shot George, set the bear trap and killed Roy.

Bron had needed someone – why not Ben? Certainly, Douglas MacGregor hadn't been around!

Bronwen's clear voice broke through his self-censure. "Douglas, why were you and Frank arguing about John?"

Almost to himself he whispered. "The police arrested Parr yesterday on drug trafficking charges. They had evidence from my lawyer and my godson, Kenjiro."

"And John Barsoti?" she asked.

Douglas' glanced at her a desolate blankness in his eyes. "When Parr confessed, he said John was his accomplice. They picked John up, but that must have been after he'd already cut the post."

"What time did they arrest him?"

"He could have hired someone to cut it."

"Anybody could have hired someone. How did that someone get up the road? How did he know you were gone? How did he know when to be there?"

Watching Douglas wrestle with answering questions and with his feelings of betrayal, Bronwen's heart sank. "You think John set the trap, killed Roy and beat Robbie?"

"And shot George," he added.

Bronwen hurt for him. Though she'd been the one pushing him to suspect a friend, a sense of wrongness about Parr's accusation settled in her. "John's running for senator, for goodness sake! Why would he get mixed up in a thing like this?" she asked.

"According to Parr, he covered a drug habit. Parr said he could get him to do anything to keep that out of the newspapers."

"Have you talked to John?"

Douglas looked miserable. "Yes. But how can I know what's true?"

"How can you not?" Bronwen leaned forward, a fervent determination in her voice. "For days, you've been telling me you won't suspect your friends. And his Mary sings like a woman who is happy. Husband with a drug habit, would she be happy?"

"But all the evidence – the truck, the trap and the crook, the snow tires and now even Parr …"

"Did Kenjiro ever see John with Parr?"

"I don't know."

Bronwen threw back her covers and pulled her sore legs over the side of the bed. "If I were you, I'd be listening to John's side of the story."

"I talked to him yesterday at the police station."

She glanced up at him. "He's arrested?"

"Out on recognizance. No one else knows."

Pushing up from the mattress, she took two steps and realized her legs were still cramped. Too late she turned back to the bed.

*　*

Douglas saw the surprised grimace cross her face and reached out, pulling her onto the bed just before she collapsed.

"What is it?"

She laughed, a bit tightly, "Darned legs. They're still in knots."

"You can't spend the day in the oak tree and the night under barn beams and not expect to be sore." He attempted to sound light-hearted as she massaged her calf. Her slow pulling motion proved an exquisite torture for him.

He looked away from her soft dishevelment. "I'll go see John. You're right about that, but you have to go back to Portland."

"Just like that?" Bronwen asked in a tight voice.

"I can't let you stay here to be a target for John or Parr or . . ."

"I'm not the target," she said. "You are. You'd just like me out of your sight so you can go on hiding from friends and the truth, pretending you don't care about us."

"I care about you – there can't be an Us." he stated flatly.

Bronwen tried to lurch from the covers. His hands held her in place. "I can't help it that I'm not much fun in bed," she whispered, "or on the hearth rug, for that matter."

"Bron, please understand . . ."

"I think I already understand. The big question here is do you ever intend to let yourself care enough to take a chance."

"It has nothing to do with how you are in bed. You were wonderful, giving, generous." Douglas swallowed hard. "But that's just it. It's me. I hurt you, instead of loving you. I care enough to send you away from me." Bronwen started to protest, but he added, "And I send you away from whatever anyone plans . . . as long as you're here, every scheme aimed at me hurts you as well."

"Yes, it does. No matter where I am." She held his gaze with her attention.

"All right," he admitted. "I understand. But I need to not worry about you."

"You should talk again to John," she whispered. "You've accused yourself of all kinds of crimes, falsely. You'd better make sure you're not doing the same to him."

Douglas's surprise shut him up for thirty seconds. Then he said, "Bronwen, I know what I'm like. And this other stuff isn't going to stop, whether or not it's John. I want you gone."

"All right. I'll get out." She pushed from the bed, biting down a cry as her back muscles cramped.

"Bron, you need help. I'll send for mother or a doctor or . . ."

She stood, and just as quickly sank back down on the bed. "No. No one please."

*   *

Bronwen just wanted to be alone to get over the ache in her heart as much as those in her body. She sat again. "I'll be fine. All I need is this breakfast and another nap." Tears filled her eyes, so she fixed her attention on the tray he'd brought, on the banana next to the cereal bowl.

She picked it up. "Potassium's supposed to be good for muscles, isn't it?"

While unpeeling the banana, she tried to pull her legs up onto the bed. They wouldn't mind.

Just as she was biting off a sweet chunk, Douglas put an arm under her knees and another around her shoulders. When he lowered her into the middle of the bed, she looked up at him over the ripe fruit. His gaze was on her fingers which enveloped the banana – a bleak helplessness in his eyes.

Bron felt herself blush. "I guess I need a nap first."

He took the banana, replaced it on the tray and stepped backward toward the door. "I'll go see John while you sleep. When I come back, I'll take you to Portland."

His dark gaze swept over her once more. As he reached for the doorknob, his attention rested on the banana. "You do need the potassium – a massage too, but I'll be damned if I can give them to you."

CHAPTER THIRTY-THREE

Hopping into the truck, Douglas decided to leave Bronwen in Frank's capable hands. She was going to be in bed all day, and he had to follow through on her belief that he should hear more of John's side of this mess.

He left a note for his mother and talked to Frank, who cleared wood from the damaged addition and promised to keep track of Bronwen when she awoke.

Then Douglas drove recklessly down the entry road.

* *

A mere two hours later, Bronwen woke up. She dressed and hobbled downstairs, surprised to find herself alone in the kitchen until she realized this was not one of Alice's two days at the ranch.

She wasn't sure where Margaret had gone, but she could see Frank at the barn, clearing up the rubble of the night before.

She needed to return to Portland for a few days to get a fresh perspective on things. She hated to leave this landscape not quite done, but Margaret's project would hold until she returned with a fresh mind.

And there were jobs in Portland that needed her attention. The vest pocket park needed to be ready for Larry and his backhoe. She wished she were more excited about going, but she still knotted with stiffness from the hours spent in the tree and under barn beams.

She needed to say good-bye to Margaret. There'd be worry and concern in Margaret's eyes, and Bronwen wouldn't be able to give her any answers.

As long as she remained here, Douglas would work himself to the bone in an effort to avoid her. Her presence created discomfort at a time when he couldn't afford to be distracted. She had to leave, but she didn't want Douglas MacGregor driving her home. Two hours in the car with him would be sheer torture – loving him, knowing he didn't love her enough.

She went out to the vegetable garden, but didn't find Margaret there.

So, she walked up toward the barn, thinking she might be there. She could hear Frank and his crew cleaning the mess of the collapse.

"No, I think Margaret is getting Mrs. Smith from her home," Frank said. "I thought you were asleep."

"I was, but I'm better now. Douglas wants me to go back to Portland."

Frank raised an eyebrow. "Seems like whatever they plan to do to him, you become the unintended victim. I'm real sorry about this barn collapse, Honey."

"It certainly wasn't your design or building skill that made this happen," she said.

"Want me to drive you back to Portland?"

"No Frank. I can do that now. But you and Margaret are no more safe than Douglas."

"I understand Parr is in jail and confessing."

"Yes, but I don't think it's just Parr." She didn't want to mention John in front of Frank's crew. Besides, she had a strong feeling that

Mary's husband could not be such a crazy man as it would take to do all this.

"Well, you drive safely."

"I will."

Bronwen started back to the house, but as she came to the intersection with the road to the north, she glanced to the dirt at her feet.

And froze. The studded tire tracks were here – the same chevron pattern as the tracks she'd seen on the entry road the morning after Robbie was hit.

But those tires were now in the custody of the Eugene Police department.

Or were they? Did they belong to the person who cut the support post?

She followed the tracks for another hundred yards before she went back to the ranch. She heard Frank's chain saw from the vicinity of the barn.

Margaret wasn't in the nearby fields.

In the house, she found two notes, one on the breakfast table and the other on her desk in the den.

The first read: "Mom, I'm going to talk to John and figure out what's real and what is not. Back this afternoon to take Bronwen to Portland when she wakes. D."

The second was in Margaret's handwriting: "Frank and Bronwen, Helen Smith called. Couldn't understand her. Am going up to bring her back here. I think she's not eating again, and not making any sense. Back in an hour, around ten a.m.."

It was now noon.

Douglas would come in and eat soup first, so she left him a note next to his mother's note, explaining what she'd seen on the north road.

Then she added:

"Your mother has gone up the north road to Helen's and is two hours later than she promised. I want to be sure she's safe, so I'm going to tell Frank. We'll probably drive up the north road and check on her before I go on home. I'll let you know if I find anything. Bron"

Bronwen left the papers by the soup bowl she'd set out for him, and then drove up to the barn.

"Frank, I can't find Margaret. She's two hours late coming back from Helen Smith's and I can't raise her by phone."

He dropped his hammer. "God, no." He pulled his phone out, tried Margaret's cell and then Helen's house phone.

"Helen's phone has been disconnected," He yanked his car keys from his pocket. "I'm going up there."

Bronwen said, "I'll follow."

As they drove off, she noticed that George cleaned dead wood out of the burned cottonwood stand.

George frowned when their two cars took the road to the north instead of the entry drive to the freeway. He put down his saw and went in search of Margaret MacGregor.

CHAPTER THIRTY-FOUR

"**Y**our Bronwen is right." Mary Barsoti said to Douglas. "This information and these attacks are coming from someone who knows you well."

They faced each other in the long driveway of the Barsoti ranch, in the shade of an old elm tree. The dust of Douglas' arrival had settled long ago. But the tension in Douglas and Mary had risen.

Douglas leaned on the bumper of his truck and watched Mary avoid eye contact by scratching the ears of Prince Charlie, their border collie.

Mary took a deep breath. "If John hated you, he'd tell you to your face. There's no way you wouldn't know that."

Douglas knew she was right. Everything about John was straight-forward, blunt honesty. That was why he would be such a good state senator. The man told you what he thought, and he listened to your ideas with an open mind.

"Mary," he started, but she waved her hand to stop his apology. "Let's see that list," she said. "And then let's call John to see if he has some insight."

"He's at the campaign office?"

"Yes. Chief Wilson thinks they'll be letting him go on his next campaign trip – off to Lebanon, Donald, Aloha, and the other

Willamette Valley towns, so not too far away to reappear in case Parr's accusations heat up."

Douglas hauled out his list, and the lists Margaret and Bronwen had made. "Here's what we've got so far."

Ten minutes later, on the cell phone with John, they'd decided to get David Brock to subpoena the financial books of Sheriff Crawley and start a suit against Crawley's accusation. If Brock didn't go along with that, they would have a better idea about his possible guilt, at least in the embezzlement situation.

"But," John pointed out, "Embezzlement is a far cry from setting a monster trap on your property and clawing your dog to death.

Douglas stopped breathing, thinking of Roy's last moments. Mary is right, he thought. John never holds back, even when it hurts.

"Okay then," John went on. "How do we approach Phil?"

"We go up to his old place and figure out that he's not got that ancient truck, not even at his Mom's.

"As far as I know," John said, "he got rid of that joy ride long ago."

"And then," Douglas said, "we're back to knowing nothing."

"Well, what about this new assessor from Chico, California."

"Even there, we have to ask who's feeding him information."

Douglas and John agreed to meet before John's trip up the valley, then signed off.

Mary, who had set a cold beer on the truck hood, took a swig of her own beer and then asked. "Jealousy?"

Douglas flashed on his damned feelings about Ben Llewellyn, but Mary said, "Who wishes you were not so successful? Or maybe wishes you didn't seem so. . . I don't know, so honest, so put together?"

"I'm none of the above."

"That's your point of view. But who might see that differently?" Douglas had a hard time imagining it. He felt so un-put-together, especially after hurting Bronwen. He turned away from Mary's gaze.

Mary said, "This started before you met Bronwen."

He stared at her.

Is she clairvoyant? Or does it all show on my face?

Mary went on, "So, it's not got to do with stealing her from some old beau."

"No," he said, and found his voice nearly swallowed in his chagrin at the truth. He pushed his throat to work, and said, "I guess Leonard Parr has pestered her to date, but she doesn't give him the time of day."

"I've pegged her for a smart one," Mary said. "Like to meet her."

"I'm sending her back to Portland until this is all over."

"Think she'll go this time?"

Again, he stared.

"Talk gets around," she said. "Bar tender at Harry's heard you and George. Tells that you've got a lady friend who doesn't go when you say 'go'. That stuff comes home from the crowd at the campaign office, or the old basketball buddies, or anyone else that John sees regularly."

His brain jumped to a new track. "That's it, then," he said. "It isn't a friend that's doing this. It's somebody who listens to bar-room talk and puts it all together for Parr."

Mary smiled at him. Then shook her head. "Doug, I'm glad you hate to suspect John and your old friends, but there are things that have happened out there that are vengeance, not just a bully wanting your land."

"Vengeance?" He asked, "For what?"

"Linda have a dad or brothers?"

"Only her mom, and she's in a nursing home. Says she talks to Linda once a week."

"You visit her?"

"Yeah, when I'm out visiting . . . visiting some other friends in the same hospital."

CHAPTER THIRTY-FIVE

Frank's car raised all kinds of dust, so Bronwen slowed to get a better view of details along the road. At one turn, she thought she saw a battered truck lying on its side and fallen down the drop off to the left. When she stopped, she realized it was an ancient Model T Ford, and so rusted out, it could not have been running in the last twenty years or more.

Back in her car, she tried to catch up with Frank for a couple of miles. Then the road turned toward the right and she caught a flash of sunlight on metal in the trees above her.

She thought, that's on Douglas' ranch and he's never mentioned any building or shed up here. What or who put metal up there?

Bronwen turned her car onto a logging spur off the main north road.

She tried to call Frank but got no signal on her phone.

At about five miles from the ranch house, she left her car hidden deep in the woods, and began climbing a steep narrow path, navigating by the memory of that one quick flare.

She debated, even as she climbed.

I'm certain that flash has something to do with the sheep, but what about Margaret and Helen? Should I back off and go figure out what is keeping Margaret?

Well, what if the sheep rustler has Margaret up there?

I'll see what I can see. If Margaret isn't there, I'll retreat without causing a ruckus and catch up with Frank.

The clouds moved into the valley, obscuring the sun. Above her the snowberries and sea foam were just beginning to leaf out. A large animal had been eating at the newer leaves of huckleberries. A cud chewer, so not a threat, she decided.

As she neared the top, voices carried across an open field.

*   *

After Bronwen and Frank left the ranch using the north road, George wished he had a car to follow her. He could have used the old Buick if he'd known where the keys were, but after he'd looked around the ranch house in the obvious places, he began pawing through drawers. Still he worried about her, especially when he found the notes on the breakfast table.

Earlier this afternoon, George had spoken to Margaret as she took off to the north in answer to a call from Helen. George knew Frank and Bronwen worried about her late return. He felt the need to tell someone that Frank and the young garden lady were following those tracks up the north road. But he was aware that if only he knew, he would be one old man on a Don Quixote quest, like that story Douglas senior had told his boy so long ago.

And right now, he felt more helpless than Sancho Panza.

"Damn fool truck tires," he muttered to himself. "Coulda told the police those tires at Barsoti's wouldn't be the right ones. This rustler is someone with a big hate and John Barsoti's never been much fashed over anythin'. A gentle lad he is . . ."

George's shoulder wound ached as he tried to figure what to do. In the house, he tried to call Douglas, then Margaret and then Helen, whose number was on the refrigerator. He got no one, and became even more worried when he discovered that Helen's phone had been disconnected.

At last, decisions became unnecessary when the MacGregor truck crawled up the entry drive. Fishing in his pocket for Bronwen's note, he hustled out to meet Douglas.

*   *

Bronwen lay several miles north, among the huckleberries and Oregon grape surrounding an open meadow of old tree stumps. She watched Parr's man, Ralph, waving his arms at a second man she vaguely recognized. With them was a much younger man she didn't know at all. She saw no sign of Margaret, or Margaret's car.

Why isn't Ralph in jail? she wondered. The other man . . . oh, that's Mrs. Smith's son, Phil – the deputy who arrested Ralph.

Bronwen remembered Phil well, tall, except for his stooped shoulders. He was one of the three men who'd helped Douglas put up the gate posts. He'd also been at the morning's conference at the ranch two weeks ago, back when she surveyed the MacGregor's hill. She'd seen him helping around the ranch since then. He was a big man, sunburnt up to his hat-line, and seemed older than Douglas' other friends.

As she watched, Phil peeled several bills from a heavy roll of money.

He handed the bills to Ralph.

The youngest of the three men was wiry and nervous. Ralph called him Dick. Repeatedly, Dick sighted down his rifle at nearby trees and rocks. Bron held very still so he would find no reason to aim at her. Dick didn't stand still the entire time he talked. The thrust of his jaw indicated habitual belligerence.

Ralph had more silent ways and though small, gave off an aura of untapped power. Whenever Ralph spoke, Douglas' big friend, Phil, took an involuntary step backwards. Ralph intimidated him far more than the cocky anger and the rifle of young Dick.

"Tomorrow night?" queried Ralph, taking off his stocking cap and scratching his thin hair. "Dick and me just got here and I ain't had time to scout out things real good."

Phil answered, "There isn't any better time, Ralph. It isn't my fault you had to lay low so long after you let MacGregor's dog catch you. You should never have stuck around to watch the fire."

Ralph cackled, "I understand you ripped open MacGregor's collie the other day."

"Had to. He kept makin' a ruckus every time I came to visit – like he knew I was the one who hit on his brother. But I found a way to make it look like someone else killed the cur."

"You always got a way to pin it on someone else, don't you?" snarled Ralph.

The man shrugged, "I know what I'm doing."

"Maybe you do, but I don't like going blind into some other man's plan," Ralph warned.

"That sheep's about dead right now. It can't wait for your fears to calm down."

"Not fears – caution. When you gonna "plant" that varmint?"

"We steal the rest of the flock tomorrow night. The next morning I'll pull that wooly ace out of my sleeve and "plant" her under his big Maple. After that, MacGregor will be in jail and unable to look for you."

A slow grin spread over Ralph's face as Phil talked.

Bronwen tried to move away but found herself waiting to see what else Phil had planned.

"How we goin' to set about stealing this flock?" whined Dick, nervously clicking the catch on his rifle. "We haven't had a good look at what we're doing?"

"Look, Dick," Phil said, "stop fiddling with that thing. You and Ralph meet me at the exit to MacGregor's at 4 a.m. I'll take you on a hike to where you can see the whole set up. Got your approach figured out a couple of weeks ago, when I was there."

Ralph, put his ragged hat back over his stringy hair and sat down on a worn camp stool. "I don't know 'bout this. You may have put his dogs out of the picture but there's other fellas still down there, from what I see."

Phil had grown impatient with their questioning. "Those men are old – Ian's not even very bright. Besides, they'll be busy with the other flocks. It was MacGregor's dogs you had to worry about."

Dick, twitchy as a snake, stepped closer. "I'm not worried about no dog. The whole thing don't make no sense to me. If it don't make sense, I don't like it and I don't do it."

Phil clenched his fists and moved toward Dick. Ralph jumped to his feet with extraordinary speed and silence.

Phil shrugged his shoulders, dropped his fists and laughed. "It's simple. I hate MacGregor and his do-good Mother."

At the mention of Margaret, Bronwen felt a cold ball turn in her stomach. She made herself put aside feeling and listen.

"He sets great store by these sheep," Phil said, "enough to insure them for a very large amount. He always did think a great deal of himself. So, I saw a way to get at him and earn a little on the side. I offered the sheep to Parr instead of some money I owed him."

The younger man seemed satisfied, but Ralph asked, "Why's this dead sheep s'pose to put MacGregor in jail?"

"Anthrax," said Phil. "One of his ewes just happens to have gotten a bad case of anthrax. It's gonna look like he was hidin' a epidemic. Not nice to put your neighbors' lives in danger that way, no it's not! Not legal, neither."

"Anthrax!" shouted Dick. "Did you inject her with it? Where you keeping her? She's not one of them we've got already is she?" Dick looked petrified by the disease.

Phil laughed and pointed at Dick. "That's exactly the effect she's going to have on all the ranchers in this valley. Fear is going to keep MacGregor locked up a long time. Don't worry. She's not here. Before I injected her, I kept her in a little shed on my property."

Bronwen remembered the long tufts of wool in the barbed wire in Helen's tool shed.

Phil explained to Ralph and Dick. "That ewe is in a safe place. The morning after you steal the rest of the flock, she's going to be found on MacGregor's ranch. You won't ever have seen such a hoop-te-doo as that's going to create. I'm going to let the law find the sheep and the frightened ranchers will carry the ball for me!"

Dick slapped his thigh and cackled with the humor of it all. "Whew! You take the cake! You must hate him somethin' fierce to pull this."

"I do, gentlemen. I do."

*   *

So, this was the man who'd broken Robbie's hip and killed Roy and the Blackwatch ewe. Bronwen looked at Phil carefully because she wanted to know his face whenever she saw him again. As he moved to his old Ford truck, Bronwen saw the chevron pattern of his studded tires. There was snow still in the tread.

She thought he must keep this truck up in the mountains.

Then a memory hit her – Crawley staring at himself in her dark glasses and saying, "Phil had an old truck, back in high school. That'd be ancient by now, but I ain't seen him in it for a good ten year."

The sun came out from behind another cloud. Phil looked in Bronwen's direction. She held very still, sure that, in this bright light, he would soon see her dark red blouse.

Instead, he opened the door of his battered truck and turned to talk to Ralph. "Meet me tomorrow morning – four o'clock sharp. We got a lot to do."

The sun shone briefly on the front door window. The reflection blinded her.

There it was! That was the mirrored light she'd seen from the road. Bronwen waited for some time after Phil drove down the rutted road.

She lay there, remembering the woman in the worn sweater, shuffling toward her off the porch, babbling nonsense about her son's sheep and the sheep shearers whose trucks trampled her daffodils. Poor Helen. She was no more senile than her son had made her, lying to her about what he was doing.

When Dick and Ralph were busy about camp, Bronwen backed down the steep slope and dropped to the narrow path. As she ran, she marshalled her evidence to convince Douglas MacGregor of what she had seen.

From all she knew about Douglas' past, Bronwen understood why Phil Smith hated him. If she was right, he would stop at nothing to hurt both Douglas and Margaret.

*   *

At one-twenty in the afternoon, Douglas stared at the note George had found. Margaret was on the phone to Portland, searching for Bronwen. Helen sat at the table in the kitchen, knitting a baby sweater for Phil. No one told her Phil was a grown man.

Margaret said, "Frank and I didn't pass her as we drove back from Helen's. Either she's on her way to Portland, or she took another road."

"Damn," Douglas said, "I should have tied her in that bed, or taken her with me to town."

Douglas impatiently watched his phone for a message from the secretary at Frank's Portland office. He muttered, "Those damn tracks again. How does this guy drive on the north road without passing our gate?"

He stayed in the kitchen long enough for the return call from Frank's office. Bronwen was not in Portland and wasn't at her apartment either. No one had been able to raise her on her phone.

"She dropped back out of my dust and then disappeared," Frank said.

With that, Douglas hit the porch on the run, and ran for the truck with Frank close on his heels.

They leapt in and left faster than was safe for the condition of the shock absorbers. Douglas scanned the tell-tale studded tire tracks and drove on the left side of the road to avoid obliterating them, just as he saw Bronwen had done before him.

At mile four, Frank said, "Stop."

They both hopped out and discovered Bronwen's tire tracks where they pulled to one side at the sight of the ancient Ford. "That's been there since before you were born," Frank said.

"But Bron didn't know that. She just knows we're looking for an ancient truck."

"This is about where I last saw her in my rearview mirror."

"What did you do, Girl?" Douglas whispered, staring around them at the road and the ravine below them. "What did you see?"

Frank said, "She was as worried about your mom as I was. Maybe she saw something she thought was a threat to Margaret, or to you."

The hills and forest surrounding them seemed vast and silent.

*   *

After they drove off, Margaret called detective David Brock, asking him to come help in the search.

Helen knitted, and kept whispering, "Slip one, knit one, pass the slipped stitch over the knit stitch, yarn over."

*   *

At two-twenty in the afternoon, Bronwen ran around the last turn in the trail. In the grove of hemlock and cedar, her hidden Peugeot looked comforting. In a moment, she'd opened the front door and inserted the key in the ignition, ready to go back to the ranch and tell Douglas what she'd discovered.

As she tried to turn the car on, a meaty hand covered her mouth and jerked her head back against the seat, making her right foot kick out reflexively. The pain in her foot and the greater pain in her neck stunned her. For an instant, she didn't realize that the blaring noise was her hand on the horn.

"Damn you, stop! Stop!"

She recognized Phil's voice just before he shoved her head forward into the steering wheel. Blinded by pain and propelled by fear, Bronwen rolled out the open driver's door into the gravel and mud of the woods.

She pushed herself to her feet and ran.

"Not so fast, little lady," Phil laughed as his big hands made a grab for her. Bronwen twisted away from him and tried to run down what she thought was the road. Her vision greyed with dizziness. Every muscle in her body slowed and became heavy. As she toppled over, she felt something warm running down the side of her face. She couldn't even get her hands to reach out and stop her fall.

*   *

Laughing, Phil Smith turned over the body of the woman. He couldn't remember her name, but, through the trees, he'd recognized that car well enough from the day she'd driven into the ranch. He'd known then that she was MacGregor's. He'd hated her from the day she and MacGregor had come out of the woods unhurt by his big trap.

He liked it that she'd tried to fight him, tried to get away even though she hadn't had a chance. It made what he planned to do promise to be more fun. He reached down and brushed the blood from her face back into her hair.

"Pretty." He muttered and lifted her over his shoulder to carry her up the trail to his camp.

*   *

At six o'clock, Bronwen awoke under a dirty blanket, twenty feet from a small campfire. She saw that her car had been driven up here.

Douglas won't even know I'm not in Portland.

The blanket smelled of tobacco and stale sweat. She cringed under it, trying to keep her revulsion from making her any sicker. Her hands had been tied behind her back. Her fingers were numb and her wrists burned under the rough hemp. Leather thongs hobbled her ankles together.

When she tried to open her eyes, her head throbbed. Damn, she thought. I've made a mess for everyone.

Her head ached. After a time, she could see a dim grayness, darkening until she blacked out again.

*   *

In the deep darkness of midnight, ten miles from his ranch and five miles from Bronwen, Douglas argued with David. "Men are easier to find at night," Douglas explained. "They betray themselves because they think they can't do without coffee or heat. Let me keep looking for her. You go back and tell mother I'm all right."

"But you're not all right. If you were, you'd realize that Frank's got the right idea. He's probably found her at some friend's house in Portland, or at Llewellyn's in whatever little town that was . . ."

"Beavercreek." Douglas' voiced held little patience.

"Yeah. Even if he hasn't turned her up that way, the more you drive on this road, the more you wipe out the evidence she wrote about.

"You've been over this road," David went on. "I've been over this road. We haven't found her car at all. If we're very lucky, we've only partially wiped out the tracks by now. We've got to wait till dawn."

Wary of trusting anyone, Douglas was silent for a long time. Finally, he spoke, "Okay, David. You're the detective. But I'm taking off again at first light."

*   *

Long before dawn, the noise of a truck dragging something very heavy awoke Bronwen. She heard Ralph's voice. "That's Smith wipin' everything out down there. They won't find her car's tracks or the old truck tracks either."

Bronwen shivered. Her head was a continuous pressure. When she moved, the pressure became sharp pain behind her eyes.

"What about his dame? Is she dead?"

"Nah, but he sure knocked her a good 'un."

"Why do you think she was down there? Who is she? What are we gonna do with a sick dame?"

Ralph seemed tired of the questions. "We ain't gonna do nothin' with her. She's a MacGregor somehow or other – was at MacGregor's, the day of the fire. Now, she's Smith's package. He ain't gonna do no more than keep her trussed up until this is over. Then we have some fun before she gets dumped in the desert on our way to Utah."

"But what was she down there for?"

"I don't know. Shut up, I tell ya. We got to get out of here to meet Smith. Move."

Bronwen heard one of the two trucks drive off. The noise of its studded tires could be heard for a long time, cracking and spewing out gravel as the truck jounced down a logging road. From inside the other truck that they had left in camp, she could hear two dogs barking.

She tried her arms against the ropes, and felt blood running into her palms. After countless times, fingering the knots, a few strands came loose, but the rope still held tight.

Bronwen fell into a shivering sleep.

*   *

Long before dawn, Douglas was up, unable to do anything but watch for the little bit of sunrise that would allow him to see the tracks in the road. Hours before, Frank had called from Portland, still unable to turn up Bronwen.

Douglas paced the den, stopping often to stare at the map of his home which Bronwen had drawn. On it, the north road turned and went off toward the upper framing lines, ending about two hundred yards from the junction.

He leaned over the map, his hands gripping the sides of the table they'd set up together in what seemed now like another age.

Her italic lettering moved with grace, the contour lines swept firmly. The house and great barn were drawn with assurance. In the left-hand corner, she had written:

"Landscape Design for the home of Margaret and Douglas MacGregor, MacGregor Road, Lane County, Oregon, Bronwen Llewellyn, A.S.L.A."

In all his life, he'd never thought of it as "MacGregor Road". To him, it had always been the road up the hill. Now it would be the road where . . .

His head ached as he staved off foreboding. He stood up, walking away from the table. Premature for grief. He had to get out and do something before he was of no use to Bronwen at all. How could he clear his mind of her, so that he could think for her?

Waiting for light was the hardest. At least Frank was doing something. He had the state police looking for her in the rest areas on both sides of the freeway and at filling stations along the old highway.

Maybe they'd already found Bronwen – but Frank had said he would call, no matter what time. Anything could have happened . . .

Out on the freeway, Douglas heard truck drivers able to go about their business, not having this infernal wait for the sun. Some distance away, he heard a truck dragging something heavy.

He went out on the front porch to look for the source of the sound.

The Celebration Grove prevented a clear view across the mile to the freeway. The sound was far off and receding. Perhaps not a freeway sound.

He was through waiting.

David's truck barreled up the entry road as Douglas got into the Chevy. David hopped out and ran to join Douglas. Swinging into the passengers' side, he shouted over the noise of the cold engine, "Let's go!"

Douglas dropped all thought that David could be false to him. "Thanks, David."

"I knew you wouldn't be able to wait for sunrise. I cut it kind of thin, though."

They turned onto the north road, peering through the beam of the headlights for any sign of the track they'd both seen the night before.

David talked to Douglas while staring out the front window. "Barsoti and Phil called last night."

That worried Douglas. "Did you tell them about Bronwen? I don't want them to get Crawley bumbling around in the woods today."

"I didn't even tell them that Bronwen was missing, because I was afraid they'd call Crawley. We can tell them about that when they show up."

Relieved not to have to explain his suspicions of Phil and John, Douglas watched the road. He was glad to have David's help. They always had made a good team, in the fields, logging, playing basketball. "Tell Angie thanks for loaning you to me."

"She wouldn't have you out here alone any more than I would. Shouldn't we be seeing those tire tracks by now? Hasn't it been a mile?"

"At least."

"Stop, Douglas. I'll get out and walk in front of the truck until we spot them and can get going again."

They progressed slowly for about twenty minutes. Finally, David signaled Douglas to join him on the road. Douglas could see that David was worried.

"Look at this! Somebody has dragged this road with a log."

A mile later, in a ditch at the side of the road, Douglas saw the log, covered with mud and rocks, the bark scraped away by repeated use. On either end were heavy S-hooks by which it had been connected to a truck.

Douglas paced the road from side to side, his sharp eyes looking for any sign of the track. It was gone – completely gone. A wave of nausea hit him. She had been out all night – all night!

"Bronwen!" Douglas slumped against the warm truck hood, his head sinking to his fists. "I heard them doing this. Ten minutes before you came, I heard this happening. If I'd come then, I'd have caught them. I'd have her."

He looked up at the cold dark hills. "There's a truck fixed to hold this log somewhere. They've got her out there, somewhere."

David stood by, helpless. If Angie were out like this all night, he'd be crazy frantic. "Doug, we've gotta get help. You have to trust John and Phil on this, or we'll never stand a chance."

The dark shadows under Douglas's eyes deepened. "We have to find her, and I don't know who to trust."

* *

She awoke to a feeble sun and a wind, raising her head slowly, painfully. The rustlers hadn't returned. Bronwen was sure Phil had taken her captors to the high meadow of crocuses on Samson's mountain where they could see the whole ranch. She remembered the view herself from the day of their run-in with Samson. That meadow was a hike of about two hours. Two hours up, one hour down and a half hour drive would bring them back about seven-thirty. It was about six or six thirty now – sunrise. Not very long to work out an escape.

She sat up and tested the cords that bound her, cutting into her arms.

It was frosty cold and windy. Frost had soaked her blanket, as well as her hair and clothes. Before her, she could see an open slope falling away toward the cliff and the sheep path. Off to her left, were the bushes in which she'd hidden yesterday. The rest of the area had been logged over sometime in the last twenty or thirty years and never replanted. The lodge-pole pine was the one type of tree that had self-seeded.

She worked at the knots with her fingernails. Not a chance. Plus, she knew that if she escaped in this open country during daylight, Phil would find her easily. She had to escape at night. But how?

Could she roll anywhere, tied up this way?

She lay down, clutching the blanket, so as not to lose its flimsy protection. She did a test roll. After two controlled rolls, she was able stop herself by flattening her hands behind her and digging in her feet.

Her head brought unbelievable pain. She lay very still trying to contain her nausea.

Slow, wretched, she crawled back up the hill and rolled to within six feet of the cliff edge – seven rolls from her original position. She was not sure if the sickness that waved through her was from her head wound or her fear of the cliff.

She crawled uphill again, this time to the front of the tent. After resting to settle her head, she rolled. Nine rolls from the tent front. She felt warmer from the exertion. But her arms and shoulders were shaking tired.

She was crawling back to her original position when she heard the truck on the road. She slumped under the blanket and hoped he didn't notice the pine needle debris on her clothes.

She could escape, if they left her here tonight.

*   *

The younger man got out of the truck, grinning at Bronwen. "Look what fell out of the eagle's nest, Ralph. Smith caught himself a good one this time."

"Leave go of it, Dick." said Ralph. He sat down next to Bronwen with a concerned look on his face. "How is that bump, little lady? You took a nasty fall. That's a lot of blood."

He reached out to touch the wound on her head. She flinched. "Now, don't you worry, I'll take good care of you. You got to stay tied up till we're done with our job, here. But soon as that's over, we'll take you someplace nice and let you go."

Dick snickered as he poured himself some coffee.

"Shut up, Dick. You're scaring the little lady. You're sure safe with me, honey," he said patting her shoulder.

She made herself not draw away. She'd seen the satisfaction her fear had given him and knew better than to feed it. She sat, shivering from her wet clothes and the frost of spring.

The two men argued with each other, cursed their dogs and packed things into the first truck. Occasionally, Dick would sit down and talk to her in an insinuating tone. Ralph would send Dick on some trumped-up errand and give her a saccharin apology for the other man's behavior. He would test his effect by touching her hair or face.

She knew that if she flinched, he would be pleased and try some new and more disgusting gesture on her.

He smiled, "You'll be all right, Honey. We'll get along fine."

*   *

The morning wore on. Ralph put a greasy lunch before her to signal the end of half a day. He made no attempt to untie her hands so she could deal with the lunch. She'd grown so cold that she was afraid she'd be sick if she ate it. So, it stayed there until one of their sheep dogs got interested.

Late in the afternoon, Phil came into camp. He swung down from his truck and grinned at her. Ralph and Dick pretended not to be around.

Phil ambled over to her, sat down and put an arm around her shoulders. "Are you all right, missy?"

"Cold." As soon as she said it, she wished she hadn't.

"Well, I can help you with that. You can wait for me in the tent.

That'd be a little warmer. "Dick? Help me get the lady in the tent. She's cold."

Alarmed, Bronwen stiffened. It would be harder to escape from the tent. These ropes had done nothing but make her wrists bleed since she began trying to get them off. How would she unzip the tent door? She couldn't think about what she would do when he came back if she was still here.

She wouldn't be here.

He lifted her over his shoulder, her throbbing head down, his shoulder jabbing her stomach. When Dick opened the tent, Phil dropped her inside, letting her back hit the tent floor, snapping her head. "There you go, honey," he sneered as he zipped up the mosquito netting.

As she lay there losing consciousness, Phil spoke to Dick and Ralph. "You two're goin' to sleep in the truck tonight. And don't give me no lip."

CHAPTER THIRTY-SIX

As they pulled up to the house, David took a deep breath and plunged into it with Douglas.

"The reason I know you need help is that your mother took that decision out of your hands."

Douglas nodded.

David's eyes blazed with fury. "Are you going to make us pay the rest of our lives for listening to Linda's lies? We didn't know what to do! Will you never understand? We just didn't know . . ."

"It's not got anything to do with Linda." Douglas turned to him slowly. "I have to trust somebody, but each of you is a suspect in this affair."

"A suspect?"

"There are things that have been done that only you three could have known were important to me."

David's voice was tight with frustration and anger. "For years, we didn't know whether to trust you. Now you don't know whether to trust us. Where does it stop?"

"It has to stop here," said Douglas. "I can't find her without you. I have to trust you or there's no chance for her."

"'Bout time! What'll we do?"

"For two of you, my trust is warranted. But the third has been trying to kill me. I don't know who that third is."

David let out a low whistle. "Rock and a hard place. I'll tell you this, I'm not your suspect and I'd be willing to wager you're wrong about John and Phil as well. So, let's plan the search."

Douglas stared at the dashboard, trying to think straight. "They have Bronwen, but they don't have all the Blackwatch. I have to believe they want the Blackwatch and she just happened to get in their way."

He grimaced at the specter that thought raised. "They'll stay within striking distance of the ranch until they have the sheep. They're up that road somewhere."

David added, "The state police are looking for her, her Peugeot and that old truck you've described to me."

"So, my ranch and Smith Ranch are our responsibility. We'll divide the area and cover the grid, one man per section."

"One?"

"Pairing would slow us down. It's cold. We have to find her fast."

"John and Phil will be here soon," David said.

"One precaution . . . when they get here where we can see their reaction, tell 'em we believe the stolen Blackwatch are hidden in this area. That way, if one of them knows I should be looking for Bronwen instead, his surprise may give him away."

*   *

In the tent, Bronwen shivered under the dirty blanket. It was long after noon, she guessed. Without the sun, it was difficult to tell just how much after. The cold hours seemed interminable. Could she last until they left? Where was Douglas now? What had Phil done to him? Phil could have trapped him alone while he searched for her – trapped him and killed . . .

Oh God, don't let Douglas trust him. He wants so desperately to trust his friends. And please, don't let Frank come out here.

What would happen to Frank if she died? She had no illusions about how deeply Ben's death had affected Frank. It had been like losing a son.

Her semi-conscious wanderings were interrupted by the grate of Ralph's angry voice hissing at Dick.

"Phil Smith is on his way here. I saw him comin' over the hill to the south."

Minutes later, she heard the tent door unzip. Phil's face appeared in front of hers. "How are you, Babe?" he asked.

When she opened her mouth to reply, he shoved a dirty rag in it and began tying another around her head to hold the first. She gagged and choked.

"Breathe through your nose! Your nose, you hear me?" He finished tying and smiled at her fear. He reached out and caressed her face and throat. "You look real good, Babe. If you're a good girl, I'll keep you alive. Otherwise, there are lots of cliffs between here and Utah."

She closed her eyes and shrank into herself.

"Your man's looking for you. Real frantic he is – even willing to trust his old pals to help out, except he pretends it's the fool sheep he's got us lookin' for.

"I'll help him out," Phil went on in a singsong tone. "I've always been willing to help MacGregors, like they were always willing to help me. I'll help him into jail for your murder. I'll help him think it was John who did it all. They were always so tight, him and John, and always looking down their noses at poor Phil with the drunk for a dad. Always helpful to me and Mom. Just a friendly bunch o' cozy neighbors."

Phil snorted, and let his hand run across her breasts and hips as he backed out of the tent. "Cozy neighbors takin' good care of each other."

The sound of the zipper allowed her to breathe again. How many hours left? What if he came back? She was so cold. How could she fight him? What weapons were there?

The stale sweat smell of the man made her sick. She had to keep from throwing up or she might kill herself, choking. She tried to breathe more deeply through her nose. The smell of oil on the rag made the nausea worse. She took shallower breaths. In the increasing cold, it was difficult to breathe.

As she lost consciousness, her body relaxed. Her breathing became more natural. From far away, she heard Ralph arguing with Phil about where he'd hidden her car . . . was it today? yesterday? Was this the night he would take the rest of the Blackwatch?

Douglas, be careful of him. Her shivering muscles were so tired.

*　*

Near sunset, in his quadrant of the search area, Douglas found one piece of the puzzle – an old Ford truck which carried no license plates. It lay rolled on its side in small draw. No attempt had been made to cover it with camouflage.

"Phil's old truck," Douglas muttered as he clambered down the loose sides of the basin toward it. "Why would he do this?"

He stared at the welded eye-bolts on the back of the truck bed. The rubbing of metal on metal had left shiny spots on the back side of each eye. "That's where the log's S-hooks were attached."

He pulled himself into the bed and began to climb up to the cab door. As he swung his leg over the truck-bed wall, the bottom of his right pant leg caught on a rusty edge. When he pulled it, loose a long, white wool tuft came with it.

"Blackwatch! Why? And why take Bronwen? Why do all this and then dump the truck in such an obvious place?" Douglas yanked open the passenger door and lowered himself into the cab searching for signs that Bronwen had been there. Almost immediately, he found a long blond hair on the seat and another at the inner side of the window. The cracked rubber surrounding the window had blood in it – still red, not browned with age.

Bronwen.

Douglas stared at the evidence, disbelief, and then horror, paralyzing him. Images of Bronwen passed before him. Her gentle face alternated with images of Phil – Phil, his friend of a lifetime, Phil as a child, accepting offers of food and clothes, yet turning away in shame, Phil as a teenager, sarcastically cynical. Phil as a man, touchy and closed.

"No! He can't be consumed by his father even now. Where is he? I have to find her . . ."

Douglas pushed against the dashboard to scramble out of the cab. His hand landed on a slip of paper. Hoping for a note, some hint, he turned it over. It was a gasoline receipt, signed by John Barsoti.

Not Phil? John? How did John get Phil's truck?

He recalled the day in the meadow. I was lucky enough to have someone bash my truck, Phil laughed. I've got the insurance money. You've still got the Chevy.

Which one of them was it? John? Covering up a drug habit according to Parr.

Phil? John? How will I know? Can I go back up there and meet them not knowing? Can I pretend I've seen nothing? Can I even look at them without letting go and . . .

Douglas passed his hand with the receipt over his face. "I have to meet them. I have to get them to give me some hint of which one it is. Some hint, anything.

*   *

In the eerie after-light of sunset, Douglas and David greeted John at the planned rendezvous point. John was late. The spring warmth had turned so cold that every breath hung in the air. Douglas had become ominously silent. Bronwen had been exposed to the elements for over thirty hours.

David, believing he understood Douglas's worry, asked the necessary questions. "John, you're late. Where's Phil? What did you come up with?"

"Not a thing. Lots of animal sign. I got side-tracked by the smell of smoke, but I couldn't find the source. Phil and I met at the section line, but I don't know why he isn't here. Maybe he ran into something in that last quarter mile."

"Let's give him the fifteen minutes we agreed on before we look for him," suggested David.

Douglas's hands were in his pockets as he approached John. "You been out recently, checking on that anthrax rumor, John?"

"I was, before I left to campaign in eastern Oregon."

"You remember using this filling station up at Harrisburg?" Douglas pulled out the sales receipt and shoved it in front of John.

John glanced at Douglas's steel eyes before he looked at the paper. "Harrisburg is off my beaten path. Those are mostly ryegrass farmers up that way, and few sheep."

"Not all," said Douglas. "Close to the river, a few still grow mint and run sheep on the fallow fields. Look at the date."

"What's going on, Doug? Where'd you find this thing?"

Douglas's voice was rough with controlled anger. "Just look at the date and tell me where you were."

John took a close look this time. "That's my signature, but on that day, I was in Pendleton."

"And somebody can vouch for. . ."

"About six hundred democrats will vouch for me," John's face went red with indignation. "My speech put a few to sleep, but not all! What's gotten into you? Decided to take Parr's word over mine?"

David stepped between the two of them. "Whoa up, guys. Right now, we got important things to do." He glanced at Douglas. "Can't this wait till we find your . . . uhm, your sheep?"

"It may have a lot to do with finding my sheep. John, have you used this gas station in Harrisburg, lately?"

"Not on that date, but I've used it, yeah."

"And do you normally use plastic to pay for gas?"

"Not when I can help it, but sometimes I'm stuck with no cash." Douglas turned away, his shoulders heavy with tired anxiety. He scanned the section from which Phil would emerge. John wasn't going to let Douglas's suspicions go that easily. He grabbed Douglas by the arm. "You better tell me what this is all about. I don't like being accused in silence, and with no hope of a jury."

"I can't tell you," said Douglas, removing his arm. "For the safety of others, I have to keep my thoughts to myself for now." He looked at John with a mixture of resignation and apology. "I hope we won't need a jury to settle this."

"Damn you!" John hissed, then, deflated, he whispered, "Damn this whole business."

Douglas glanced at John, frowned and looked at his watch again. "What's keeping him?" He paced up the road toward Phil's quadrant, watching.

John pursed his lips in concern for his silent friend. He spoke in a low tone to David, "I don't know what he thinks I did."

David shrugged, "He's got a lot of reasons to be wary of all of us. Let's just hang in there for a while, until he figures out what's going down."

"If something's going on, he'd be a lot better off telling us and getting help." said John.

"If he knew which of us to tell."

That silenced John for a moment, but only a moment. "Heck! If these rustlers are after the rest of MacGregor's Blackwatch, we'd be better off setting a good trap – bait it with something they can't resist. Why are we scouring the woods for sheep instead of enticing the rustlers out into the open?"

David was stumped. Under ordinary circumstances, he would have told John that they searched for Bronwen Llewellyn. For Douglas's sake, he had to respect the request for secrecy.

So, he tried another tack. "John, Doug's a logical man. He must have some reason for extra concern. Let's just do it his way, today."

"I'll give it my best, but I think we're more likely to catch them with bait than by stalking them."

David looked up at the sound of snapping branches. "Here comes Phil. Where you been?"

Phil slapped his arms together to keep warm. "I got hung up in a boggy area. Thought maybe the mud would yield some track." He glanced around, "Is Douglas late, too? Did he go in after me? We better find him. Which way did he go?"

David said, "He's just pacing the road." David whistled and soon Douglas was back in sight, striding toward them, his face strained with worry. Phil smiled and reported nothing unusual in his area of Turkey Vulture Mountain.

"Your old Ford," said Douglas. "Where is it?"

Phil looked surprised. "That old thing? It's in the junk yard, I bet. The insurance agent from the Sheep Ranchers Association limped away with it ten years ago. You know him, don't you John? Isn't he the guy that's running your campaign?"

*   *

Bronwen lay unconscious in the tent, unaware that Ralph and Dick had taken their trucks out of camp late in the afternoon. The two men drove around the most northern mountain on the Smith Ranch, turned south on an old macadamized road and came to rest, well after dark on a logging spur in the property of John Barsoti to the south of MacGregor's barn. It was a hundred yards across the marsh to MacGregor's barn, a half mile if you had to skirt the marsh.

In the dark, Ralph and Dick acted like a team for the first time that day, taking rolls of old carpet out of the truck and spreading them across the marsh, then returning for another roll until they were within the thirty dry feet behind the barn.

Inside the barn, David slept while Olin Thompson took the first watch. The Blackwatch ewes were restless tonight.

"Getting ready to drop their lambs," Olin thought.

He heard snuffling near the back door to the barn, the door near the marsh. He got up to investigate the sound. It sounded like a dog. Olin thought perhaps Mr. MacGregor's lame Robbie had gotten out of the house. Robbie wouldn't be safe if the thieves came, Olin figured as he opened the door and looked out into the dark, cold night.

*   *

Here's where it starts, MacGregor. I don't touch a thing tonight, yet all is lost – your friends, your woman, the Blackwatch, tomorrow your freedom and then your ranch. I'll take everything you're proud of – smash it to pulp, and when you get out of jail, I'll hunt you down, just like I did her. She was too good for me, but in the end, she begged.

You're gonna beg too. All her fine pride was in the dust, in the dust where I left her.

*   *

In the tent, Bronwen worked to rouse herself. Dark. No human sound in the camp . . . only the crackle of a dying fire.

They are gone. My chance. They will come back and take me. I have to get up. But first, I must be able to breathe.

Bronwen worked her tongue behind the rags, pushing forward over and over. Each thrust gained her a little more space at the back of her mouth. The rags couldn't come out because of the scarf Phil had tied around her face.

Moving her head back and forth to loosen the scarf, Bronwen grew sure she was tightening the knot. She could feel it dig into the base of her skull. She tried rubbing her face along the floor of the tent to pull the rag down, but the pain from her head wound grew so great she feared she would pass out. She had to have her hands in front of her for this job.

Bronwen hadn't practiced gymnastics since high school, but she'd once been able to step through her clasped hands and step back out again. This wasn't quite the same. Her hands were tied together at the wrists, giving her a lot less slack, but she had to try. Wishing that women were built more like men, she lay on her side, pushing her hips toward her wrists and then into the space between her arms.

Her head throbbed. Her arms ached, but the prospect of facing Phil again tonight made her continue her efforts long past pain and into numbness.

Agonizing moments later, her hands were behind her knees. Little by little, she worked to pull each leg through until her heels rested on her wrists. With a final thrust, her right heel pushed her wrists away from her shoulders. Her left foot popped out of the circle of her arms. She heard the muscles in her right shoulder tear but could no longer distinguish new pain from old. She pulled the other foot through her hands and lay back sweating.

Steam rising from her body was a presage of colder body temperatures. She recognized the danger of dying from exposure just as Ben had done. Still, she had to escape the tent and hope for rescue before the night air killed her.

She pulled her numbed hands toward her mouth and yanked down the scarf. At last she was able to spit out the rags and breathe. For several minutes, she filled her lungs with dangerously cold, but sweet-smelling air.

Without opening her eyes, she pulled her feet toward her, tried to open her cold, cramped hands to untie her feet but found the tight knots were going to take too much time. She would work on that after she was out and in hiding.

She pushed on the floor to raise her body to all fours. Once up, she had to hold very still to stop the spinning of her world.

At last, she moved toward the tent door on her knees, steadying herself with her head, like a tripod.

She thought of one of Ben's crazy models where the first floor was very narrow (`More room for gardens' he'd laughed) and the succeeding floors wider.

She was afraid that she would topple as the model had always done.

Bronwen opened her eyes to the flashing patterns of pain from her head wound. In a numbed fog, she searched for the door zipper. Her fingers could grip nothing, so she pressed the zipper between her palms, and pulled up.

The fabric came up with the zipper. No resistance. She let it back down and moved close enough to get one knee on the bottom of the door fabric. The zipper slipped from her palms. Grabbing it again took a nightmare's effort. Her head . . .

"Do it!" she ordered herself. "No feeling! Just do!"

Over many false starts, the zipper rose one foot. She dropped to her side and began to push herself out. Her head met a rock just outside the front. She pushed past it, beyond thought, only doing. Cold was complete in her. The outside added wet to cold.

How many rolls from the tent to the cliff? Five or seven, and then crawl to the shrubs. No, no! brush your tracks over the edge of the cliff. Make it look like you went over. Then crawl. Where is a branch of pine? How did I use that? The blanket. I'll use the blanket.

Roll! Roll! Roll!

Am I straight?

Four. Five.

Am I going the right way? Six. Seven.

Open your hands! Dig in feet! Stop! Stop! Don't move. My head – stop my head.

She pushed up and fell back to a spinning universe. The spinning slowed, she could make out the edge of the cliff.

Oh, God, so close!

She could move again. She pushed rocks and dirt over the edge. The shackles and ropes cut into her skin with every motion, but she was beyond feeling. It was too important to convince Ralph that she'd rolled off the cliff. She hoped in the dark it looked believable.

Bronwen pulled the blanket after her as she backed with an awkward crawl toward the Oregon grape and huckleberries in which she had hidden two afternoons before. She found them, but was afraid to stop, so continued feeling her way with her feet, crawling another thirty feet into the thickest part of the undergrowth. She came up against a small pine tree, lay down on its years of dropped needles, pulled the blanket as much as she could over the ball of her curled-up body and listened for their return.

The shivering of her whole body became uncontrollable. Her shoulders ached from the muscle tear and from ceaseless motion. Now that she needed to be quiet, she realized how little her body had been still for twenty-four hours. She tried to control the motion of her body in its attempts to keep warm. Anyone in the camp would be able to hear the sound of her teeth.

She turned her face away from the camp. A horror took hold of her spine as she saw the looming shadow of an enormous ram. His eyes flashed in the low light of the campfire. She knew he was looking at her. A marble stiffness replaced her shivering. She kept her gaze on him as he swung his head from side to side, in ever widening arcs. Their eyes locked. Back and forth, back and forth. He grew larger with each swing.

She was Roy, with a gaping neck, fixing the ram with his eye. "Go way to me. Turn him. Turn him."

Her spinning head took over her mind as she relaxed. She was falling over the cliff – off a bridge.

Ben smiled at her. "Come, Bron. I'll take you where I am warm. Always warm. Let go and become warm, again."

She opened her eyes. "I can't, now. I have to listen for them. They'll have Douglas's sheep. I want to stay . . ."

"Come, Bronwen."

"No, Ben. I want to stay . . . to warn Douglas."

*   *

In the house, Frank sat, staring at his dinner. Phil and John had returned home for a few hours after a futile day of searching. David stayed in the barn with Olin Thompson for the night. Douglas remained outside, looking for George. Phil's mother slept in Margaret's bed. Frank and Margaret were silent.

A knock on the door aroused Frank's attention. A faint glimmer of hope lit his eyes. Margaret opened the door to her son.

Beside Douglas, George Conall entered, his gnarled hands creasing his hat back and forth. "'Scuse me, ma'am." he said to Margaret. "Young Douglas and I need to talk to you."

"Of course," said Margaret, "Come in, George."

He placed his hat on the table and sat across from Douglas, who lay a worn map of the ranch on the kitchen table.

"Lad, forget findin' out who the Judas is," George broke in. "Instead, think like the thief and find a spot on your land where he can stay well hidden, graze sheep and bring a truck in and out without being seen – a small meadow, a logged over area with an access road, even an old one."

Douglas spread the tattered paper on the table, pushing aside the plates and silverware.

"This place," said George, pulling the map to him, "would have to be well away from the road or on a slope which faces away from the road."

All four of them bent over the map, Frank and Margaret adding to George and Douglas's memory of the places which had been harvested in their timber holdings. They marked each on the map.

Two of them fit the characteristics that George was looking for, Twinberry Lake and Grant's Camp.

Frank leaned into the light. "There are other logged-over areas on the ranch your father bought from Kenneth Smith. When you were a toddler, before George came from Scotland, I helped your father and Kenneth log up here at Madrone Bluff. That was over thirty years ago and here at Turkey Vulture Mountain the year after that. Both of those places are within that eight miles you scouted today, and they can't be seen from the road. We had to walk to the edge of the cliff at Turkey Vulture Mountain to see the road and it was so far below us that we couldn't hear log trucks on it if we were sawing."

"Okay, that's four possibilities," said Douglas. "Let's look at the access."

Frank took the map and began studying it. He penciled in the abandoned logging roads from each site to the north road.

Douglas began preparing to get in the truck as soon as they chose the most probable site. He lifted his pack and sleeping bag from near the wood stove, hoping they would stay warmed by the truck heater until he found Bronwen. He stopped by the back door, waiting.

Suddenly he remembered something. "Samson!"

"Who?" Frank asked.

"Samson, that wild ram – Bronwen guessed that something drove him south – made him jittery and angry. His habit is to roam around Turkey Vulture Mountain."

"That's it then!" George stood, folding the map into his pocket. He turned to Douglas. "Your lame Robbie knows Mrs. Llewellyn, doesn't he?"

"Yes, why?"

"We'll need him. With his nose, we won't be looking for a needle in a haystack."

"But . . .."

"A good dog would find her quick."

"I'll get him," said Margaret and started up the stairs.

"Listen!" shushed Douglas, opening the door. He knew that deep, slow bleating better than any other. "Blackwatch! Outside the barn!"

He turned off the porch lights and ran outside followed by George and Frank, with Margaret close behind.

They ran in the dark across the road, through the lower meadow toward the back of the barn. As they rounded the back corner, Douglas could see the last of his Blackwatch on the far side of the marsh. Two men and two dogs harried the sheep into two trucks.

"Damn, David! Where are you? Did you do this?" Even as he blamed David, Douglas was afraid for David's safety. He knew he'd rather be betrayed by David and Olin than find them dead in the barn.

*   *

Ralph swore when he heard the creak of the back door to the house. He and Dick cussed the dogs and sheep across the last of the carpeting path and into the trucks. Then they turned to fire at the pursuers.

Ralph's first shot caught Frank.

George and Douglas dropped down beside him. Douglas shouted, "Mother! Stop!"

Margaret hesitated as another bullet splintered the top of a fence post. "Go back. An Ambulance! Go back!" Douglas watched her turn slowly and begin to run. A bullet thumped into the pine to her right. Douglas leapt, knocking her to the ground. Sure that he'd knocked her out, he turned her over.

Her small fists pushed at his chest, "Get off me, boy! I've got to get an ambulance. Get off me, now. Mind me!"

Startled, he backed off, regained presence of mind enough to tell her to crawl until she reached the back gate and then he crawled back to Frank. Frank lay in pain, but conscious.

"George," whispered Douglas. "Get Frank to the house as soon as they stop shooting. I'm going after them. Those guys are a sure way to find Bronwen when they talk."

He ran in a low crouch behind scrub bushes at the edge of the marsh. After a few moments, he stood up to run across the open space as fast as he could. During the last eighth of a mile, Ralph's dogs became aware of his presence. They broke away from the thieves and ran at him. Dick, seeing what they were running for, raised his rifle. The faster dog leapt at Douglas' throat. Douglas was ready for him, hitting him in the ribs with a left upper-cut and chopping at his neck with his right forearm.

The dog fell aside, unconscious in the wet marsh.

The second dog leapt. Dick fired twice. The dog screamed in pain as the first bullet hit him. The second bullet seared into Douglas' head and he fell in the marsh between the two dogs.

The truck doors slammed and the engines roared to life.

CHAPTER THIRTY-SEVEN

The scream of sirens jolted Douglas awake. He felt cool marsh mud and scrawny arms strong enough to lift him onto a stretcher. A merciful unconsciousness protected him.

"He's lucky the dog jumped, ma'am. That shot would have killed him."

Margaret's reply seemed far away. "But the head wound. There's so much blood . . ."

"Head wounds bleed more'n they're worth. The very divil it'll hurt, but it just took the outside off his scalp on the way by – a lousy shot i' truth. That scrawny thief was all speed and no think."

Douglas recognized George's style. He managed to open a dry mouth and murmur something he could not, himself, understand.

When next he was aware of the world, he realized he was on the library couch. Margaret leaned over her son, "Douglas, the doctor is looking over Frank and David, right now. David was hit with a rifle butt. Olin took a nasty knock on the head too, but he's all right."

Douglas managed to push one word out. "Thanks."

Bronwen! The thieves escaped! I blew it – all speed and no think!

He turned his face into the rough cover of the couch and willed himself back into control of his body. By the time the paramedics arrived, he was sitting up, his head in his hands, talking to George about going out in search of Bronwen.

Outside, Margaret walked next to the stretcher, holding Frank's hand as they trundled him into the waiting ambulance. The bullet sat dangerously close to an artery. Frank's voice grew weak. He whispered a stream of anxiety. "Margaret, they have to find Bronwen, now. The thieves have the sheep. There is nothing to keep them in this county or even in the state. This is a fight for her life. She's . . ."

Margaret held in check the despair they both felt. "Quiet, Frank. If no one else, I will go. I know this ranch like the back of my hand."

This thought agitated Frank even more. He tried to sit up. "No, Margaret. I can't lose you, too. Not now, when we've just begun."

"Hush, Frank. I'll work out something. I'll get the help of somebody big and fast. I'll take care of her. Frank, hush." She kissed his damp forehead and lingered over the pine needle and marsh flower smell of this gentle man. How could she have been so unaware of his love through all the years of his friendship with her husband? He was in deed a gentleman – too good to hint at anything other than friendly affection.

She turned her thoughts to his Bronwen. She knew Douglas's wound wouldn't stop him from searching for Bronwen. The guns worried her the most. Her heart stopped at the thought of how close Douglas had come to sharing the death of the luckless dog.

*   *

Near midnight, after the ambulance driver left, Margaret drove George, Douglas and the collie, Robbie, up the north road to the Turkey Vulture Mountain cut-off, four miles from the ranch. David and Olin were left guarding the house and recuperating from deep and debilitating blows to the head. David's wife, Angie, was on her way.

There had been a mysterious consultation between Douglas and David. Something, more than Samson's unexplained migrations, made them believe Turkey Vulture Mountain had been purposefully overlooked in yesterday's group search.

Margaret accepted Douglas's silence. He wouldn't discuss his suspicions with her, probably hoping that he was right and they would find Bronwen soon – yet hoping that he was wrong, and his friends guiltless.

But David had remembered that John and Phil had each arrived late at the four-mile check point – Phil a little later than John. Frank's clear memory of the Turkey Vulture Mountain logging area had placed it within the area those two should have covered just before that meeting. Samson's migrations plus the delay of both John and Phil during the search were the strongest clues that this might be where Bronwen was held captive.

*   *

Near midnight, Ralph and Dick pulled into the camp. Ralph hissed as he slammed the truck door. "Damn, Dick! You shouldn't have killed him. Now, they'll be after us for MacGregor's murder! We can't stay here any longer than to pack up the camp. Get on it!"

"We were already going to get it for kidnapping that dame!" Dick spat out. "What's the difference? Don't get so high and mighty on me – at least I stopped him. Shit, he was fast! We never would have seen him if the dogs hadn't been along."

"You shot the dog, too. My one good dog!"

"Your dog was in the way of my one good shot!"

"Shut up and get to the top of the hill. Get them other sheep into the truck from the pen back there. I got to get the dame in my truck."

*   *

Margaret parked the truck well beyond the entrance to the spur road.

With George following, Douglas pushed himself the half mile to the bluff where Frank had told them there'd be an animal path to the top. Douglas was glad for the bandages and the wool cap. He felt the need for something to hold his head together as he ran. It threatened to split apart at some invisible seam.

George had always been able to think like an animal. That talent, and Frank's vivid description, helped them find the animal path even in the blackness of night. George turned to Douglas, "This is where the dog comes in."

Before they could put Robbie down, a cloud of dirt hit the path in front of them. Rocks fell from the cliff top above. They crouched against the sheer wall and listened. On the path in front of them, they could see the light of a lantern and the dark shadow of a man whose anger rang out over the void.

"Damn! She rolled right over the cliff. That bitch had guts. How could she get out of the tent? She couldn't have untied those ropes."

Douglas felt a knot of impending grief tighten around his chest.

Another shadow appeared at the edge of the cliff, "That's two murders they'll get us for. She can't survive a fall like that, not in the shape we left her this evening. Let's get out before they trace us." Their voices grew fainter as the men moved away from the bluff.

George shook Douglas. "If she's down here, the dog can find her. There may be a chance."

"She's so afraid of falling," Douglas' whispered.

George took the dog from Douglas's arms and put him down on the rocky path. He let him sniff her towel that would give her scent.

The dog whined and nosed around the path. He stopped whining and broke for the top – a direction that took both George and Douglas by surprise. With his nose to the path and to the wall of the cliff, Robbie ran on his three good legs upward instead of down. Douglas ran twenty feet behind him.

Ralph and Dick argued too much to hear anything, laying blame and packing up.

Robbie entered the shrubs at the top of the cliff and stopped for a time, before the camp. Soon, he was back, jumping on Douglas, who stilled his agitation with a hand signal. The dog led him far into the shrubs, to the prone body of Bronwen.

Douglas fell to his knees beside her. He could feel the coldness of her through his jacket. He pulled her close to him and tried to untie the knots at her hands. He leaned into her feeling for her breath, her pulse. Robbie lay down, pushing close, warming her as Roy had done on the night Robbie was beaten.

George dropped down beside Bronwen, pulling off Douglas's pack and getting out the sleeping bag. He whispered, "Move away, so I can get her ropes."

Douglas leaned back and was surprised by the quick flash of a switch blade. In three deft cuts, the ropes fell away.

Douglas whispered. "Let's get her into the bag while we figure a way out of here."

George's whisper was harsh. "She needs your heat." George helped him pull the sleeping bag around them. Douglas rubbed her arms and back.

"Do whatever it takes to get her blood moving again," George said, taking off his cap. He put it on her head and pulled the bag close around Douglas' shoulders and Bronwen's head. "I'm going to check the place out," said George, "and see if I can make it hard to start the trucks. Warm her up!" He was gone into the dark.

Douglas rubbed Bronwen's arms and back, holding her close inside his jacket. Her cold crept into him, but he could not feel much change in her temperature. His hands kept moving over her, the exertion rewarming him until finally, he could feel the effect on her. She moved in his arms and mumbled something.

He renewed his efforts. She murmured, "Ben, please. Have to stay. Danger . . . Douglas. . ."

He kept warming her while his throat constricted and the cry in his mind exploded. "Don't die like this! Stay for me!"

She pushed into his body, warming her wounded wrists and hands at his chest. She seemed to come to, a little. He bent down to whisper encouragement. "Bron, live! Work at it Bronwen. Frank wants you with him. Think about Frank."

She turned her head up toward his face. "Douglas. Samson."

"What do you mean?"

"Samson – sheep attracted him." She lost her voice and fell still again after the effort.

He looked around him. In the dark, he sensed the glaring eyes he knew so well. The ram stood statue still.

Bronwen made a last effort, "Go way to me, Robbie. Go way. Turn Samson."

He tried to make sense of her weak whisper. Then her thought came to him. Use Robbie and Samson to create havoc – a diversion. "You clever girl!" he whispered. "God, let her live!"

His hands continued to warm her. He kept an eye on the still form of Samson and watched what little he could see of the thieves from his prone position in the trees.

Neither John nor Phil was with them. Thank God! His friends must have missed this place during yesterday's search. Or, perhaps the camp wasn't here then. Douglas felt a pang of guilt for his suspicions of them. He should have known how easy it was to suspect others. He owed both an apology when all this was over – when Bronwen was well again . . .

George returned with two rifles and two sets of keys from the rustler's trucks. "They won't be going anywhere. And there'll be no more potshots unless they carry side arms. The problem now, is to get by them, carrying her. I'd sure like to get those sheep back at the same time."

"Bronwen has given me an idea," said Douglas.

"She's talking?"

"A little. Look behind me at the shadow of the big wild ram." George's eyes grew wide. "Whoa! The Lincoln!"

"The dog could convince him to go. We have to help Robbie create enough chaos for us to get down the trail."

"Yup. Let's do it now. You get out o' there and carry her. I'll cover our tails and pick up old Robbie."

When Douglas had Bronwen in the sleeping bag and in his arms, he stood up and spoke to the dog. "Go way to me, Robbie"

Robbie leapt up and went to the ram, circling the heavy head.

George snarled low in his throat. The ram wheeled away from the humans.

Robbie darted to the ram's right and wheeled him toward the camp.

He snapped at the heels and the ram kicked out.

Douglas was afraid for a moment that Samson would turn and attack Robbie, but George growled once more, and the big animal moved into the camp.

Robbie followed Douglas' quiet directions. He took the ram past the trucks and into the camp so fast that Ralph was not aware of him until Samson knocked over the old camp stool.

Dick poked his head out of the tent, saw the animal coming at him and dove out the door to the right, yelling, "Ralph, get him off me!"

Douglas whistled Robbie back and started for the path. "Wait!" George took his arm. "Look at what's happening."

The ram was angry at being forced into the open by the dog. Samson took his temper out on the tent and then attacked Dick. His big nose shoved under Dick's prone body and threw him ten feet down the slope toward Ralph. Ralph grabbed at Dick's arm and pulled him scrambling toward the path down the cliff, the ram chasing them.

George handed Douglas the keys. "Get her in their first truck. Do you know where this old logging spur joins the main one?"

"Yes," Douglas said, running for the truck. "Frank drew it on the map."

George called after him, "I've got a score to settle with these guys." Douglas shook his head, but George pushed him. "I've two good arms now and two good rifles. Take Mrs. Llewellyn quickly."

Douglas knew George could handle the situation and Bronwen was in grave danger. He ran to the truck that had no dogs, and lay Bronwen in the sleeping bag on the right seat close to the heater vent. Keeping an arm over her, he started down the old road. The lights of the truck were dim and miss-aimed, barely showing him the turns. Straining his eyes made him aware again of his head wound. His whole body cried out for the rest he'd missed while searching for her, but anger and fear drove him on.

The logging road joined the main north road after two miles.

Another hundred yards brought him to Margaret. She saw what was happening at once, climbed out of his truck and into the rustlers' to hold Bronwen while he sped home.

"Where's George?"

"He's guarding the rustlers with Robbie. They left the keys and their firearms in the trucks, so George has them. See if the heater works, Mother. She's dy... she's in the late stages of hypothermia."

His mother tried the heater dials, unsuccessfully and soon turned to kneading Bronwen's arms and back. "When we get home, take her upstairs, Douglas, and get these wet clothes off of her. I'll fix hot water bottles and call the hospital. Pray the helicopter is available. It took too long for the ambulance to come for Frank this evening."

Douglas handed her his phone. "Call now."

Douglas turned the truck through the last curve. In the dark, he could see several trucks and a sheriff's car parked across his road. A crowd of men milled around the yard and on the porch.

Margaret gaped, "Did you ask them to come help?"

"No. Just John and Phil were going to come back just before dawn. I'll have to stop out here and carry her the rest of the way. Call the hospital before we deal with them. She's so close!"

He jumped out of the truck, took Bronwen from his Mother's arms and then ran toward the house.

As he approached, the crowd closed ranks before him. He knew most of these women and men to be neighbor ranchers. He could see the anger and fear on their faces but knew no reason for it.

*   *

The crowd could see the dark anxiety and determination on his face. His long strides did not falter as he approached them. The pale woman in his arms puzzled them. They fell away before his power and stood back for his mother.

The MacGregors had been people they liked and the situation they found themselves in now, at once angered and mystified them. That Douglas MacGregor endangered them, most of his neighbors found difficult to believe. That Margaret MacGregor would countenance it, was impossible. Yet, the ewe had died of anthrax. They could tell that, even in the early light of dawn.

*   *

Douglas mounted the porch and was surprised to see David with his head bandaged. With him were Phil and John.

John explained, "David called me about this gathering."

David glanced at Margaret. "Angie called the hospital, too. Frank's operation went very well."

"Thanks, David."

Douglas was brusque. "Come into the kitchen with me, all three of you, please. I have to warm her up, then I want your help picking up the thieves."

One of the men in the crowd hollered, "MacGregor, you beat on that woman, too?"

Douglas's whole body jerked as if he'd been shot. Without turning around to face his accuser, he asked David stiffly. "Why?"

"They found a ewe on the hill. She was dead and they claim the symptoms are anthrax – a lot of bleeding and . . ."

Douglas jaw clamped tight and he started to push into the house. A hand grabbed at his shoulder from behind. "You don't think we're gonna just let you go hide in your house do ya?"

Douglas turned to glare at his accuser. "If you stop me, this woman will die from exposure. As soon as the ambulance has taken her, I will come out here and talk to you about any crime you think you can pin on me."

Phil said, "I'll stay out here and keep the crowd calm. You go on in."

Douglas glanced at him, wondering how he ever could have suspected him of kidnapping. "Thanks, Phil."

As they entered the house, Phil was saying, "Now neighbors, let's give MacGregor a chance to clear himself. We don't want to jump to conclusions just because the evidence is so . . ."

Alice closed the kitchen door behind them. When she saw the blue of Bronwen's lips, her eyes widened. "I'll have hot water for her right away, Douglas. I been keeping a warming brick in her bed, just in case."

"Good. Thanks." He carried her swiftly up the stairs to her room leaving the three men in the kitchen.

Margaret held up his phone and told those in the kitchen, "They're expecting the helicopter back at the hospital in a few minutes." She lit the oven as she talked. "They'll take her to Sacred Heart in Eugene. There's a special Hypothermia Unit there."

Margaret explained to Alice, "I'm going to heat sheet blankets to wrap her in. As soon as the hot water bottles are filled bring them to me."

David stopped pacing the kitchen and started up the steps talking to himself as much as to anyone, "He can't lose her now. She is the only one ever to get through to him . . ."

At the head of the stairs, he heard his friend's disjointed pleading.

Through the doorway to Janet's room, David could see Douglas's grieving fear as he pulled at her wet, muddy clothes.

David strode into Douglas's room, to find a robe and into the bathroom for towels. He returned to Bronwen's room. Douglas glared as he entered. "David!"

David ignored him and wrapped the towel around Bronwen's wet hair. "If you insist on doing everything alone, you'll lose her, forever. The faster we rid her of these wet clothes, the better."

Douglas nodded and tugged off her red blouse while David wrapped the robe around her. Their eyes met. David whispered, "May she live to cure you, my friend."

"Get my wool socks from the second drawer."

When Douglas had the socks on her feet, he said, "I'll care for her now. Help George at Turkey Vulture Mountain. Damn where is that helicopter? . . . David . . . Thanks."

David met Margaret on her way up with the hot water bottles and a cotton blanket.

CHAPTER THIRTY-EIGHT

A half hour later, after the helicopter and the medical team had taken Bronwen from him, Douglas lay back on the bed and let the emptiness come. His arms ached from his efforts to revive her. His body ached with the remembered feel of her coldness. She'd not said a word since he'd carried her to the truck. Fear gripped him and refused to let go.

But soon he'd have to deal with the men on the porch. He could hear their talk growing less controlled by the minute.

Before Margaret had left in the helicopter with Bronwen, she'd told him of the dead ewe the neighbors had found under the Big Leaf Maple. An anonymous caller had sent the sheriff and these ranchers to the exact spot, saying they should "get there before Douglas MacGregor has time to bury more of his sheep."

As soon as he learned of the accusation, Douglas realized he'd have to talk fast and convincingly to stay out of jail. The crowd, it seemed, believed the theft Douglas claimed, was his attempt to hide this fast spreading disease in his flocks. To each rancher, the mysterious caller had whispered, "Who knows where he's buried them all? He might even have hidden them on some other man's land."

Anthrax could ruin all the ranchers. Once it was in the soil, it threatened the land for generations, affecting the lungs of any mammal living on their ranches, including their families. They couldn't afford to ignore the dead ewe lying under his Maple.

Douglas's feet hit the floor, anger growing with every step. He stomped into his own room and grabbed a dry shirt and levis, dragged them on and stuffed his feet in his boots, ready to take on the restless crowd.

If Douglas hadn't made it a point to know all he could about the diseases of sheep, he would never have guessed how the anthrax symptoms had been produced. Someone had done a good job of setting him up for a fall. And if he hadn't found the rustler's camp and the healthy Blackwatch, it would look as if the rumored anthrax burials might be true.

In his anger, he remembered his father's thunderous voice quoting, "Save me from malignant men and liars!" He strode down the stairs, braced by the thought that someone, centuries before, had felt as he felt now.

Grabbing his wool coat, he spat out another ancient curse. "He's made a pit and dug it deep and he himself shall fall into the hole."

On the porch, he faced forty men and women in varying degrees of anger and fear. He looked each in the eye, acknowledging their long acquaintance and their right to be here. Surprisingly, Kenjiro Eguchi's father stood among them. Ken senior had not spoken to Douglas since just before he signed his strawberry farm over to Leonard Parr.

"Ken," Douglas nodded. Ken Eguchi gave him a nod and a small smile of support.

Douglas turned to the larger crowd. "Thank you for waiting, neighbors. I had to take care of Mrs. Llewellyn."

Sheriff Crawley interrupted, "Has she got the anthrax, too?"

"Mrs. Llewellyn was missing in the forest for two days." Douglas tried to keep his voice even. "She was kidnapped by the same men who took my Blackwatch sheep. She's suffering from hypothermia."

His eyes had dark circles under them. His voice didn't seem to be the resonant voice they knew in him. Most of his neighbors were uneasy with what they had to do.

Yet, an insistent voice called out, "These guys that kidnapped Mrs. Llewellyn, they the same that took Kenjiro Eguchi right after he came to see you?"

Kenjiro's father stepped up on the porch. His voice grew deep and strong. "Douglas MacGregor helped my son. Thanks to him, my son is recovering from drug addiction and will soon be able to return to our home."

It took courage for Ken to speak publicly of his son in this way. "Thank you, Ken," Douglas whispered.

Ken turned toward him, his eyes bright with unshed tears. "I heard the rumors. You are a true godfather. I could not let them think you hurt Kenjiro."

Douglas nodded his thanks and turned toward the crowd again, searching for John and Phil. He couldn't see either, so assumed they had gone with David to Turkey Vulture Mountain.

"Is Arne Alverson among you?" asked Douglas.

"No"

"Then your caller knew enough not to call him. He's been out here helping me guard my sheep. He'd be able to tell you that there's been no anthrax. His right-hand man, Olin Thompson, has been knocked on the head last night when the thieves broke into the barn and stole the rest of my flock. Your caller didn't tell you that, did he?"

"Ian told us about that, but that still don't explain this dead sheep." said Crawley.

"Some of you probably know," said Douglas, "that anthrax can be injected into an animal to induce the disease." Douglas sat on the porch rail to ease the distance and tension between him and his neighbors. "The thief could inject one sheep, return it here to die and then call all of you with a rumor about the whole flock."

"That makes sense," said one of the ranchers. "Somebody could have given it only to this ewe."

"But," started Crawley, "who'd hate you so much as to do any such of a thing, MacGregor?"

"I've been asking myself that same question," Douglas said. "But out there where I found Mrs. Llewellyn, I found only two men. One works for Leonard Parr. The other, I don't know at all. They were hidden in an area of the old Smith property that I haven't seen for a long time."

"MacGregor," called out Tom Broughton, another rancher, "if you've found your sheep and this Mrs. Llewellyn in the same place, can we see the sheep?"

"I've recovered half of the flock in that old truck. The other half are in a second truck, still out there. I have no dog, at the moment, so you'll have to help me turn these into the barn pens."

"Ya got no dogs?" said Gerald Crawley. "Are they sick with hyper-thermal or anthrax?"

Douglas held his tired anger in check. Gerald's insistence on the anthrax required unusual energy. Douglas wondered how Gerald might fit into the whole system of sheep rustling.

"Gerald," said Douglas, "One dog is out with my crofter, George Conall, helping keep track of the thieves until David can bring them in. My dog, Roy, was killed by the thieves."

Gerald shut up. The other ranchers shied away from him, disassociating themselves from his harping. Douglas noticed the crowd's reaction to Crawley and breathed a little easier. At that point, Alice stepped out with the coffee.

A few minutes later, all could see that despite their night in the truck, the sheep were in good health. The men began to disperse, offering their help and their apologies as Ian cared for the ewes and Douglas gathered the oil and matches to burn the anthraxed ewe's carcass.

As Crawley began to slink off, Douglas called to him. Head down, Crawley turned back.

"Sheriff, who called you about this little party?" Douglas asked.

"No call. Phil come in the office and told me he'd heard the neighbors was perty mad at you. I thought I ought to come see it didn't get out o' hand." Crawley twisted his hat brim and hitched up his low slung levis.

Douglas scalp tightened as it always did when an ugly thought slipped up on him. He let the thought batter his heart for a moment before he turned it over to his mind. As they faced each other, Douglas stood as still as stone. Crawley itched to move away, but seemed rooted to the spot, watching the changes of mood register in Douglas's face. Finally, Douglas broke the silence with questions.

"Why is Parr's man Ralph out of jail?"

"Out of jail? Why shouldn't he be? He was only arrested on a drunk and disorderly charge."

"That's what Phil arrested him for?"

"Drunk and disorderly – that Ralph Birch kin swear like a trapped polecat!"

"It was Phil who told you about the rumor of anthrax back last month?"

"Yup."

"It was Phil who took over the investigation of the thefts at the Sheep Ranchers Association when David left?"

"Well, sure."

"Was it Phil who pointed out to you the discrepancies in David's book keeping?"

"He saw David was spending a lot more than the others for travel."

"And Phil who told you he'd heard I had tax troubles and wanted the insurance money for the Blackwatch?" Douglas's voice was growing rougher.

Crawley stepped back as if threatened. "It made sense to me."

"Does Phil check in with you by car radio whenever he's out on the road?"

"Of course."

"But you can't tell if he's really where he says he is, can you?"

"Why wouldn't he be?"

"Do you ever wonder? Do you ever call anybody in these little towns where he says he's busting up fights or checking out possible burglaries?"

"Course not!"

Douglas's voice exuded pure ice. "You should. You should get off your backside and do your job. Where's Phil now?"

"He said he was going to check out the place where you found Mrs. Llewellyn – See if there was any clues as to what happened there."

"He left before David?"

"Before David and John," said Crawley.

"Damn, Crawley. Didn't you even ask yourself how he knew where to go?"

"No. That is . . . I figured . . ."

Douglas already reached inside his back door for his rifle. "Where you goin'?" whined Crawley.

"I'm going to see if anybody's left alive."

"I'll come with ya. You never know. . . "

Douglas rounded on him. "I do know. I know you should clear out your desk. I know you should find yourself a job that requires sitting down. And I know I don't want you with me when I'm trying to rescue the people who trusted me."

Crawley scowled and stomped off toward his flashy car.

As Douglas swung off the back porch, Alice ran out with a phoned message from Margaret. She'd written it verbatim.

"Son, Bronwen is frightened for you – roused herself to warn me. She said `Phil Smith' several times. 'Watch out for Phil Smith.' She said something like 'Helen's not crazy, Phil is.' She whispered "anthrax" several times."

Douglas' heart filled with dread. "Alice, did Mother say how Bron is doing?"

"She said they're working on her body temperature. The doc said it was a good sign that she could talk even this much."

He jerked his head up toward the mountains. "I'm going back to Turkey Vulture Mountain. Would you call the state police and tell them how to get there. I've got to get to David and John before Phil does something drastic. They're out there with him! And he's gone off it this time."

"I'll take care of it. You be careful, young Douglas."

Douglas nodded grimly, stuffed the note into his pocket and hollered for Ian to burn the carcass of the diseased ewe for him. He climbed into the thieves' truck and tore off down the north road toward the mess he'd created by wanting to trust Phil Smith as much as Crawley did.

*   *

The spring warmth pushed higher into the mountains, aided by a south wind. The peach of sunrise warmed the purple-gray clouds as they uncurled toward the north.

Douglas saw the fair signs of spring that were too late to warm Bronwen. He watched for signs of David's truck, but came across Phil's new red truck at the logging spur near the animal path he and George had used last night. He couldn't approach the camp this way – too exposed and too easy to pick him off as he climbed. Douglas got out and ran to the truck. Phil's cab was still warm. The gun rack was empty.

Back in the Chevy, Douglas drove at breakneck speed past his mother's car and up the rutted back road which approached the thieves' camp from the east. His mind raced faster than his truck.

Helen Smith has not been confused. She's been lied to. He's used her to throw us off – going to visit her, but coming up here instead, telling her he was working, but hanging around my home, waiting.

David's truck stood in the road, stuck in the mud, half-way up the east logging spur. No one seemed to be in it. It, too, was warm. David didn't habitually carry a rifle, only his deputy sheriff's revolver. Douglas couldn't remember if John had brought one or not, but he often had a rifle when he went into the woods.

Douglas left his truck and ran toward the camp.

It had been two hours since he'd left George here with the dog, two rifles, one ram and a switch blade knife.

Douglas kept to the pine trees as much as he could. There wasn't much undergrowth to hide in. He ran away from the road, about twenty feet uphill, before he turned toward the rustlers' camp.

He came upon the camp from the east. Below him, he could see the second truck. Inside the vehicle's metal sides, he could hear Blackwatch sheep. The body of Ralph hung out of the cab on the driver's side. His wound was minutes old.

Douglas crouched down near a pine and listened. He scanned the hillside below him for signs of any motion. It took him a long time to spot George and the younger thief, prone in the winter dry grass just downhill and to his right. George held a rifle at the ready in his right hand. He protected the young punk from Phil and at the same time protected himself from the punk. Douglas wished he had brought a rope to toss to George. If he didn't have the young rustler to guard, George could be a help.

George motioned to Douglas to stay down. Robbie lay down, not ten feet from George, wagging his tail at Douglas's approach but minding the old man's whispered, "Stay".

Where are David and John?

Where's Phil?

As the actors in the scene waited their cue, Douglas went over in his mind all the signs in his relationship with Phil. He should have picked up on the hints. As soon as Phil came back from San Francisco without Linda, Douglas had known there'd been a change for the worse in him.

He wouldn't look me in the eye – wouldn't talk to me.

The slight shift of the wind brought Douglas' mind back to the present, alert for any sound that would give away the location of his quarry.

Or of Phil's victims.

David! Why did Phil need that money from David's travel funds?

Did he owe Crawley? Or someone else?

Constantly, Phil had compared his life with Douglas's. Even from his wheelchair, Douglas's father taught boys the skills they needed for life.

Phil's father had drunk away most of the time he could have spent with his son.

Every sign of friendship and every proffer of help had been stored as a source of resentment. And when seductively helpless Linda had turned to Phil with her insatiable need, she had provided a focus for festering hate.

Sitting still and listening was Douglas's best protection. For fifteen minutes, nothing moved except the rising sun and the skudding pink and gray clouds.

The rising sun helped him at last. It flashed on a rifle barrel near the top of the rise, on the far side of the camp. The barrel's light led his eyes to the thinning hair atop Phil's head. Douglas dropped down the hillside below Phil's sight line. He ran around the back side of the hill, keeping to the trees at the edge of the logged meadow. He skirted the temporary pen where his sheep had been kept and slowed to position himself downhill behind Phil.

He didn't know yet where David and John were. He didn't want to start anything until he did know. The other thing he couldn't bring himself to do was to shoot Phil in the back. He moved uphill until he had Phil well within range of his charge.

At that moment, Phil stood and pumped shots into the truck full of sheep. Douglas lunged, tackling him around the legs. The rifle fired once more as Douglas knocked it from his hands. It lay a few feet from Phil. Phil turned to fight him off. "Damn you MacGregor!" He kicked at Douglas' chest and hit out at him.

Douglas recovered his breath and scrambled uphill again. On higher ground, Phil had the advantage. He struck out with his foot, catching Douglas in the ribs. As Douglas fell to the side, he grabbed at Phil's outstretched leg. But Phil twisted away and came up with his rifle cocked.

Douglas looked at the barrel of a Remington 700, enough power to put a very big hole in Douglas's chest.

"Thought that'd make you sit still, MacGregor."

"Where'd you get that thing, Phil?" Douglas asked as calmly as possible.

"It's a little souvenir of Crawley's days in munitions supply. Don't ask me how he smuggled it back home from that little banana state you two were in. Once it turned up missing, he could hardly ask the government to help him find a gun he wasn't supposed to have, now could he?"

"That what you used to shoot George?"

"Sure."

Douglas hoped to keep Phil talking long enough for George to show up, or maybe David and John were still alive. "I figured you had to have something very high powered to shoot him with such accuracy from so far across the draw."

"Ian's Draw. Your old man always named places after the nothingest people. Why'd he name that little valley after such a stupid old man?"

"Ian was always a good friend to my father. Truthful, and loyal . . ."

"And carried your useless old man whenever the wheelchair got stuck."

Douglas's vision of his father was very different from Phil's, but he held in his heart the image of Ian carrying his father on his back so that they could fish together in Ian's favorite stream.

Douglas continued to talk to Phil and to stall. "That trap and the shepherd's crook – that was pretty clever. The trap almost got Mrs. Llewellyn. And after the crook, I became convinced John did it all. I just couldn't figure out why."

"You heard it from Parr. Old Johnny boy has a drug problem. I got him trapped now too and when they find everybody, it's gonna look like John shot you all. Parr gave me a little something to needle into John before I kill him. The whole state's gonna know that the man who wanted to be senator was a crazy druggie."

Douglas felt the sweat break out on his palms. Phil talked as if John were still alive. He hadn't mentioned David. "Who else have you got trapped, Phil?'

"Why your old buddy David, the embezzler."

"You set David up too?"

"Why not. Discredit the great high school triumvirate – take you all down to size at last."

Douglas felt the adrenaline drain out of him. All he felt now was sadness in the face of Phil's long-term bitterness.

"We were a quartet, Phil."

Phil didn't seem to hear him. He just rambled on. "I didn't plan on the girl. She found us, so I had to take her, to shut her up. I didn't want her like I wanted Linda. It was just your sheep. I only wanted to take your sheep."

"Linda? Is that what all this was about? You blamed me for Linda?"

"She didn't want me to touch her, kept saying she was gonna come back to you, no matter what."

"She never came back, Phil. She lied to you about that – about everything."

"She never came back 'cause I wouldn't let her." Phil pulled a small plastic bag from his shirt pocket. Inside, a tress of white-blond hair lay curled.

Douglas looked at the hair and at the gleam of triumph in Phil's dark eyes. Waves of sickness washed over him. "Where is she, Phil?"

"Had to do it, finally. Had to stop hearin' her whimpering."

"Where?" Douglas whispered.

"In the Chico Canyon. It's hard digging in the Chico Canyon."

So, that's the hold Parr has over Phil. Douglas thought. That crooked tax assessor's from Chico.

"That tax assessor see you burying her? That why he's got a job here now – so he can bleed you for what he saw?"

"Can't bleed a dry vein. Nothing to bleed. He tried that for a while, then he went to Parr. Parr made sure he got the job here. The two of them're doing funny things all over the county. And they both try to bleed me."

"You mean they get you to do things to me?"

"That's not hard. I don't mind mussing with your life." Phil shifted his Remington. "'Course, I don't know what I'll do for entertainment after you're gone."

At that moment, just above the rise in the hill behind Phil, Douglas saw black and tan fur fluff in the wind. He looked at Phil's gun and hoped Phil hadn't noticed his glance toward Robbie. Phil had relaxed his grip on the rifle as he talked, but he was too far away for Douglas to reach in one motion.

"Well, Phil. What now?"

"Now, I kill you. You're weak, MacGregor. You had two chances to shoot me – one in Ian's Draw when you were sneaking up behind me. You coulda shot me in the back. Instead, you let me escape."

"I recognized something about you that day. In spite of your baseball cap and the big shirt, there was something familiar – the way you run, or something."

Douglas saw the collie move to Phil's left. All but Robbie's eyes and ears were below the hill. Douglas tensed for the dog's attack. "I didn't even know why I didn't shoot you that day," Douglas went on, "I didn't understand until today, when I had you cold and I still couldn't do it."

"You always were soft, MacGregor. That's why Linda got you to marry her. She didn't no more love you than . . ."

As if triggered by Linda's name, Robbie leapt at Phil's left arm. He snarled as he flew toward the startled man. The dog's forty pounds knocked the rifle out of his hands. Douglas dove for Phil's knees and toppled him into the rocky hillside. Both men rolled down the hill, sending small rocks careening toward the bluff.

Douglas' hold on Phil's foot was vise-like. As they struck ground, Douglas pulled Phil's leg under his arm pit. Phil's other foot struck out at his bandaged head, catching him on the right ear. Blinding light filled Douglas's vision and the roar of a vast crowd covered all other sound except the excited yap and snarl of the collie.

Only his grip on Phil's leg and the sharp stab of rocks in his chest helped him orient his body to the fight. He jammed his fist into the other man's stomach and felt, rather than heard, the crumpling of Phil's body. Douglas scrambled up onto his opponent while he had a temporary advantage. His legs straddled Phil's, pinning him in an awkward position.

And then, Phil glanced up at the rifle in George's hands. At that moment, Douglas knew they'd stopped all fight in the man. Douglas bent over to regain his breath as he held Phil's arms. His sight and hearing began to return while Robbie licked his face.

"Where's the kid, George?" he asked.

"Had to knock him out so as to help you, Lad. Won't be out long though and his shoelaces weren't much good for tying him up."

"Damn you," Phil whined. "Damn all of you."

Douglas felt his scalp pull tight. A cold dread possessed him. "Where are David and John?"

Phil's glance slid to the truck with the bullet holes in the side.

"Oh, God," Douglas grabbed up the high-powered rifle and, pulling Phil with him, stumbled toward the truck. The words of the ancient curse propelled him toward his worst fears.

"You've dug it deep . . ." He yanked at the door handle at the back of the truck. "Your mischief will recoil upon you and . . ."

The door fell open, letting in the sunlight.

"and violence shall fall upon your head" finished David, smiling out at him.

Relief flooded through Douglas as John also raised his big body from the truck floor.

"This," said John, looking at himself with disgust, "This is one kind of dirt I never want to hit again."

"Really, old buddy," said David, "You ought to breed a better smell of sheep." Both men smiled grimly at their attempts to make light of a close brush with death and insanity.

"Douglas," David went on, "he'd shot Ralph by the time we arrived. But we didn't see that until he opened up on us as well. We took to this place fast." John said, "He shot a couple of your lambing ewes who were next to me. If you'll work on one . . ."

George dumped the sullen kid at Phil's feet and hopped in the truck with one of the ewes before John finished his sentence. In a few minutes, he had a lamb out of her – healthy and angry. John, still dazed by his close call, moved a little slower. George helped him get the lamb out of the second dead ewe and then went back after the twin.

Sirens wailed as the state police drove up the road below the bluff.

When the cars screeched to a halt at the logging spur that led to this site, Douglas knew someone from the ranch must be with the police and had shown them the turn off. In his exhaustion and light-headedness, Douglas hoped they'd hurry. They would climb the animal path and take over the investigation.

For a moment, all four childhood friends were silent, each wondering what had brought them to this. Phil's sullen face was the same one they had known in boyhood, but his boyish shame had turned him into an angry, unbalanced man.

Could they have blocked the coming of this day with a word? a gesture before it came to this?

Or should they have faced the tough facts sooner?

*   *

"MacGregor! Where's my brother?" Ian Conall's bull head and shoulders appeared above the bluff as he climbed the path. Behind him were two state troopers and two of Eugene's finest, Captain Jules Wilson and Officer Boyce.

"Where's George?" demanded Ian. "I want to see George."

George popped out of the truck and ran to his brother. "I'm fine Ian. Don't fash yerself so – You'll not have to learn how to do your own cookin'. Not fer a long while yet."

Douglas watched the two old men embrace. Wearily, he handed Phil's rifle over to the state trooper. Through the fog of his head pain and unfocused eyes, he saw Officer Jules approaching him.

"MacGregor. I just came from the hospital with your mother. Frank Bauman is doing well. Mrs. Llewellyn is unconscious, but breathing on her own, so far."

Douglas sat down hard on the tail gate, closed his eyes and leaned his aching head into the nearest Blackface wool. "Thank God!"

A deep slow-bleating chorus surrounded him.

CHAPTER THIRTY-NINE

Bronwen awoke to a rhythmic "blip, hum, blip, hum" and the subdued whispers of a darkened hospital. She remembered hearing the repeated ringing of bells and the rush of stiff fabric into her room. There'd been anxiety in the faces of strangers who came into her view. She'd been able to see the blue-haze aura of florescent lights. She'd been able to hear the murmurs and the feet but could not make herself understand what they were trying to do.

At one crisis, Bronwen, freed of pain, floated above her bed. Her Self watched herself as seven people, inserted needles and tubes in her arms, monitored gauges, listened to her body's messages.

Now, in the "blip, hum" of her awareness, Bronwen tried to recapture the wonderful sensation of floating, but the drip-line in her arm, kept her firmly in bed.

At the end of her bed, on a wall, she saw two drawings, done by herself at age five. How could those be there?

She slept again.

* *

The sun enlivened the wall in front of her with the shadows of her own wires. Each time she opened her eyes, the shadows had moved further along, changing shape and clarity. At dusk, she awoke to see a freckled, smiling face under a froth of dark hair.

"Good afternoon, Mrs. Llewellyn. I'm glad you decided to stick with us."

Bronwen smiled at the lighthearted welcome back from death's threshold. Glancing at the I.V. she quipped, "It isn't so much that I stuck with you as that you tied me down."

The nurse quirked up one eyebrow, "Ah, a joke. Well, that's a good sign. We had to make you stay, you know. Mrs. MacGregor was adamant on that subject."

"Mrs. MacGregor? Is she here now?"

"I believe Mr. Bauman took her home to get some rest. Your husband has been here, but he had to go back to court – something about testifying about the murder."

"My husband?"

"He's fine. That head wound was painful, but not permanent."

"A head wound?"

"He's fine – kinda got battered up wrestling that Smith guy, but he'll be fine. Now lie back or you'll come unglued."

Bron lay back, thoroughly confused. Then she realized what the nurse had said. "What murder?"

"According to the morning papers, one of the sheep rustlers."

"And my . . . husband?"

"Oh, he saved everybody else."

Bronwen sank back into the pillows, "Better read me the reviews, blow by blow. I think I missed the whole last reel."

*   *

After hearing the Oregon Daily's jumbled version of what had happened, Bronwen, relieved that everyone was safe, slept and woke several times throughout the night. Each time, the hospital became quieter and the lights were more subdued. Twice she thought that the vision of Douglas standing in the doorway might be real. But when she tried to reach out to him, the vision disappeared, and the night seemed much darker.

Just before dawn she felt him sit on her bed and hold her hand. When he leaned down to kiss her, she tried to speak to him, but her body wouldn't allow her to respond. She felt his hands brush over her face and down her throat.

His kisses on her closed eyes and her mouth were of an airy softness.

He brushed her cheek bones and her temple with his gentle lips and rested his head next to hers on the pillow, his breath warming her ear as he whispered to himself, "Thank God!"

His thumb felt the soft thump of the pulse in her throat. "Oh, Bronwen, I need you."

He groaned, "Please! You have to fight this fever, Bron and come home to me soon. I can't . . ."

He sat up and caressed her hand. "I can't take Ben's place. I know that," he whispered harshly, "but I don't want to be without you."

She floated through a mist of the mind, reaching out for him, comforting him. Her mind, but not her inert body, held him.

He sat for minutes. At last he whispered, "I'll be back, Bron. I'm needed at Phil's hearing, but I'll be back."

He rose from her bed and left the room.

*   *

Douglas returned from the hearing, saddened by Phil's state and his unrelenting hate. He stood in the hall outside Bronwen's room, thinking about what Phil had told the detectives. Linda had said she wanted to come back to Douglas, and Phil couldn't let her do that, so he'd killed her in the desert.

Phil would never understand that Linda had been maneuvering Phil toward jealousy, toying with his emotions the way she had toyed with every man both during and after their marriage.

She'd never intended to do more than rouse Phil's anger. The result had been way more than she'd ever imagined, and for those days of fear that she had suffered, Douglas felt great remorse.

He steeled himself to put those images out of his mind and be present for Bronwen.

*   *

As he entered her room, he noticed two childish drawings taped on the wall at the foot of her bed. Thinking they were from David's kids, he stood in front of them to study them, putting both hands on the wall to be able to lean closer in the low light.

They were mirror images, facing each other. Each featured a blond man in a hospital bed with humans flying above. The drawings were of such detail that he could tell the pattern on the pajamas. The drawings showed great skill for a child.

In a very child-like lettering in blue crayon, the left one said "Fy nhad, mae yn engel yn ehedeg drosot ti."

The right said, "Daddy, the engel watches oer you."

At the bottom, in the same blue crayon, the left one said, "Yr wyf i yn hoffi yn eistedd yn yr ysbyty gennyt ti. Caru a ti, Bronwen, yr aderyn bach."

The right one said, "I want to bee with you in the yspital. I luve you, Sparrow".

Douglas leaned on the wall, hanging his head, overwhelmed with sadness for her. This, in the bed, was her father. Someone had kept these drawings for her and brought them down here. Ben's parents – her foster parents.

The angels watched over her.

He turned toward her silent self and stood by the chair next to her bed. She opened her eyes as if she felt his presence. She smiled and reached a hand for his.

"Bore da, f'ynghariad," she said.

He recognized those lovely words, laughed, and sat down to hold her hand.

"Your parents have been here, I see." He waved toward the drawings.

She smiled at them. "I thought I saw those in my sleep. I hope Mam and Da will come back to meet you."

An hour later, as she slept and he rested his aching head next to her hand, the door opened. He sat up. The small woman who walked in wore a plaid shirt and levis. The man was tall and sandy haired. Douglas knew in a moment that these were Ben's parents.

He stood, but Mrs. Llewellyn waved him down. Mr. Llewellyn extended his hand. He whispered, "Douglas MacGregor, I assume."

Douglas nodded.

The man waved to include his wife, "Evan and Mora Llewellyn." Mr. Llewellyn glanced at Bronwen, and then stepped to the other side of the bed, taking her other hand.

Her eyes flicked open. Mr. Llewellyn said, "Hello, Little Bird. Are you quite through with adventures?"

"I think," she whispered, "that I'm just starting on them." And then she turned her loving smile toward Douglas.

CHAPTER FORTY

The lights blazed at the MacGregor House. The fires in the living room and den crackled and the doors stood open to let in the spring air.

Douglas had brought Bronwen home from the hospital this morning so that she could help celebrate Frank and Margaret's marriage. The couple had been to the justice of the peace in Lane County on the day Bronwen came out of her long sleep.

In anticipation of the party, the house glowed with signs of warmth, good humor and happiness.

When she had arranged the last flowers and set them on the den mantel, Bronwen went upstairs to change her clothes. In the kitchen, chatting with George, Ian and John Barsoti, Douglas became aware of her footsteps above him.

She'd become his fiancée a week ago, at Sacred Heart Hospital, but this was their first day together and he grew impatient to be with her, to test their new understanding of each other.

He knew when she stepped into the shower. The sound of the water running up the pipes reminded him of the first time she'd showered in this house. She always had the power to distract him, even at distances like this.

He found himself thinking about going upstairs, greeting her as she came out, helping her put salve on her rope-burned wrists, aid her maneuver around the sling for her dislocated shoulder, watching her dress, maybe even . . . no, there were too many people already in this creaky house.

He tried to concentrate on the story John told about Eugene politics.

Sometime during the weeks of Bronwen's convalescence, Crawley had resigned as sheriff and bought a car dealership. The police had charged Parr with enough crimes to keep him in jail for a long time. Jules had also arrested the tax assessor. The state justice department now entered the cases, charging the two of them with fraud and illegal use of the assessor's office.

Phil's lawyer insisted that Phil plead insanity. Mrs. Smith now received an appointed legal guardian. She lived in a care home where she had friends and a garden to work.

Even better news came from Portland. Leonard Parr Senior had been appalled at the destruction his son had caused among the valley families. The poor man walked a fine line between supporting and condemning his son. He couldn't do much until after the trial finished, but he'd talked to Frank Bauman about ways to restore the land his son had extorted from Eguchi.

Of course, the land under Parr's administration building had been ruined, no longer good for strawberries, but Parr Senior intended to help Ken Eguchi find land equivalent to it. A good deal of Leonard's land and buildings would probably be used to pay reparations to the farmers he had ruined.

All this had happened with vague awareness on Douglas's part. Off and on, between calls from the hospital, he'd worked with the police investigators, in a concussion induced fog. Afterward, he'd had barely enough energy to convince the county auditor to look at certain things he was sure would show up in the sheriff's accounts.

And then he'd fallen asleep on a sofa in the hospital for twenty-four straight hours, before spending the next days at Bronwen's bedside.

During that first day, the auditor had cleared David and charged Phil with embezzling.

Bronwen had been coming in and out of consciousness. As a result, for the rest of the week, Douglas might as well have been in Ashtabula for all the attention he'd paid to anything besides Bronwen's recovery.

*   *

Today, Douglas welcomed all kinds of guests from Portland and the valley ranches who had come to celebrate Frank and Margaret Bauman, newlyweds. His sister Janet and her family arrived. Douglas and Jim, Janet's husband, to set up tables in the yard. Janet and the kids helped Bronwen decorate the house with flowers from the garden.

Evan and Mora Llewellyn arrived while Bronwen was upstairs, changing. They had known Frank all the time that Ben and Bronwen worked in his offices and had come to like Margaret very much during the weeks at the hospital.

Douglas heard Bronwen come out of the bathroom and skip into the bedroom. She didn't usually hurry from one room to another like that. Perhaps she remembered his arrival at the head of the stairs and . . .

He could feel those beautifully smooth shoulders beneath his fingers even now. And see her startled green eyes . . .

The sound of the doorbell took all indecision and temptation from him. He pushed away from the counter and went to the door to greet guests.

"David! Angie! I'm glad you're here."

David grasped Douglas with intensity. "Can't thank you enough for figuring out how Phil did it. I never would've connected the embezzling with Parr and the new tax assessor. Blackmailing Phil because of Linda's death seems to have been the first thing that California tax assessor did for Parr."

Angie kissed Douglas on the cheek. "David knew the embezzler had to be Phil, but he didn't want to believe it. He sure couldn't prove it. You've given him back his self-respect. Thanks."

Douglas put an arm around both of them and walked them into the living room. "David, you two-faced buzzard! You're always ragging on me for keeping problems to myself."

David laughed and then announced proudly, "As of yesterday, I'm a detective on the Eugene police force."

"That's great to know. You'll like Jules and Boyce. Good men," Douglas said.

David leaned toward Douglas and whispered, "Parr goes to court next month and the government thinks it has a pretty tight case, especially now that Roger Hargert and James Macklin will testify with Kenji Eguchi."

"That's great." Douglas beamed, "The boys and their folks will all be here for the party."

"And Lloyd Jones?" asked Angie, a twinkle in her eye. "He'll be pontificating as usual."

"He's a good lawyer," laughed David, "but somebody should grease his soap box."

"I'm just glad he's on our side," said Douglas. "He got Parr and Phil so tied up with confessing each other's sins that neither of them will get loose for a long time."

David shook his head. "Parr claims that encouraging Phil to harass you was all Phil's idea.

"Stop beating yourselves for Phil," Angie whispered. "Neither you nor Parr had any real control over Phil. He'd become controlled by his own jealousy and hate."

Douglas glanced around for the Brock children who were following. He knelt down, lifted little Sarah in his arms and spoke to her brother. "Johnny, I want to show you and Sarah the sheep before dark. Come on into the kitchen with me, then I'll run up and see if Aunt Bronwen is ready to go with us."

After introducing Angie and the kids to everyone in the kitchen, Douglas started up the steps two at a time. He rounded the corner of the first landing and looked up at the slender legs of his wife-to-be. She descended the stairs, clad in a dress the green of new fir needles.

"No sling?"

"Not for this afternoon."

Her skirt moved about her 'each way free'. He moved up the stairs, taking her in his arms as she came down.

"I thought you wore Osh-Koshes or corduroy," he whispered as his lips caressed her throat. "Oh, Bronwen! This is going to be a long party!" He moved his hands up to feel the smoothness of her back – a little surprised at just how smooth it was.

"Not even under this?"

"I don't own any. Does it bother you?"

"Me? Yes! No one else could tell. And with this neckline . . ."

He paused to run a finger around the scalloped edge. "With this neckline and your face, no one will be looking down long enough to figure it out."

She shivered under his light caress. "Whoa! When did you become so glib-tongued?"

His finger continued tracing across her collar bone, up over her shoulder and across her back. He stopped, his other hand playing with the buttons in the front of the dress.

A triumphant smile creased his face. "Lots of buttons, eh? I like this dress more and more."

She laughed and winked down at him, lowering her head to give him soft butterfly kisses. His hunger made him reach for more substantial fare, but she drew back. "That will have to hold us for the duration. I believe you left some friends in the kitchen whose children are now peeking around the corner."

He turned swiftly to see two smiling faces. To cover his embarrassment, he pulled Bronwen down to meet them. "Well, gang, this is Aunt Bronwen. She's ready to go out to the barn with us and see the sheep and lambs. Bronwen, I'd like you to meet my very good friends. Little John Brock, named for Uncle John Barsoti. And this is Sarah Brock."

John said, I'm John Douglas Brock, 'cause I got two uncles."

"I've heard good things about both of you from your Uncle Douglas," said Bronwen.

Little John reached out a hand to shake with her. Sarah reached out a hand to feel her skirt. Douglas lifted Sarah and little John held onto Bronwen's hand as they entered the kitchen.

Everyone in the room appeared to smother a laugh. David spoke for all, "We thought you might not reappear downstairs. I volunteered to go after you, but everybody else voted to send the kids."

Angie nudged David's ribs playfully. "The kids are more discreet than their daddy."

* *

When the new bride and groom arrived, Douglas felt pleased at the glow that happiness gave his mother. He hugged her tight and whispered in her ear.

"Mother, you are beautiful!"

"I feel beautiful. I didn't think I ever would again."

"You're always beautiful to me."

"Say it often and say it loud."

"Especially in front of Frank?"

"Good plan, son."

Just then, John Barsoti popped the champagne cork, lifted the bottle and toasted, "To Frank and Margaret Bauman. May they have many years, filled with happiness."

*   *

For the rest of the afternoon and evening, there were friends going back and forth through the kitchen to the barn for a look at the soft wool of the Blackwatch sheep, and to admire the additions to the barn, the new gardens and the pond with the ducks.

In the evening, Ole, Ian, George and Arne set up dominoes and chess games in the library and taught the children how to play. As Arne and George played the winning chess game, they suffered the advice of many kibitzers.

Douglas stood near the living room fireplace. His sister stood next to him, holding her youngest asleep in her arms.

"Great to see you happy, Brutha," she said. "She's a keeper. I'm so glad."

He looked at Janet and the little one. "She'll want you to bring the kids in winter. Christmas?"

Janet nodded, "Bron already showed me where they can sled from the pond clear to the old oak tree."

He smiled, remembering the creeper vine in Bronwen's hair. "She plans a danged great garden."

Janet faced him. "It is gorgeous. But, Doug, no more adventures, please. Mom doesn't need any more heartbreak."

"Nor do I, Janny. Nor do I."

Janet nodded, and allowed her five-year-old to tug her out to the barn. Doug stayed by the fire, greeting friends and enjoying the mix of farmers, weavers, sheep ranchers, city police, sheriff's staff, architects and landscapers that filled his home. He watched indulgently, loving all these people and a little amazed that a loner like him could be happy in such a crowd.

Of course, he wouldn't mind seeing them head for home, either. He wanted Bronwen very much this night.

*   *

Much later, Bronwen walked out to car with her parents. "Honey," Mora said, "He's a fine man. I'm very glad for you."

"I think we're doing the right thing, Mam. I do love him."

"And it's pretty obvious he cares deeply about you," Mora said.

Evan Llewellyn took her hand in his. "Little Sparrow, you loved Ben and he loved you. You made it all work – his quick, darting ideas needed your calming, safe port. You've got to be proud of the life you made with Ben, but now it's time to make this new life. It's different, maybe riskier with a man you haven't known all your life, but I like him. Go for it."

"Thank you, Dad." Bronwen hugged her parents goodnight.

*   *

By midnight, Douglas and Bronwen helped pack Margaret and Frank into a car for their drive to the historic Bed and Breakfast at nearby Coburg. Frank kissed Bronwen, whispered something that made her laugh, and he ducked into his car. He warmed the motor while Douglas talked to Margaret.

"Good night, Mother. When will we be seeing you two here again?"

"Oh, I don't know yet. We'll let you know before we come back for a visit. This is your home now – yours and Bronwen's. You be good to that young lady, son."

"Could I be otherwise? She has me in her spell!"

"Now, Douglas, Bronwen was a queen not a witch. And, if I remember my old tales, it was the jealousy of her husband that brought on her imprisonment and finally war. Let's have none of that."

Douglas raised his right hand and grinned at his mother. "Solemn word. None of that. Now off with you mother. It's late and this man is impatient to be with his woman."

"Which man?"

"Both."

"Good."

*   *

Bronwen waved Frank and Margaret around the last bend. As she retraced her steps up the hill toward him, Douglas' watchful eyes enjoyed the motion of her green silk. His thoughts came out, unbidden, `How sweetly flows that liquefaction of her clothes.'

She laughed and imitated his sensuous motion from days ago. "At least this time it is liquid." She put her arms up to his shoulders. His hands ran up her back in the motion they had started that afternoon on the stairwell. She was a little off balance. Her foot swung between his legs to catch herself. The contact cut through any reserves he might have had.

With a groan of long deferred desire, he lifted her in his arms and carried her up the veranda steps and into the living room. The fire still burned. He flipped off the lights as he entered, set her feet on the hearth rug and took the ribbon from her hair.

As Bronwen felt her hair fall, she looked up to see that the old gaunt darkness had taken over his face. She touched his cheek, bringing his faraway look back to her. Warmth again entered him, and joy.

A sigh escaped him as he kissed her. "Darling." He touched her lips with the gentleness of controlled desire.

"How can I ever get enough of you?" he moaned. "I want so much to taste you in small portions, but I can't help it. After all these nights, I'm afraid I'll devour you, all at once."

"We have time. Time will let us love slowly."

Settling her in the crook of one arm, he began studying the intricate, twisted closure at the top of her dress. A frown drew his dark brows together. "Now this is "Much Ado About Nothing"!"

His fingers began to fumble with the twisted threads – a task made difficult by her teasing retreat.

"I give up. Why do you always twist your shirt cuffs and your buttons so torturously?" He lowered his mouth to her collar bone and began kissing his way down to the button in spite of her squirming laughter.

When he arrived, he took its weakened thread in his teeth and bit it off. Suddenly, neither of them laughed. The button fell from his mouth.

His eyes followed the button's fall to the exposed half-moon of her breast. His gaze rested there as he whispered the line that echoed in his mind.

"Your love is more fragrant than wine, And your perfumes sweeter than any spices."

His voice caught.

She took up the song.

"Awake, north wind, and come, south wind; Blow upon my garden that its perfumes may pour forth, That my beloved may come to his garden

And enjoy its rare fruits."

Douglas's dark eyebrows relaxed. "My love."

"You needn't hide in the hills any longer," she whispered. "The garden is yours."

He bit his lip and looked away as if still afraid of his desire for her.

Bronwen began unbuttoning his shirt. She opened it and put her arm around him, massaging his muscles, while her other hand opened his belt.

He stopped her hand. "The last time you did this, I lost all restraint. I think this better be my job."

He removed his Levis and stood up enjoying the sensation of being watched by her. He felt his whole being grow taut with awareness of her gaze. The look of love he saw erased the last of his doubts.

Douglas stepped toward her and worked to unbutton the rest of her dress.

She stopped his suddenly fumbling hands and slipped the silk off for him, letting it drop around her bare feet.

He had known that her body was beautiful. But the night when he had taken her so quickly in the den, he'd been dimly aware of anything other than the sensation of touch. And after her rescue, when he believed she was dying in his arms, he remembered an icy beauty.

This woman before him became a revelation to all his senses. Her cream and rose skin promised warmth. The shadows of her curves invited exploration. As she moved toward him, he caught the scent of the wind through sun dried wheat. Her soft lips promised the taste of honey. Her sea green eyes drew him into their depths.

*   *

Douglas lifted her in his arms and lay her on the hearth rug. She reached out for him with an urgency akin to his own. Eagerly, he lay beside her, feeling the curves and planes of her and letting his kisses touch off sparks of fire in the childlike folds at her arms and in the small valley between the peaks of her breasts.

He touched her wrists where the rope burns began to disappear, and asked, "How is your shoulder? Do you want that sling?"

She laughed. "I just won't hug you as well with that arm. It's getting better."

"I'll steer clear of it."

His hands moved down her body until they met at the lace of her underwear. As his thumbs caressed just inside the barrier of the lace, her hips pushed toward him. He groaned, his body responding to the passion in her.

He pulled off the lace pants and returned to her, his fingers moving up her legs, his thumbs drawing a path up her soft inner thighs. Gently, he pushed her legs apart. His hands met at the golden hairs on the mound between her legs. His thumbs touched the most feminine part of her and began to stroke.

Her reaction came, immediate and startling. She grabbed at his arms and jerked back.

He stopped, looking at her in dismay. A dark thought crossed his mind and then he erased it in concern for her.

"Bronwen? I won't hurt you like that first time in the library."

"I don't fear you . . ." she whispered. "I just didn't know it could be like that, no one has ever touched me like . . ."

She drew in a sharp sob and turned away, realizing what she'd just revealed about Ben.

He was on his knees in an instant, holding her to his chest and rocking her as she wept. After a moment, he brushed her hair back from her ears and kissed her.

"Darling, he never hurt you on purpose, did he?"

"No! Never!"

"I thought not." He closed his eyes, understanding at last, just how impetuous Benjamin Llewellyn had been. She had loved Ben and given herself to him believing that the joy in marriage for her had been to satisfy his need. And now, she understood something it was too late to change. There could have been a different, more complete joy for both of them.

"It's all right, Bronwen. He loved you, very much."

"He wasn't selfish." She defended.

"I know, Bron. You were both children, with no experience outside of each other. You have grown from a girl into a woman since. He would have grown, too. He just didn't get the chance."

Douglas lay down. He spoke gently, reassuringly to her. "Bronwen, let me give you this pleasure. Let your mind trust me. I won't hurt you as I did that night."

Her voice broke through her confused emotions. "Douglas, that night it was my own tension that hurt me. I trust you. Talk to me."

He moved his hands over her again, talking about his love, his longing, his plans for their life.

She relaxed under the sound of his voice and the gentleness of his hands, her body responded with waves of sensations she had never felt. She was both afraid to let them happen to her and afraid to stop them. At last, she had no choice. Her body took over from her mind, accepting his gift without reservations while he whispered encouragement.

"Douglas," she whispered urgently, "Come to me."

She took him in. Her breathing stopped with the surprise of how much she needed this moment of joining. Never before had she felt the shared sensuousness of this act. This was their desire.

* *

A lovely eternity later, he lay next to her, exhausted with the joy of knowledge. She ran her fingers over his breasts. He turned on his side and mimicked the motions of her hands with his own until he felt her nipples respond. He bent to kiss them and then silently he caressed her, finally letting his hand rest on that muscle just above her knee, the place where he wanted to be, it seemed so long ago.

After a few moments, he trusted his voice again.

"Bronwen, I have much to teach you and much to learn from you."

Bron spoke softly, holding his gaze. "I'm here. I'll not leave your hearth, no matter how far into the hills you may want to go."

His voice was barely a tense whisper, "I won't be wanting to go into the hills without you, Bronwen. Sheep herding need not be done alone."

She smiled up at him. "I love the hills."

*   *

In the meadow of crocus flowers, the dark figure of the ram stood rigidly still, looking out over the valley. As the lights in the house blinked out, Samson snorted, raised his unblinking gaze to the ridge of hemlock and fir which protected his solitude. He turned slowly away from the human place.

ABOUT THE AUTHOR

Rae Richen is the author of adventures for adults and young adults, of romantic suspense and of the recent Glyn Jones and Grandma Willie mystery series. Join Rae Richen as we explore fear and power, greed and human need in short stories and novels, articles, interviews and essays.

Using family relationships and the backdrop of historical events, Rae Richen writes to bring focus to the themes that drive each of us.

The characters in these stories face a confusing world of hypocrisy with courageous honesty. The humor, friendships, and caring they bring to these situations help them forge new solutions to age-old problems.

Learn more about this author at www.raerichen.com or contact her at rae@raerichen.com .

For a good read of all first chapters, and the history and back story of these novels, sign in as the author's friendly reader at https://www.raerichen.com/guest-area .

THANK YOU, ALL

Thank you to that huge, red-eyed and tenaciously territorial wild ram who met and challenged me in the hills just north of the Wayne Morse Ranch, in Oregon. Thank you to Gary, Sheila and Emmy Seitz and Woody Richen who came along in time to distract him from his lonely prey and help us all make it back to the valley.

I've thought of him as Sampson ever since.

Thank you to my father-in-law, forester Clarence Richen, who introduced me to the woods of Oregon and the idea of cottonwood as a cash crop on boggy lands.

And a tip of the hat to the lovely barns of Beaulieu, England, especially Great Coxwell, and to the grand Swiss and monastery style barns that are still working in the Willamette Valley of Oregon. What beautiful architecture! They serve their purpose exceeding well.

Thank you to the students of Eugene and Harrisburg, Oregon who showed me your farms and ranches, you barns, and your creeks. I learned as much from you during those years as you ever learned from me. You taught me to love the wilderness of your hills and your valley, your rye grass, mint and your sheep.

Thank you to the parents of my students who accepted a whole passel of university mathematicians and their spouses into your grange and your square-dancing fun. You taught us how to stop counting footsteps, let go and enjoy motion. I hate to tell you that some of us still think in terms of squares, triangles, circles and parabolas as we dance. It works, but it's awfully cerebral.

Sincerely,
Rae Richen

OTHER BOOKS BY RAE RICHEN

Visit www.raerichen.com/blog for stories and ideas about life and writing and just plain fun.

For more stories, here are novels by Rae Richen.

Uncharted Territory – a father-son adventure in the mountains and in learning to accept and love despite the fragility of life. Learn more: https://www.raerichen.com/books

Scapegoat: The Price of Freedom – a teen and his friends struggle with a culture of easy accusation during the McCarthy Anti-Communist era. Learn more: https://www.raerichen.com/books

Scapegoat: The Hounded – after September 11, 2001, a grandfather and grandson work to create safety and freedom for friends falsely accused of treason. Learn more: https://www.raerichen.com/books

In Concert – A novel of suspense and romance when a famous musician is stalked by a vicious man who wants to own her and her son. Visit https://www.raerichen.com/in-concert and read the first chapter for free.

Frozen Trust – a novel of espionage and romance within the United States during World War II. Visit https://www.raerichen.com/frozen-trust or https://www.raerichen.com/guest-area and read the first chapter of all the books for free.

Sentinels of Solitude – a novel of suspense and love during a murderous land grab in the lush Willamette Valley of Oregon. Visit https://www.raerichen.com/guest-area for the stories behind the story.

A Fool's Gold – a novel of treachery and romance in the Rocky Mountains of Colorado during the mining fever of the 1880s. Visitwww.raerichen.com/books for more information

Those Who Curse You --A Murder Mystery of Unlikely Bonds and Unrelenting Peril – Can inner-city architect, Sarah Rohann ,and her client, Abraham Hallowell save their families from the murderous drug gang that threatens all of their lives? Visit https://www.raerichen.com/the-ones-who-curse-you

Without Trace: A Glyn Jones and Grandma Willie Mystery –
When Trace Gowan, drummer in Glyn Jones' hip-hop band, goes missing, Glyn and his friends involve Grandma Willie and her connections to prison and police in the search. They find there is a lot more than a kidnapping going on and all of them are in danger. www.raerichen.com/books or https://www.raerichen.com/without-trace

Coming Soon: *Calling The Shots, An Anthology of Short Stories:* A confection especially for readers who asked "What happened to Elizabeth in The *Price of Freedom*? To Dick Street of *In Concert* and in *Those Who Curse You*?"

Learn what caused Gryf and his brother Sam to be the targets of a madman even before they came to the United States – the back story of *A Fool's Gold.* And see what happened to Lewis James's missing brother, Dicken – a follow-up on Lewis's search for Dicken during *In Concert.*

In this and other anthologies soon to be published, Rae Richen will give us short stories to reveal where these characters lives intersected with the stories in the novels and where they went after we last saw them.

At the same time, in other stories, Rae Richen also has created whole new worlds and characters that you will want to follow and cheer for as they attempt to untangle their complicated lives.